MUZAK FOR TORSO MURDERS

I hit him on the head with a marble ashtray. I take the saws out of my briefcase, spread plastic on the floor, and cut him up as quickly as I can. I wrap the pieces separately in the plastic, cover them in brown butcher paper, type out the address labels, and drop them in the mail . . .

GOODBYE, DARK LOVE

One by one she left tiny burns across his chest. The sound, like a distant cat's hiss, soothed her. Pulling back her robe, she looked down at the heart shape tattooed long ago on her stomach. She did not smile. It was not beautiful to her. Nor would it be to anyone else. He'd known that. She put the cigarette out in his navel . . .

PAIN

We went together down a dark stairway into that other world. We were in the back room, the one I had not seen. Against one wall was a small steel closet. Her arm slipped around my waist. In a soft voice, she explained the purpose of the steel closet. "It's called the Standing Room. You can't stand up, not quite, and you can't sit down. It is what I have chosen for you. Would you like to try it? It won't be fatal—not this time . . ."

CUTTING EDGE

DENNIS ETCHISON, Editor

ST. MARTIN'S PRESS/NEW YORK

All of the characters in this book are fictitious, and any resemblance to actual persons, living or dead, is purely coincidental.

CUTTING EDGE

Copyright © 1986 by Dennis Etchison

All rights reserved.

Published by arrangement with Doubleday & Company, Inc.

Library of Congress Catalog Card Number: 86-8854

ISBN: 0-312-90772-9   Can. ISBN: 0-312-90773-7

Printed in the United States of America

First St. Martin's Press mass market edition/October 1987

10 9 8 7 6 5 4 3 2 1

to
KIRBY McCAULEY
and
CARL FABER

Contents

Introduction

There are seasons of pain. I have assembled this book because the blood is on the rock. It is my blood.

When I started reading and writing in the 1950s, much of my attention was given to science fiction, a very exciting field indeed to grow up with. At that time a boom of sorts was on and the literature was alive with promise. Brave new writers were everywhere, and it was my impression that they not only were content with their lot as outcasts but were busily forging an alternative to the protections of the larger society. And so, tentatively at first and then with the naïve self-assurance of my own awakening consciousness, I decided to join them. The rock, I thought, was not such a bad place to be.

After a while, either the field or my perception of it changed. Did it overreach itself, or had I merely misread its potential? In any event, eventually a split seemed to occur.

While one faction retreated to the less ambiguous ray guns and rocket ships of its space opera past, another channeled its imaginative energies into fabricating ever more baroque variations on heroic medieval pageant plays. By the 1970s this latter, heretofore but a splinter of a literary subgenre, moved into a position of dominance—or so it appeared from my perspective.

Perhaps it was tight money that frightened publishers into playing it safe with imitations of the phenomenally successful Tolkien books and T. H. White's *The Once and Future King;* or perhaps it was the readers who lost faith after a baptism of unrest and social upheaval. Whatever the cause, booksellers became convinced that their customers were more interested in pseudo-historical pastiches about attractive role models engaged in quests for grails beyond mysterious forests, aided by gnomes with crossbows, elves in chain mail and magic—in other words, in adolescent fantasies of potency disguised as rite-of-passage fairy tales—than in any further confrontation with a future of scaled-down expectations. "Hard" science fiction went retrograde and began eating itself, excreting shiny but sterile wet dreams of a Fourth Reich in space, while behind the backs of the technocrats the feyest of the fans marshaled their forces and took over the asylum.

Those misfits among us who could not find nourishment in such reactionary enclaves discovered that we were stranded. Further, by embracing a protean life at the expense of membership in the social collective, a price had been set without our realizing it. The tide shifted, revealing the extent of the break, and dues were now to be extracted. In my youthfulness I hadn't expected that. As James Baldwin has put it, I didn't even know what dues were. But in that moment the benefits of consensus were lost; the tide was out and the separation from the mainland was complete.

At high noon on the rock, I began to write of the pain.

Or more accurately to focus directly on my isolation, in the belief that I might forge from it something stronger and more beautiful than what had been lost as the illusion of membership crumbled; I vowed that I would make of it my strength. And then, because this is a just universe, I would be permitted to rejoin the world before it was too late, and on my own terms.

Time passed, and the shadows lengthened.

At some point it became clear to me that what I was undergoing was not a trial. It was my life. And, never satisfied, the rock continued to take my blood.

It was only then, when I knew that I must embrace my lot or die, that my Heracles appeared. . . .

In the questioning, uprooted sixties, some of the more poetic and humanistic writers within the science fiction community chose to concentrate on the "soft" sciences and explorations of the inscape, incorporating attitudes of contemporary existential philosophy and metaphysics via the fractured artistic techniques of an unsettled time. But this attempt at evolution within a commercial category was quickly defused by the field, which borrowed a shopworn term from another medium and pigeon-holed this latest development as a temporary aberration called "the New Wave," thereby effectively cutting its authors out of the herd and abandoning their revisionist efforts to stillbirth before they could carry the field into riskier, less insurable territory.

During the same period a much older form of fantastic story-telling, predicated on a philosophy of pessimism and despair, gained a broadened base of support. Morbid allegorists of the non-scientific variety such as Poe and Lovecraft were discovered to hold strong emotional appeal for growing numbers of people unable to find succor within the monolithic gates of the futurist establishment. Ancient belief systems derived from mysticism and the occult recruited new converts by the millions as the horror tale grew more popular than ever before, and an alternative brand of moral fable became viable in the marketplace.

With no relief forthcoming from the power complex, the seventies saw reflections of malaise spread through the popular media on an even greater scale than in former crisis pockets of depression and world war. Paranoid melodramas of suspense and terror became bankable as best-selling books, while filmgoers refused to tire of obsessively blood-spattered portents of impending death and destruction. Like the nightmares of apocalypse and atomic mutation that had haunted Japanese films, Western pop culture drenched itself ever deeper in the sacrificial blood of its own darkening unconscious.

Unfortunately the horror novel has fared little better than science fiction or fantasy. Supermarket racks continue to stock a never-ending farrago of flashy paperbacks, their lurid covers competing with *The National Enquirer* and *People,* each one promising to render previous best-sellers about unruly children (possession!) or suburban unrest (poltergeists!) as passé as last week's *TV Guide.* Like fad diets and astrological predictions of disaster, such pandering seeks to exploit middle-class unease with the latest prepackaged devil theory. Those old standbys the Communists (or Terrorists, now) may or may not be lurking just around the corner and up your street this month, according to the editors of *Time* and *Newsweek,* but Something Not from Around Here is surely behind the ubiquitous disintegration of the American family, and an endless supply of facile excuses is being marketed to housewives hungry for answers at $3.50 a shot. . . .

Watchman, what of the night?

Only character remains alive in the silence, in the hour when the scales are lifted from our eyes and we finally see what is there—what is really at the end of every fork, as William Burroughs put it. Only after the failure of consciousness can the dream come.

It is at this edge that change takes place.

Sometime around the beginning of the last decade, something happened. It was a strange awakening. Within the decaying manse of horror literature, of all places, a surprising and unexpectedly fecund movement began, one that has not yet been defused or aborted.

I am not speaking now of your meat-market authors who stuff books like sausages by the pound, but of those who never came in from the cold and yet were not broken by the night. Most of them were, as I am, primarily short-story writers, who in this country are considered to be only one step up from poets, who are considered to be only one step up from bums. Soon, what I thought was only a wish-fulfillment hallucination turned out to be something more along the lines of a miracle.

Consider the unlikelihood of it all.

The climate was hardly encouraging for readers or writers who sought a fiction not bounded by the homeostatic limitations of mainstream literature. The old futures of the science-fictioneers had become quaint anachronisms, no more relevant to the crucible of contemporary life than visions of zeppelins over Broadway. And the haunted houses and fetid graveyards of traditional horror were being strip-mined and bulldozed for the prefab market, jerry-built into hermetically sealed tombs with a view. The forms which previously gave shape and meaning to our dreams were moribund, and there was nowhere left to turn. Darkness wove ever closer, warning us to make peace with the long night of the soul. There was, it seemed, little left of a once so rich art to give courage during the human winter to come. I remember composing a bitter poem: *The snow on the wheel / turns, and the / century ices.* We could no longer ask our doctors, psychiatrists, politicians, intellectuals for a candle to light the way; they were all sick from the same thing. Our artist-philosophers busied themselves programming their word processors to churn out fast-food fiction for a drive-thru society dangerously close to running out of gas, scrambling after trilogies about an elfinland that never was and never will be; or they were lost and gone mad in the mirrored halls of academe, posturing and twitching like hebephrenics in what might as well have been the private language of terminal schizophrenia.

Readers and writers alike had been trapped between a stainless-steel rock and a moss-covered hard place, so to speak. One could buy into the propaganda machine of the engineer-litterateurs with their germ-free O'Neill Colonies, seeking redemption in some robotized orbiting womb. Or wallow in the fatalism of popular horror, with its Ancient Ones still bumping around in the cellar and the Antichrist forever bestirring in the woodpile. Pick your poison, either one will do. Consensus is everything in this society; without it you are damned, or on your own, which is presumed to be the same thing. . . .

Well, in the words of Kenneth Patchen: *It may be a long time till morning, but there's no law against talking in the dark.*

I first heard it in the pages of *Whispers* magazine, which I stumbled across quite by accident. Formerly *Whispers from Arkham,* under the editorship of a dentist and collector named Stuart David Schiff this small-circulation periodical endeavored to offer a platform for the voices of the disenfranchised, some of them exiles from science fiction, alongside more traditional material. The most authentic signs of life I had seen in some time were glimpsed there, as a new generation of dark fantasists—as how could they not be in such times?—gathered together to keep each other warm. Then came Whispers Press and other lines of limited-edition hardcovers (culminating in the 1980s with the spectacular success of Scream/Press). And then original anthologies through established publishers, after former fan and neophyte agent Kirby McCauley fired the opening gun with his landmark *Frights.*

In short, a kind of renaissance began to happen under so many turned-up noses. Iconoclastic reviewers predisposed to the outré—Jack Sullivan, Douglas Winter, others—pointed the way, and so did some admirably unprejudiced and independent

editors, including Gerald Page, Karl Edward Wagner, Charles L.
Grant and Ramsey Campbell. The last three are also now
among the most important writers in the field. Perhaps they
became editors by default, because in the beginning few others
were willing to take the job. And because they were excited
about what was happening.

Readers kept the night watch and demanded more titles.
*Whispers, Shadows, Terrors, New Terrors, Fears, Night Chills,
Horrors, Death,* the milestone *Dark Forces* . . . the list reads
deceptively like a litany of the perverse. We have an adventur-
ous audience and brave compilers to thank for providing a fo-
rum for this activity, for taking chances on defiantly
idiosyncratic stories that really do not fit the category as it has
been known but which probably would have found no other
home; many of the stories in these books have been like no
others anywhere, stories which with rare power and immediacy
addressed the ordeal of preserving our humanity through the
rigors of 1984 and beyond. The fact that these extraordinary
volumes, caskets overflowing with bright and dark jewels, managed to slip into the racks next to so much old wine in so many
garish bottles is a special grace for which we should be grateful.
Their numbers multiply as the readership expands, at least partially because of beachheads established by so many sensation-
mongering macaberesques. Out of the mud grows the lotus.

When this parturient new field opened up I had already been
writing for many years, placing my stories wherever I could in
science fiction and literary publications, in girlie books and slick
magazines. In one of my regular perusals of market lists in *Writer's Digest,* I came upon Stu Schiff's modest solicitation. My
contact with him (and later with others like him) led to accept-
ances for stories that in some cases had gone begging for years.
One manuscript in particular I remember had been in submis-
sion continuously for more than half a decade. My work was too
soft for what sf had become by then, too speculative for the
mainstream markets, too hard-edged and disquieting for the
slicks, and too downbeat for the fantasy field.

Then, after thirteen or fourteen years as a professional writer,
I received a humble letter from Kirby McCauley. He had seen
something of mine in *Whispers,* claimed to like the way I wrote,
and asked if I had a story for a new anthology he was putting

together. I did. Shortly thereafter McCauley was instrumental in organizing the World Fantasy Convention. At its third meeting in Los Angeles I was astounded to learn that after years of obscurity I was now suddenly a minor celebrity, at least at that gathering, my contribution to *Frights* having been voted a place on the final ballot of the World Fantasy Awards by popular tally. I didn't win, but my life has not been the same since.

I had never considered myself a horror writer in any traditional sense, so I was naturally reluctant to claim membership in that camp. However, through no particular plan but rather by following the path of least resistance, I found my work being accepted more often in their publications than anywhere else. In most cases I am convinced that these stories could have found a home nowhere else; in some cases I have absolute proof. As the field developed, McCauley took me on as a client, and the rest is as improbable as any bizarrerie I have ever written. He taught me that I could, after all, survive without altering what I wrote, and that I was not alone on the rock.

This book, then, is my offering of gratitude to those who have made the fever dream of safe harbor a reality, not the least of whom is Pat LoBrutto of Doubleday, who agreed to publish it. Many of them are represented here, though not all, of course, because of the limitations of space. If you have been reading in the field, you know who they are. If you have not, then it is my hope that *Cutting Edge* will introduce you to some of them.

It is my little song to Kirby McCauley and the field that miraculously appeared at the nadir of my despair and took me in at my darkest hour, when I had lost hope of surviving by doing what means more to me than anything else: art without compromise. "Once you have truly given up the ghost," wrote Henry Miller, "everything follows with absolute certainty, even in the midst of chaos." It is also my fervent wish that this book will serve as a kind of beacon for others who may believe that they have been left to sink or swim on their own and who doubt their own strength. I, too, was lost before I was found. The blood is on the rock, but I know now that it is not mine alone.

Dennis Etchison

PART I

Bringing It
All Back Home

PETER STRAUB

Blue Rose

(for Rosemary Clooney)

On a stifling summer day the two youngest of the five Beevers children, Harry and Little Eddie, were sitting on cane-backed chairs in the attic of their house on South Sixth Street in Palmyra, New York. Their father called it "the upstairs junk room," as this large irregular space was reserved for the boxes of tablecloths, stacks of diminishingly sized girl's winter coats, and musty old dresses Maryrose Beevers had mummified as testimony to the superiority of her past to her present.

A tall mirror that could be tilted in its frame, an artifact of their mother's onetime glory, now revealed to Harry the rear of Little Eddie's head. This object, looking more malleable than a head should be, an elongated wad of Pla-Do covered with straggling feathers, was just peeking above the back of the chair. Even the back of Little Eddie's head looked tense to Harry.

"Listen to me," Harry said. Little Eddie squirmed in his chair, and the wobbly chair squirmed with him. "You think I'm kidding you? I had her last year."

"Well, she didn't kill *you*," Little Eddie said.

"Course not, she liked me, you little dummy. She only hit me a couple of times. She hit some of those kids every single day."

"But teachers can't *kill* people," Little Eddie said.

At nine, Little Eddie was only a year younger than he, but Harry knew that his undersized fretful brother saw him as much a part of the world of big people as their older brothers.

"Most teachers can't," Harry said. "But what if they live right in the same building as the principal? What if they won *teaching awards,* hey, and what if every other teacher in the place is scared stiff of them? Don't you think they can get away with murder? Do you think anybody really misses a snot-faced little brat—a little brat like you? Mrs. Franken took this kid, this runty little Tommy Golz, into the cloakroom, and she killed him right there. I heard him scream. At the end, it sounded just like bubbles. He was trying to yell, but there was too much blood in his throat. He never came back, and nobody ever said boo about it. She killed him, and next year she's going to be your teacher. I hope you're afraid, Little Eddie, because you ought to be." Harry leaned forward. "Tommy Golz even looked sort of like you, Little Eddie."

Little Eddie's entire face twitched as if a lightning bolt had crossed it.

In fact, the young Golz boy had suffered an epileptic fit and been removed from school, as Harry knew.

"Mrs. Franken especially hates selfish little brats that don't share their toys."

"I do share my toys," Little Eddie wailed, tears beginning to run down through the delicate smears of dust on his cheeks. "Everybody *takes* my toys, that's why."

"So give me your Ultraglide Roadster," Harry said. This had been Little Eddie's birthday present, given three days previous by a beaming father and a scowling mother. "Or I'll tell Mrs. Franken as soon as I get inside that school, this fall."

Under its layer of grime, Little Eddie's face went nearly the same white-gray shade as his hair.

An ominous slamming sound came up the stairs.

"Children? Are you messing around up there in the attic? Get down here!"

"We're just sitting in the chairs, Mom," Harry called out.

"Don't you bust those chairs! Get down here this minute!"

Little Eddie slid out of his chair and prepared to bolt.

"I want that car," Harry whispered. "And if you don't give it to me, I'll tell Mom you were foolin' around with her old clothes."

"I didn't do nothin'!" Little Eddie wailed, and broke for the stairs.

"Hey, Mom, we didn't break any stuff, honest!" Harry yelled. He bought a few minutes more by adding, "I'm coming right now," and stood up and went toward a cardboard box filled with interesting books he had noticed the day before his brother's birthday, and which had been his goal before he had remembered the Roadster and coaxed Little Eddie upstairs.

When, a short time later, Harry came through the door to the attic steps, he was carrying a tattered paperback book. Little Eddie stood quivering with misery and rage just outside the bedroom the two boys shared with their older brother Albert. He held out a small blue metal car, which Harry instantly took and eased into a front pocket of his jeans.

"When do I get it back?" Little Eddie asked.

"Never," Harry said. "Only selfish people want to get presents back. Don't you know anything at all?" When Eddie pursed his face up to wail, Harry tapped the book in his hands and said, "I got something here that's going to help you with Mrs. Franken, so don't complain."

His mother intercepted him as he came down the stairs to the main floor of the little house—here were the kitchen and living room, both floored with faded linoleum, the actual "junk room" separated by a stiff brown woolen curtain from the little makeshift room where Edgar Beevers slept, and the larger bedroom reserved for Maryrose. Children were never permitted more than a few steps within this awful chamber, for they might disarrange Maryrose's mysterious "papers" or interfere with the rows of antique dolls on the window seat, which was the sole, much-revered architectural distinction of the Beevers house.

Maryrose Beevers stood at the bottom of the stairs, glaring suspiciously up at her fourth son. She did not ever look like a woman who played with dolls, and she did not look that way now. Her hair was twisted into a knot at the back of her head. Smoke from her cigarette curled up past the big glasses like bird's wings which magnified her eyes.

Harry thrust his hand into his pocket and curled his fingers protectively around the Ultraglide Roadster.

"Those things up there are the possessions of my family," she said. "Show me what you took."

Harry shrugged and held out the paperback as he came down within striking range.

His mother snatched it from him, and tilted her head to see

its cover through the cigarette smoke. "Oh. This is from that little box of books up there? Your father used to pretend to read books." She squinted at the print on the cover. *"Hypnosis Made Easy.* Some drugstore trash. You want to read this?"

Harry nodded.

"I don't suppose it can hurt you much." She negligently passed the book back to him. "People in society read books, you know—I used to read a lot, back before I got stuck here with a bunch of dummies. *My* father had a lot of books."

Maryrose nearly touched the top of Harry's head, then snatched back her hand. "You're my scholar, Harry. You're the one who's going places."

"I'm gonna do good in school next year," he said.

"Well. You're going to do well. As long as you don't ruin every chance you have by speaking like your father."

Harry felt that particular pain composed of scorn, shame, and terror that filled him when Maryrose spoke of his father in this way. He mumbled something that sounded like acquiescence, and moved a few steps sideways and around her.

2

The porch of the Beevers house extended six feet on either side of the front door, and was the repository for furniture either too large to be crammed into the junk room or too humble to be enshrined in the attic. A sagging porch swing sat beneath the living-room window, to the left of an ancient couch whose imitation green leather had been repaired with black duct tape; on the other side of the front door, through which Harry Beevers now emerged, stood a useless icebox dating from the earliest days of the Beeverses' marriage and two unsteady camp chairs Edgar Beevers had won in a card game. These had never been allowed into the house. Unofficially, this side of the porch was Harry's father's, and thereby had an entirely different atmosphere, defeated, lawless, and shameful, from the side with the swing and couch.

Harry knelt down in neutral territory directly before the front door and fished the Ultraglide Roadster from his pocket. He placed the hypnotism book on the porch and rolled the little metal car across its top. Then he gave the car a hard shove and watched it clunk nose-down onto the wood. He repeated this several times before moving the book aside, flattening himself out on his stomach, and giving the little car a decisive push toward the swing and the couch.

The Roadster rolled a few feet before an irregular board tilted it over on its side and stopped it.

"You dumb car," Harry said, and retrieved it. He gave it another push deeper into his mother's realm. A stiff, brittle section of paint which had separated from its board cracked in half and rested atop the stalled Roadster like a miniature mattress.

Harry knocked off the chip of paint and sent the car backwards down the porch, where it flipped over again and skidded into the side of the icebox. The boy ran down the porch and this time simply hurled the little car back in the direction of the swing. It bounced off the swing's padding and fell heavily to the wood. Harry knelt before the icebox, panting.

His whole head felt funny, as if wet hot towels had been stuffed inside it. Harry picked himself up and walked across to where the car lay before the swing. He hated the way it looked, small and helpless. He experimentally stepped on the car and felt it pressing into the undersole of his moccasin. Harry raised his other foot and stood on the car, but nothing happened. He jumped on the car, but the moccasin was no better than his bare foot. Harry bent down to pick up the Roadster.

"You dumb little car," he said. "You're no good anyhow, you low-class little jerky thing." He turned it over in his hands. Then he inserted his thumbs between the frame and one of the little tires. When he pushed, the tire moved. His face heated. He mashed his thumbs against the tire, and the little black doughnut popped into the tall thick weeds before the porch. Breathing hard more from emotion than exertion, Harry popped the other front tire into the weeds. Harry whirled around, and ground the car into the wall beside his father's bedroom window. Long deep scratches appeared in the paint. When Harry peered at the top of the car, it too was scratched. He found a nailhead which protruded a quarter of an inch out from the front of the house, and scraped a long paring of blue paint off the driver's side of the Roadster. Gray metal shone through.

Harry slammed the car several times against the edge of the nailhead, chipping off small quantities of paint. Panting, he popped off the two small rear tires and put them in his pocket because he liked the way they looked.

Without tires, well scratched and dented, the Ultraglide Roadster had lost most of its power. Harry looked it over with a bitter, deep satisfaction and walked across the porch and shoved it far into the nest of weeds. Gray metal and blue paint shone at him from within the stalks and leaves. Harry thrust his hands into their midst and swept his arms back and forth. The car tumbled away and fell into invisibility.

When Maryrose appeared scowling on the porch, Harry was seated serenely on the squeaking swing, looking at the first few pages of the paperback book.

"What are you doing? What was all that banging?"

"I'm just reading, I didn't hear anything," Harry said.

3

"Well, if it isn't the shitbird," Albert said, jumping up the porch steps thirty minutes later. His face and T-shirt bore broad black stripes of grease. Short, muscular, and thirteen, Albert spent every possible minute hanging around the gas station two blocks from their house. Harry knew that Albert despised him. Albert raised a fist and made a jerky, threatening motion toward Harry, who flinched. Albert had often beaten him bloody, as had their two older brothers, Sonny and George, now at Army bases in Oklahoma and Germany. Like Albert, his two oldest brothers had seriously disappointed their mother.

Albert laughed, and this time swung his fist within a couple of inches of Harry's face. On the backswing he knocked the book from Harry's hands.

"Thanks," Harry said.

Albert smirked and disappeared around the front door. Almost immediately Harry could hear his mother beginning to shout about the grease on Albert's face and clothes. Albert thumped up the stairs.

Harry opened his clenched fingers and spread them wide, closed his hands into fists, then spread them wide again. When he heard the bedroom door slam shut upstairs, he was able to get off the swing and pick up the book. Being around Albert made him feel like a spring coiled up in a box. From the upper rear of the house, Little Eddie emitted a ghostly wail. Maryrose screamed that she was going to start smacking him if he didn't shut up, and that was that. The three unhappy lives within the house fell back into silence. Harry sat down, found his page, and began reading again.

A man named Dr. Roland Mentaine had written *Hypnosis Made Easy*, and his vocabulary was much larger than Harry's. Dr. Mentaine used words like "orchestrate" and "ineffable" and "enhance," and some of his sentences wound their way through so many subordinate clauses that Harry lost his way. Yet Harry, who had begun the book only half expecting that he would comprehend anything in it at all, found it a wonderful book. He had made it most of the way through the chapter called "Mind Power."

Harry thought it was neat that hypnosis could cure smoking, stuttering, and bedwetting. (He himself had wet the bed almost nightly until months after his ninth birthday. The bedwetting stopped the night a certain lovely dream came to Harry. In the dream he had to urinate terribly, and was hurrying down a stony castle corridor past suits of armor and torches guttering on the walls. At last Harry reached an open door, through which he saw the most splendid bathroom of his life. The floors were of polished marble, the walls white-tiled. As soon as he entered the gleaming bathroom, a uniformed butler waved him toward the rank of urinals. Harry began pulling down his zipper, fumbled with himself, and got his penis out of his underpants just in time. As the dream-urine gushed out of him, Harry had blessedly awakened.) Hypnotism could get you right inside someone's mind and let you do things there. You could make a person speak in any foreign language they'd ever heard, even if they'd only heard it once, and you could make them act like a baby. Harry considered how pleasurable it would be to make his brother Albert lie squalling and red-faced on the floor, unable to walk or speak as he pissed all over himself.

Also, and this was a new thought to Harry, you could take a person back to a whole row of lives they had led before they were born as the person they were now. This process of rebirth was called reincarnation. Some of Dr. Mentaine's patients had been kings in Egypt and pirates in the Caribbean, some had been murderers, novelists, and artists. They remembered the houses they'd lived in, the names of their mothers and servants and children, the locations of shops where they'd bought cake and wine. Neat stuff, Harry thought. He wondered if someone who had been a famous murderer a long time ago could remember pushing in the knife or bringing down the hammer. A lot of the books remaining in the little cardboard box upstairs, Harry had noticed, seemed to be about murderers. It would not be any use to take Albert back to a previous life, however. If Albert had any previous lives, he had spent them as inanimate objects on the order of boulders and anvils.

Maybe in another life Albert was a murder weapon, Harry thought.

"Hey, college boy! Joe College!"

Harry looked toward the sidewalk and saw the baseball cap and T-shirted gut of Mr. Petrosian, who lived in a tiny house next to the tavern on the corner of South Sixth and Livermore Street. Mr. Petrosian was always shouting genial things at kids, but Maryrose wouldn't let Harry or Little Eddie talk to him. She said Mr. Petrosian was common as dirt. He worked as a janitor in the telephone building and drank a case of beer every night while he sat on his porch.

"Me?" Harry said.

"Yeah! Keep reading books, and you could go to college, right?"

Harry smiled noncommittally. Mr. Petrosian lifted a wide arm and continued to toil down the street toward his house next to the Idle Hour.

In seconds Maryrose burst through the door, folding an old white dish towel in her hands. "Who was that? I heard a man's voice."

"Him," Harry said, pointing at the substantial back of Mr. Petrosian, now half of the way home.

"What did he say? As if it could possibly be interesting, coming from an Armenian janitor."

"He called me Joe College."

Maryrose startled him by smiling.

"Albert says he wants to go back to the station tonight, and I have to go to work soon." Maryrose worked the night shift as a secretary at St. Joseph's Hospital. "God knows when your father'll show up. Get something to eat for Little Eddie and yourself, will you, Harry? I've just got too many things to take care of, as usual."

"I'll get something at Big John's." This was a hamburger stand, a magical place to Harry, erected the summer before in a vacant lot on Livermore Street two blocks down from the Idle Hour.

His mother handed him two carefully folded dollar bills, and he pushed them into his pocket. "Don't let Little Eddie stay in the house alone," his mother said before going back inside. "Take him with you. You know how scared he gets."

"Sure," Harry said, and went back to his book. He finished the chapter on "Mind Power" while first Maryrose left to stand up at the bus stop on the corner and then Albert noisily departed. Little Eddie sat frozen before his soap operas in the living room. Harry turned a page and started reading "Techniques of Hypnosis."

4

At eight-thirty that night the two boys sat alone in the kitchen, on opposite sides of the table covered in yellow bamboo Formica. From the living room came the sound of Sid Caesar babbling in fake German to Imogene Coca on *Your Show of Shows*. Little Eddie claimed to be scared of Sid Caesar, but when Harry had returned from the hamburger stand with a Big Johnburger (with "the works") for himself and a Mama Marydog for Eddie, double fries, and two chocolate shakes, he had been sitting in front of the television, his face moist with tears of moral outrage. Eddie usually liked Mama Marydogs, but he had taken only a couple of meager bites from the one before him now, and was disconsolately pushing a french fry through a blob of ketchup. Every now and then he wiped at his eyes, leaving nearly symmetrical smears of ketchup to dry on his cheeks.

"Mom *said* not to leave me alone in the house," said Little Eddie. "I heard. It was during *The Edge of Night* and you were on the porch. I think I'm gonna tell on you." He peeped across at Harry, then quickly looked back at the french fry and drew it out of the puddle of ketchup. "I'm ascared to be alone in the house." Sometimes Eddie's voice was like a queer speeded-up mechanical version of Maryrose's.

"Don't be so dumb," Harry said, almost kindly. "How can you be scared in your own house? You live here, don't you?"

"I'm ascared of the attic," Eddie said. He held the dripping french fry before his mouth and pushed it in. "The attic makes noise." A little squirm of red appeared at the corner of his mouth. "You were supposed to take me with you."

"Oh jeez, Eddie, you slow everything down. I wanted to just get the food and come back. I got you your dinner, didn't I? Didn't I get you what you like?"

In truth, Harry liked hanging around Big John's by himself because then he could talk to Big John and listen to his theories. Big John called himself a "renegade Papist" and considered Hitler the greatest man of the twentieth century, followed closely by Paul VI, Padre Pio who bled from the palms of his hands, and Elvis Presley.

All these events occurred in what is usually but wrongly called a simpler time, before Kennedy and feminism and ecology, before the Nixon presidency and Watergate, and before American soldiers, among them a twenty-one-year-old Harry Beevers, journeyed to Vietnam.

"I'm still going to tell," said Little Eddie. He pushed another french fry into the puddle of ketchup. "And that car was my birthday present." He began to snuffle. "Albert hit me, and you stole my car, and you left me alone, and I was scared. And I don't wanna have Mrs. Franken next year, cuz I think she's gonna hurt me."

Harry had nearly forgotten telling his brother about Mrs. Franken and Tommy Golz, and this reminder brought back very sharply the memory of destroying Eddie's birthday present.

Eddie twisted his head sideways and dared another quick look at his brother. "Can I have my Ultraglide Roadster back, Harry? You're going to give it back to me, aren'cha? I won't tell Mom you left me alone if you give it back."

"Your car is okay," Harry said. "It's in a sort of a secret place I know."

"You hurt my car!" Eddie squalled. "You did!"

"Shut up!" Harry shouted, and Little Eddie flinched. "You're driving me crazy!" Harry yelled. He realized that he was leaning over the table, and that Little Eddie was getting ready to cry again. He sat down. "Just don't scream at me like that, Eddie."

"You did something to my car," Eddie said with a stunned certainty. "I knew it."

"Look, I'll prove your car is okay," Harry said, and took the two rear tires from his pocket and displayed them on his palm.

Little Eddie stared. He blinked, then reached out tentatively for the tires.

Harry closed his fist around them. "Do they look like I did anything to them?"

"You took them *off!*"

"But don't they look okay, don't they look fine?" Harry opened his fist, closed it again, and returned the tires to his pocket. "I didn't want to show you the whole car, Eddie, because you'd get all worked up, and you gave it to me. Remember? I wanted to show you the tires so you'd see everything was all right. Okay? Got it?"

Eddie miserably shook his head.

"Anyway, I'm going to help you, just like I said."

"With Mrs. Franken?" A fraction of his misery left Little Eddie's smeary face.

"Sure. You ever hear of something called hypnotism?"

"I heard a hypmotism." Little Eddie was sulking. "Everybody in the whole world heard a that."

"Hypnotism, stupid, not hypmotism."

"Sure, hypmotism. I saw it on the TV. They did it on *As the World Turns.* A man made a lady go to sleep and think she was going to have a baby."

Harry smiled. "That's just TV, Little Eddie. Real hypnotism is a lot better than that. I read all about it in one of the books from the attic."

Little Eddie was still sulky because of the car. "So what makes it better?"

"Because it lets you do amazing things," Harry said. He called on Dr. Mentaine. "Hypnosis unlocks your mind and lets you use all the power you really have. If you start now, you'll really knock those books when school starts up again. You'll pass every test Mrs. Franken gives you, just like the way I did." He reached across the table and grasped Little Eddie's wrist, stalling a fat brown french fry on its way to the puddle. "But it won't just make you good in school. If you let me try it on you, I'm pretty sure I can show you that you're a lot stronger than you think you are."

Eddie blinked.

"And I bet I can make you so you're not scared of anything anymore. Hypnotism is real good for that. I read in this book, there was this guy who was afraid of bridges. Whenever he even *thought* about crossing a bridge he got all dizzy and sweaty. Terrible stuff happened to him, like he lost his job and once he just had to ride in a car across a bridge and he dumped a load in his pants. He went to see Dr. Mentaine, and Dr. Mentaine hypnotized him and said he would never be afraid of bridges again, and he wasn't."

Harry pulled the paperback from his hip pocket. He opened it flat on the table and bent over the pages. "Here. Listen to this. 'Benefits of the course of treatment were found in all areas of the patient's life, and results were obtained for which he would have paid any price.'" Harry read these words haltingly, but with complete understanding.

"Hypmotism can make me strong?" Little Eddie asked, evidently having saved this point in his head.

"Strong as a bull."

"Strong as Albert?"

"A lot stronger than Albert. A lot stronger than me, too."

"And I can beat up on big guys that hurt me?"

"You just have to learn how."

Eddie sprang up from the chair, yelling nonsense. He flexed his stringlike biceps and for some time twisted his body into a series of muscleman poses.

"You want to do it?" Harry finally asked.

Little Eddie popped into his chair and stared at Harry. His T-shirt's neckband sagged all the way to his breastbone without ever actually touching his chest. "I wanna start."

"Okay, Eddie, good man." Harry stood up and put his hand on the book. "Up to the attic."

"Only, I don't wanna go in the attic," Eddie said. He was still staring at Harry, but his head was tilted over like a weird little echo of Maryrose, and his eyes had filled with suspicion.

"I'm not gonna *take* anything from you, Little Eddie," Harry said. "It's just, we should be out of everybody's way. The attic's real quiet."

Little Eddie stuck his hand inside his T-shirt and let his arm dangle from the wrist.

"You turned your shirt into an armrest," Harry said.

Eddie jerked his hand out of its sling.

"Albert might come waltzing in and wreck everything if we do it in the bedroom."

"If you go up first and turn on the lights," Eddie said.

5

Harry held the book open on his lap, and glanced from it to Little Eddie's tense smeary face. He had read these pages over many times while he sat on the porch. Hypnotism boiled down to a few simple steps, each of which led to the next. The first thing he had to do was to get his brother started right, "relaxed and receptive," according to Dr. Mentaine.

Little Eddie stirred in his cane-backed chair and kneaded his hands together. His shadow, cast by the bulb dangling overhead, imitated him like a black little chair-bound monkey. "I wanna get started, I wanna get to be strong," he said.

"Right here in this book it says you have to be relaxed," Harry said. "Just put your hands on top of your legs, nice and easy, with your fingers pointing forward. Then close your eyes and breathe in and out a couple of times. Think about being nice and tired and ready to go to sleep."

"I don't wanna go to sleep!"

"It's not really sleep, Little Eddie, it's just sort of like it. You'll still really be awake, but nice and relaxed. Or else it won't work. You have to do everything I tell you. Otherwise everybody'll still be able to beat up on you, like they do now. I want you to pay attention to everything I say."

"Okay." Little Eddie made a visible effort to relax. He placed his hands on his thighs and twice inhaled and exhaled.

"Now close your eyes."

Eddie closed his eyes.

Harry suddenly knew that it was going to work—if he did everything the book said, he would really be able to hypnotize his brother.

"Little Eddie, I want you just to listen to the sound of my voice," he said, forcing himself to be calm. "You are already getting nice and relaxed, as easy and peaceful as if you were lying in bed, and the more you listen to my voice, the more relaxed and tired you are going to get. Nothing can bother you. Everything bad is far away, and you're just sitting here, breathing in and out, getting nice and sleepy."

He checked his page to make sure he was doing it right, and then went on.

"It's like lying in bed, Eddie, and the more you hear my voice, the more tired and sleepy you're getting, a little more sleepy the more you hear me. Everything else is sort of fading away, and all you can hear is my voice. You feel tired but good, just like the way you do right before you fall asleep. Everything is fine, and you're drifting a little bit, drifting and drifting, and you're getting ready to raise your right hand."

He leaned over and very lightly stroked the back of Little Eddie's grimy right hand. Eddie sat slumped in the chair with his eyes closed, breathing shallowly. Harry spoke very slowly.

"I'm going to count backwards from ten, and every time I get to another number, your hand is going to get lighter and lighter. When I count, your right hand is going to get so light it floats up and finally touches your nose when you hear me say 'one.' And then you'll be in a deep sleep. Now I'm starting. Ten. Your hand is already feeling light. Nine. It wants to float up. Eight. Your hand really feels light now. It's going to start to go up now. Seven."

Little Eddie's hand obediently floated an inch up from his thigh.

"Six." The grimy little hand rose another few inches. "It's getting lighter and lighter now, and every time I say another number it gets closer and closer to your nose, and you get sleepier and sleepier. Five."

The hand ascended several inches nearer Eddie's face.

"Four."

The hand now dangled like a sleeping bird half of the way between Eddie's knee and his nose.

"Three."

It rose nearly to Eddie's chin.

"Two."

Eddie's hand hung a few inches from his mouth.

"One. You are going to fall asleep now."

The gently curved, ketchup-streaked forefinger delicately brushed the tip of Little Eddie's nose, and stayed there while Eddie sagged against the back of the chair.

Harry's heart beat so loudly that he feared the sound would bring Eddie out of his trance. Eddie remained motionless. Harry breathed quietly by himself for a moment. "Now you can lower your hand to your lap, Eddie. You are going deeper and deeper into sleep. Deeper and deeper and deeper."

Eddie's hand sank gracefully downward.

The attic seemed hot as the inside of a furnace to Harry. His fingers left blotches on the open pages of the book. He wiped his face on his sleeve and looked at his little brother. Little Eddie had slumped so far down in the chair that his head was no longer visible in the tilting mirror. Perfectly still and quiet, the attic stretched out on all sides of them, waiting (or so it seemed to Harry) for what would happen next. Maryrose's trunks sat in rows under the eaves far behind the mirror, her old dresses hung silently within the dusty wardrobe. Harry rubbed his hands on his jeans to dry them, and flicked a page over with the neatness of an old scholar who had spent half his life in libraries.

"You're going to sit up straight in your chair," he said.

Eddie pulled himself upright.

"Now I want to show you that you're really hypnotized, Little Eddie. It's like a test. I want you to hold your right arm straight out before you. Make it as rigid as you can. This is going to show you how strong you can be."

Eddie's pale arm rose and straightened to the wrist, leaving his fingers dangling.

Harry stood up and said, "That's pretty good." He walked the two steps to Eddie's side and grasped his brother's arm and ran his fingers down the length of it, gently straightening Eddie's hand. "Now I want you to imagine that your arm is getting harder and harder. It's getting as hard and rigid as an iron bar.

Your whole arm is an iron bar, and nobody on earth could bend it. Eddie, it's stronger than Superman's arm." He removed his hands and stepped back.

"Now. This arm is so strong and rigid that you can't bend it no matter how hard you try. It's an iron bar, and nobody on earth could bend it. Try. Try to bend it."

Eddie's face tightened up, and his arm rose perhaps two degrees. Eddie grunted with invisible effort, unable to bend his arm.

"Okay, Eddie, you did real good. Now your arm is loosening up, and when I count backwards from ten, it's going to get looser and looser. When I get to *one*, your arm'll be normal again." He began counting, and Eddie's fingers loosened and drooped, and finally the arm came to rest again on his leg.

Harry went back to his chair, sat down, and looked at Eddie with great satisfaction. Now he was certain that he would be able to do the next demonstration, which Dr. Mentaine called "The Chair Exercise."

"Now you know that this stuff really works, Eddie, so we're going to do something a little harder. I want you to stand up in front of your chair."

Eddie obeyed. Harry stood up too, and moved his chair forward and to the side so that its cane seat faced Eddie, about four feet away.

"I want you to stretch out between these chairs, with your head on your chair and your feet on mine. And I want you to keep your hands at your sides."

Eddie hunkered down uncomplainingly and settled his head back on the seat of his chair. Supporting himself with his arms, he raised one leg and placed his foot on Harry's chair. Then he lifted the other foot. Difficulty immediately appeared in his face. He raised his arms and clamped them in so that he looked trussed.

"Now your whole body is slowly becoming as hard as iron, Eddie. Your entire body is one of the strongest things on earth. Nothing can make it bend. You could hold yourself there forever and never feel the slightest pain or discomfort. It's like you're lying on a mattress, you're so strong."

The expression of strain left Eddie's face. Slowly his arms extended and relaxed. He lay propped string-straight between the two chairs, so at ease that he did not even appear to be breathing.

"While I talk to you, you're getting stronger and stronger. You could hold up anything. You could hold up an elephant. I'm going to sit down on your stomach to prove it."

Cautiously, Harry seated himself down on his brother's midriff. He raised his legs. Nothing happened. After he had counted slowly to fifteen, Harry lowered his legs and stood. "I'm going to take my shoes off now, Eddie, and stand on you."

He hurried over to a piano stool embroidered with fulsome roses and carried it back; then he slipped off his moccasins and stepped on top of the stool. As Harry stepped on top of Eddie's exposed thin belly, the chair supporting his brother's head wobbled. Harry stood stock-still for a moment, but the chair held. He lifted the other foot from the stool. No movement from the chair. He set the other foot on his brother. Little Eddie effortlessly held him up.

Harry lifted himself experimentally up on his toes and came back down on his heels. Eddie seemed entirely unaffected. Then Harry jumped perhaps half an inch into the air, and since Eddie did not even grunt when he landed, he kept jumping, five, six, seven, eight times, until he was breathing hard. "You're amazing, Little Eddie," he said, and stepped off onto the stool. "Now you can begin to relax. You can put your feet on the floor. Then I want you to sit back up in your chair. Your body doesn't feel stiff anymore."

Little Eddie had been rather tentatively lowering one foot, but as soon as Harry finished speaking he buckled in the middle and thumped his bottom on the floor. Harry's chair (Maryrose's chair) sickeningly tipped over, but landed soundlessly on a neat woolen stack of layered winter coats.

Moving like a robot, Little Eddie slowly sat upright on the floor. His eyes were open but unfocused.

"You can stand up now and get back in your chair," Harry said. He did not remember leaving the stool, but he had left it. Sweat ran into his eyes. He pressed his face into his shirt sleeve. For a second, panic had brightly beckoned. Little Eddie was sleepwalking back to his chair. When he sat down, Harry said, "Close your eyes. You're going deeper and deeper into sleep. Deeper and deeper, Little Eddie."

Eddie settled into the chair as if nothing had happened, and Harry reverently set his own chair upright again. Then he picked up the book and opened it. The print swam before his eyes. Harry shook his head and looked again, but still the lines of print snaked across the page. (When Harry was a sophomore at Adelphi College he was asked to read several poems by Guillaume Apollonaire, and the appearance of the wavering lines on the page brought back this moment with a terrible precision.) Harry pressed the palms of his hands against his eyes, and red patterns exploded across his vision.

He removed his hands from his eyes, blinked, and found that although the lines of print were now behaving themselves, he no longer wanted to go on. The attic was too hot, he was too tired, and the toppling of the chair had been too close a brush with actual disaster. But for a time he leafed purposefully through the book while Eddie tranced on, and then found the subheading "Post-Hypnotic Suggestion."

"Little Eddie, we're just going to do one more thing. If we ever do this again, it'll help us go faster." Harry shut the book. He knew exactly how this went; he would even use the same phrase Dr. Mentaine used with his patients. *Blue rose*—Harry did not quite know why, but he liked the sound of that.

"I'm going to tell you a phrase, Eddie, and from now on whenever you hear me say this phrase, you will instantly go back to sleep and be hypnotized again. The phrase is 'blue rose.' 'Blue rose.' When you hear me say 'blue rose,' you will go right to sleep, just the way you are now, and we can make you stronger again. 'Blue rose' is our secret, Eddie, because nobody else knows it. What is it?"

"Blue rose," Eddie said in a muffled voice.

"Okay. I'm going to count backward from ten, and when I get to 'one' you will be wide awake again. You will not remember anything we did, but you will feel happy and strong. Ten."

As Harry counted backwards, Little Eddie twitched and stirred, let his arms fall to his sides, thumped one foot carelessly on the floor, and at "one" opened his eyes.

"Did it work? What'd I do? Am I strong?"

"You're a bull," Harry said. "It's getting late, Eddie—time to go downstairs."

Harry's timing was accurate enough to be uncomfortable. As

soon as the two boys closed the attic door behind them they heard the front door slide open in a cacophony of harsh coughs and subdued mutterings followed by the sound of unsteady footsteps proceeding to the bathroom. Edgar Beevers was home.

6

Late that night the three homebound Beevers sons lay in their separate beds in the good-sized second-floor room next to the attic stairs. Directly above Maryrose's bedroom, its dimensions were nearly identical to it except that the boys' room, the "dorm," had no window seat and the attic stairs shaved a couple of feet from Harry's end. When the other two boys had lived at home, Harry and Little Eddie had slept together, Albert had slept in a bed with Sonny, and only George, who at the time of his induction into the Army had been six feet tall and weighed two hundred and one pounds, had slept alone. In those days, Sonny had often managed to make Albert cry out in the middle of the night. The very idea of George could still make Harry's stomach freeze.

Though it was now very late, enough light from the street came in through the thin white net curtains to give complex shadows to the bunched muscles of Albert's upper arms as he lay stretched out atop his sheets. The voices of Maryrose and Edgar Beevers, one approximately sober and the other unmistakably drunk, came clearly up the stairs and through the open door.

"*Who* says I waste my time? I don't say that. I don't waste my time."

"I suppose you think you've done a good day's work when you spell a bartender for a couple of hours—and then drink up your wages! That's the story of your life, Edgar Beevers, and it's a sad, sad story of w-a-s-t-e. If my father could have seen what would become of you . . ."

"I ain't so damn bad."

"You ain't so damn good, either."

"Albert," Eddie said softly from his bed between his two brothers.

As if galvanized by Little Eddie's voice, Albert suddenly sat up in bed, leaned forward, and reached out to try to smack Eddie with his fist.

"I didn't do nothin'!" Harry said, and moved to the edge of his mattress. The blow had been for him, he knew, not Eddie, except that Albert was too lazy to get up.

"I hate your lousy guts," Albert said. "If I wasn't too tired to get out of this-here bed, I'd pound your face in."

"Harry stole my birthday car, Albert," Eddie said. "Makum gimme it back."

"One day," Maryrose said from downstairs, "at the end of the summer when I was seventeen, late in the afternoon, my father said to my mother, 'Honey, I believe I'm going to take out our pretty little Maryrose and get her something special,' and he called up to me from the drawing room to make myself pretty and get set to go, and because my father was a gentleman and a Man of His Word, I got ready in two shakes. My father was wearing a very handsome brown suit and a red bow tie and his boater. I remember just like I can see it now. He stood at the bottom of the staircase, waiting for me, and when I came down he took my arm and we just went out that front door like a courting couple. Down the stone walk, which my father put in all by himself even though he was a white-collar worker, down Majeski Street, arm in arm down to South Palmyra Avenue. In those days all the best people, all the people who counted, did their shopping on South Palmyra Avenue."

"I'd like to knock your teeth down your throat," Albert said to Harry.

"Albert, he took my birthday car, he really did, and I want it back. I'm ascared he busted it. I want it back so much I'm gonna die."

Albert propped himself up on an elbow and for the first time really looked at Little Eddie. Eddie whimpered. "You're such a twerp," Albert said. "I wish you *would* die, Eddie, I wish you'd just drop dead so we could stick you in the ground and forget about you. I wouldn't even cry at your funeral. Prob'ly I wouldn't even be able to remember your name. I'd just say, 'Oh yeah, he was that little creepy kid used to hang around cryin' all the time, glad he's dead, whatever his name was.' "

Eddie had turned his back on Albert and was weeping softly,

his unwashed face distorted by the shadows into an uncanny image of the mask of tragedy.

"You know, I really wouldn't mind if you dropped dead," Albert mused. "You neither, shitbird."

". . . realized he was taking me to Alouette's. I'm sure you used to look in their windows when you were a little boy. You remember Alouette's, don't you? There's never been anything so beautiful as that store. When I was a little girl and lived in the big house, all the best people used to go there. My father marched me right inside, with his arm around me, and took me up in the elevator and we went straight to the lady who managed the dress department. 'Give my little girl the best,' he said. Price was no object. Quality was all he cared about. 'Give my little girl the best.' *Are you listening to me, Edgar?*"

Albert snored face-down into his pillow; Little Eddie twitched and snuffled. Harry lay awake for so long he thought he would never get to sleep. Before him he kept seeing Little Eddie's face all slack and dopey under hypnosis—Little Eddie's face made him feel hot and uncomfortable. Now that Harry was lying down in bed, it seemed to him that everything he had done since returning from Big John's seemed really to have been done by someone else, or to have been done in a dream. Then he realized that he had to use the bathroom.

Harry slid out of bed, quietly crossed the room, went out onto the dark landing, and felt his way downstairs to the bathroom.

When he emerged, the bathroom light showed him the squat black shape of the telephone atop the Palmyra directory. Harry moved to the low telephone table beside the stairs. He lifted the phone from the directory and opened the book, the width of a Big 5 tablet, with his other hand. As he had done on many other nights when his bladder forced him downstairs, Harry leaned over the page and selected a number. He kept the number in his head as he closed the directory and replaced the telephone. He dialed. The number rang so often Harry lost count. At last a hoarse voice answered. Harry said, "I'm watching you, and you're a dead man." He softly replaced the receiver in the cradle.

7

Harry caught up with his father the next afternoon just as Edgar Beevers had begun to move up South Sixth Street toward the corner of Livermore. His father wore his usual costume of baggy gray trousers cinched far above his waist by a belt with a double buckle, a red-and-white plaid shirt, and a brown felt hat stationed low over his eyes. His long fleshy nose swam before him, cut in half by the shadow of the hat brim.

"Dad!"

His father glanced incuriously at him, then put his hands back in his pockets. He turned sideways and kept walking down the street, though perhaps a shade more slowly. "What's up, kid? No school?"

"It's summer, there isn't any school. I just thought I'd come with you for a little."

"Well, I ain't doing much. Your ma asked me to pick up some hamburg on Livermore, and I thought I'd slip into the Idle Hour for a quick belt. You won't turn me in, will you?"

"No."

"You ain't a bad kid, Harry. Your ma's just got a lot of worries. I worry about Little Eddie too, sometimes."

"Sure."

"What's with the books? You read when you walk?"

"I was just sort of looking at them," Harry said.

His father insinuated his hand beneath Harry's left elbow and extracted two luridly jacketed paperback books. They were titled *Murder, Incorporated* and *Hitler's Death Camps.* Harry already loved both of these books. His father grunted and handed *Murder, Incorporated* back to him. He raised the other book nearly to the tip of his nose and peered at the cover, which depicted a naked woman pressing herself against a wall of barbed wire while a uniformed Nazi aimed a rifle at her back.

Looking up at his father, Harry saw that beneath the harsh line of shadow cast by the hat brim his father's whiskers grew in different colors and patterns. Black and brown, red and orange, the glistening spikes swirled across his father's cheek.

"I bought this book, but it didn't look nothing like that," his father said, and returned the book.

"What didn't?"

"That place. Dachau. That death camp."

"How do you know?"

"I was there, wasn't I? You wasn't even born then. It didn't look anything like that picture on that book. It just looked like a piece a shit to me, like most of the places I saw when I was in the Army."

This was the first time Harry had heard that his father had been in the service.

"You mean, you were in World War II?"

"Yeah, I was in the Big One. They made me a corporal over there. Had me a nickname too. 'Beans.' 'Beans' Beevers. And I got a Purple Heart from the time I got a infection."

"You saw Dachau with your own eyes?"

"Damn straight, I did." He bent down suddenly. "Hey— don't let your ma catch you readin' that book."

Secretly pleased, Harry shook his head. Now the book and the death camp were a bond between himself and his father.

"Did you ever kill anybody?"

His father wiped his mouth and both cheeks with one long hand. Harry saw a considering eye far back in the shadow of the brim.

"I killed a guy once."

A long pause.

"I shot him in the back."

His father wiped his mouth again, and then motioned forward with his head. He had to get to the bar, the butcher, and back again in a very carefully defined period of time. "You really want to hear this?"

Harry nodded. He swallowed.

"I guess you do, at that. Okay—we was sent into this camp, Dachau, at the end of the war to process the prisoners and arrest the guards and the commandant. Everything was all arranged. A bunch of brass hats from Division were going to come on an inspection, so we had to wait there a couple days. We had these guards lined up, see, and these skinny old wrecks would come up and give 'em hell. We wasn't supposed to let 'em get too near."

They were passing Mr. Petrosian's little tar-paper house, and Harry felt a spasm of relief that Mr. Petrosian was not out on his tiny porch working on his case of beer. The Idle Hour was only a few paces ahead.

"Anyhow, one of these guards, one of the worst ones, suddenly decided he's going to run for it. He takes off, runnin' like crazy toward the woods. What do I do? I ask. Nobody knows what the hell to do. Shoot him, somebody says. So I shot him in the back. That was all she wrote."

Now they had reached the screen door which led into the Idle Hour, and the smells of malt and hops filled the air. "See you back at the house," his father said, and disappeared through the screen door like a magician.

8

After Harry had read a hundred pages of *Murder, Incorporated*, his favorite murderers were Louis "Lepke" Buchalter and Abe "Kid Twist" Reles. They were dependable professionals. A kind of black light surrounded them and made them glitter. Lepke Buchalter and Abe Reles looked out at the world from the shadows of their hat brims. They lived in shadowy rooms and peered out through the curtains. They appeared on a dark corner before their terrified victim, did their work, and walked away, turning up their coat collars.

Suppose you had some kind of job that took you around the country, like a salesman's job, Harry thought as he read away the afternoon in the porch swing; suppose you had a job that took you from one town to another. Suppose you killed someone in each one of those towns, carefully and quietly, and hid the bodies so it would take people a long time to find them. Your work would never be done.

9

"Blue rose," Harry said.

Little Eddie sagged openmouthed against the cane of his chair, his hands loose in his lap.

It had worked. Harry looked around as if he expected applause, and did feel that all the things in the attic looked back at him with warm approval. It was nine-thirty at night; he and Eddie, alone in the house, occupied the attic in perfect safety.

Harry wanted to see if he could put other people under and make them do things, but for now, for tonight, he was content to experiment with Eddie.

"You're going deeper and deeper asleep, Eddie, deeper and deeper, and you're listening to every word I say. You're just sinking down and down, hearing my voice come to you, going deeper and deeper with every word, and now you are real deep asleep and ready to begin."

Little Eddie sat sprawled over Maryrose's cane-backed chair, his chin touching his chest and his little pink mouth drooping open. He looked like a slightly undersized seven-year-old, like a second-grader instead of the fourth-grader he would be when he joined Mrs. Franken's class in the fall. Suddenly he reminded Harry of the Ultraglide Roadster, scratched and dented and stripped of its tires.

"Tonight you're going to see how strong you really are. Sit up, Eddie."

Eddie pulled himself upright and closed his mouth, almost comically obedient.

Harry thought it would be fun to make Little Eddie believe he was a dog and trot around the attic on all fours, barking and lifting his leg. Then he saw Little Eddie staggering across the attic, his tongue bulging out of his mouth, his own hands squeezing and squeezing his throat. Maybe he would try that too, after he had done several other exercises he had discovered in Dr. Mentaine's book. He checked the underside of his collar for maybe the fifth time that evening, and felt the long thin shaft of the pearl-headed hatpin he had stopped reading *Murder, Incorporated* long enough to smuggle out of Maryrose's bedroom after she had left for work.

"Eddie," he said, "now you are very deeply asleep, and you will be able to do everything I say. I want you to hold your right arm straight out in front of you."

Eddie stuck his arm out like a poker.

"That's good, Eddie. Now I want you to notice that all the feeling is leaving that arm. It's getting number and number. It doesn't even feel like flesh and blood anymore. It feels like it's made out of steel or something. It's so numb that you can't feel anything there anymore. You can't even feel pain in it."

Harry stood up, went toward Eddie, and brushed his fingers along his arm. "You didn't feel anything, did you?"

"No," Eddie said in a slow gravel-filled voice.

"Do you feel anything now?" Harry pinched the underside of Eddie's forearm.

"No."

"Now?" Harry used his nails to pinch the side of Eddie's biceps, hard, and left purple dents in the skin.

"No," Eddie repeated.

"How about this?" He slapped his hand against Eddie's forearm as hard as he could. There was a sharp loud smacking sound, and his fingers tingled. If Little Eddie had not been hypnotized, he would have tried to screech down the walls.

"No," Eddie said.

Harry pulled the hatpin out of his collar and inspected his brother's arm. "You're doing great, Little Eddie. You're stronger than anybody in your whole class—you're probably stronger than the whole rest of the school." He turned Eddie's arm so that the palm was up and the white forearm, lightly traced by small blue veins, faced him.

Harry delicately ran the point of the hatpin down Eddie's pale, veined forearm. The pinpoint left a narrow chalk-white scratch in its wake. For a moment Harry felt the floor of the attic sway beneath his feet; then he closed his eyes and jabbed the hatpin into Little Eddie's skin as hard as he could.

He opened his eyes. The floor was still swaying beneath him. From Little Eddie's lower arm protruded six inches of the eight-inch hatpin, the mother-of-pearl head glistening softly in the light from the overhead bulb. A drop of blood the size of a watermelon seed stood on Eddie's skin. Harry moved back to his chair and sat down heavily. "Do you feel anything?"

"No," Eddie said again in that surprisingly deep voice.

Harry stared at the hatpin embedded in Eddie's arm. The oval drop of blood lengthened itself out against the white skin and began slowly to ooze toward Eddie's wrist. Harry watched it advance across the pale underside of Eddie's forearm. Finally he stood up and returned to Eddie's side. The elongated drop of blood had ceased moving. Harry bent over and twanged the hatpin. Eddie could feel nothing. Harry put his thumb and forefinger on the glistening head of the pin. His face was so hot he might have been standing before an open fire. He pushed the pin a further half inch into Eddie's arm, and another small quantity of blood welled up from the base. The pin seemed to be moving in Harry's grasp, pulsing back and forth as if it were breathing.

"Okay," Harry said. "Okay."

He tightened his hold on the pin and pulled. It slipped easily from the wound. Harry held the hatpin before his face just as a doctor holds up a thermometer to read a temperature. He had imagined that the entire bottom section of the shaft would be painted with red, but saw that only a single winding glutinous streak of blood adhered to the pin. For a dizzy second he thought of slipping the end of the pin in his mouth and sucking it clean.

He thought: Maybe in another life I was Lepke Buchalter.

He pulled his handkerchief, a filthy square of red paisley, from his front pocket and wiped the streak of blood from the shaft of the pin. Then he leaned over and gently wiped the red smear from Little Eddie's underarm. Harry refolded the handkerchief so the blood would not show, wiped sweat from his face, and shoved the grubby cloth back into his pocket.

"That was good, Eddie. Now we're going to do something a little bit different."

He knelt down beside his brother and lifted Eddie's nearly weightless, delicately veined arm. "You still can't feel a thing in this arm, Eddie, it's completely numb. It's sound asleep and it won't wake up until I tell it to." Harry repositioned himself in order to hold himself steady while he knelt, and put the point of the hatpin nearly flat against Eddie's arm. He pushed it forward far enough to raise a wrinkle of flesh. The point of the hatpin dug into Eddie's skin but did not break it. Harry pushed harder, and the hatpin raised the little bulge of skin by a small but appreciable amount.

Skin was a lot tougher to break through than anyone imagined.

The pin was beginning to hurt his fingers, so Harry opened his hand and positioned the head against the base of his middle finger. Grimacing, he pushed his hand against the pin. The point of the pin popped through the raised wrinkle.

"Eddie, you're made out of beer cans," Harry said, and

tugged the head of the pin backwards. The wrinkle flattened out. Now Harry could shove the pin forward again, sliding the shaft deeper and deeper under the surface of Little Eddie's skin. He could see the raised line of the hatpin marching down his brother's arm, looking as prominent as the damage done to a cartoon lawn by a cartoon rabbit. When the mother-of-pearl head was perhaps three inches from the entry hole, Harry pushed it down into Little Eddie's flesh, thus raising the point of the pin. He gave the head a sharp jab, and the point appeared at the end of the ridge in Eddie's skin, poking through a tiny smear of blood. Harry shoved the pin in further. Now it showed about an inch and a half of gray metal at either end.

"Feel anything?"

"Nothing."

Harry jiggled the head of the pin, and a bubble of blood walked out of the entry wound and began to slide down Eddie's arm. Harry sat down on the attic floor beside Eddie and regarded his work. His mind seemed pleasantly empty of thought, filled only with a variety of sensations. He *felt* but could not hear a buzzing in his head, and a blurry film seemed to cover his eyes. He breathed through his mouth. The long pin stuck through Little Eddie's arm looked monstrous seen one way; seen another, it was sheerly beautiful. Skin, blood, and metal. Harry had never seen anything like it before. He reached out and twisted the pin, causing another little blood-snail to crawl from the exit wound. Harry saw all this as if through smudgy glasses, but he did not mind. He knew the blurriness was only mental. He touched the head of the pin again and moved it from side to side. A little more blood leaked from both punctures. Then Harry shoved the pin in, partially withdrew it so that the point nearly disappeared back into Eddie's arm, moved it forward again; and went on like this, back and forth, back and forth as if he were sewing his brother up, for some time.

Finally he withdrew the pin from Eddie's arm. Two long streaks of blood had nearly reached his brother's wrist. Harry ground the heels of his hands into his eyes, blinked, and discovered that his vision had cleared.

He wondered how long he and Eddie had been in the attic. It could have been hours. He could not quite remember what had happened before he had slid the hatpin into Eddie's skin. Now his blurriness really was mental, not visual. A loud uncomfortable pulse beat in his temples. Again he wiped the blood from Eddie's arm. Then he stood on wobbling knees and returned to his chair.

"How's your arm feel, Eddie?"

"Numb," Eddie said in his gravelly sleepy voice.

"The numbness is going away now. Very, very slowly. You are beginning to feel your arm again, and it feels very good. There is no pain. It feels like the sun was shining on it all afternoon. It's strong and healthy. Feeling is coming back into your arm, and you can move your fingers and everything."

When he had finished speaking Harry leaned back against the chair and closed his eyes. He rubbed his forehead with his hand and wiped the moisture off on his shirt.

"How does your arm feel?" he said without opening his eyes.

"Good."

"That's great, Little Eddie." Harry flattened his palms against his flushed face, wiped his cheeks, and opened his eyes.

I can do this every night, he thought. I can bring Little Eddie up here every single night, at least until school starts.

"Eddie, you're getting stronger and stronger every day. This is really helping you. And the more we do it, the stronger you'll get. Do you understand me?"

"I understand you," Eddie said.

"We're almost done for tonight. There's just one more thing I want to try. But you have to be really deep asleep for this to work. So I want you to go deeper and deeper, as deep as you can go. Relax, and now you are really deep asleep, deep deep, and relaxed and ready and feeling good."

Little Eddie sat sprawled in his chair with his head tilted back and his eyes closed. Two tiny dark spots of blood stood out like mosquito bites on his lower right forearm.

"When I talk to you, Eddie, you're slowly getting younger and younger, you're going backward in time, so now you're not nine years old anymore, you're eight, it's last year and you're in the third grade, and now you're seven, and now you're six years old . . . and now you're five, Eddie, and it's the day of your fifth birthday. You're five years old today, Little Eddie. How old are you?"

"I'm five." To Harry's surprised pleasure, Little Eddie's voice actually seemed younger, as did his hunched posture in the chair.

"How do you feel?"

"Not good. I hate my present. It's terrible. Dad got it, and Mom says it should never be allowed in the house because it's just junk. I wish I wouldn't ever have to have birthdays, they're so terrible. I'm gonna cry."

His face contracted. Harry tried to remember what Eddie had gotten for his fifth birthday, but could not—he caught only a dim memory of shame and disappointment. "What's your present, Eddie?"

In a teary voice, Eddie said, "A radio. But it's busted and Mom says it looks like it came from the junkyard. I don't want it anymore. I don't even wanna *see* it."

Yes, Harry thought, yes, yes, yes. He could remember. On Little Eddie's fifth birthday, Edgar Beevers had produced a yellow plastic radio which even Harry had seen was astoundingly ugly. The dial was cracked, and it was marked here and there with brown circular scablike marks where someone had mashed out cigarettes on it.

The radio had long since been buried in the junk room, where it now lay beneath several geological layers of trash.

"Okay, Eddie, you can forget the radio now, because you're going backwards again, you're getting younger, you're going backwards through being four years old, and now you're three."

He looked with interest at Little Eddie, whose entire demeanor had changed. From being tearfully unhappy, Eddie now demonstrated a self-sufficient good cheer Harry could not ever remember seeing in him. His arms were folded over his chest. He was smiling, and his eyes were bright and clear and childish.

"What do you see?" Harry asked.

"Mommy-ommy-om."

"What's she doing?"

"Mommy's at her desk. She's smoking and looking through her papers." Eddie giggled. "Mommy looks funny. It looks like smoke is coming out of the top of her head." Eddie ducked his chin and hid his smile behind a hand. "Mommy doesn't see me. I can see her, but she doesn't see me. Oh! Mommy works hard! She works hard at her desk!"

Eddie's smile abruptly left his face. His face froze for a second in a comic rubbery absence of expression; then his eyes widened in terror and his mouth went loose and wobbly.

"What happened?" Harry's mouth had gone dry.

"No, Mommy!" Eddie wailed. "Don't, Mommy! I wasn't spying, I wasn't, I promise—" His words broke off into a screech. "NO, MOMMY! DON'T! DON'T, MOMMY!" Eddie jumped upward, sending his chair flying back, and ran blindly toward the rear of the attic. Harry's head rang with Eddie's screeches. He heard a sharp *crack!* of wood breaking, but only as a small part of all the noise Eddie was making as he charged around the attic. Eddie had run into a tangle of hanging dresses, spun around, enmeshing himself deeper in the dresses, and was now tearing himself away from the web of dresses, pulling some of them off the rack. A long-sleeved purple dress with an enormous lace collar had draped itself around Eddie like a ghostly dance partner, and another dress, this of dull red velvet, snaked around his right leg. Eddie screamed again and yanked himself away from the tangle. The entire rack of clothes wobbled and then went over in a mad jangle of sound.

"NO!" he screeched. "HELP!" Eddie ran straight into a big wooden beam marking off one of the eaves, bounced off, and came windmilling toward Harry. Harry knew his brother could not see him.

"Eddie, stop," he said, but Eddie was past hearing him. Harry tried to make Eddie stop by wrapping his arms around him, but Eddie slammed right into him, hitting Harry's chest with a shoulder and knocking his head painfully against Harry's chin; Harry's arms closed on nothing and his eyes lost focus, and Eddie went crashing into the tilting mirror. The mirror yawned over sideways. Harry saw it tilt with dreamlike slowness toward the floor, then in an eye blink drop and crash. Broken glass sprayed across the attic floor.

"STOP!" Harry yelled. "STAND STILL, EDDIE!"

Eddie came to rest. The ripped and dirty dress of dull red velvet still clung to his right leg. Blood oozed down his temple from an ugly cut above his eye. He was breathing hard, releasing air in little whimpering exhalations.

"Holy shit," Harry said, looking around at the attic. In only a few seconds Eddie had managed to create what looked at first like absolute devastation. Maryrose's ancient dresses lay tangled in a heap of dusty fabrics from which wire hangers skeletally protruded; gray Eddie-sized footprints lay like a pattern over the muted explosion of colors the dresses now created. When the rack had gone over, it had knocked a section the size of a dinner plate out of a round wooden coffee table Maryrose had particularly prized for its being made from a single section of teak—"a single piece of *teak,* the rarest wood in all the world, all the way from Ceylon!" The much-prized mirror lay in hundreds of glittering pieces across the attic floor. With growing horror, Harry saw that the wooden frame had cracked like a bone, showing a bone-pale, shockingly white fracture in the expanse of dark stain.

Harry's blood tipped within his body, nearly tipping him with it, like the mirror. "Oh God oh God oh God."

He turned slowly around. Eddie stood blinking two feet to his side, wiping ineffectually at the blood running from his forehead and now covering most of his left cheek. He looked like an Indian in war paint—a defeated, lost Indian, for his eyes were dim and his head turned aimlessly from side to side.

A few feet from Eddie lay the chair in which he had been sitting. One of its thin curved wooden arms lay beside it, crudely severed. It looked like an insect's leg, Harry thought, like a toy gun.

For a moment Harry thought that his face too was red with blood. He wiped his hand over his forehead and looked at his glistening palm. It was only sweat. His heart beat like a bell. Beside him Eddie said, "Aaah . . . what . . . ?" The injury to his head had brought him out of the trance.

The dresses were ruined, stepped on, tangled, torn. The mirror was broken. The table had been mutilated. Maryrose's chair lay on its side like a murder victim, its severed arm ending in a bristle of snapped ligaments.

"My head *hurts,*" Eddie said in a weak, trembling voice. "What happened? Ah! I'm all blood! I'm all blood, Harry!"

"You're all blood, you're all blood?" Harry shouted at him. "Everything's *all blood,* you dummy! Look around!" He did not recognize his own voice, which sounded high and tinny and seemed to be coming from somewhere else. Little Eddie took an aimless step away from him, and Harry wanted to fly at him, to pound his bloody head into a pancake, to destroy him, smash him . . .

Eddie held up his bloodstained palm and stared at it. He wiped it vaguely across the front of his T-shirt and took another wandering step. "I'm ascared, Harry," his tiny voice uttered.

"Look what you did!" Harry screamed. "You wrecked everything! Damn it! What do you think is going to happen to us?"

"What's Mom going to do?" Eddie asked in a voice only slightly above a whisper.

"You don't know?" Harry yelled. "You're dead!"

Eddie started to weep.

Harry bunched his hands into fists and clamped his eyes shut. They were both dead, that was the real truth. Harry opened his eyes, which felt hot and oddly heavy, and stared at his sobbing, red-smeared, useless little brother. "Blue rose," he said.

10

Little Eddie's hands fell to his sides. His chin dropped, and his mouth fell open. Blood ran in a smooth wide band down the left side of his face, dipped under the line of his jaw, and continued on down his neck and into his T-shirt. Pooled blood in his left eyebrow dripped steadily onto the floor, as if from a faucet.

"You are going deep *asleep*," Harry said. Where was the hatpin? He looked back to the single standing chair and saw the mother-of-pearl head glistening on the floor near it. "Your whole body is *numb*." He moved over to the pin, bent down, and picked it up. The metal shaft felt warm in his fingers. "You can feel no *pain*." He went back to Little Eddie. "Nothing can *hurt* you." Harry's breath seemed to be breathing itself, forcing itself into his throat in hot harsh shallow pants, then expelling itself out.

"Did you *hear* me, Little Eddie?"

In his gravelly, slow-moving hypnotized voice, Little Eddie said, "I heard you."

"And you can feel no *pain?*"

"I can feel no pain."

Harry drew his arm back, the point of the hatpin extending forward from his fist, and then jerked his hand forward as hard as he could and stuck the pin into Eddie's abdomen right through the blood-soaked T-shirt. He exhaled sharply, and tasted a sour misery on his breath.

"You don't feel a thing."

"I don't feel a thing."

Harry opened his right hand and drove his palm against the head of the pin, hammering it in another few inches. Little Eddie looked like a voodoo doll. A kind of sparkling light surrounded him. Harry gripped the head of the pin with his thumb and forefinger and yanked it out. He held it up and inspected it. Glittering light surrounded the pin too. The long shaft was painted with blood. Harry slipped the point into his mouth and closed his lips around the warm metal.

He saw himself, a man in another life, standing in a row with men like himself in a bleak gray landscape defined by barbed wire. Emaciated people in rags shuffled up toward them and spat on their clothes. The smells of dead flesh and of burning flesh hung in the air. Then the vision was gone, and Little Eddie stood before him again, surrounded by layers of glittering light.

Harry grimaced or grinned, he could not have told the difference, and drove his long spike deep into Eddie's stomach.

Eddie uttered a small *oof*.

"You don't feel anything, Eddie," Harry whispered. "You feel good all over. You never felt better in your life."

"Never felt better in my life."

Harry slowly pulled out the pin and cleaned it with his fingers.

He was able to remember every single thing anyone had ever told him about Tommy Golz.

"Now you're going to play a funny, funny game," he said. "This is called the Tommy Golz game because it's going to keep you safe from Mrs. Franken. Are you ready?" Harry carefully slid the pin into the fabric of his shirt collar, all the while watching Eddie's slack blood-streaked person. Vibrating bands of light beat rhythmically and steadily about Eddie's face.

"Ready," Eddie said.

"I'm going to give you your instructions now, Little Eddie. Pay attention to everything I say and it's all going to be okay. Everything's going to be okay—as long as you play the game exactly the way I tell you. You understand, don't you?"

"I understand."

"Tell me what I just said."

"Everything's gonna be okay as long as I play the game exactly the way you tell me." A dollop of blood slid off Eddie's eyebrow and splashed onto his already soaked T-shirt.

"Good, Eddie. Now the first thing you do is fall down—not now, when I tell you. I'm going to give you all the instructions, and then I'm going to count backwards from ten, and when I get to *one*, you'll start playing the game. Okay?"

"Okay."

"So first you fall down, Little Eddie. You fall down real hard. Then comes the fun part of the game. You bang your head on the floor. You start to go crazy. You twitch, and you bang your hands and feet on the floor. You do that for a long time. I guess you do that until you count to about a hundred. You foam at the mouth, you twist all over the place. You get real stiff, and then you get real loose, and then you get real stiff, and then real loose again, and all this time you're banging your head and your hands and feet on the floor, and you're twisting all over the place. Then when you finish counting to a hundred in your head, you do the last thing. You swallow your tongue. And that's the game. When you swallow your tongue you're the winner. And then nothing bad can happen to you, and Mrs. Franken won't be able to hurt you ever ever ever ever."

Harry stopped talking. His hands were shaking. After a second he realized that his insides were shaking too. He raised his trembling fingers to his shirt collar and felt the hatpin.

"Tell me how you win the game, Little Eddie. What's the last thing you do?"

"I swallow my tongue."

"Right. And then Mrs. Franken and Mom will never be able to hurt you, because you won the game."

"Good," said Little Eddie. The glittering light shimmered about him.

"Okay, we'll start playing right now," Harry said. "Ten." He went toward the attic steps. "Nine." He reached the steps. "Eight."

He went down one step. "Seven." Harry descended another two steps. "Six." When he went down another two steps, he called up in a slightly louder voice, "Five."

Now his head was beneath the level of the attic floor, and he could not see Little Eddie anymore. All he could hear was the soft, occasional plop of liquid hitting the floor.

"Four."

"Three."

"Two." He was now at the door to the attic steps. Harry opened the door, stepped through it, breathed hard, and shouted "One!" up the stairs.

He heard a thud, and then quickly closed the door behind him.

Harry went across the hall and into the dormitory bedroom. There seemed to be a strange absence of light in the hallway. For a second he saw—was sure he saw—a line of dark trees across a wall of barbed wire. Harry closed this door behind him too, and went to his narrow bed and sat down. He could feel blood beating in his face; his eyes seemed oddly warm, as if they were heated by filaments. Harry slowly, almost reverently extracted the hatpin from his collar and set it on his pillow. "A hundred," he said. "Ninety-nine, ninety-eight, ninety-seven, ninety-six, ninety-five, ninety-four . . ."

When he had counted down to "one," he stood up and left the bedroom. He went quickly downstairs without looking at the door behind which lay the attic steps. On the ground floor he slipped into Maryrose's bedroom, crossed over to her desk, and slid open the bottom right-hand drawer. From the drawer he took a velvet-covered box. This he opened, and jabbed the hatpin in the ball of material, studded with pins of all sizes and descriptions, from which he had taken it. He replaced the box in the drawer, pushed the drawer into the desk, and quickly left the room and went upstairs.

Back in his own bedroom, Harry took off his clothes and climbed into his bed. His face still burned.

He must have fallen asleep very quickly, because the next thing he knew Albert was slamming his way into the bedroom and tossing his clothes and boots all over the place. "You asleep?" Albert asked. "You left the attic light on, you fuckin' dummies, but if you think I'm gonna save your fuckin' asses and go up and turn it off, you're even stupider than you look."

Harry was careful not to move a finger, not to move even a hair.

He held his breath while Albert threw himself onto his bed, and when Albert's breathing relaxed and slowed, Harry followed his big brother into sleep. He did not awaken again until he heard his father half screeching, half sobbing up in the attic, and that was very late at night.

11

Sonny came from Fort Sill, George all the way from Germany. Between them, they held up a sodden Edgar Beevers at the gravesite while a minister Harry had never seen before read from a Bible as cracked and rubbed as an old brown shoe. Between his two older sons, Harry's father looked bent and ancient, a skinny old man only steps from the grave himself. Sonny and George despised their father, Harry saw—they held him up on sufferance, in part because they had chipped in thirty dollars apiece to buy him a suit and did not want to see it collapse with its owner inside into the lumpy clay of the graveyard. His whiskers glistened in the sun, and moisture shone beneath his eyes and at the corners of his mouth. He had been shaking too severely for either Sonny or George to shave him, and had been capable of moving in a straight line only after George let him take a couple of long swallows from a leather-covered flask he took out of his duffel bag.

The minister uttered a few sage words on the subject of epilepsy.

Sonny and George looked as solid as brick walls in their uniforms, like prison guards or actual prisons themselves. Next to them, Albert looked shrunken and unfinished. Albert wore the green plaid sport jacket in which he had graduated from the eighth grade, and his wrists hung prominent and red four inches below the bottoms of the sleeves. His motorcycle boots were visible beneath his light gray trousers, but they, like the green jacket, had lost their flash. Like Albert, too. Ever since the discovery of Eddie's body, Albert had gone around the house looking as if he'd just bitten off the end of his tongue and was trying to decide whether or not to spit it out. He never looked anybody in the eye, and he rarely spoke. Albert acted as though a gigantic padlock had been fixed to the middle of his chest and *he* was damned if he'd ever take it off. He had not asked Sonny or George a single question about the Army. Every now and then he would utter a remark about the gas station so toneless that it suffocated any reply.

Harry looked at Albert standing beside their mother, kneading his hands together and keeping his eyes fixed as if by decree on the square foot of ground before him. Albert glanced over at Harry, knew he was being looked at, and did what to Harry was an extraordinary thing. Albert *froze*. All expression drained out of his face, and his hands locked immovably together. He looked as little able to see or hear as a statue. *He's that way because he told Little Eddie that he wished he would die*, Harry thought for the tenth or eleventh time since he had realized this, and with undiminished awe. Then was he lying? Harry wondered. And if he really did wish that Little Eddie would drop dead, why isn't he happy now? Didn't he get what he wanted? Albert would never spit out that piece of his tongue, Harry thought, watching his brother blink slowly and sightlessly toward the ground.

Harry shifted his gaze uneasily to his father, still propped up between George and Sonny, heard that the minister was finally reaching the end of his speech, and took a fast look at his mother. Maryrose was standing very straight in a black dress and black sunglasses, holding the straps of her bag in front of her with both hands. Except for the color of her clothes, she could have been a spectator at a tennis match. Harry knew by the way she was holding her face that she was wishing she could smoke. Dying for a cigarette, he thought, ha-ha, the Monster Mash, it's a graveyard smash.

The minister finished speaking, and made a rhetorical gesture with his hands. The coffin sank on ropes into the rough earth. Harry's father began to weep loudly. First George, then Sonny, picked up large damp shovel-marked pieces of the clay and dropped them on the coffin. Edgar Beevers nearly fell in after his own tiny clod, but George contemptuously swung him back. Maryrose marched forward, bent and picked up a random piece of clay with thumb and forefinger as if using tweezers, dropped it, and turned away before it struck. Albert fixed his eyes on Harry—his own clod had split apart in his hand and crumbled away between his fingers. Harry shook his head *no*. He did not want to drop dirt on Eddie's coffin and make that noise. He did not want to look at Eddie's coffin again. There was enough dirt around to do the job without him hitting that metal box like he was trying to ring Eddie's doorbell. He stepped back.

"Mom says we have to get back to the house," Albert said.

Maryrose lit up as soon as they got into the single black car they had rented through the funeral parlor, and breathed out acrid smoke over everybody crowded into the back seat. The car backed into a narrow graveyard lane, and turned down the main road toward the front gates.

In the front seat, next to the driver, Edgar Beevers drooped sideways and leaned his head against the window, leaving a blurred streak on the glass.

"How in the name of hell could Little Eddie have epilepsy without anybody knowing about it?" George asked.

Albert stiffened and stared out the window.

"Well, that's epilepsy," Maryrose said. "Eddie could have gone on for years without having an attack." That she worked in a hospital always gave her remarks of this sort a unique gravity, almost as if she were a doctor.

"Must have been some fit," Sonny said, squeezed into place between Harry and Albert.

"Grand mal," Maryrose said, and took another hungry drag on her cigarette.

"Poor little bastard," George said. "Sorry, Mom."

"I know you're in the armed forces, and armed forces people speak very freely, but I wish you would not use that kind of language."

Harry, jammed into Sonny's rock-hard side, felt his brother's body twitch with a hidden laugh, though Sonny's face did not alter.

"I said I was sorry, Mom," George said.

"Yes. Driver! Driver!" Maryrose was leaning forward, reaching out one claw to tap the chauffeur's shoulder. "Livermore is the next right. Do you know South Sixth Street?"

"I'll get you there," the driver said.

This is not my family, Harry thought. I came from somewhere else and my rules are different from theirs.

* * *

His father mumbled something inaudible as soon as they got in the door and disappeared into his curtained-off cubicle. Maryrose put her sunglasses in her purse and marched into the kitchen to warm the coffee cake and the macaroni casserole, both made that morning, in the oven. Sonny and George wandered into the living room and sat down on opposite ends of the couch. They did not look at each other—George picked up a *Reader's Digest* from the table and began leafing through it backward, and Sonny folded his hands in his lap and stared at his thumbs. Albert's footsteps plodded up the stairs, crossed the landing, and went into the dormitory bedroom.

"What's she in the kitchen for?" Sonny asked, speaking to his hands. "Nobody's going to come. Nobody ever comes here, because she never wanted them to."

"Albert's taking this kind of hard, Harry," George said. He propped the magazine against the stiff folds of his uniform and looked across the room at his little brother. Harry had seated himself beside the door, as out of the way as possible. George's attentions rather frightened him, though George had behaved with consistent kindness ever since his arrival two days after Eddie's death. His crew cut still bristled and he could still break rocks with his chin, but some more violent demon seemed to have left him. "You think he'll be okay?"

"Him? Sure." Harry tilted his head, grimaced.

"He didn't see Little Eddie first, did he?"

"No, Dad did," Harry said. "He saw the light on in the attic when he came home, I guess. Albert went up there, though. I guess there was so much blood Dad thought somebody broke in and killed Eddie. But he just bumped his head, and that's where the blood came from."

"Head wounds bleed like bastards," Sonny said. "A guy hit me with a bottle once in Tokyo. I thought I was gonna bleed to death right there."

"And Mom's stuff got all messed up?" George asked quietly. This time Sonny looked up.

"Pretty much, I guess. The dress rack got knocked down. Dad cleaned up what he could, the next day. One of the cane-back chairs got broke, and a hunk got knocked out of the teak table. And the mirror got broken into a million pieces."

Sonny shook his head and made a soft whistling sound through his pursed lips.

"She's a tough old gal," George said. "I hear her coming, though, so we have to stop, Harry. But we can talk tonight."

Harry nodded.

12

After dinner that night, when Maryrose had gone to bed—the hospital had given her two nights off—Harry sat across the kitchen table from a George who clearly had something to say. Sonny had polished off a six-pack by himself in front of the television and gone up to the dormitory bedroom by himself. Albert had disappeared shortly after dinner, and their father had never emerged from his cubicle beside the junk room.

"I'm glad Pete Petrosian came over," George said. "He's a good old boy. Ate two helpings too."

Harry was startled by George's use of their neighbor's first name—he was not even sure that he had ever heard it before.

Mr. Petrosian had been their only caller that afternoon. Harry had seen that his mother was grateful that someone had come, and despite her preparations wanted no more company after Mr. Petrosian had left.

"Think I'll get a beer, that is if Sonny didn't drink it all," George said, and stood up and opened the fridge. His uniform looked as if it had been painted on his body, and his muscles bulged and moved like a horse's. "Two left," he said. "Good thing you're underage." George popped the caps off both bottles and came back to the table. He winked at Harry, then tilted the first bottle to his lips and took a good swallow. "So what the devil was Little Eddie doing up there anyhow? Trying on dresses?"

"I don't know," Harry said. "I was asleep."

"Hell, I know I kind of lost touch with Little Eddie, but I got the impression he was scared of his shadow. I'm surprised he had the nerve to go up there and mess around with Mom's precious stuff."

"Yeah," Harry said. "Me too."

"You didn't happen to go with him, did you?" George tilted the bottle to his mouth and winked at Harry again.

Harry just looked back. He could feel his face getting hot.

"I just was thinking maybe you saw it happen to Little Eddie, and got too scared to tell anybody. Nobody would be mad at you, Harry. Nobody would blame you for anything. You couldn't know how to help someone who's having an epileptic fit. Little Eddie swallowed his tongue. Even if you'd been standing next to him when he did it and had the presence of mind to call an ambulance, he would have died before it got there. Unless you knew what was wrong and how to correct it. Which nobody would expect you to know, not in a million years. Nobody'd blame you for anything, Harry, not even Mom."

"I was asleep," Harry said.

"Okay, okay. I just wanted you to know."

They sat in silence for a time, then both spoke at once.

"Did you know—"

"We had this—"

"Sorry," George said. "Go on."

"Did you know that Dad used to be in the Army? In World War II?"

"Yeah, I knew that. Of course I knew that."

"Did you know that he committed the perfect murder once?"

"What?"

"Dad committed the perfect murder. When he was at Dachau, that death camp."

"Oh Christ, is that what you're talking about? You got a funny way of seeing things, Harry. He shot an enemy who was trying to escape. That's not murder, it's war. There's one hell of a big difference."

"I'd like to see war someday," Harry said. "I'd like to be in the Army, like you and Dad."

"Hold your horses, hold your horses," George said, smiling now. "That's sort of one of the things I wanted to talk to you about." He set down his beer bottle, cradled his hands around it, and tilted his head to look at Harry. This was obviously going to be serious. "You know, I used to be crazy and stupid, that's the only way to put it. I used to look for fights. I had a chip on my shoulder the size of a house, and pounding some dipshit into a coma was my idea of a great time. The Army did me a lot of good. It made me grow up. But I don't think you need that, Harry. You're too smart for that—if you have to go, you go, but out of all of us, you're the one who could really amount to something in this world. You could be a doctor. Or a lawyer. You ought to get the best education you can, Harry. What you have to do is stay out of trouble and get to college."

"Oh, college," Harry said.

"Listen to me, Harry. I make pretty good money, and I got nothing to spend it on. I'm not going to get married and have kids, that's for sure. So I want to make you a proposition. If you keep your nose clean and make it through high school, I'll help you out with college. Maybe you can get a scholarship—I think you're smart enough, Harry, and a scholarship would be great. But either way, I'll see you make it through." George emptied the first bottle, set it down, and gave Harry a quizzical look. "Let's get one person in this family off on the right track. What do you say?"

"I guess I better keep reading," Harry said.

"I hope you'll read your ass off, little buddy," George said, and picked up the second bottle of beer.

13

The day after Sonny left, George put all of Eddie's toys and clothes into a box and squeezed the box into the junk room; two days later, George took a bus to New York so he could get his flight to Munich from Idlewild. An hour before he caught his bus, George walked Harry up to Big John's and stuffed him full of hamburgers and french fries and said, "You'll probably miss Eddie a lot, won't you?" "I guess," Harry said, but the truth was that Eddie was now only a vacancy, a blank space. Sometimes a door would close and Harry would know that Little Eddie had just come in; but when he turned to look, he saw only emptiness. George's question, asked a week ago, was the last time Harry had heard anyone pronounce his brother's name.

In the seven days since the charmed afternoon at Big John's and the departure on a southbound bus of George Beevers, everything seemed to have gone back to the way it was before, but Harry knew that really everything had changed. They had been a loose, divided family of five, two parents and three sons. Now they seemed to be a family of three, and Harry thought that the actual truth was that the family had shrunk down to two, himself and his mother.

Edgar Beevers had left home—he too was an absence. After two visits from policemen who parked their cars right outside the house, after listening to his mother's muttered expressions of disgust, after the spectacle of his pale, bleary, but sober and clean-shaven father trying over and over to knot a necktie in front of the bathroom mirror, Harry finally accepted that his father had been caught shoplifting. His father had to go to court, and he was scared. His hands shook so uncontrollably that he could not shave himself, and in the end Maryrose had to knot his tie—doing it in one, two, three quick movements as brutal as the descent of a knife, never removing the cigarette from her mouth.

Grief-stricken Area Man Forgiven of Shoplifting Charge, read the headline over the little story in the evening newspaper which at last explained his father's crime. Edgar Beevers had been stopped on the sidewalk outside the Livermore Avenue National Tea, T-bone steaks hidden inside his shirt and a bottle of Rheingold beer in each of his front pockets. He had stolen two steaks! He had put beer bottles in his pockets! This made Harry feel like he was sweating inside. The judge had sent him home, but home was not where he went. For a short time, Harry thought, his father had hung out on Oldtown Road, Palmyra's Skid Row, and slept in vacant lots with winos and bums. (Then a woman was supposed to have taken him in.)

Albert was another mystery. It was as though a creature from outer space had taken him over and was using his body, like *Invasion of the Body Snatchers*. Albert looked like he thought somebody was always standing behind him, watching every move he made. He was still carrying around that piece of his tongue, and pretty soon, Harry thought, he'd get so used to it that he would forget he had it.

Three days after George left Palmyra, Albert had actually tagged along after Harry on the way to Big John's. Harry had turned around on the sidewalk and seen Albert in his black jeans and grease-blackened T-shirt halfway down the block, shoving his hands in his pockets and looking hard at the ground. That was Albert's way of pretending to be invisible. The next time he turned around, Albert growled, "Keep walking."

Harry went to work on the pinball machine as soon as he got inside Big John's. Albert slunk in a few minutes later and went straight to the counter. He took one of the stained paper menus from a stack squeezed in beside a napkin dispenser and inspected it as if he had never seen it before.

"Hey, let me introduce you guys," said Big John, leaning against the far side of the counter. Like Albert, he wore black jeans and motorcycle boots, but his dark hair, daringly for the nineteen-fifties, fell over his ears. Beneath his stained white apron he wore a long-sleeved black shirt with a pattern of tiny azure palm trees. "You two are the Beevers boys, Harry and Bucky. Say hello to each other, fellows."

Bucky Beaver was a toothy rodent in an Ipana television commercial. Albert blushed, still grimly staring at his menu sheet.

"Call me Beans," Harry said, and felt Albert's gaze shift wonderingly to him.

"Beans and Bucky, the Beevers boys," Big John said. "Well, Buck, what'll you have?"

"Hamburger, fries, shake," Albert said.

Big John half turned and yelled the order through the hatch to Mama Mary's kitchen. For a time the three of them stood in uneasy silence. Then Big John said, "Heard your old man found a new place to hang his hat. His new girlfriend is a real pistol, I heard. Spent some time in County Hospital. On account of she picked up little messages from outer space on the good old Philco. You hear that?"

"He's gonna come home real soon," Harry said. "He doesn't have any new girlfriend. He's staying with an old friend. She's a rich lady and she wants to help him out because she knows he had a lot of trouble and she's going to get him a real good job, and then he'll come home, and we'll be able to move to a better house and everything."

He never even saw Albert move, but Albert had materialized beside him. Fury, rage, and misery distorted his face. Harry had time to cry out only once, and then Albert slammed a fist into his chest and knocked him backwards into the pinball machine.

"I bet that felt real good," Harry said, unable to keep down his own rage. "I bet you'd like to kill me, huh? Huh, Albert? How about that?"

Albert moved backward two paces and lowered his hands, already looking impassive, locked into himself.

For a second in which his breath failed and dazzling light filled his eyes, Harry saw Little Eddie's slack, trusting face before him. Then Big John came up from nowhere with a big hamburger and a mound of french fries on a plate and said, "Down, boys. Time for Rocky here to tackle his dinner."

That night Albert said nothing at all to Harry as they lay in their beds. Neither did he fall asleep. Harry knew that for most of the night Albert just closed his eyes and faked it, like a possum in trouble. Harry tried to stay awake long enough to see when Albert's fake sleep melted into the real thing, but he sank into dreams long before that.

He was rushing down the stony corridor of a castle past suits of armor and torches guttering in sconces. His bladder was bursting, he had to let go, he could not hold it more than another few seconds . . . at last he came to the open bathroom door and ran into that splendid gleaming place. He began to tug at his zipper, and looked around for the butler and the row of marble urinals. Then he froze. Little Eddie was standing before him, not the uniformed butler. Blood ran in a gaudy streak from a gash high on his forehead over his cheek and right down his neck, neat as paint. Little Eddie was waving frantically at Harry, his eyes bright and hysterical, his mouth working soundlessly because he had swallowed his tongue.

Harry sat up straight in bed, about to scream, then realized that the bedroom was all around him and Little Eddie was gone. He hurried downstairs to the bathroom.

14

At two o'clock the next afternoon Harry Beevers had to pee again, and just as badly, but this time he was a long way from the bathroom across from the junk room and his father's old cubicle. Harry was standing in the humid sunlight across the street from 45 Oldtown Way. This short street connected the bums, transient hotels, bars, and seedy movie theaters of Oldtown Road with the more respectable hotels, department stores, and restaurants of Palmyra Avenue—the real downtown. 45 Oldtown Way was a four-story brick tenement with an exoskeleton of fire escapes. Black iron bars covered the ground-floor windows. On one side of 45 Oldtown Way were the large soapsmeared windows of a bankrupted shoe store, on the other a vacant lot where loose bricks and broken bottles nestled amongst dandelions and tall Queen Anne's lace. Harry's father lived in that building now. Everybody else knew it, and since Big John had told him, now Harry knew it too.

He jigged from leg to leg, waiting for a woman to come out through the front door. It was as chipped and peeling as his own, and a broken fanlight sat drunkenly atop it. Harry had checked the row of dented mailboxes on the brick wall just outside the door for his father's name, but none bore any names at all. Big John hadn't known the name of the woman who had taken Harry's father, but he said that she was large, black-haired, and crazy, and that she had two children in foster care. About half an hour ago a dark-haired woman had come through the door, but Harry had not followed her because she had not looked especially large to him. Now he was beginning to have doubts. What did Big John mean by "large" anyhow? As big as he was? And how could you tell if someone was crazy? Did it show? Maybe he should have followed that woman. This thought made him even more anxious, and he squeezed his legs together.

His father was in that building now, he thought. Harry thought of his father lying on an unmade bed, his brown winter coat around him, his hat pulled low on his forehead like Lepke Buchalter's, drawing on a cigarette, looking moodily out the window.

Then he had to pee so urgently that he could not have held it in for more than a few seconds, and trotted across the street and into the vacant lot. Near the back fence the tall weeds gave him some shelter from the street. He frantically unzipped and let the braided yellow stream splash into a nest of broken bricks. Harry looked up at the side of the building beside him. It looked very tall, and seemed to be tilting slightly toward him. The four windows on each floor looked back down at him, blank and fatherless. Just as he was tugging at his zipper, he heard the front door of the building slam shut.

His heart slammed too. Harry hunkered down behind the tall white weeds. Anxiety that she might walk the other way, toward downtown, made him twine his fingers together and bend his fingers back. If he waited about five seconds, he figured, he'd know she was going toward Palmyra Avenue and would be able to get across the lot in time to see which way she turned. His knuckles cracked. He felt like a soldier hiding in a forest, like a murder weapon.

He raised up on his toes and got ready to dash back across the street, because an empty grocery cart closely followed by a moving belly with a tiny head and basketball shoes, a cigar tilted in its mouth like a flag, appeared past the front of the building. He could go back and wait across the street. Harry settled down and watched the stomach go down the sidewalk past him. Then a shadow separated itself from the street side of the fat man, and the shadow became a black-haired woman in a long loose dress now striding past the grocery cart. She shook back her head, and Harry saw that she was tall as a queen and that her skin was darker than olive. Deep lines cut through her cheeks. It had to be the woman who had taken his father. Her long rapid strides had taken her well past the fat man's grocery cart. Harry ran across the rubble of the lot and began to follow her up the sidewalk.

His father's woman walked in a hard, determined way. She stepped down into the street to get around groups too slow for her. At the Oldtown Road corner she wove her way through a group of saggy-bottomed men passing around a bottle in a paper bag and cut in front of two black children dribbling a basketball up the street. She was on the move, and Harry had to hurry along to keep her in sight.

"I bet you don't believe me," he said to himself, practicing, and skirted the group of winos on the corner. He picked up his speed until he was nearly trotting. The two black kids with the basketball ignored him as he kept pace with them, then went on ahead. Far up the block, the tall woman with bouncing black hair marched right past a flashing neon sign in a bar window. Her bottom moved back and forth in the loose dress, surprisingly big whenever it bulged out the fabric of the dress; her back

seemed as long as a lion's. "What would you say if I told you
. . ." Harry said to himself.

A block and a half ahead, the woman turned on her heel and
went through the door of the A&P store. Harry sprinted the rest
of the way, pushed the yellow wooden door marked ENTER, and
walked into the dense, humid air of the grocery store. Other
A&P stores may have been air-conditioned, but not the little
shop on Oldtown Road.

What was foster care anyway? Did you get money if you gave
away your children?

A good person's children would never be in foster care, Harry
thought. He saw the woman turning into the third aisle past the
cash register. He saw with a small shock that she was taller than
his father. If I told you, you might not believe me. He went
slowly around the corner of the aisle. She was standing on the
pale wooden floor about fifteen feet in front of him, carrying a
wire basket in one hand. He stepped forward. What I have to
say might seem. . . . For good luck, he touched the hatpin
inserted into the bottom of his collar. She was staring at a row of
brightly colored bags of potato chips. Harry cleared his throat.
The woman reached down and picked up a big bag and put it in
the basket.

"Excuse me," Harry said.

She turned her head to look at him. Her face was as wide as it
was long, and in the mellow light from the store's low-wattage
bulbs her skin seemed a very light shade of brown. Harry knew
he was meeting an equal. She looked like she could do magic, as
if she could shoot fire and sparks out of her fierce black eyes.

"I bet you don't believe me," he said, "but a kid can hypnotize people just as good as an adult."

"What's that?"

His rehearsed words now sounded crazy to him, but he stuck
to his script.

"A kid can hypnotize people. I can hypnotize people. Do you
believe that?"

"I don't think I even care," she said, and wheeled away toward the rear of the aisle.

"I bet you don't think I could hypnotize you," Harry said.

"Kid, get lost."

Harry suddenly knew that if he kept talking about hypnotism

the woman would turn down the next aisle and ignore him no matter what he said, or else begin to speak in a very loud voice about seeing the manager. "My name is Harry Beevers," he said to her back. "Edgar Beevers is my dad."

She stopped and turned around and looked expressionlessly into his face.

Harry dizzyingly saw a wall of barbed wire before him, a dark green wall of trees at the other end of a barren field.

"I wonder if you maybe call him Beans," Harry said.

"Oh, great," she said. "That's just great. So you're one of his boys. Terrific. *Beans* wants potato chips, what do you want?"

"I want you to fall down and bang your head and swallow your tongue and *die* and get buried and have people drop dirt on you," Harry said. The woman's mouth fell open. "Then I want you to puff up with *gas.* I want you to *rot.* I want you to turn green and *black.* I want your *skin* to slide off your bones."

"You're crazy!" the woman shouted at him. "Your whole family's crazy! Do you think your mother wants him anymore?"

"My father shot us in the back," Harry said, and turned and bolted down the aisle for the door.

When he got outside he began to trot down seedy Oldtown Road. When he came to Oldtown Way he turned left. When he ran past number 45, he looked at every blank window. His face, his hands, his whole body felt hot and wet. Soon he had a stitch in his side. Harry blinked, and saw a dark line of trees, a wall of barbed wire before him. At the top of Oldtown Way he turned into Palmyra Avenue. From there he could continue running past Alouette's boarded-up windows, past all the stores old and new, to the corner of Livermore, and from there, he only now realized, to the little house that belonged to Mr. Petrosian.

15

On a sweltering midafternoon eleven years later at a camp in the Central Highlands of Vietnam, Lieutenant Harry Beevers closed the flap of his tent against the mosquitoes and sat on the edge of his temporary bunk to write a long-delayed letter back to Pat Caldwell, the young woman he wanted to marry—and to whom he would be married for a time, after his return from the war to New York State.

This is what he wrote, after frequent crossings-out and hesitations. Harry later destroyed this letter.

Dear Pat:

First of all I want you to know how much I miss you, my darling, and that if I ever get out of this beautiful and terrible country, which I am going to do, that I am going to chase you mercilessly and unrelentingly until you say that you'll marry me. Maybe in the euphoria of relief (YES!!!), I have the future all worked out, Pat, and you're a big part of it. I have eighty-six days until DEROS, when they pat me on the head and put me on that big bird out of here. Now that my record is clear again, I have no doubts that Columbia Law School will take me in. As you know, my law board scores were pretty respectable (modest me!) when I took them at Adelphi. I'm pretty sure I could even get into Harvard Law, but I settled on Columbia because then we could both be in New York.

My brother George has already told me that he will help out with whatever money I—you and I—will need. George put me through Adelphi. I don't think you knew this. In fact, nobody knew this. When I look back, in college I was such a jerk. I wanted everybody to think my family was well-to-do, or at least middle-class. The truth is, we were damn poor, which I think makes my accomplishments all the more noteworthy, all the more loveworthy!

You see, this experience, even with all the ugly and self-doubting and humiliating moments, has done me a lot of good. I was right to come here, even though I had no idea what it was really like. I think I needed the experience of war to complete me, and I tell you this even though I know that you will detest any such idea. In fact, I have to tell you that a big part of me loves being here, and that in some way, even with all this trouble, this year will always be one of the high points of my life. Pat, as you see, I'm determined to be honest—to be an honest man. If I'm going to be a lawyer, I ought to be honest, don't you think? (Or maybe the reverse is the reality!) One thing that has meant a lot to me here has been what I can only call the close comradeship of my friends and my men—I actually like the grunts more than the

usual officer types, which of course means that I get more loyalty
and better performance from my men than the usual lieutenant.
Some day I'd like you to meet Mike Poole and Tim Underhill
and Pumo the Puma and the most amazing of all, M. O. Dengler, who of course was involved with me in the Ia Thuc cave
incident. These guys stuck by me. I even have a nickname,
"Beans." They call me "Beans" Beevers, and I like it.

There was no way my court-martial could have really put me in
any trouble, because all the facts, and my own men, were on my
side. Besides, could you see me actually killing children? This is
Vietnam and you kill people, that's what we're doing here—we
kill Charlies. But we don't kill babies and children. Not even in
the heat of wartime—and Ia Thuc was pretty hot!

Well, this is my way of letting you know that at the court-
martial of course I received a complete and utter vindication.
Dengler did too. There were even unofficial mutterings about
giving us medals for all the BS we put up with for the past six
weeks—including that amazing story in Time magazine. Before
people start yelling about atrocities, they ought to have all the
facts straight. Fortunately, last week's magazines go out with the
rest of the trash.

Besides, I already knew too much about what death does to
people.

I never told you that I once had a little brother named Edward.
When I was ten, my little brother wandered up into the top floor
of our house one night and suffered a fatal epileptic fit. This
event virtually destroyed my family. It led directly to my father's
leaving home. (He had been a hero in WWII, something else I
never told you.) It deeply changed, I would say even damaged, my
older brother Albert. Albert tried to enlist in 1964, but they
wouldn't take him because they said he was psychologically unfit.
My mom too almost came apart for a while. She used to go up in
the attic and cry and wouldn't come down. So you could say that
my family was pretty well destroyed, or ruined, or whatever you
want to call it, by a sudden death. I took it, and my dad's deser-
tion, pretty hard myself. You don't get over these things easily.

The court-martial lasted exactly four hours. Big deal, hey?—as
we used to say back in Palmyra. We used to have a neighbor
named Pete Petrosian who said things like that, and against what
must have been million-to-one odds, who died exactly the same

*way my brother did, about two weeks after—lightning really did
strike twice. I guess it's dumb to think about him now, but maybe
one thing war does is to make you conversant with death. How it
happens, what it does to people, what it means, how all the dead
in your life are somehow united, joined, part of your eternal family. This is a profound feeling, Pat, and no damn whipped-up
failed court-martial can touch it. If there were any innocent children in that cave, then they are in my family forever, like little
Edward and Pete Petrosian, and the rest of my life is a poem to
them. But the Army says there weren't, and so do I.*

*I love you and love you and love you. You can stop worrying
now and start thinking about being married to a Columbia Law
student with one hell of a good future. I won't tell you any more
war stories than you want to hear. And that's a promise, whether
the stories are about Nam or Palmyra.*

> *Always yours,*
> *Harry*
> *(aka "Beans!")*

PETER STRAUB is the author of *Julia, If You Could See Me
Now, Ghost Story, Shadowland* and *Floating Dragon,* as well as
The Talisman, written in collaboration with Stephen King. The
first two titles, along with a previously unreleased novel, *Under
Venus,* have been collected in one volume as *Wild Animals.*
Forthcoming are two books: the novel *Koko* and a collection of
novellas.

JOE HALDEMAN

The Monster

Start at the beginning? Which beginning?

Okay, since you be from Outside, I give you the whole thing. Sit over there, be comfort. Smoke em if you got em.

They talk about these guys that come back from the Nam all fucked up and shit, and say they be like time bombs: they go along okay for years, then get a gun and just go crazy. But it don't go nothing like that for me. Even though there be the gun involved, this time. And an actual murder, this time.

First time I be in prison, after the court martial, I try to tell them what it be and what they get me? Social workers and shrinks. Guy to be a shrink in a prison ain't be no good shrink, what they can make Outside, is the way I figure it, so at first I don't give them shit, but then I always get Discipline, so I figure what the hell and make up a story. You watch any TV you can make up a Nam story too.

So some of them don't fall for it, they go along with it for a while because this is what crazy people do, is make up stories, then they give up and another one comes along and I start over with a different story. And sometime when I know for sure they don't believe, when they start to look at me like you look at a animal in the zoo, that's when I tell them the real true story. And that's when they smile, you know, and nod and the new guy come in next. Because if anybody would make up a story like that one he'd have to be crazy, right? But I swear to God it's true.

Right. The beginning.

I be a lurp in the Nam, which means Long Range Recon Patrol. You look in these magazines about the Nam and they

56

make like the lurps be always heroes, brave boys go out and face Charlie alone, bring down the artillery on them and all, but it was not like that. You didn't want to be no lurp where we be, they make you be a fuckin lurp if they want to get rid of your ass, and that's the God's truth.

Now I can tell you right now that I don't give a flyin fuck for that U.S. Army and I don't like it even more when I be drafted, but I got to admit they be pretty smart, the way they do with us. Because we get off on that lurp shit. I mean we be one bunch of bad ass brothers and good old boys and we did love that rock an roll, and God they give us rock an roll—fuck your M-16, we get real tommy guns with 100-round drum, usually one guy get your automatic grenade launcher, one guy carry that starlite scope, another guy the full demo bag. I mean we could of taken on the whole fuckin North Vietnam Army. We could of killed fuckin Rambo.

Now I like to talk strange, though any time I want, I can talk like other people. Even Jamaican like my mama ain't understand me if I try. I be born in New York City, but at that time my mama be only three months there—when she speak her English it be island music, but the guy she live with, bringing me up, he be from Taiwan, so in between them I learn shitty English, same-same shitty Chinese. And live in Cuban neighborhood, *por el español* shitty.

He was one mean mother fuckin Chinese cab driver, slap shit out of me for twelve year, and then I take a kitchen knife and slap him back. He never come back for the ear. I think maybe he go off someplace and die, I don't give a shit any more, but when I be drafted they find out I speak Chinese, send me to language school in California, and I be so dumb I believe them when they say this means no Nam for the boy: I stay home and translate for them tapes from the radio.

So they send me to the Nam anyhow, and I go a little wild. I hit everybody that outranks me. They put me in the hospital and I hit the doctor. They put me in the stockade and I hit the guards, the guards hit back, some more hospital. I figure sooner or later they got to kill me or let me out. But then one day this strac dude come in and tell me about the lurp shit. It sound all right, even though the dude say if I fuck up they can waste me and it's legal. By now I know they can do that shit right there in

LBJ, Long Binh Jail, so what the fuck? In two days I'm in the jungle with three real bad ass dudes with a map and a compass and enough shit we could start our own war.

They give us these maps that never have no words on them, like names of places, just "TOWN POP. 1000" and shit like that. They play it real cute, like we so dumb we don't know there be places outside of Vietnam, where no GIs can go. They keep all our ID in base camp, even the dog tags, and tell us not to be capture. Die first, they say, that shall be more pleasant. We laugh at that later, but I keep to myself the way I do feel. That the grave be one place we all be getting to, long road or short, and maybe the short road be less bumps, less trouble. Now I know from twenty years how true that be.

They don't tell us where the place be we leave from, after the slick drop us in, but we always sure as hell head west. Guy name Duke, mean honky but not dumb, he say all we be doin is harassment, bustin up supply lines comin down the Ho Chi Minh Trail, in Cambodia. It do look like that, long lines of gooks carryin ammo and shit, sometime on bicycles. We would set up some mine and some Claymores and wait till the middle of the line be there, then pop the shit, then maybe waste a few with the grenade launcher and tommy guns, not too long so they ain't regroup and get us. Duke be taking a couple Polaroids and we go four different ways, meet a couple miles away, then sneak back to the LZ and call the slick. We go out maybe six time a month, maybe lose one guy a month. Me and Duke make it through all the way to the last one, that last one.

That time no different from the other times except they tell us try to blow a bridge up, not a big bridge like the movies, but one that hang off a mountain side, be hard to fix afterward. It also be hard to get to.

We lose one guy, new guy name of Winter, just tryin to get to the fuckin bridge. That be bad in a special kind of way. You get used to guys gettin shot or be wasted by frags and like that. But to fall like a hundred feet onto rocks be a different kind of bad. And it just break his back or something. He laying there and crying, tell all the world where we be, until Duke shut him up.

So it be just Duke and Cherry and me, the Chink. I am for goin back, no fuckin way they could blame us for that. But Duke crazy for action, always be crazy for killing, and Cherry would follow Duke anywhere, I think he a fag even then. Later I do know. When the Monster kill them.

This is where I usually feel the need to change. It's natural to adjust one's mode of discourse to a level appropriate to the subject at hand, is it not? To talk about this "Monster" requires addressing such concepts as disassociation and multiple personality, if only to discount them, and it would be awkward to speak of these things directly the way I normally speak, as Chink. This does not mean that there are two or several personalities resident within the sequestered hide of this disabled black veteran. It only means that I can speak in different ways. You could as well, if you grew up switching back and forth among Spanish, Chinese, and two flavors of English; chocolate and vanilla. It might also help if you had learned various Vietnamese dialects, and then spent the past twenty years in a succession of small rooms, mainly reading and writing. There still be the bad mother fucker in here. He simply uses appropriate language. The right tool for the job, or the right weapon.

Let me save us some time by demonstrating the logical weakness of some facile first-order rationalizations that always seem to come up. One: that this whole Monster business is a bizarre lie I concocted and have stubbornly held on to for twenty years —which requires that it never have occurred to me that recanting it would result in much better treatment and, possibly, release. Two: that the Monster is some sort of psychological shield, or barrier, that I have erected between my "self" and the enormity of the crime I committed. That hardly holds up to inspection, since my job and life at that time comprised little more than a succession of premeditated cold-blooded murders. I didn't kill the two men, but if I had, it wouldn't have bothered me enough to require elaborate psychological defenses. Three: that I murdered Duke and Cherry because I was . . . upset at discovering them engaged in a homosexual act. I am and was indifferent toward that aberration, or hobby. Growing up in the ghetto and going directly from there to an Army prison in Vietnam, I witnessed perversions for which you psychologists don't even have names.

Then of course there is the matter of the supposed eyewitness. It seemed particularly odious to me at the time that my government would prefer the testimony of an erstwhile enemy soldier over one of its own. I see the process more clearly now, and realize that I was convicted before the court-martial was even convened.

The details? You know what a *hoi chan* was? You're too young. Well, *chieu hoi* is Vietnamese for "open arms"; if an enemy soldier came up to the barbed wire with his hands up, shouting *chieu hoi*, then in theory he would be welcomed into our loving, also open, arms and rehabilitated. Unless he was killed before people could figure out what he was saying. The rehabilitated ones were called *hoi chans*, and sometimes were used as translators and so forth.

Anyhow, this Vietnamese deserter's story was that he had been following us all day, staying out of sight, waiting for an opportunity to surrender. I don't believe that for a second. Nobody moves that quietly, that fast, through unfamiliar jungle. Duke had been a professional hunting guide back in the World, and he would have heard any slightest movement.

What do I say happened? You must have read the transcript . . . I see. You want to check me for consistency.

I had sustained a small but deep wound in the calf, a fragment from a rifle grenade, I believe. I did elude capture, but the wound slowed me down.

We had blown the bridge at 1310, which was when the guards broke for lunch, and had agreed to rendezvous by 1430 near a large banyan tree about a mile from the base of the cliff. It was after 1500 when I got there, and I was worried. Winter had been carrying our only radio when he fell, and if I wasn't at the LZ with the other two, they would sensibly enough leave without me. I would be stranded, wounded, lost.

I was relieved to find them still waiting. In this sense I may *have* caused their deaths: if they had gone on, the Monster might have killed only me.

This is the only place where my story and that of the *hoi chan* are the same. They were indeed having sex. I waited under cover rather than interrupt them.

Yes, I know, this is where he testified I jumped them and did all those terrible things. Like *he* had been sitting off to one side, waiting for them to finish their business. What a bunch of bullshit.

What actually happened—what *actually* happened—was that

I was hiding there behind some bamboo, waiting for them to finish so we could get on with it, when there was this sudden loud crashing in the woods on the other side of them, and bang. There was the Monster. It was bigger than any man, and black —not black like me, but glossy black, like shiny hair—and it just flat smashed into them, bashed them apart. Then it was on Cherry, I could hear bones crack like sticks. It bit him between the legs, and that was enough for me. I was gone. I heard a couple of short bursts from Duke's tommy gun, but I didn't go back to check it out. Just headed for the LZ as fast as my leg would let me.

So I made a big mistake. I lied. Wouldn't you? I'm supposed to tell them sorry, the rest of the squad got eaten by a werewolf? So while I'm waiting for the helicopter I make up this believable account of what happened at the bridge.

The slick comes and takes me back to the fire base, where the medics dress the wound and I debrief to the major there. They send me to Tuy Hoa, nice hospital on the beach, and I debrief again, to a bunch of captains and a bird colonel. They tell me I'm in for a Silver Star.

So I'm resting up there in the ward, reading a magazine, when in comes a couple of MPs and they grab me and haul me off to the stockade. Isn't that just like the Army, to have a stockade in a hospital?

What has happened is that this gook, honorable *hoi chan* Nguyen Van Trong, has come out of the woodwork with his much more believable story. So I get railroaded and wind up in jail.

Come on now, it's all in the transcript. I'm tired of telling it. It upsets me.

Oh, all right. This Nguyen claims he was a guard at the bridge we blew up, and he'd been wanting to escape—they don't say "desert"—ever since they'd left Hanoi a few months before. Walking down the Ho Chi Minh Trail. So in the confusion after the blast, he runs away; he hears Duke and Cherry and follows them. Waiting for the right opportunity to go *chieu hoi*. I've told you how improbable that actually is.

So he's waiting in the woods while they blow each other and up walks me. I get the drop on them with my Thompson. I make Cherry tie Duke to the tree. Then I tie Cherry up, facing him. Then I castrate Cherry—with my *teeth!* You believe that? And then with my teeth and fingernails, I flay Duke, skin him alive, from the neck down, while he's watching Cherry die. Then for dessert, I bite off his cock too. Then I cut them down and stroll away.

You got that? This Nguyen claims to have watched the whole thing, must have taken hours. Like he never had a chance to interrupt my little show. What, did I hang on to my weapon all the time I was nibbling away? Makes a lot of sense.

After I leave, he say he try to help the two men. Duke, he say, be still alive, but not worth much. Say he follow Duke's gestures and get the Polaroid out of his pack.

When those picture show up at the trial, I be a Had Daddy. Forget that his story ain't makin sense. Forget for Chris' sake that he be the fuckin *enemy!* Picture of Duke be still alive and his guts all hangin out, this godawful look on his face, I could of been fuckin Sister Teresa and they wouldn't of listen to me.

[At this point the respondent was silent for more than a minute, apparently controlling rage, perhaps tears. When he continued speaking, it was with the cultured white man's accent again.]

I know you are constrained not to believe me, but in order to understand what happened over the next few years, you must accept as tentatively true the fantastic premises of my delusional system. Mainly, that's the reasonable assertion that I didn't mutilate my friends, and the unreasonable one that the Cambodian jungle hides at least one glossy black humanoid over seven feet tall, with the disposition of a barracuda.

If you accept that this Monster exists, then where does that leave Mr. Nguyen Van Trong? One possibility is that he saw the same thing I did, and lied for the same reason I initially did— because no one in his right mind would believe the truth—but his lie implicated me, I suppose for verisimilitude.

A second possibility is the creepy one that Nguyen was somehow allied with the Monster; in league with him.

The third possibility . . . is that they were the same.

If the second or the third were true, it would probably be a good policy for me never to cross tracks with Nguyen again, or at least never to meet him unarmed. From that, it followed that it would be a good precaution for me to find out what had happened to him after the trial.

A maximum-security mental institution is far from an ideal place from which to conduct research. But I had several things going for me. The main thing was that I was not, despite all evidence to the contrary, actually crazy. Another was that I could take advantage of people's preconceptions, which is to say prejudices: I can tune my language from a mildly accented Jamaican dialect to the almost impenetrable patois that I hid behind while I was in the Army. Since white people assume that the smarter you are, the more like them you sound, and since most of my keepers were white, I could control their perception of me pretty well. I was a dumb nigger who with their help was getting a little smarter.

Finally I wangled a work detail in the library. Run by a white lady who thought she was hardass but had a heart of purest tapioca. Loved to see us goof off so long as we were reading.

I was gentle and helpful and appreciative of her guidance. She let me read more and more, and of course I could take books back to my cell. There was no record of many of the books I checked out: computer books.

She was a nice woman but fortunately not free of prejudice. It never occurred to her that it might not be a good idea to leave her pet darky alone with the computer terminal.

Once I could handle the library's computer system, my Nguyen project started in earnest. Information networks are wonderful, and computerized ordering and billing is, for a thief, the best tool since the credit card. I could order any book in print—after all, I opened the boxes, shelved the new volumes, and typed up the catalogue card for each book. If I wanted it to be catalogued.

Trying to find out what the Monster was, I read all I could find about extraterrestrials, werewolves, mutations; all that science fiction garbage. I read up on Southeast Asian religions and folk tales. Psychology books, because Occam's Razor can cut the person who's using it, and maybe I *was* crazy after all.

Nothing conclusive came out of any of it. I had seen the Monster for only a couple of seconds, but the quick impression was of course branded on my memory. The face was intelligent, perhaps I should say "sentient," but it was not at all human.

Two eyes, okay, but no obvious nose or ears. Mouth too big and lots of teeth like a shark's. Long fingers with too many joints, and claws. No mythology or pathology that I read about produced anything like it.

The other part of my Nguyen project was successful. I used the computer to track him down, through my own court records and various documents that had been declassified through the Freedom of Information Act.

Not surprisingly, he had emigrated to the United States just before the fall of Saigon. By 1986 he had his own fish market in San Francisco. Pillar of the community, the bastard.

Eighteen years of exemplary behavior and I worked my way down to minimum security. It was a more comfortable and freer life, but I didn't see any real chance of parole. I probably couldn't even be paroled if I'd been white and had bitten the cocks off two *black* men. I might get a medal, but not a parole.

So I had to escape. It wasn't hard.

I assumed that they would alert Nguyen, and perhaps watch him or even guard him for a while. So for two years I stayed away from San Francisco, burying myself in a dirt-poor black neighborhood in Washington. I saved my pennies and purchased or contrived the tools I would need when I eventually confronted him.

Finally I boarded a Greyhound, crawled to San Francisco, and rested up a couple of days. Then for another couple of days I kept an intermittent watch on the fish market, to satisfy myself that Nguyen wasn't under guard.

He lived in a two-room apartment in the rear of the store. I popped the back-door lock a half hour before closing and hid in the bedroom. When I heard him lock the front door, I walked in and pointed a .44 Magnum at his face.

That was the most tense moment for me. I more than half expected him to turn into the Monster. I had even gone to the trouble of casting my own bullets of silver, in case that superstition turned out to be true.

He asked me not to shoot and took out his wallet. Then he recognized me and clammed up.

I made him strip to his shorts and tied him down with duct tape to a wooden chair. I turned the television on fairly loud, since my homemade silencer was not perfect, and traded the

Magnum for a .22 automatic. It made about as much noise as a flyswatter each time I shot.

There are places where you can shoot a person even with a .22 and he will die quickly and without too much pain. There are other sites that are quite the opposite. Of course I concentrated on those, trying to make him talk. Each time I shot him I dressed the wound, so there would be a minimum of blood loss.

I first shot him during the evening news, and he lasted well into Johnny Carson, with a new bullet each half hour. He never said a word, or cried out. Just stared.

After he died, I waited a few hours, and nothing happened. So I walked to the police station and turned myself in. That's it.

So here we be now. I know it be life for me. Maybe it be that rubber room. I ain't care. This be the only place be safe. The Monster, he know. I can feel.

[This is the end of the transcript proper. The respondent did not seem agitated when the guards led him away. Consistent with his final words, he seemed relieved to be back in prison, which makes his subsequent suicide mystifying. The circumstances heighten the mystery, as the attached coroner's note indicates.]

State of California
Department of Corrections
Forensic Pathology Division
Glyn Malin, M.D., Ph.D.—Chief of Research

I have read about suicides that were characterized by sudden hysterical strength, including a man who had apparently choked himself to death by throttling (though I seem to recall that it was a heart attack that actually killed him). The case of Royce "Chink" Jackson is one I would not have believed if I had not seen the body myself.

The body is well-muscled, but not unusually so; when I'd heard how he died I assumed he was a mesomorphic weight-lifter type. Bones are hard to break.

Also, his fingernails are cut to the quick. It must have taken a burst of superhuman strength, to tear his own flesh without being able to dig in.

My first specialty was thoracic surgery, so I well know

how physically difficult it is to get to the heart. It's hard to believe that a person could tear out his own. It's doubly hard to believe that someone could do it after having brutally castrated himself.

I do have to confirm that that is what happened. The corridor leading to his solitary confinement cell is under constant video surveillance. No one came or went from the time the door was shut behind him until breakfast time, when the body was discovered.

He did it to himself, and in total silence.

GM:wr

JOE HALDEMAN is the author of *The Forever War, Mindbridge, All My Sins Remembered, Dealing in Futures* and the *Worlds* trilogy. A winner of both the Hugo and the Nebula Award, his short works have appeared in *Playboy, Omni,* and many other magazines and anthologies since the early 1970s. He recently completed a screenplay and is currently at work on new short stories and a novel.

KARL EDWARD WAGNER

Lacunae

They were resting, still joined together, in the redwood hot tub, water pushing in bubbling surges about their bodies. Elaine watched as the hot vortex caught up streamers of her semen, swirled it away like boiled confetti, dissipating it throughout the turbulence.

I'm disseminated, she thought.

Elaine said: "I feel reborn."

Allen kissed the back of her neck and brushed her softening nipples with his fingertips. "Your breasts are getting so full. Are you stepping up the estrogens?"

His detumescent penis, still slick with Vaseline, tickled as it eased out of Elaine's ass. Allen's right hand moved down through the warm water, milked the last droplets of orgasm from Elaine's flaccid cock. Gently he turned Elaine around, kissed her lovingly—probing his tongue deep into her mouth.

"Here," said Allen, breaking their kiss. He pushed down on Elaine's shoulders, urging her beneath the foaming surface. Elaine let her knees bend, ducked beneath the water that swirled about Allen's hips. As Allen's hands cupped her head, Elaine opened her mouth to accept Allen's slippery cock. She tasted the sweet smear of her own shit as she sucked in its entire length. Suddenly swelling, the cock filled her mouth, hardening as it pushed deep into her throat.

Elaine gagged and tried to pull back, but Allen's hands forced her head hard into his pubic hair. Water filled Elaine's nostrils as she choked, bit down in an uncontrollable reflex. Allen's severed cock, bitten free at the base, wriggled inward, sliding past the back of her throat and down into her windpipe.

Elaine wrenched free of Allen's hands. Blood and come filled her lungs—spewed from her mouth in an obscene fountain as her head pushed toward the surface. But her head could not break through the surface, no matter how desperately she fought. There was a black resilient layer that separated her from the air above, closed like wax over her face, pushed the vomit back into her lungs.

A vortex of blood and semen sucked her soul into its warm depths.

The first thing she heard was a monotoned *shit-shit-shit*—like autumn leaves brushing the window. She became aware of an abrupt pressure against her abdomen, of vomit being expelled from her mouth. She was breathing in gasps.

She opened her eyes. The layer of clinging blackness was gone.

"Shit goddammit," said Blacklight, wiping vomit from her face and nostrils. "Don't ever try that alone again."

Elaine stared at him dumbly, oxygen returning to her brain.

Beside her on the carpet lay the black leather bondage mask —its straps and laces cut. The attached phallus-shaped gag, almost bitten through, was covered with her vomit. A spiked leather belt, also slashed, was coiled about the mask.

"Jesus!" said Blacklight. "You OK now?"

He was wrapping a blanket around her, busily tucking it in. There was a buzzing somewhere, in her head or in her pelvis— she wasn't sure. Memory was returning.

"I dreamed I was a man," she said, forcing her throat to speak.

"Fuckin' A. You nearly dreamed you were dead. I had a buddy from Nam who used to do this kinda shit. He'd been dead two days before they found him."

Elaine looked upward at the chinning bar mounted high across her entrance hall doorway. The leather mask with its padded blindfold and gag—sensory deprivation and sensual depravity—cutting out the world. The belt, looped around her neck, free end held in her hands as she kicked away the stool. The belt buckle should have slipped free when she fainted from lack of oxygen. Instead its buckle had become entangled with the complex buckles of the bondage mask, not releasing, nearly suffocating her. Friends who had shown her how to experience visions of inner realities through this method had warned her, but until now there had been no problems. No worse than with the inversion apparatus.

"I heard you banging about on the floor," Blacklight explained, taking her pulse. He had been an army medic until he'd Section-Eighted—no future for a broad six-foot-eight medic in the paddies. "Thought maybe you were balling somebody, but it didn't feel right. I busted in your door."

Good job through two dead bolts and a chain, but Blacklight could do it. Her neighbor in the duplex loft had split last week, and the pizzeria downstairs was being redone as a vegetarian restaurant. Elaine might have lain there dead on the floor until her cats polished her bones.

"I dreamed I had a cock," she said, massaging her neck.

"Maybe you still do," Blacklight told her. He looked at his hands and went into the bathroom to wash them.

Elaine wondered what he meant, then remembered. She reached down to flick off the vibrator switch on the grotesque dildo she had strapped around her pelvis. Gathering the blanket about herself, she made it to her feet and waited for Blacklight to come out of the bathroom.

When she had removed the rest of her costume and washed herself, she put on a Chinese silk kimono and went to look for Blacklight. She felt little embarrassment. Between cheap smack in Nam and killer acid in the Haight, Blacklight's brain had been fried for most of his life. He was more reliable for deliveries than the Colombians, and old contacts supported him and his habit.

Blacklight was standing in the center of her studio—the loft was little more than one big room with a few shelves and counters to partition space—staring uncertainly at an unfinished canvas.

"You better look closer at your model, or else you got a freak." The canvas was wall-sized, originally commissioned and never paid for by a trendy leather bar, since closed. Blacklight pointed. "Balls don't hang side by side like that. One dangles a little lower. Even a dyke ought to know that."

"It's not completed," Elaine said. She was looking at the bag of white powder Blacklight had dropped onto her bar.

"You want to know why?"

"What?"

"It's so they don't bang together."

"Who doesn't?"

"Your balls. One slides away from the other when you mash your legs together."

"Terrific," said Elaine, digging a fingernail into the powder.

"You like it?"

"The thing about balls." Elaine tasted a smear of coke, licking her fingertip.

"Uncut Peruvian flake," Blacklight promised, forgetting the earlier subject.

Elaine sampled a nailful up each nostril. The ringing bitterness of the coke cut through the residues of vomit. Good shit.

"It's like Yin and Yang," Blacklight explained. "Good and Evil. Light and Dark."

One doesn't correct a large and crazed biker. He was wrestling his fists together. "Have you ever heard the story of Love and Hate?"

Across the knuckles of his right fist was tattooed LOVE; across those of his left: HATE.

Elaine had seen *The Night of the Hunter,* and she was not impressed.

"An ounce?"

"One humongous oh-zee." Blacklight was finger-wrestling with himself. "They got to be kept apart, Love and Hate, but they can't keep from coming together and trying to see which one's stronger."

Elaine opened the drawer beneath her telephone and counted out the bills she had set aside earlier. Blacklight forgot his Robert Mitchum impersonation and accepted the money.

"I got five paintings to finish before my show opens in SoHo, OK? That's next month. This is the end of this month. My ass is fucked, and I'm stone out of inspiration. So give me a break and split now, right?"

"Just don't try too much free-basing with that shit, OK?" Blacklight advised. He craned his thick neck to consider another unfinished canvas. It reminded him of someone, but then he forgot who before he could form the thought.

"Your brain is like your balls, did you know that?" He picked up the thread of the last conversation he could remember.

"No, I didn't know that."

"Two hunks rolling around inside your skull," Blacklight said, knotting his fists side by side. "They swim in your skull side by side, just like your balls swing around in your scrotum. Why are there two halves of your brain instead of just one big chunk—like, say, your heart?"

"I give up."

Blacklight massaged his fists together. "So they don't bang together, see. Got to keep them apart. Love and Hate. Yin and Yang."

"Look. I got to work." Elaine shook a gram's worth of lines out of the Baggie and onto the glass top of her coffee table.

"Sure. You sure you're gonna be OK?"

"No more anoxic rushes with a mask on. And thanks."

"You got a beer?"

"Try the fridge."

Blacklight found a St. Pauli and plinked the non-twist-off cap free with his thumb. Elaine thought he looked like a black-bearded Wookie.

"I had a buddy from Nam who offed himself trying that," Blacklight suddenly remembered.

"You told me."

"Like, whatever turns you on. Just don't drop the hammer when you don't mean to."

"Want a line?"

"No. I'm off Charlie. Fucks up my brain." Blacklight's eyes glazed in an effort to concentrate. "Off the goddamn dinks," he said. "Off 'em all." There were old tracks fighting with the tattoos, as he raised his arm to kill the beer. "Are you sure you're gonna be OK?" He was pulling out a fresh beer from behind the tuna salad.

Elaine was a foot shorter and a hundred pounds lighter, and acrobicise muscles weren't enough to overawe Blacklight. "Look. I'm all right now. Thanks. Just let me get back to work. OK? I mean, deadline-wise, this is truly crunch city."

"Want some crystal? Got a dynamite price."

"Got some. Look, I think I'm going to throw up some more. Want to give me some privacy?"

Blacklight dropped the beer bottle into his shirt pocket. "Hang loose." He started for the door. The beer bottle seemed no larger than a pen in his pocket.

"Oh," he said. "I can get you something better. A new one. Takes out the blank spots in your head. Just met a new contact who's radically into designer drugs. Weird dude. Working on some new kind of speed."

"I'll take some," said Elaine, opening the door. She really needed to sleep for a week.

"Catch you later," promised Blacklight.

He paused halfway through the door, dug into his denim jacket pocket. "Superb blotter," he said, handing her a dingy square of dolphin-patterned paper. "Very inspirational. Use it and grow. Are you sure you're gonna be OK?"

Elaine shut the door.

Mr. Fix-it promised to come by tomorrow, or the next morning after that, for sure.

Elaine replaced the chain with one from the bathroom door, hammered the torn-out and useless dead bolts back into place for her own peace of mind, then propped a wooden chair against the doorknob. Feeling better, she pulled on a leotard, and tried a gram or so of this and that.

She was working rather hard, and the airbrush was a bit loud, although her stereo would have drowned out most sounds of entry in any event.

"That blue," said Kane from behind her. "Cerulean, to be sure—but why? It impresses me as antagonistic to the overdone flesh tones you've so laboriously mulled and muddled to confuse the faces of the two lovers."

Elaine did not scream. There would be no one to hear. She turned very cautiously. A friend had once told her how to react in these situations.

"Are you an art critic?" The chair was still propped beside her door. Perhaps it was a little askew.

"Merely a dilettante," lied Kane. "An interested patron of the arts for many years. *That* is not a female escutcheon."

"It shouldn't be."

"Possibly not."

"I'm expecting my boyfriend at any minute. He's bringing over some buyers. Are you waiting for them?"

"Blacklight contacted me. He thought you'd like something stronger to help you finish your gallery collection."

Elaine decided to take a breath. He was big, very big. His belted trenchcoat could have held two of her and an umbrella. A biker friend of Blacklight's was her first thought. They hadn't quite decided whether to be hit men for the Mafia or their replacements in the lucrative drug trade. He was a head shorter than Blacklight, probably weighed more. There was no fat. His movements reminded Elaine of her karate instructor. His face, although unscarred, called to mind an NFL lineman who'd flunked his advertising screen test. His hair and short beard were a shade darker than her hennaed Grace Jones flattop. She did not like his blue eyes—quickly looked away.

"Here," said Kane.

She took from his spadelike hand a two-gram glass phial—corner headshop stuff, spoon attached by an aluminum chain.

"How much?" There was a can of Mace in the drawer beneath the telephone. She didn't think it would help.

"New lot," said Kane, sitting down on the arm of her largest chair. He balanced his weight, but she flinched. "Trying to re-create a lost drug from long ago. Perfectly legal."

"How long ago?"

"Before you'd remember. It's a sort of superspeed."

"Superspeed?"

Kane dropped the rest of the way into the chair. It held his weight. He said: "Can you remember everything that has happened to you, or that you have done, for the past forty-eight hours?"

"Of course."

"Tell me about eleven thirty-eight this morning."

"All right." Elaine was open to a dare. "I was in the shower. I'd been awake all night, working on the paintings for the show. I called my agent's answering machine, then took a shower. I thought I'd try some TM afterward, before getting back to work."

"But what were you thinking at eleven thirty-eight this morning?"

"About the showing."

"No."

Elaine decided it was too risky to jump for the phone. "I forget what I was thinking exactly," she conceded. "Would you like some coffee?" Scalding coffee in the face might work.

"What was on your mind at nine forty-two last night?"

"I was fixing coffee. Would you like some . . . ?"

"At nine forty-two. Exactly then."

"All right. I don't remember. I was flipping around the cable dial, I think. Maybe I was daydreaming."

"Lacunae," said Kane.

"Say, what?"

"Gaps. Missing pieces. Missing moments of memory. Time lost from your consciousness, and thus from your life. Where? Why?"

He rolled the phial about on his broad palm. "No one really remembers every instant of life. There are always forgotten moments, daydreams, musings—as you like. It's lost time from your life. Where does it go? You can't remember. You can't even remember forgetting that moment. Part of your life is lost in vacant moments, in lapses of total consciousness. Where does your conscious mind go? And why?

"This"—and he tossed the glass phial toward her—"will remove those lost moments. No gaps in your memory—wondering where your car keys are, where you left your sunglasses, who called before lunch, what was foremost in your mind when you woke up. Better than speed or coke. Total awareness of your total consciousness. No more lacunae."

"I don't have any cash on hand."

"There's no charge. Think of it as a trial sample."

"I know—the first one is free."

"That's meant to be a mirror, isn't it." Kane returned to the unfinished painting. "The blue made me think of water. It's someone making love to a reflection."

"Someone," said Elaine.

"Narcissus?"

"I call it: *Lick It Till It Bleeds.*"

"I'll make a point of attending the opening."

"There won't be one unless people leave me alone to work."

"Then I'll be getting along." Kane seemed to be standing without ever having arisen from the chair. "By the way, I wouldn't shove that. New lab equipment. Never know about impurities."

"I don't like needlework anyway," Elaine told him, dipping into the phial with the attached spoon. She snorted cautiously, felt no burn. Clean enough. She heaped the spoon twice again.

She closed her eyes and inhaled deeply. Already she could feel a buzz. Trust Blacklight to steer her onto something good.

She was trying another spoonful when it occurred to her that she was alone once again.

Blacklight secured the lid of the industrial chemical drum and finished his beer. The body of the designer drug lab's former owner had folded inside nicely. Off to the illegal toxic waste dump with the others. Some suckers just can't tell which way the wind blows.

"Did you really land in a flying saucer?" he asked, rummaging in the cooler for another beer.

Kane was scowling over a chromatogram. "For sure. Looked just like a 1957 Chrysler 300C hubcap."

Blacklight puzzled over it while he chugged his beer. The prettiest girl in his junior high—her family had had a white 300C convertible. Was there a connection?

"Then how come you speak English so good?"

"I was Tor Johnson's stand-in in *Plan 9 from Outer Space*. Must have done a hundred retakes before we got it down right."

Blacklight thought about it. "Did you know Bela Lugosi?"

Kane jabbed at the computer keyboard, watching the monitor intently. "I've got to get some better equipment. There's a methyl group somewhere where it shouldn't be."

"Is that bad?"

"Might potentiate. Start thinking of another guinea pig."

At first she became aware of her hands.

It was 1:01:36 A.M., said the digital clock beside her bed. She stepped back from the painting and considered her hands. They were tobacco-stained and paint-smeared, and her nails needed polish. How could she hope to create with hands such as these?

Elaine glared at her hands for forty-three seconds, found no evidence of improvement. The back of her skull didn't feel quite right either; it tingled, like when her mohawk started to grow out last year. Maybe some wine.

There was an opened bottle of Liebfraumilch in the refrigerator. She poured a glass, sipped, set it aside in distaste. Elaine thought about the wine for the next eighty-six seconds, reading the label twice. She made a mental note never to buy it again. Stirring through a canister of artificial-sweetener packets, she found half a 'lude, washed it down with the wine.

She returned to *Lick It Till It Bleeds* and worked furiously, with total concentration and with mounting dissatisfaction, for the next one hour, thirty-one minutes, and eighteen seconds.

Her skin itched.

Elaine glowered at the painting for another seven minutes nineteen seconds.

She decided to phone Allen.

An insomniac recording answered her. The number she had dialed was no longer in service. Please . . .

Elaine tried to visualize Allen. How long had it been?

Her skin itched.

Had she left him, or had he driven her out? And did it really matter? She hated him. She had always hated him. She hated all that she had previously been.

Her body felt strange, like a stranger's body. The leotard was binding her crotch. Stupid design.

Elaine stripped off her leotard and tights. Her skin still itched. Like a caterpillar's transformation throes. Death throes of former life. Did the caterpillar hate the moth?

She thought about Allen.

She thought about herself.

Love and hate.

There was a full-length mirror on her closet door. Elaine stared at her reflection, caressing her breasts and crotch. She moved closer, pressed herself to the mirror, rubbing against her reflection.

Making love to herself.

And hating.

Pressed against her reflection, Elaine could not ignore the finest of scars where the plastic surgeon had implanted silicone in her once-flat breasts. Fingering her surgically constructed vagina, Elaine could not repress the memories of her sex-change operation, repress the awareness of her former maleness.

Every instant remembered. Of joy. Of pain. Of longing. Of rage. Of hatred. Of self-loathing.

Of being Allen.

Her fists hammered her reflection, smashing it into a hundred brittle moments.

Blood trickled from her fists, streamed along her arms, made curling patterns across her breasts and belly.

She licked her blood, and found it good. It was shed for herself.

Gripping splinter shards of mirror, Elaine crossed to her unfinished painting. She stood before the life-sized figures, loving and hating what she had created.

Her fists moved across the canvas, slashing it into mad patterns.

Take. This is my body. Given for me.

Blacklight was finishing a cold anchovy-and-black-olive pizza. He considered his greasy sauce-stained hands, wiped them on his jeans. Stains were exchanged, with little disruption of status quo. He licked his tattooed knuckles clean.

It was raining somewhere, because the roof of the old warehouse leaked monotonously away from the light. He watched Kane. Maybe Lionel Atwill's caged gorilla on the loose in the lab. Maybe Rondo Hatton as Mr. Hyde.

"So what are lacunae?"

Kane was studying a biochemical supply catalogue. "Gaps. Cavities. Blank spaces."

"Spaces are important," Blacklight said. He knotted his pizza-stained fists and rolled their knuckles together. "Do you know how atomic bombs work?"

"Used to build them," Kane said. "They're overrated."

"You take two hunks of plutonium or something," Blacklight informed him. "Big as your fist. Now then, keep spaces between them, and it's on safety. But"—and he knocked his fists against one another—"take away the spaces, slam 'em together. Critical mass. Ker-blooie."

He punctuated the lecture with an explosive belch. "So that's why there's always got to be spaces in between," Blacklight concluded. "Like the two halves of your brain. Id and Ego. Yin and Yang. Male and Female. Even in your thoughts you've got to have these gaps—moments to daydream, to forget, to be absentminded. What happens when you fill in all the lacunae?"

"Critical mass," said Kane.

The mirror was a doorway, clouded and slippery with the taste of blood. Clutching angry shards of glass, Allen and Elaine waited on opposite sides, waited each for the other to break through.

KARL EDWARD WAGNER's books include *Darkness Weaves, Death Angel's Shadow, Bloodstone, Dark Crusade, Night Winds, The Road of Kings* and *In A Lonely Place.* A former psychiatrist, he is the publisher of books under the Carcosa imprint, as well as editor of the annual series *The Year's Best Horror Stories.* He has won the British Fantasy Award four times and the World Fantasy Award twice.

PART II

They're Coming for You

W. H. PUGMIRE AND
JESSICA AMANDA SALMONSON
"Pale Trembling Youth"

Dykes, kikes, spics, micks, fags, drags, gooks, spooks . . . more
of us are outsiders than aren't; and *that's* what the dear young
ones too often fail to see. They think they've learned it all by
age fifteen. Perhaps they have. But they're not the only ones
who've learned it.

They're wise youngsters, no doubt about it, and I wish them
all survival, of one kind or another, though few of them will
have it. They're out there on the streets at night; they've spiked
their hair and dyed it; they've put roofing nails through their
earlobes and scratched their lovers' initials in the whites of their
eyes. And they're such beauties, these children. I have empathy
for them, though by their standards, at thirty, I'm an old man.
Am I a dirty old man? Perhaps. But I keep my hands to myself
and am outraged by the constant exploitation I have seen. I help
who I can, when I can. They laugh at me for it; I don't mind.
Much as they hate to admit it, they appreciate the helping
hand; they assuredly need it.

The new bands have power. They have raw, wild, gorgeous,
naïve energy. The temporary nature of these bands, the tran-
sience of the sound they create, the ephemeral nature of their
performances *and their youth* has a literal and symbolic truth to
it that breaks my heart. Ah, the dear young ones! Their own
parents hate them. Their parents hate themselves. How mo-
rosely, pathetically beautiful it all is!

But I have my criticisms. I don't tell them what to do with
their lives, but I do tell them they're not the first and only ones
to *know*. They all think they've invented it; invented everything.
Twelve-year-old artists of the street—don't *ever* doubt that some

81

of them are geniuses—their music, dress, and Xerox flyers are undeniably brilliant works of art. Stripped of technical gaudiness and the veneer of social dishonesty, these kids and their art alienate people because of the reality that's exposed.

Reality is pain.

But none of it is new. A punk who's a good friend, a good kid, I gave him a rare old dada poster for his birthday. He loved it. He thought it was something new. "No, sir," I told him. "It was printed before World War I." He was impressed. He got some white paste and smeared it onto the window of an uptown jewelry store. What brilliance! It breaks my heart.

So there's nothing new. Least of all pain. It's the oldest thing around. I want to tell them, "Yes, you're outsiders. Yes, this thing you're feeling really is pain. But you're not alone." Or you're not alone in being alone. A poison-bad planet. For everyone.

On the north side of Lake Union, visible from about any high point in and around the city, is a little spot called Gas Works Park. Considering how visible it is on the lake's edge, it's rather out of the way. It has the appearance of war's aftermath—a bombed factory. When the gasworks closed shop several decades back, no one knew what to do with that extraordinary network of chimneys and pipes and silos. For years they sat rusting. Then someone had the fat idea of painting the whole thing, laying a lawn, and calling it a park. It looks good. It looks monstrous. It is urban decadence at its best and worst. It's not much frequented at night.

A pathetic old faggot took me across on his sailboat. He's not only pathetic, but rich; spent his whole life "buying" his way to the inside. But he's an outsider, too. We met in a downtown park in the days of my own alienated childhood, when he wasn't much younger but his gums were less black; and we've pretended we're friends ever since.

I'd been on his boat most of the late afternoon and early evening, until the sun was going down. Then I said, "I don't need to go back into town. Let me ashore at Gas Works Park."

He let me off. I stood on the concrete landing and waved to the old man, who looked almost heroic pulling at the rigging—but not quite.

The sun had set. The last streaks of orange were visible beyond the city's silhouette. The skyscrapers south of the lake were shining like boxes full of stars. I turned my back, climbed the grassy knoll, and gazed toward the antiquated gasworks. The garish paint had been rendered invisible by the darkness.

I breathed deeply of the cold, clean evening air and felt invigorated. The decayed structure before me was huge, the skeleton of a gargantuan beast. Its iron pipes, winding steel stairs and catwalks, variety of ladders, planks, chains, and tanks had a very real aesthetic charm. "Danger—keep off," a sign read on a chain-link fence. Even in the darkness, the evidence of the structure's conquerors—their graffiti—was palely visible on the surface of its heights.

Hearing footsteps in the gravel behind me, I turned and saw a tall skinhead punk shambling toward the fence. He nodded and smiled at me, then leaned toward the fence, curling fingers around the links. I thought I detected a sadness in his eyes. He was looking upward into one particular part of the gasworks, with such intensity that I could not help but follow his gaze. It seemed that he was staring at a particular steel stairway that led up and into a long pipe.

The sound of his deep sigh made me look at him again. He had taken a pack of cigarettes from a pocket in his black leather jacket. "Smoke?" he offered, holding the pack toward me.

"No, thank you," I replied. Kindness and gentility, contrasted against a violent image, no longer surprised me in these youths.

"Something else, ain't it?" he said, nodding at the structure.

"It is," I replied, not in a mood for conversation.

He continued: "My band and I used to come here at midnight to record tapes of us banging on parts of it. Fucking inspiration! You get some really cool sounds."

"You're in a punk band?" I asked lamely.

"Naw. Industrial band. Kind of an offshot of punk and hardcore, a lot of screaming and banging on pipes and weird electronic sounds. Put it all together and it makes an intense noise."

"Hmm," I said, having trouble imagining why anyone would want to sit around banging on pipes and screaming. I must, occasionally, admit to a gap between this generation and mine.

"But we broke up," he continued in a quiet voice. "Our singer hanged himself. Up there." He turned to gaze once more at that particular section of the structure. I felt a chill. Talk of death was unpleasant to me, and this was too sudden an introduction of the subject.

"I'm sorry," I said.

"Yeah, it's sad. He had a great voice. He could scream and make you feel like you'd die. Then he could sing so tenderly you couldn't hold back tears. But he was messed up. His dad was always getting drunk and beating on him, so he took to the streets. Came to live with me and some others in an abandoned building. We called him Imp, he was so small. He'd never eat, just drink coffee and do a lot of speed. He shook all the time and he had so little color to his skin that some of us took to calling him the 'pale trembling youth,' which he didn't like as much as Imp."

He paused to take a drag from his cigarette. The night had grown especially dark. The gasworks stood silently before us and seemed to listen to the young man's tale.

"He really loved this place. Used to come at night with a wrench or hammer to investigate sounds. He slept here a lot. He'd bring his girls here."

He stopped again, his face sad.

"His last girlfriend killed herself with sleeping pills. He loved her like none of the others. A few days later he was found up there, swinging from that pipe, his studded belt around his broken neck."

"How old was he?"

"Sixteen." After a pause, he tossed his cigarette to the ground and shoved his hands into pockets. "Well, it's getting cold. Think I'll head on back to the District and find me some anarchy and beer." He smiled kindly. I returned his smile. "Nice talking to you." We nodded to each other. He turned and stalked into the darkness.

It had indeed grown cold, but as I turned to look once more at the weird structure, I felt drawn near. Looking with dismay at the fence before me, I took hold of it and began to climb.

When I reached the top of the fence, I moaned softly at the difficulty climbing over and down the other side. I felt cold air against my neck. Looking at a section of the gasworks where the punk had taken his life, I thought I saw a shadowy figure watching me. Then the shadows blended and the image was gone.

Wind played with my hair. With sudden resolve, I climbed over the top of the fence, almost falling down the other side.

I stood near a huge rusted pipe. It was perhaps forty feet long and five feet high. I felt a thrill of boyish excitement, for I have had a love of tunnels since I was small. Going to one end of the pipe, I stood to look inside.

I entered.

My footfalls echoed weirdly as my boots hit the metal surface. The sides felt cold and rough. When I reached the middle, I sat down, bending knees to chest, listening to the sounds of evening. Then I heard a pinging, coming from the end of the pipe that I had entered. I looked and saw a small person standing there, looking at me. From its stance I took it to be a boy. The figure held something in its hand, which it slowly, nonchalantly struck against the pipe. Then my vision seemed to blur. I rubbed my eyes with shaky fingers; when I looked again, I saw nothing.

I sat for what seemed endless moments. Finally, I raised myself on unsteady legs.

From above came a sudden banging, a horrible and ferocious sound, as though a madman were leaping from place to place and violently striking at pipes and metal surfaces with something large. The sound of it shook the pipe I was in. I felt the reverberations like a throbbing pain in my skull. Shouting in alarm, I fell to my knees, covering my ears with moist palms. On and on it went, until I was sure that I would lose my mind.

Then it stopped. For a few moments all I could hear was the ringing in my ears. Then another sound came to me: low sobbing. I had never heard such misery and loneliness in a voice. It tore my heart to listen to it. It froze my soul. Gradually it faded into silence.

I was too weak to rise. When at last I found the strength, I crawled weakly out of the pipe, into the waiting dark.

W. H. PUGMIRE claims to be "a militant punk rock homosexual who worships death and reads H. P. Lovecraft religiously." He was the publisher of *Midnight Fantasies*, a magazine devoted to Lovecraft, and of the regional rock magazine *Punk Lust*.

JESSICA AMANDA SALMONSON has published five novels, of which *Ou Lu Khen and the Beautiful Madwoman* is the most recent. She is also a poet *(Innocent of Evil)* and World Fantasy Award-winning anthologist *(Amazons!)*. Her latest books are the collection *A Silver Thread of Madness*, and the anthology *Heroic Visions II*. Forthcoming is a contemporary horror novel, *Anthony Shriek*.

MARC LAIDLAW

Muzak for
Torso Murders

Donny gets to work with the quick-setting cement; it will probably have hardened before most of the blood has congealed in the
chest's cavities. The brass lion's feet on the antique bathtub
gleam from his attentive polishing, as does the porcelain interior, scoured so many times with Bon Ami that the scratch
marks of steel-wool pads appear in places. Shiny black plastic-
wrapped parcels almost fill the basin.

Whistle while you work, he thinks, but the cement is so heavy
that he hasn't any breath to spare for frivolities. This is the part
of his work that he likes less every time: messy cement, sweaty
grunting labor, disgusting slopping sounds as the viscous mixture
oozes over the plastic bundles and fills the tub to brimming.
There it sits like his mother's oatmeal, untouched by any spoon.
He can hear her in the kitchen while he works in the garage, her
radio perpetually tuned to an easy-listening station while you-
know-what bubbles in a cauldron on the stove and her knife
chops, chops, chops along with a thousand strings. He prefers
Bernard Herrmann —the score from *Psycho*—but she never lets
him play his albums while she's in the house. "Too disturbing,"
she says. If only she knew how much her Muzak disturbs him.

"Donny, are you almost done in there? Your dinner's ready."

"Be right there," he calls.

"Hands clean this time?"

"I'll use Boraxo, honest." Under his breath he allows himself
a brief curse: *"Christmas."*

Of course, nothing ever goes right when he hurries, and
thanks to his mother he tips the wheelbarrow in which he'd
mixed the cement, and the muck drips over his oxfords. His new

87

shoes! Another pair for the furnace, another sweaty chore. It's only a movie, he tells himself, to make himself relax. Sometimes Mom makes his life unbearable. True, she feeds him, provides a home, sews his clothes, and buys him most (though not all) of the things he wants. The videocassette player, for instance, was her idea, but he'd had to purchase *TCM* secretly with his own allowance. Despite all she does for him, her regimen is at times too much for a son to endure. Hot meals at the same hour every day, always accompanied by oatmeal ("Just to fill you up, dear!"), and regular vegetable snacks in between. She doesn't believe in dessert. It's no wonder that he's had to develop outlets for his energy, secret pastimes, forbidden games.

As he scrubs his hands with gritty powder, he feels the ever-present thrill of potential discovery. He doesn't fear the police, but if Mother ever finds out what goes on beneath her roof, well, he could get in real trouble—

"Donny, it's getting cold!"

—but that is all part of the fun. Sometimes he wishes he could tell her; she is, after all, his only possible confidante. She might approve. On the other hand . . .

"Look at your nails," she says as he raises the first forkful of salad to his lips. Red dressing splatters the tablecloth.

"I thought you said you washed up. What is that?"

He examines his thumbnail and discovers a traitorous crescent of dark red film clotted up to the quick. He swallows the leaf of romaine and quickly digs under his nail with a tine of the fork. The deposit comes away in a rubbery lump.

"It's only Russian dressing," he lies. "Dried stuff from the mouth of the jar, when I twisted the cap off—"

"Don't talk with food in your mouth."

He nods and stabs a tomato, takes another bite. Too late, he remembers the blob on the end of the fork. He's a cannibal now, how about that?

"Have you decided what to do about a job?"

He nods, wishing she would turn down the radio. "Send in the Clowns" is playing again. Sure, send them into the garage and he'd take care of them: pull off their noses, shave their frizzy wigs, paint their mouths red with their own—

"I thought that woman from the agency called you."

He shrugs and gives the ineluctable bowl of oatmeal a stir. As usual, it's much too sweet.

"She just wanted to find out my birthday," he says. "I forgot to put it on the form."

"Well, wasn't that nice of her? Maybe they'll throw you a party."

"Maybe." He smiles to himself. She believes anything he tells her. The agency lady had called to ask if he wanted to work in a mail room downtown, and of course he'd said he couldn't go that far because Mother was ill and he had to be able to get home quickly to fix her lunch and put her on the toilet—and by the time he'd gotten that far, the lady had said, "I'm sorry, but all of our jobs are in the financial district. Maybe you should try an agency out in your neighborhood. Perhaps one specializing in manual labor."

Ugh! That was when he'd hung up. But it was fine with him; now they should leave him alone. He doesn't like the thought of risking himself at a job anyway. He had almost come undone at the agency interview, and that was nothing.

They'd given him forms on which to answer a great many personal questions. He had raced through them, neatly slashing the sections concerning work history. Then he had come to the tricky part: essay questions.

"What would you do in this situation? Your superior comes into your office complaining that you scheduled her for two crucial meetings at the same time."

His neck itched with sweat; the office air-conditioning chilled him. He felt as if he had swallowed a mouthful of monosodium glutamate: throbbing spine, burning cheeks, torpid muscles.

He scrawled: "Apologize."

"Your supervisor makes a mistake on a memorandum and you are blamed for the error. What would you do?"

Is it a man or a woman? he thought, as the fluorescent lights began to strobe. He carefully penciled: "Explain to my supervisor's supervisor."

From somewhere in the walls or acoustic-tile ceiling of the office, sweet voices sang "Raindrops Keep Fallin' on My Head" as though it were a hymn. So sincere, so saccharine.

"For the third time in a week, a mail-room employee delivers your mail to the wrong address. You call him into your office and

he claims that your handwriting is illegible and he cannot read the destination. What do you do?"

The Bacharach tune drove pins into his brain. Three times this week, he thought. God, that Muzak!

"I ask him if he has seen the view from my window, and while he is looking away I hit him on the head with a marble ashtray. Then I lock the door. I take the saws out of my brief-case, spread plastic on the floor, and cut him up as quickly as I can, even working into my lunch hour to get the job done. I wrap the pieces separately in the plastic, cover them in brown butcher paper, type out address labels, and drop them in the mail."

An advertisement for secluded retirement homes rescued him from committing this response to the agency files. He crumpled the form, staggered to the desk with hands dripping, and asked if he could have another. The secretary had stared at him as if he were an ape from the zoo: he felt enormous and ungainly, surrounded by polite clerks. "I made a mistake," he said.

The second form took hours to complete because he worked only during commercial breaks in the Muzak.

And why had he gone to all that trouble in the first place? Because Mother had insisted. She had money, plenty of money, but she said a job would do him good. He had gone thirty-five years without a job; he saw no reason to start now. Besides, he had his own work to pursue. Sometimes it paid in cash, but the true rewards were hardly monetary.

"More oatmeal, Donny?"

"No, thanks, Mom. I'm stuffed."

"You just go watch TV. I'll do the dishes and come join you."

"Okay, Mom."

He slouches into the living room, turns on the VCR, and takes an oft-handled cassette out of the rack. It is labeled: "The Care Bears in the Land Without Feelings," a title he was sure would never interest his mother when he glued it to the cassette. He slips it into the player, turns on the set with the sound down low, listens to the dishes clinking in the kitchen. The remote control stays in his hand, in case Mom should come in at a bad time.

And in this movie, all times are bad. Outside of a fever dream, the Care Bears could never have found themselves in a land so devoid of human or ursine sentiment as the one on the screen. Images swim out of his memory, merging with the light that plays across his eyes. It's only a movie, he tells himself. What have we here? Cross sections of red meat, stumped limbs or trunks? No, it's the infernal sun, with flares strung out and heaving across the void—the raw stuff of violence on a cosmic scale. The sight of it makes him feel significant, attuned. His breathing comes swiftly, in shallow gulps. The miasma of night begins to gather in his eyes and the pit of his gut, as if he's about to black out. He can hardly see the TV anymore; the volume is turned down so low that his mother's Muzak overwhelms the ominous sound track. Strings and synthesizers sigh; a chorus of castrati whimpers, "Please, mister, please," as *Texas Chainsaw Massacre* buries itself in his eyes.

"Donny, how about some iced tea?"

He jerks and switches from video to live TV. A news anchorwoman mouths at him, apparently concerned for his well-being.

"What was that?" she says.

"Ad for some shocker, Mom."

"Oh, those horrid things. I swear I don't know what the world is coming to."

"Who does?"

To the left of the newscaster's head, bright letters appear beneath a stylized cartoon toilet bowl whose rim is stained red: BASIN BUTCHER. He taps the volume control slightly, until he can hear the TV over his mother's voice.

"—fifth in a series of apparently linked murders. Police say the body of another unidentified male was cut into pieces, wrapped in Mylar, and embedded in cement inside five antique porcelain sinks."

"Did you know that someone set fire to Gracie's poodle? The poor little thing, really. First the poison bait and now this."

The TV news team switches to field coverage, the same it showed last night. He sits up to appreciate this replay; Channel 2 has the best footage. Policemen scramble down a dusky shore of the bay, stumbling among concrete blocks and rusting wrecks of old cars. The camera zooms in on five gleaming white sinks, standing out like porcelain idols against the choppy water. Sea gulls dive to peck hungrily at the basins. The taps and handles gleam in the light of the setting sun, and so does he. An ambitious trick, but not as neat as the tub will be. The toilets had been a coarse guffaw of a murder, an attention-getter. Soon he will run out of the fixtures left over from his father's business; after one more tub, the next stage of his work will commence. There are dozens of statuary molds waiting to be filled with his homemade cement-and-flesh porridge, and more than enough cement powder to fulfill his dreams for the indefinite future. He need never expose himself by purchasing supplies.

"I hear that another poor woman was mugged at Safeway yesterday—right at the checkout counter," his mother says.

"The search continues for the person or persons responsible for the killings. Police seek information regarding a vehicle seen in the Bayshore area Wednesday night. An old-model truck with wooden paneling—"

He switches the channel quickly, unnerved, and looks at his mother to make sure she hasn't been paying attention. She watches him steadily over her bifocals.

"What's wrong with you, Donny? You haven't been yourself lately."

"I don't know what you mean, Mom."

"You don't talk to me anymore. You're a stranger. You're tuckered out all the time and I never see you when you're working. What are you doing out there, anyway?"

"I told you, Mom, it's a surprise. You're not supposed to know."

She smiles, a prim expression that reassures him that she won't press any further, never fear. He gets up and gives her a kiss on the cheek. "I love you, Mom. Why don't you sit down and I'll bring *you* some iced tea."

"Would you? What a darling. All right, I'll plump my fat old fanny down and take a rest."

She chatters on as he enters the kitchen, opens the icebox and takes out a tray, finds two tall glasses and loads them with cubes. The tea is in a pitcher on the counter, next to the radio. In here the Muzak is deafening, but he doesn't dare turn it down, though it makes the glasses chatter in his hands.

"Who's looking out from under the stairway? Everyone knows it's—"

"Donny!"

He forces his fingers to relax before they crush the glasses. His teeth are clamped together, there is fog in his eyes and fear on his breath. He stands in darkness, fumbling for a way back to the light. His hands encounter a drawer.

"Donny, come in here!"

He walks toward her voice like a servile mummy, stiff-legged, carrying drinks; the gleeful Muzak dictates his steps, sets the pace of his heart. He reaches the coffee table and starts to set down the drinks, only to find that he is not holding beverages after all. In either hand is a knife: not as sharp as his special knives, being for domestic use, but still sufficient for his purposes.

On the screen, to which Mother draws his eyes with a bony finger, is frozen a frame from his video: a flayed corpse in a cemetery. *TCM.* He almost drops the knives.

"I put on the Care Bears," she says.

His hands begin to shake as the Muzak blasts at his shoulders, pushing him closer to her. Closer.

"Aren't they wonderful?" he whispers. "Such feeling. Such care . . ."

"Why, yes," she answers, looking past the knives that almost touch her throat. She doesn't see them. She smiles at Donny. "I thought we could watch them together. What's this cute fellow's name?"

He looks at the screen and lowers the knives. "He never has a name. But later . . ." He sets the knives on the coffee table, iced tea forgotten, and seats himself beside her. "Later, you'll meet Leatherface."

"Leatherface? And is he very nice?"

"Oh yes," he says. "Very, very nice."

"And these are the Care Bears you watch every day?"

"That's right." He nods eagerly, amazed by her blindness. She must see only what she wants to see. How could she believe anything but the best of her son? Her first sight of the corpse—where she had expected to find an animated teddy bear—must have snapped her mind. What a relief! It means he can finally be honest with her: after so much furtiveness, he can tell her his secrets and bask in her praise. She should be as proud of him as she'd be if he'd found a job or built a birdhouse.

The video player whirrs, begins to move again.

"Oh, Donny, I see," she says in high-pitched merriment. "I'm so glad we're together, just you and me."

"So am I, Mom. I have to tell you—"

The confessions are ready to come bubbling up, but she interrupts him.

"It was you who poisoned Gracie's noisy little dog, wasn't it?" Her tone is comforting. "And set the fire?"

He blushes, but when she gives his knee a gentle squeeze, he nods shyly. "Yes, Mom, and—"

"You don't know how relieved I am to hear it. And it's you who've been taking out Dad's truck late at night, isn't it?"

He straightens. "Oh no, Mom, honest! I wouldn't do that without asking, you know I . . ."

Her eyes begin to wander. "Then I must be losing my mind," she says gently. "Try to Remember" filters in from the kitchen. "I'm so old I've started hearing things."

"No, Mom, don't say that." He chokes back a sob. "Okay, I have gone out. That was me you heard. I won't do it anymore, though. I promise I won't use the woody." That's a true lie; he'll have to use the other car from now on, since the woody was spotted.

"I know where you've been going, Donny."

"Do you, Mom?"

"Of course I do. I'm not senile, you know."

"No, Mom, you're sharp as a tack. I was going to tell you about it, really I—"

"Hush, I know you better than that." She puts a finger to her lips, rises from the sofa, goes to the stereo. She takes out an album and puts it on the player. He's so excited that he doesn't even care that it's Lawrence Welk. As the schmaltzy music fills the air and a slaughterhouse on the television brightens the room, she comes back and kisses him on the crown.

"I've heard them, you see," she says.

"Oh, that," he says, feeling awkward.

"Now be honest. I've heard them come in with you, and the noises. You make them squeal, don't you? They like you very much, isn't that so?"

"Like me?" He stretches his collar, clears his throat. "You don't think I . . ."

"I've told you not to lie to me, Donny," she snaps. "What's

been going on in my house? Something dirty? Something shameful?"

Black champagne bubbles float up and gather against the ceiling, filling the room from the top to the bottom. That music—Muzak.

"Take off this record, Mom, please."

"Are you doing wicked things in there?"

"No, Mom, no . . . it's nothing like that."

"Vile things? Evil?"

"Mom, I kill them! That's all, I swear. I keep them tied up for a while and then I chop them into pieces."

"Don't lie to me, Donny."

She glares at him, one finger tapping in time to Lawrence Welk. There's nothing else in the room, none of the comfort of the TV massacres; only Mom and her accusations, which are brutal as blows because unjust. He tries to rise but the music beats him down. Where are the knives? He squints through the black ballooning air, but the only blades he sees are in her hands.

"Don't lie to me."

"No, Mama, I'm not lying. Please don't punish me, I'll be good."

Muzak thicker than murder. He bolts through his muddled thoughts, escaping in the only direction open to him with his body paralyzed and his mother waiting for him out there in the land without feelings. This proves to be a dead end, but by the time he has backed out to consciousness, he is truly immobilized. Ropes cut into his wrists and ankles. He lies cramped on his side in a cold coffin. Is it only a movie? he asks himself.

"—never, never do it again," his mother is saying. "You'll never—"

"I won't," he tries to promise, but his mouth is plugged with a kitchen sponge. He opens his eyes to stare at a shiny white wall high as a cliff, all porcelain. Mom stands looking down at him, humming to a saccharine tune from the other room. He fights the Muzak's spell, but he cannot fight the ropes.

"You've been a very bad boy," she says. "I have to see to it that you don't bring any more trouble to this house."

Over the cliff, the lip of the tub, the edge of the barrow appears. Her shoulders strain to lift it. Not cement, he thinks.

Oh no, not cement. A grey flood drools steadily toward his face. There's a sickly sweet smell. "Just to fill you up," she says. The basin reverberates with the sound of his struggles as the clammy mixture spreads across his cheeks. What a stupid sound!

And the last thing he hears, as oatmeal seals his ears, is pure schmaltz.

MARC LAIDLAW sold his first short story at the age of seventeen. Since then his work has appeared in such diverse publications as *Omni, Creepy*, Ramsey Campbell's *New Terrors*, and *Contemporary Literary Criticism*. A novel, *Dad's Nuke*, was published in 1986. He is currently employed at the University of California Medical Center, where he peruses *The Journal of Trauma* in search of inspiration for further stories and novels.

ROBERTA LANNES

Goodbye, Dark Love

Marla ran her fingers down to the fold in her chenille robe and parted the front. She leaned into the bed where the body lay, still and very dead.

She let the robe drop from her shoulders. It made a muffled sound, like that of a swan's wing flapping, as it hit the floor. She looked down at her breasts, then at the slowly graying form. Grasping one nipple, she reached with her other hand to the body and the exquisite erection that rose over the wide elastic band. Her hand enveloped the shaft as she manipulated her nipple to hardness. Her breath came in gasps as she jerked the stony cock while kneading, teasing, exciting herself. Her fingers moved down to her crotch, parting the lips, feeling for the nub of flesh. Touching. Tingling. Vibrating with urgency. She felt herself dipping close to climax.

"No, no," she whispered. "Not this way."

She released him, pulled herself, her mind, from the place she had been. She made herself think about the outside, the bus stop where people were waiting for their lives to begin again, exchanging lies and wary glances. She listened to their distant voices. Motor noises. She heard his wristwatch. The radio playing softly in the front room. Music. Playful. Far away. Calming.

A cry. The baby. Mrs. Lopez's baby.

Marla smiled.

So perfect.

So new.

So un . . . —but no.

She grabbed the erection more firmly. Lusting. She could only want. She mounted him. She pushed the beet-colored rod to the mouth of her heat and plunged down on it. Orgasm. Again and again. Driving it in. An icicle unrelenting in its cold against her living warmth.

Suddenly the acrid stench of urine overpowered her. There was no ignoring it now. The memories of rest rooms in parks, in town, on the boardwalk, the bus station. Stinking. Cold. Dark gray walls with white turbans of paper toweling hurled against them, fecal arcs like a mad artist's attempts at a statement. Why there? Why had he always wanted to do it there?

There. Then. The better days. The time he'd taken her to the pike. It was hot, sunny. She wore the new sundress he had bought her. Pink. Scant. He won her a stuffed octopus, bought her a Sno-cone, rode on the roller coaster with her. When they ran into two of the men he worked with, he introduced her as "my lady." They smiled at her and told him she was gorgeous. A knockout. He'd looked at her that day. Really looked. Like he was seeing her for the first time. It made her hope things would change. Maybe. Someday.

She saw herself then, grimaced, then saw herself here, now, impaled on his lifeless cock, ecstatic. On her terms for once.

The knock at the front door tore into her.

She froze. Her foot began to cramp. She could hear no voices, no sound but her own ragged breath. Like a shot, another knock. It couldn't be anyone important. There *was* no one. Panic roiled inside her. She clenched her teeth. Then, quietly, footsteps marked the retreat of the stranger, whoever it was.

Marla sighed, relieved.

A soft heartache, a little pain rose up from deep inside, breaking the angry lust, crawling up her throat until a small cry passed her lips. Her friends. Where were they now? He'd once welcomed them, enjoyed their laughter, their warm company. Then, one by one, they were forbidden to her. His friends she never saw. They were a part of his world, a world he told her she was better off not knowing. A world she never allowed herself to be curious about. After all, she had someone who loved her, someone to protect her. Her friends had not. She let him become her world, let herself be whatever part of his world she could.

Then the day came when she knew he had protected her too well.

She pulled herself from him and got up. She paced around the bed, pulling on her robe, looking at him. His face was still handsome in death. Clear blue eyes staring wide. Flared nostrils. Aquiline nose. Lips full, parted. Inviting. She put her face close to his. She could smell the familiar alcohol. Sour. She covered his lips with hers. Her tongue searched for warmth, familiar places. He took her warmth, but did not hold it.

She nuzzled him and felt the five o'clock shadow growing on his cold cheeks.

Murky amber light from drawn old yellowed shades gave the room a dream ambience. Alone now, beside him, she had her dream. The dream she had been too frightened to acknowledge, even to herself, for so long. The dream was of choice. *Another man, anyone but him.*

She didn't know when her love, her lust, her need of him turned. When his arrival made her cringe. When the scent of him made her turn away. When his touch reviled her. But when it changed, so did she. Slowly. Steadily. Finally, irrevocably, completely. What was between them seemed no longer bitter-sweet, electric. She became aware he was waging a battle, she the unwilling enemy. It was he, victorious, sabotaging, cunning, brutal, unrelenting. An army of one in a war without political cause, without provocation, without reason. One day he was playful, toying. The next day he was cruel. And all the days after, until something in her turned her devotion into a grain of anger. The grain multiplied into a handful, a bucket, a barrel, until nothing could contain it all. Until today.

He left her his money, his belongings, but they were unimportant to her now. She wanted someone else. A man who would love her tenderly, openly, kindly. Any man would do. She could choose now. She was leaving the chains behind. His death was the ultimate permission. He left her her own life. That she would cherish.

She looked hard at him. A new power flowed into her.

"You will never again tell me that no one else can have me. And I'll never hear your lie—that no one else but you could make me come."

She stood on her knees near his face, letting the robe fall open. Her fingers went to the slash between her legs, parting the swollen lips, touching the growing bud of skin inside. Her fingers moved quickly, hungrily. Her other hand pushed one breast up to her mouth. Her tongue darted out over her nipple, flicking it until it raged red, hard.

"Watch me . . ." Her voice was a husky whisper. She rocked over her fingers, moaning.

Falling back on the bed, spent, she gasped, choked. It had wasted her. She lay there a few minutes until her breathing slowed.

Then she propped herself up on a pillow and reached for the pack of cigarettes on the nightstand. She lit one. She blew smoke in his face. As she took long drags she played with the small round scars over her stomach and chest. Turning the butt in her fingers, she pressed the lit end into the flesh that fell wrinkled and moist from his jaw. The cigarette went out with a spitting sound.

In that instant, she recalled an evening after a long day on the beach. She was severely sunburned, blistering. He'd been so concerned. He put ointment on her, cool compresses. All night, until she finally fell asleep, he held her hand, held an ice cube to her swollen lips, cooed soothing words. The next morning, before she was fully awake, he was on her, taking what he said was owed him. The pain . . .

"Does it feel good? You told me that pain and pleasure were so close. So close. Does it feel the same to you? You bastard! What did you know? You just wanted to mark me for life so no one else would want me. You made sure, didn't you? You loved it. Hurting me. Knowing I would have to lie to anyone who found them. Knowing the lies would be useless because everyone could tell what they were. Knowing no one would dare suspect you. No. Only weird Marla could do that to herself. Ha!"

She lit another cigarette.

The air-conditioner wheezed, then chugged once before purring again. Its rusty dark bulk in the window allowed street sounds to filter through. She had often imagined that it was a huge radio transmitting the music of the city. The raw beat. The wails. The whistle of the wind. The roar of engines. The pounding of the rain. The sirens. The music only she could understand. He'd called her bizarre, silly. He had never understood anything. She burned his cheek. Hair sizzled. Stank.

She could hear the bus pull up. Brakes screamed. All the liars, the rapists, the cheats, the motherfuckers, the phony assholes, the teasers, the pleasers, the real crazies there. Packed in for rides to their individual hells. Soon more would come. Standing in their rootless anger, littering their disappointments, waving false hope behind TV smiles. After all, what else was there in the world? What?

One by one, she left tiny burns across his chest until a heart began to take shape. The sound, like a distant cat's hiss, soothed her. Pulling back her robe, she looked down at the heart shape long ago tattooed into her stomach. She did not smile. It was not beautiful to her. Nor would it be to anyone else. He'd known that. She put the cigarette out in his navel.

He was beginning to stink. Like shit. Like spoiled canned vegetables. Like mold and piss and sweat and vomit and sickness. She gagged. She turned up the flame on the lighter so that it shot out like a blowtorch. She touched the tip of the flame to one of his eyes. She almost expected it to close in reflex. It sizzled and popped. She held her breath. The flame slowly burned the entire eye away, leaving a deep smoking black pit. She began on the other eye. Gagging, she quit.

It was time. She went into the kitchen and found a large carving knife, a box of scented candles, and six heavy-duty trash bags.

She lit the candles first, scattering them around the room. The odors of him seemed to lessen. She then set about carefully dismembering the body. She tried to be neat. It was much more difficult than she had expected. The knife required her full weight behind it to go through bone.

She filled the six bags with the now simplified body, the bed-sheets, and her robe. She knotted the tops. In the kitchen, she washed off the knife and put it back where she found it. She then took a long hot shower, dried off, dressed, packed three suitcases and began to straighten up.

Room by room she went, reminiscing. They were full of memories, many good ones. The curtains he bought her that she just had to have. The sofa and loveseat she saw in the Sears catalogue that *he* just had to have. There was his brush on the sink, still full of his soft graying brown hair. The pair of reading glasses he wore to read the *TV Guide*. She loved watching TV with him.

She went to the phone and called a taxi.

She cursed herself for being too young to drive. In a few months she would be sixteen. Then she would come back and take his car. Until then she would have to be patient.

Lastly she dragged the six bags, one by one, to the back door. She opened the door and set them outside in the alley. She locked the door, staring down at the six neatly tied, shiny black sacks. Wistfully, she turned away.

The taxi horn sounded out front.

"Well, I guess it's time to say goodbye, Daddy. Thanks for everything." She shrugged. "Thanks for nothing."

She let the taxi driver take her suitcases out. She stood at the front door trying to remember what it felt like to love him. She felt nothing.

She locked the door and walked out to the waiting world.

ROBERTA LANNES is a fine artist and illustrator, as well as a teacher of English, art, journalism, creative writing and photography. She is also the designer of graphics for a number of corporations. Though she has been writing since the age of eight, this is her first professionally published horror story. She is presently at work on a novel of obsession and murder, *The Hallowed Bed*.

CHARLES L. GRANT

Out There

When Rick looked in the bathroom mirror, there was blood on his cheek. He watched, fascinated, as his finger drifted down the length of the scratch without touching his skin, from just under his right eye to the edge of his jaw. Along the way, small red bubbles slipped out and quivered, and he daubed at them with a tissue, wincing though he didn't even feel the beginning of a sting.

Odd, he thought.

His head tilted to the left, lifting the cut to the light above the glass, probed from the inside with his tongue, poked with a clean tissue, and frowned.

While he was asleep, he decided; he must have done it while he was sleeping. A check of his stubbed fingernails, and he shrugged; they weren't sharp enough to dent butter, but it could have happened in a dream. He could have had a nightmare, thrashed around, and done it without knowing it. That he didn't remember the nightmare didn't bother him. He knew he'd been having them for a month or so now, but once morning woke him they were gone, and all that was left was a residue of apprehension that had him looking over his shoulder once or twice before he fully awakened, as if expecting to see someone in the bed beside him.

It didn't seem serious, more than likely pressure from the job, and after-the-fact qualms about his decision to accept a new position in the firm's San Francisco branch. The first time in almost two decades he would be living anywhere else but here.

He touched the cut again top and bottom, then proceeded to finish his toilet, knocking rather than brushing his hair away from his forehead, doing his teeth with scarcely any toothpaste, soaping and rinsing his face with a washcloth that skirted the wound gingerly, close enough to rid the skin of the dried blood and far enough away to keep from aggravating it with soap. When he was done, he stepped back, adjusted the knot of his tie, and reached for his suit jacket on the hook on the back of the door. A cursory turn for wrinkles on the sides and back, and he left with a slap of his hand on the light switch.

The kitchen was neat without being pristine, and when breakfast was over it remained that way.

The living room was neat without being a showcase, and as he sipped his coffee and stared out the window, he felt a great satisfaction that another day had begun.

Across the street was an apartment building similar to his—all brownstone and high windows, shades midway to the sill, venetian blinds open to catch the morning's warmth. Below, on the street, pedestrians were already on their way to work, wearing winter coats that were, he noticed, mostly unbuttoned. Cool, then, but not as cold as it had been over the past few days. A nod of approval, and he returned the cup to the sink, rinsed it, lay it on the drainboard, and fetched his overcoat from the closet. A quick swipe of his shoes against the backs of his trouser legs, and he draped the coat over his arm, picked up his briefcase, and left.

There was no one in the elevator. A rare treat—no artificial conversations to be made, no false smiles, no comments on the weather. The only person he would have liked to see this morning was Fred Alleta, an old man who lived three doors down from his own apartment. A fellow historian, he liked to think, but the man hadn't been seen in a while, wasn't answering his telephone, and most of the neighbors had decided he'd gone on vacation, to his place up in Maine, a small home on the coast where he was going to retire at the end of the year.

Rick wasn't worried. He had his own life to fuss over, and Alleta was more than capable of taking care of himself. A reminder then to make a point of calling before Fred left for good.

And the moment he stepped outside, his cheek felt as if someone had laid a branding iron on it.

He gasped and staggered, his free hand instantly clamping to his face. His vision blurred with tears, and he shook his head to clear it, moved a tentative step sideways, and straightened. Someone asked if he was all right, and he managed a nod, a weak smile, and mumbled something about a toothache. A second step, a third, and the pain subsided, the skin on his cheek feeling as though it were drawn taut over wire.

God, he thought, lengthening his stride to normal, cautiously lowering his hand; it must have been a delayed reaction. But damn, that hurt!

At the first opportunity he checked himself in a shop window. There was no blood that he could see, only the angry red line that now seemed more like a gash. He shuddered, held his coat to his chest, and moved on to work, five blocks away.

Listening to the morning sounds that hadn't changed in a hundred years, listening to the old men muttering to themselves, watching the old women in their war paint heading for the department stores with their purses against their stomachs as if they'd been wounded; stopping only once—when a trio of young men, in leather and boots and glaring decorative chains too bright for the sun, stepped in front of him from a doorway and stared at him, waiting, and grinning when he finally swerved and moved on, head down.

He didn't think about them.

He didn't look back.

But his teeth ground together, and the cut on his face throbbed like a toothache.

Jesus, he thought; Jesus, that hurts.

And thought it once again when he reached his destination, glanced over his shoulder, and saw the three young men push their way onto a bus.

Brother, he thought, and touched the marble façade for luck.

The office building was black glass and chrome; the lobby was potted plants; the elevator was brass and wood; all of them were filled with hurrying workers, not one of whom spoke to him all the way to his cubicle on the eleventh floor. Once there, and once his briefcase had been placed on end beside his desk, his coat hung on the hook beside the door, he sat, patted the computer terminal a fond good morning, leaned back, and closed his eyes.

The pain was gone, but he was as breathless as if he'd just run ten miles.

"You really ought to stop living it up like that, Rick," a woman's voice said. "It's hell on productivity."

"Funny, Roberta, very funny."

He opened his eyes then and gave the pale-skinned woman a sour smile, winced before he felt the stab in his cheek, and just barely stopped his hand from coming up to touch it.

Roberta Young moved to the side of the desk. "Cut yourself shaving?"

He hesitated before nodding. "I was half asleep. Five minutes earlier and I would have cut my throat."

She barked a single laugh and dumped a low pile of folders in front of him. "Well, cut your throat on this one, Ricky. The hotshots upstairs want the information by this afternoon."

He gave her the groan he knew she was expecting, and closed his eyes again to wish her gone.

"How about lunch? Kind of a farewell party?"

"God," he said, "I'm not going for another six months, for crying out loud."

"Okay." She shrugged. "Then just plain old lunch."

He shook his head, opened his eyes, pointed ruefully at the folders. "You are the bearer of your own bad tidings, kid."

With a touch of a hand to her curly black hair, she gave him a dramatic sigh. "You're a hermit, you know that, Early? You're a goddamned hermit."

Maybe he was, he thought when she left, but it was better than the way it used to be. Much better. This way it didn't hurt so much. Old Fred knew, which was why they had become . . . not friends, but occasional companions. But never outside. Always in the building the old man called the fort.

And he thought nothing more about it; and at the end of the day, when the research was completed, the writers had their facts, he picked up his empty briefcase and started home for the night.

Wincing at the shriek of the traffic, standing aside to watch himself blend into the herd, struggling toward the corners, dodging the cabs, turning away from the buses that spat fumes in his face; breaking through a line at a movie theater and seeing the eyes, the dead eyes, the wary eyes, the eyes that warned him to keep on going, don't bother to stop, a line was a line and a man's a man for a' that.

He smiled, caught himself, and went home.

He ate dinner, watched the early news, and decided that maybe he ought to see a movie. It had been a while since he'd gone, and it would help in talking with the others at the office. He knew they thought him strange; he knew, and had been working at caring.

He was reaching for the paper when the telephone rang, an occasion so rare he had to stare at it for several seconds before grabbing the receiver.

"Rick?"

No, he said silently; it's the masked man and the Indian.

"What do you want, Ann?"

There was a pause.

"You haven't changed. Always the charmer."

"What do you want?" he said again.

"God! All I wanted was to thank you for sending the check early, that's all. It was a help. God."

He sagged in his armchair and toed off his shoes. "Sorry. A bad day."

"Yeah. Sure. Well, thanks anyway. I appreciate it."

The urge to ask her out, to go to the movies, was so sudden, so strong, he could only grunt, and his ex-wife took it as she usually did—she hung up, and he listened to the dial tone for another minute more before dropping the receiver back on the cradle and turning to the television to watch the faces move around.

The next morning he didn't see the cut until he stepped into the shower, and had to wipe the soap away from his belly to be sure it wasn't a shadow, one that started above his left hip and ran almost to his groin. He looked at his nails, hurried out of the bathroom, and threw back the blanket on the low single bed in the bedroom that held nothing more but a secondhand dresser. A hand pressed against the sheet, swept over it, caressed it, hunting for the protrusion from the mattress below.

When he found nothing, he stripped off the sheet and tried it again, and scowled when his palm came away unscathed.

"Mr. Early," he said to his reflection in the bathroom, "you really must be having one hell of a nightmare."

One that dropped him to one knee before he was halfway to the corner, that had him scrabbling for his briefcase in perfect mime of a clumsy clerk, that had him leaning against a lamppost until the burning faded and his vision cleared and he looked up at the sky and saw the first snowflake falling.

He made it to the office, but he couldn't stand straight, and Roberta followed him to his desk.

"What you need, you know, is something more than those foul hamburgers you shove down your throat. I know this place over on Lexington where—"

He sat and slumped back, and looked at her patiently, waiting for her to continue.

She was staring at his stomach.

He looked down, and saw the blood.

"C'mon," she said urgently, and grabbed his arm, pulled him up. "Jesus, leave the damned briefcase, okay? It isn't going to walk, you know."

He didn't argue. He let her take him to the lounge, empty now, and let her put him on the plastic couch. When she pulled his shirt from his trousers gingerly, he made only a token effort to stop her, stopping himself when he saw the raw wound and heard her gasp.

"God, you were knifed!"

She ran for the company nurse, and while he lay there, wondering how he could have been stabbed and not even know it, others came in, and looked, and looked away. They muttered to themselves, they didn't talk to him; they looked away, and looked back, and he finally shouted at them to leave.

I didn't see anyone, he told himself, and closed his eyes to watch himself walk out of the building the same way he always did, check the pedestrians, check the traffic, and start up the block. He saw it all, and he saw no one who was close enough to touch him.

No one.

And he said it aloud when he was taken to the hospital and was stitched up, and was sent home. He said it to Roberta, who stayed with him, holding his hand and snapping at the interns, and goading them, chiding them, flirting with them to give her friend here priority.

"You should have been in the Army," he said later, in the elevator.

"Don't think I haven't thought about it," she said. And took his keys, helped him inside, helped him to the bed. Then she reached into her purse and pulled out a sheet of paper. "I'll get this filled, okay? You're gonna need it when that painkiller wears off."

He knew his smile was mere bravado, but he gave it to her anyway and shook his head. "You don't have to. I feel better already."

When she smiled back, it was softly. "I know I don't have to. I want to, Rick, all right? I've got the keys. I'll let myself back in."

And she was gone, the scent of her lingering, the shadow of her still standing in the doorway.

"Well," he said to the room. "I think you've got yourself an angel."

It was . . . strange. It was . . . perhaps nice. It was odd enough that he didn't question it until he'd sat up and walked into the bathroom, closed the door, and stripped. Then he looked in the full-length mirror—he knew the gash was ragged, but the Merthiolate stain on his skin and the bulk of the dressing made it look worse.

But no one had touched him.

No one.

He knew it.

And stared for ten more minutes before stumbling back to the bed, to the pillow, to an examination of the ceiling and the cracks he knew better than he knew the palm of his hand. Wondering, and not wanting to know. Thinking, and wanting to avoid it by falling asleep.

Dozing, until Roberta returned with the large orange pills, two of which she made him take before she'd taken off her coat. Then she pulled a chair in from the kitchen and sat beside him, waiting for the medication to work, saying nothing and saying it all with the round of her eyes and the set of her mouth and the way her knees shifted against the mattress, touching and falling away, touching and staying.

He closed his eyes.

He slept.

He woke just after dawn and saw her curled under a blanket, still on the chair, hair in webs over her face and her hands tucked under her chin.

Quietly, he slipped out of bed and padded into the bathroom, closed the door, switched on the light, and saw the cut that ran the length of his left arm from elbow to wrist.

He wasn't sure if he screamed, but the next thing he knew Roberta was beside him, paying no attention to his nakedness as she traced the red line with a finger and shook her head.

"Jesus."

He tried a laugh. "You attacked me while I was asleep."

"It's hardly bleeding. You're lucky." She shook her head. "God, you're beginning to look like Frankenstein, y'know? You look like you've been stitched together or something. God."

"I think . . ." He passed a hand over his eyes. "I think I'm going to sit down now."

She grinned and held his arm, brought him back to the bed and sat him gently, at the same time draping a corner of the sheet over his lap. "Somnambulist," she said with a sharp nod.

"Huh?"

"You sleepwalk, dope. You move around, cut yourself, go back to bed, and are none the wiser. You'd better watch them California hills, boy; you'll fall off and split your skull and good old Roberta won't be around to take care of you." A laugh. A finger to her cheek. "Either that, or it's ghosts. You have any ghosts here, Rick? Anybody die in this place in the last ten years?"

He laughed. He couldn't help it, not knowing if she was serious and deciding she'd better not be. "I hate to disappoint you, but *I've* lived here for almost twelve years. And I don't think I'm haunting myself."

"Twelve years?" She was astounded, and looked around the room as if hunting for its age.

"It must be sleepwalking," he said. "I mean, it must be."

As far as he knew, he'd never walked in his sleep before, but that didn't mean he wasn't doing it now. He had to be. Cuts, bruises, just didn't appear, rabbits out of the hat. And if he was, then he would have to see a doctor; if he kept it up, he'd slice himself to death.

"Imagine that," Roberta said. "Twelve years in one place. In the city. That's incredible, you know?"

"Ever since the old lady left me," he said, making it sound partly a matter of pride, partly a sentence the judge had handed down. "Don't get me wrong, though. I love it here. I have a friend, he calls it the fort. Keeps the Indians out there from getting our scalps, if you know what I mean."

Then he gestured her out of the room and dressed, moving stiffly for the bandage, keeping an eye on his arm, rolling up the sleeve to give the cut air. When he finished, he found her in the kitchen, breakfast already on the table.

He wanted to be annoyed, but there was no mess.

The frying pan had already been rinsed off and was drying on the drain.

He sat, uneasy that she was still there. "You're going to be late for work."

"They'll live," she said, sitting opposite.

"I don't want you to get in trouble on my account."

Her frown was attractive. "Like I said yesterday, I do it because I want to. You want to deny me my heart's desire before you zap off to California and leave me to the vultures?"

They laughed, awkwardly, and stopped only when a neighbor knocked on the door. Fred Alleta, the red-eyed woman said, had been found dead in his apartment by his daughter the night before. Apparently, someone had broken in to rob him, found him home, and killed him. Cut him up good and stuffed him in the closet. His suitcase was packed, like he was leaving for Maine.

"That's the fourth one," Rick said when Roberta returned with the news.

"You're kidding."

"Well, four in a dozen years isn't that bad, I guess, considering the age of most of the people who live here. Easy targets for the hoods, you know what I mean?"

She looked at him without expression, then decided aloud she might as well go to work, just to keep the bosses happy. She ordered him to finish his meal and go back to bed. The pills were in the bathroom, and she would call at lunchtime to see how he was doing.

He walked her to the door, waved as she stepped into the elevator, and spent the rest of the morning trapped by the old men and women who lived on the same floor, all of them with theories about poor old Fred's death, all of them ready to move out as soon as they could because the police don't give no protection, especially if you're old. And in the same breath they lamented his leaving, because who was going to protect them from all the monsters out there, the things, the thugs, who was going to save them when good old Rick was gone?

When he was finally able to escape back into his rooms, he was thirsty and discovered there was nothing to drink in the refrigerator. A look out the window showed him pedestrians with no coats on, and a check of his bandage showed him no further bleeding, no aches, not even a stinging. Five minutes wouldn't hurt, then, he told himself as he went to the elevator and pushed twice at the button before it would light; five minutes to the corner and back, and then a little reading, a little TV, a nap before dinner, and maybe a recovery good enough to let him take in an early movie.

At the front door he stopped. Looked out to the pavement. Felt a twinge in his side, a twinge in his cheek, and looked down at his arm and saw the first drops of blood spilling from his thumb onto the floor.

He put his hand to the doorknob and felt the twinge become a burning.

He backed away.

He blinked.

The elevator was gone and he took the worn marble stairs two at a time, hauling on the banister with his right hand, holding his left arm hard against his side. Panting by the time he reached the second floor, gasping by the third, walking by the fourth as he stumbled down the hall and pushed into his home.

The telephone was ringing.

He ignored it and went into the bathroom, stripped and looked at his face, his side, the condition of his arm.

Nothing. Scratches, no blood, and he stood there until his legs began to shake, watching himself in the mirror, half expecting a limb to crumble, an eye to bulge, his hair to fall out in radioactive clumps.

Hermit, he thought then.

And Fred sliced up, on his way to Maine.

Twelve years in the same apartment, making it his, making him as much a part of the place as Fred had been before he decided to retire to Maine.

There was a whimper.

Twelve years keeping the world away.

And now, at last, when he wanted to see more of what was out there, beyond the neighborhood, beyond his job, beyond the monsters and the things and the Indians and the thugs . . .

A hard swallow, and he hurried to his bed and propped the pillows against the headboard and sat there cross-legged with the sheet and blanket held to his chin. Staring at the light draining from the window, staring at the doorway filling with black, not bothering to reach over and turn on the lamp because when his right arm moved he saw the cut begin to form at the top of a knuckle, move down to the wrist, curl under to the thumb, where it stopped. And didn't bleed.

CHARLES L. GRANT is the author of *The Nestling, The Tea Party, Night Songs, The Bloodwind, Nightmare Seasons,* and many other books, including the popular *Oxrun Station* series. Anthologies as editor include *Nightmares, Horrors, Fears* and the ongoing *Shadows* series for Doubleday. He is a multiple winner of both the Nebula Award and the World Fantasy Award. His latest novels are *The Pet* and *The Orchard.*

STEVE RASNIC TEM

Little Cruelties

He had changed. Sometimes he didn't recognize himself. His voice sounded wrong—the timbre was unfamiliar, the vocabulary wasn't his, the opinions were unrecognizable. And he did things he could not have imagined.

Again and again, Paul came back to the incident with the chicks. It had been only a little thing, a small cruelty. Something he could never feel proud of, certainly, but not an act that deserved such intense shame. Ten years ago, for Christ's sake. Joey had been only five. He couldn't have taken care of the chicks, anyway. He wasn't old enough. He was old enough for resentment, however. He'd always been old enough for that.

It had been their last Easter in the old house. Joey had wanted chicks. Paul had explained very carefully how they had no place to keep pets like that in the city—their yard was too small, and he didn't want animals smelling up the basement or the garage. They had a nice old urban home; they didn't live on a farm, for Christ's sake. And he was too little to take proper care of them anyway. Mom or Dad would end up taking care of them and that wasn't very fair, now was it?

Joey had cried so much that weekend that Eve had finally given in, going out the Saturday before Easter and coming back with the three yellow chicks. Paul hadn't even known about it until Joey'd brought the basket in for him to see, all excited and thanking him profusely, climbing up on his lap—basket and chicks tipping precariously—to kiss him sloppily on the cheek.

Paul had been furious, but he couldn't say no. Joey was too excited. Besides, Paul couldn't let himself be the bad guy.

It snowed in April that year. Freakishly late, and heavy. The yard and the hill behind the house were white ice. The chicks were sick, losing feathers, near death. Joey had failed to take care of them, just as Paul had predicted. He didn't take any pleasure in that; it was just simple fact.

They were suffering. Paul felt terrible about it—it was his responsibility. He was Joey's father, after all. He had to do the right thing. He got up at dawn, dressed warmly, and sneaked into Joey's bedroom to get the chicks. They were so sick, he would take pains to remember, that they barely made any noise when he picked up the box. Joey was dead to the world, the covers twisted tightly around his legs. Paul stopped for a moment, set the chicks down, and freed his son.

He walked up the slight hill in his heavy winter boots, the ice-covered snow crackling with each step. The chicks began to shiver, but remained silent. When he reached the top of the hill he found he couldn't go any farther, and he also couldn't see himself setting the chicks gently down into the snow. It was a failure of nerve. He'd wanted to do the right thing. He suddenly tossed the box over to the other side and turned away. A cat, maybe a dog, would take care of them.

On his way back into the house he thought about fraternity pranks he'd heard about in college. Pig embryos left in a sorority house. Dead dogs mailed to opposing football coaches. A snow-ball of frozen chicks. But he'd wanted to do the right thing.

It was ridiculous to think that the death of chicks might diminish him somehow.

Paul told Joey that the chicks had died during the night and that he'd disposed of them. The boy cried most of the next day. "I wanted to bury 'em," he'd said between sniffles. "They were *mine.*"

"It's too cold outside. The ground's frozen."

"Then how did you do it?"

Paul couldn't look him directly in the eyes. "I'm a grown-up man. I can shovel better than you can."

"I don't think I believe you. You buried 'em? Good?" His son moved closer. Paul never failed to be surprised, almost appalled, by the directness of the little boy.

"Yes, I . . . I buried them." From the way Joey nodded, Paul knew he'd believed that, at least at the moment. But the doubt was still obviously latent in his son.

Paul was up at dawn the next day, raking gloved fingers through the top layers of snow that still covered the shaded hill. Every few minutes he found a clump of wet mud and leaves, or dog shit masquerading as one of the rancid little corpses, but the dead chicks eluded him. He thought maybe he'd been lucky and a neighborhood animal had in fact eaten them or dragged them away.

He gave up when he saw Joey's bedroom light come on. In a few minutes the child would be down in the family room for his morning cartoons.

Later Paul would think that all these actions were not normal for him. If he'd just had time to think about it, plan it out, then maybe he would have behaved better. As it was, he could not recognize himself. He could not fully accept the things he was doing.

Two days after the thaw, he saw Joey playing with the desiccated chick corpses in the backyard, passing them from hand to hand like lumps of gray modeling clay. Paul had to restrain himself from going out and stopping it, from explaining how dead things bore germs, how dead things might make a little boy sick.

Joey had to know what his father had done. But they never talked about it; neither of them could even bring it up. Paul had just wanted to do the right thing.

What Joey would never understand, what none of them seemed to understand, was how much it pained Paul to hurt his son. It happened too often, he knew, and always in such little ways, but it wasn't as if he *wanted* the hurt to happen. He just couldn't stop the little cruelties from happening to Joey (even when he seemed to be so much a part of them), any more than he could stop the little cruelties from happening to himself. Sometimes Paul didn't understand the situation, and so Joey was punished unnecessarily. Sometimes Paul did something—like take a particular toy away from his son, or deny him a trip to a neighbor's house, or devise a particular kind of punishment— that was meant to help the child grow up. But sometimes it backfired, and on reminiscence it appeared to be a *cruel* thing. But Paul had tried to do the right thing—he'd done the best he could. That was the way of things; that was the way the world usually worked. For Christ's sake—he loved his son.

In any case, the city was no place for animals.

Sometimes he imagined he heard his son crying in the night.

Little cruelties. It was the small malevolences, the tiny hatefulnesses, the lesser portions of ruthlessness which had always made Paul's life in the city seem a little sour, and which finally led him to move his family out of the old house on Parker Street.

Joey hadn't wanted to go—all his friends were there, friends he'd be starting first grade with. Paul tried to be reasonable, but how many close friends could a six-year-old have, anyway?

Eve hadn't liked the idea either, but was willing to go along with whatever Paul thought was right.

Paul had no doubts.

He didn't know what it was about the city that made people act the way they did—whether it was because of overcrowding (he thought often of those experiments in which mice were packed into a confined space), or lack of contact with the ground (you spent 99 percent of your time on concrete or asphalt), or the deterioration in municipal services (on how many mornings was the first thing he smelled garbage?), or some sort of degeneration of the species. But every day he saw more and more tense people, more and more crazy people.

He saw people trapped in the middle of traffic jams, going berserk when someone cut in front of them—ramming the other car repeatedly with their own, getting out and trying to drag the other driver out through a window.

He had neighbors who couldn't keep a sprinkler head, or a hose, or even a trash can for more than a few months at a time, before it was stolen or destroyed. Security lights didn't make any difference, and small nightly destructions had become so commonplace you didn't bother to distinguish the sounds.

Every day someone was insulted. Saying it made it sound banal, but Paul had become convinced that the little insults people had to endure each day—the "We can't do it, it's not procedure," delivered by a minor government official, the "How many other stores have you stuck?" from some anonymous bill collector on the phone, the "You have to do something about your weight," from an employer—were dragging people down gradually to the level of the animals. People stepped on you, and there really wasn't a lot you could do without getting yourself into a great deal of trouble.

Paul himself felt slighted a dozen different ways each week. No one seemed capable of seeing that he was hurt by their remarks. He did his best—surely that was worth a great deal in the scheme of things. And yet every encounter hid a potential insult.

Little cruelties. He didn't discuss them aloud with anyone— more often than not, putting his complaints into words made them sound faintly ridiculous. Occasionally he was moved to write a letter to the editor concerning the latest such lapse in human compassion: the woman who got rid of the cookies molding in her cookie jar by passing them out to kids on Halloween, the man who was charged for leaving a puppy tied to a tree for two days in the pouring rain, the neighbor's little girl who sneaked into her best friend's closet and tore up all her dresses when she wouldn't lend her doll. These people never murdered anybody. These were little crimes, little cruelties. But as these unkind examples accumulated Paul began to see them as monstrous in their implications. His letters were eloquent, but he rarely mailed them.

The little cruelties were the worst. They made each day a series of subliminal defeats. Trying to stop them seemed futile— they were too much a part of life in the city. He could never decide if it was the city changing the people, or the people changing the city.

Sometimes he thought he could hear his son crying in the night. It had been like that for a very long time—the faintest echo of a wail, or a howl, as if the boy had shrunk back to embryonic size or smaller and was being tortured in some other world. He used to check on his son, climb down the two flights of stairs to his room, where he always slept soundly, where the covers had been knocked awry with his feet, and Paul was compelled to fix them, tuck his beautiful boy in, kiss him lovingly somewhere in the nimbus of down that covered his face, awed still again by the sweet smell of him. After a few years he finally stopped the checking—he now knew it probably wasn't his son who'd cried out, and there no longer was any excuse for the nocturnal visitation.

Sometimes he thought he could hear his son crying in the night. But he knew that could not be. Particularly now, when Joey no longer lived there. He wondered how many times it had happened that you heard a distressed voice in the night—someone crying or screaming, someone asking for help—but you did nothing, because that sort of thing happens all the time in the city, and you didn't know if the person crying was drunk or stoned or just crazy. And there was always the possibility that there might be danger for you there, even from a phone call, because they always seemed to know who had complained. And in any case you'd give it away by your actions—standing by the windows and holding the curtains apart, to see what the police were going to do.

But Paul still believed it was a bad thing not to call—people might die if you didn't. People died all the time because of inaction, because of all the small neglects.

The day they moved into their new house didn't go smoothly. Paul made a mistake arranging for the truck and had to pay double for a replacement. Eve complained that she didn't have adequate time to pack, and spent the last few days cramming unsorted clothing, papers, and junk into cartons and garbage bags. And at the last minute she discovered a whole new series of complaints.

"I'm going to lose my friends, my Wednesday-afternoon bridge club, the good fresh meat from Kelsey's butcher. Not to mention Jimmy the flower vendor—he's been giving me free cut flowers at the end of every weekday for over five years now!" She looked up from her packing and glared at him. "What are *you* giving up, Paul?"

Paul couldn't stand to be in the same room with her when she was like that. He headed for the door. "It's for our *safety*, for Christ's sake! I'm just trying to fulfill my responsibility, but I guess you just can't see that."

Joey had been alternatingly crying and sullen. Some of his friends had come by to see him, but he'd refused to come downstairs, even when Paul got angry with him about it. They just didn't understand what he was trying to do for them.

Christ, they thought he was being thoughtless. They thought he didn't care about their feelings. They thought he was being cruel.

The new house was meant to protect his family. He'd spent years trying to find just such a place. It wasn't actually outside the city, but in a small community called Globeville, which had been segmented and virtually torn apart when two crossing interstates were built over it. Most of the commuters who passed over it every day didn't even know it existed.

The day they drove to the new house Eve had seemed increasingly anxious. Paul found the Globeville neighborhood quaint, and appealingly isolated. Eve thought it looked like a slum.

"Half the stores are boarded up!"

"We can still do our shopping in the city, if you like." She was going to spoil their first day with an argument. She was always starting the arguments. He never could see any reason to argue.

"I haven't seen a single restaurant or grocery store that isn't out of business."

"There's a pretty good Mexican restaurant down here, and a couple of bars. And a grocery store, just a little smaller than Kelsey's, but I'm sure they stock enough for most of our needs."

"So where is everybody, Dad?" It was the first thing Joey had said since he got into the car.

"They're mostly old people. People who have lived here all their lives, even some who were here before they built the interstate—that's one of the best things about the neighborhood. I guess old people don't always get outside that often." But Paul himself was vaguely disturbed by the almost empty streets.

Somehow the neighborhood seemed shabbier to him with Joey and Eve in the car. A large percentage of the houses hadn't been repainted in years. A number of the empty buildings served as warehouses for downtown businesses who wanted storage facilities midway to the suburbs. There were delivery trucks parked along the streets, but very few cars. Most of the cars he could see were in the yards, up on blocks and overgrown with weeds, rusting to a dirty cinnamon color. For a moment Paul wondered if it might be the city air settling here.

But it could be seen as *peaceful.* Certainly he could see it that way. Despite the fact that the highways were almost on top of them, the combination of trees and elevated roadway kept the neighborhood relatively quiet.

"It is . . . *nice*, Paul." There was hesitation in her voice. Paul looked up. A slight hill on their left. They'd arrived.

The Victorian house was in great shape. Paul had checked it out with the realtor several times. Most of the exterior wood-work—the gleaming white frills and gingerbread—was intact, as if immune to the acidic pollution which had taken its toll on old houses in other parts of the city. The red brick walls and gray stone foundations were firm and showed no signs of crumbling or even discoloration. Perhaps his favorite features were the two round towers—like sentry turrets—that rose from the second story, one at each corner. And for all that sense of age, the house had a modern kitchen and a good heating plant. The house was going to keep the city available to them when they needed it, and yet still provide a sanctuary.

An evolution was afoot; human beings were being *trans-formed* within the concrete womb of the city, into what he didn't even want to speculate. The evidence was all around them, the cruelties accumulating into a disease of harshness spreading throughout every metropolitan area.

But Eve and Joey—they just didn't want to see it. He proba-bly should have moved them all to the country.

"The neighborhood's terrible!" Eve's complaints became a familiar litany. "There isn't any crime, but it's so *dirty* here, Paul. I clean the house top to bottom and it needs dusting again almost the very next day!"

"It's an old house, Eve. You get dust in old houses. But at least it's not like the pollution we had to live with before. Admit it. Wasn't that a lot worse?"

"There's nothing to *do* here!"

Maybe if he had it all to do over again he'd move them to the country, but he'd felt the need to monitor the progress of the city's disease, and Globeville provided him the perfect vantage point. . . .

Now, he would sometimes gaze out his bedroom window and see Joey digging up the backyard, straightening up occasionally to examine the balls of dirt in his hands. But Joey and Eve had been gone for years, Eve long before Joey, and in any case Joey would be at least sixteen now, and this was a younger Joey excavating his lawn, silently examining the moist dirt and drier clay, looking for dead Easter chicks.

Sometimes he did not recognize himself. His sadness belonged to someone else.

Eve left less than a year after they'd moved into the Globeville house. He supposed it was inevitable—she missed her friends and she could see nothing in Paul's theories, which even he knew were becoming a bit of an obsession.

What he could not understand was the way she left Joey behind. He was just a child, her child. He gathered she had said goodbye to the boy, but Joey never would tell him what she'd said.

He changed. Sometimes he could not recognize himself. Raising his son on his own was far different from what he'd imagined it would be. Paul never knew how to act. He didn't know how to convince his son that his intentions were good, whatever mistakes he might make.

He could not convince his son to love him.

Sometimes he hid his son's toys. Sometimes he took Joey's homework out of his Road Runner notebook and threw it away. Sometimes he slipped down to the basement and threw the circuit breakers, and the little boy who was terrified of the dark was forced to struggle through rooms of shadow and sudden night.

Sometimes he heard his son cry out faintly in the darkness and he did not come.

"Your son is bullying the other children." The voice on the phone was distant, unreliable. He should never have allowed Joey to attend school in the city.

"No, not my son. You must be mistaken."

"He curses the teachers. He writes vile things on the walls. He *defaces* school property."

"No, no. It's the school. It's *you* people. I should be educating him here, in our own home."

"He's cruel to . . ."

"What's *wrong* is you people! I've seen the way you let the children hang around outside the school, smoking and laughing, acting like little *adults* for Christ's sake! Not like children at all.

You've *robbed* them of their childhoods. No wonder they think they can say whatever they please."

He slammed the phone down, shaking. He could hear Joey moving around downstairs.

He wondered if Eve had sensed that Joey too had become infected by the cruelty.

He wondered if Eve ever suspected what had really happened to the chicks.

He had gone downstairs to talk to Joey. Maybe he was going to talk to Joey about the chicks. Maybe he was just going to discuss the boy's behavior in school. He would never be quite sure.

When he walked into the kitchen Joey was sitting cross-legged on the floor. He had two oblong lumps of clay, passing them from hand to hand. He looked serene, contented. He made no sounds, but Paul could almost hear the gentle hum the boy's mind must have made. Paul looked past his son, and saw that the floor was dirty. Gray and white animal fur adhered to the green tile. A sticky substance stained the floor and the lower part of the pale yellow cabinets. He looked back at his son. Now he could see the faint pinkness in the clay lumps, the edges of red, the small gaping mouths with sharp teeth. For several days there had been a poster on the telephone pole outside their house announcing two lost kittens. The lettering was crude, done with crayon, and above the lettering there was a crayon illustration of the two missing pets—one of them gray and one of them white.

Joey stared at him, as if waiting. Paul's lips moved silently, as if by themselves. He turned and went back up the stairs.

That night Paul heard things in the darkness, small cries and whispers. He imagined someone somewhere was in need of help. But he did not leave his bed.

The next morning Joey was gone.

Today, on foot and on his way back from the grocery store, he had seen Joey, or someone who looked like Joey, standing across the street from the Globeville house, watching it. He'd run to catch the teenager but the grocery sacks were too bulky and he didn't want to drop them.

Joey had been gone several years now. Paul couldn't even be sure he was still alive. The police were of no help—in fact, for a time they seemed to suspect that Paul had actually done something to Joey. As if he were a murderer. That had been a cruel suspicion, and by it Paul knew they'd been infected the same as everyone else. Finally they concluded that Joey had run away to, or been kidnapped by, his mother. They weren't optimistic about ever finding him.

Paul couldn't see it. Eve had abandoned Joey, so why would he leave his father? It wasn't as if his father were a murderer, a thief, a fiend. He knew his son must be dead. Someone had taken the boy from his bed, and the cruelties had just gotten out of hand. They had a way of doing that, cruelties did, as if they had a life of their own.

And yet the boy was outside, in the night, digging up his father's yard.

It was a cruel thing.

Even chicks had their place in the scheme of things. Their deaths could change how you lived within the world.

Eventually, Paul began seeing Joey, or someone who looked like Joey, nearly every afternoon. Passing in front of the Globeville house, but on the other side of the street, like a shy lover.

At night, the boy excavated his yard.

During the day, Paul could see the changes that had occurred to brick and wood, the subtle disintegrations so like plant blight, or cancer.

Paul made sure his windows and doors were locked at night. Sometimes he would wake up and watch the ceiling over his bed, where the shadows of windblown tree limbs and thick power lines tangled over a dim yellow oval of glare. He thought he could hear the sound of narrow hands sliding repeatedly into soft earth, like a dying fish flapping on a sodden wooden plank.

"It's not as if I tried to hurt anyone," he'd whisper to the dark.

He'd hear his own voice crying softly in the distance, and no one bothered to investigate.

He'd seen no one on the street in front of his house for days, but he hadn't been out, and the weather was breezy. Mostly old people, retired people lived here, and the air might have been too much for them.

Despite the breeze the pollution was bad, which was a little hard to figure. Black, cottony lines of smoke floated low over the buildings—a chimney must be working somewhere, he thought. The sunsets were soiled shades of magenta, orange, red, and bruise-colored. During Indian summer the clouds started to bleed after four o'clock.

The gutters were lined with trash, but then that had happened before. A jurisdiction problem between municipal sanitation departments. There appeared to be more cracks in the pavement out front than he remembered, but these back streets got short shrift on road repair.

Stray slivers of noxious pollution rubbed the brick edges of his house. Red decay powdered the gray-green bushes planted near the house's exterior walls. Occasionally he'd open a window but then shortly would close it because of the smell. Periods of still air trapped the stench in his neighborhood.

Eve had insisted that the house needed cleaning every other day. He had never much seen the point. He kept the garbage in airtight bags on the back porch, and someday he would haul it all out. He kept the door to the back porch closed, except when he needed to add another bag to the pile.

He watched a many-legged insect—he couldn't remember the name—leave a thin trail up the dining-room wall.

Dead insects filled the windowsills. Some nights the house grew stuffy and he ached to open the windows, but he was afraid.

Weeds grew over the curb and softened the borders of the street.

The guttering along the eaves rusted. One of the exit pipes turned brown and fell into the yard. Then he never saw it again. The grass swallowed it. The grass swallowed the walk and he became afraid of stepping into the yard.

The pipes made cracking noises in the night. He secretly hoped the pipes would break and separate completely—they linked him to the city's sewer system.

Graffiti grew along the walls of his beautiful, strong house like a vine, flowing with the grain of the brick, then separating, multiplying, seeking any empty space.

One night his garage roof fell under its own weight, crushing his car, but the gas tank had been empty anyway.

Toward the end of the month it rained for several days.

When it was over he stood out on his front porch. Water had flooded the gutters. The sewer vomited. Yolky and cinnamon-colored liquids oozed out of the sewer grates and stained the pavement. A grayish human corpse lay face-down with its skull against the opposite curb, the viscous water nudging it rhythmically. Paul had the urge to go down and touch it, pick up the lifeless arm and the head, play with it, pass the disease from hand to hand. Sores spotted his lawn. Paul went back in and secured the door.

He could never decide if it was the city changing the people, or the people changing the city.

Joey dug up his backyard. Great piles of earth lay sprawled, decayed while they slept. They cried softly in the distance, but no one called the police.

Paul wandered the darkened rooms of his sanctuary, the dried bodies of insects crackling under his old socks. Sometimes he would try to open a window, brushing leaves and wallpaper chips and brittle insect hulls from the window ledge, but the window fell apart when he lifted.

He watched Joey painting huge green, white, blue graffiti in the middle of the street. Somebody should have stopped him, but no one left their quiet, worn houses. He watched Joey breaking the windows of the house next door.

"It's not as if I were . . ." he tried to say.

Paul mourned the day and cried in his sleep. He bruised his cruel hands against the walls, and scratched at his cruel face with the broken fingernails.

All the next day Paul waited by his empty body while Joey called from the distant tunnel he had dug for himself underground, that snaked its way under the yard and curled in on itself deep under the house.

No one knew him, or recognized his absence, or the minute reduction of cruelties in the world once he had disappeared.

Around him the concrete rotted, the city pavements grew rancid.

STEVE RASNIC TEM published close to a hundred short stories between 1979 and 1986. During that time he also edited *The Umbral Anthology of Science Fiction Poetry*. His stories continue to appear in periodicals in and out of the fields of science fiction and fantasy and in many original horror anthologies. His first novel, *Excavations*, will appear shortly. At the moment he is working on the horror novel *New Blood*, about Kentucky in the thirties, snake handling, and the Melungeons.

GEORGE CLAYTON JOHNSON

The Man
with the Hoe

There is no new truth, only that which is old; there is nothing to be discovered that you have not known all along.

Fearing the hungry wolf you gathered together for protection, saying, "Surely he will not attack. There are so many of us." You felt warm and safe knowing there were others between yourself and the wolf's terrible teeth and, lulled by the lowing of the herd, you fell asleep. You did not hear the stealthy footfalls of the famished wolf or see the alarmed group scatter to leave you exposed and helpless—a sacrifice. You looked about seeking one who could save you. By that time it was too late . . .

"No," he gasps, and awakes.

He can hear his wife sleeping fitfully beside him in the darkness.

His mind is racing.

Careful not to disturb her further he rises and, following the dim flashlight beam down the carpeted hall into his book-lined den, he slumps into the familiar chair.

He turns off the heavy flashlight to save the batteries and leans back tiredly, rubbing his grainy eyes.

What a hell of a mess life is.

The gods play rough.

He cranks open the window, hearing the distant freeway sounds and the nearer cry of mating cats. From the pain and fury in the screams he pictures them clawing and snapping at each other.

He tries to focus, make sense of everything, make plans, but it is too terrible to think about. He has already considered everything.

As he looks blankly out the window into the darkness of the backyard, an odd image rises unbidden before his mind's eye: a TV image—numberless white-draped black men, arms laced together in long lines, jammed behind apartheid fences, rising and falling together. It comes back to him like a photograph. A political protest in South Africa. He'd seen it on the tube before the Department of Water and Power shut off the electricity and before he hocked the TV.

The Africans clung to each other, hip to hip, supporting each other, leaping up and down together in a slow rhythm. He couldn't tell what it was they were chanting. Moaning? Howling? The roar was drowned out by the newscaster's voice describing the protest, the racial violence, the whips, the clubs, the hostility and terror. The image had stuck in his mind. Looking at those black, straining, agonized faces he knew that they had the mentality of savages.

What was the poem?

Is this the dream he dreamed who shaped the suns
And mark't their way upon the ancient deep?

Yes. Edwin Markham— THE MAN WITH THE HOE.

Down all the caverns of Hell to their last gulf
There is no shape more terrible than this.
More tongued with censure of the world's blind greed.
More filled with signs and portents for the Soul.
More pack't with danger to the Universe.

Yes, kept separated by South African law, those illiterate brutes had become THE MAN WITH THE HOE.

He tries to imagine what will happen when those vengeful blacks break through those fences—the bloodshed.

He tries to understand what those black Africans are thinking and can't. They are a mystery from the depths of a primitive jungle.

Markham had said it.

What gulfs between him and the seraphim!
Slave of the wheel of labor what to him

Are Plato and the swing of Pleiades?
The long reaches of the peaks of song,
The rift of dawn, the reddening of the rose?

But if not *thinking*, then what are the Africans feeling? Even the dumb animals have feelings.

It is a mystery.

He breathes silently in the darkness.

Is this the thing the Lord God made and gave
To have dominion over land and sea?
To trace the stars and search the heavens for power,
To feel the passion of Eternity?

He had read somewhere that the poet got his idea from a famous painting of a French peasant working in a darkening field. Commenting on the painting in poetry, Markham had arbitrarily collaborated with Millet, the great Impressionist painter.

Betrayed, plundered, profaned and disinherited . . .

Leaning on the windowsill, remembering fragments of the poem, he thinks he sees a shadow move on the moonlit garden wall he had built to keep intruders out.

A cat: the big gray he called Bruiser because of its burly carriage and bullying manner.

Will that cat never learn?

Somewhere he had read that Man was the product of almost a hundred generations of accumulated knowledge, while each cat was the original Cat from the primeval wilderness, unaltered by time.

Silently he eases open the desk drawer and rummages among its contents, finding the slingshot and the bag of glass marbles. Putting a slippery marble in the leather pouch, he takes careful aim through the open window.

That damned cat understands territory well enough and is defying him.

Somewhere far-off thunders mutter and energies stir but he doesn't hear although he must feel the power. Were they not watching from the hidden world? Did they not care about his fate?

It is the cats' attitude: their arrogance. It is *they* who own the yard, not he, for when he shouts angrily at them they turn languidly to eye him before marking the spot with scent and sauntering insolently away.

If he chases them they are over a wall and gone where none can pursue. It is maddening.

He holds his fire as he tests the tension in the surgical-rubber tubing, stretching and releasing slightly, feeling the heavy glass pellet inside the cowhide pouch.

With the mnemonic pull in his muscles he remembers in flashes as a child, aiming and firing rocks at tin cans, glass insulators on telephone poles, streetlamps and, when that grew less challenging, at gophers on the Cheyenne prairie, frogs along Crow Creek, jackrabbits waiting hidden till the last moment before making their break, birds on limbs and wires and snowfences and on the wing, bringing them out of the sky!— remembering how he and his cousin Chuck killed a forbidden robin redbreast in Frontier Park with weapons made out of inner-tube rubber and cleverly twisted pieces of coathanger and the tongues of an old pair of shoes and kitestring and how they had put the plump bird on a stick, feathers and all, over a tiny twig fire beneath the bushes and how exultantly they ate the charred and unrecognizable results as though they were wild red Indians on the plains—Men, by God!

In the dark, aiming the slingshot, he feels rage build glowingly within him at the sly insolence of cats.

If only the whole neighborhood wasn't a single interconnected roadway to everywhere for the sneaky, treacherous things.

If only that damned woman next door didn't feed them so cheerfully, leaving out piepans of kitty vittles like bait in the driveway near the leaky water faucet for every stray. And not only the strays but even well-fed cats on the nearby streets seeking better pickings, the big males bullying the others away from the pan, or waiting patiently, ranked according to their malignant ferocity.

If only the neighborhood cats hadn't all chosen his tree-shaded trellis to do their mating, ringing in a female to stare her protests down, groaning and yowling and snarling and spitting.

Suddenly he puts his finger on it.

The dogs.

Where are the dogs that usually keep the cats under control? They are natural enemies.

For dogs there are leash laws but cats are classed as wild animals and free of regulation. They can't be leashed, is that it?

There was a time, he thinks swiftly, when the world was different. Everyone, it seemed, worked for the aircraft plant or the post office or the steel mill and they all went off to work at the same time and came home at the same time and *then* was when they thought to feed the animals and with the lure of food kept them dependent. But now, with the closing of the plants, the pattern has broken down. Now they simply ignore the animals or put out a dish of kibble and forget it till it's empty. Now they haven't a single idea where their little darling spends the night.

So it has come to this.

He blinks away tears, feeling the moistness of the cold night air from the open window. He pities his neighbors in their blindness. They can't see the signs. They aren't aware that the whole world system is breaking down, overwhelmed by numbers and greed and stupidity.

Damn you, he says to the cat-shape in his mind. I've never really liked you, nor any of your tribe. I don't like your two-faced ways, your cruelty, your spitefulness.

Now suddenly the shadows resolve themselves and he can see the big gray poised on the wall, motionless, listening, probing the neighborhood with its senses, evaluating the texture of the night. It gives a low, penetrating groan which is echoed from afar, and again from a place more distant.

He pulls back on the leather pouch, stretching the rubber tubing.

The cat-shadow moves on the garden wall.

And I don't like the way you treat your women, he says under his breath and releases the missile with a *whap!* of disturbed air.

He sees the marble fly off into the darkness and with his mind's eye he sees it arch magically as if drawn on a string to its target, guided by his confidence.

He can see the cat struck even as it turns and leaps.

Aside from a startled lurch in the air and a sharp intake of breath, the cat makes no sound as it flees back into the darkness.

There, by damn! He feels momentary satisfaction, the thrill of an act well done with accuracy and precision; the cold, solid control that is fueled by rage.

He pictures the hurt cat skirting the neighbor's shed and coming to rest beneath the jasmine bush by the poolside to lick its wounds.

He pictures the cat's eyes in the gloom: bright, sly, glowing with malevolence, filled with hatred.

He hears a long cat yowl, sustained, penetrating. Nearby, answering cat cries.

Now they'll *all* know.

He pictures cats waking in darkened rooms to heed the call. He pictures them slipping out of houses into the night to converge on his house—summoned by Bruiser, nursing his hatred, seeking revenge.

Let them come! He is ready for them. He puts another marble into the leather pouch and looks warily into the darkness. He listens intently, picturing the neighborhood cats responding, picturing them coming together from faraway places to form a group under the neighbor's jasmine bush, called forth by the injured one who nurses an age-old grudge.

Another sound!

His wife.

She has come down the hall and opened the door. He cannot see her face but he knows that she looks very tired.

Reflexively, he hides the slingshot in his lap.

"Darling?" she says hesitantly.

When he doesn't answer she says, "I'm worried. I couldn't sleep."

He waits.

"Don't you think you should talk to your cousin Chuck about this? If he knew how bad it is maybe he'd help. He *has* the money."

Cousin Chuck again. He remembers the last time he went to Chuck for the money they needed for groceries. First Chuck had to know all the details; then he'd put on that face and said, "How could you let things get this bad?" Then he talked about needing some kind of collateral for the hundred-dollar loan, the son of a bitch. He wouldn't go for the broken sewing machine that cost a bundle or the hand-carved chess set. No, Chuck wanted the rifle and shells even though he never really liked to shoot. "A rifle's more negotiable in bad times," Chuck had said, already planning how to sell it—but that was careful Chuck. He thinks about the thirty-thirty and the two boxes of cartridges lying in Chuck's carport storage cabinet, rusting. If he had his hands on that rifle those cats would learn a lesson. He imagines himself looking down the sights at Bruiser or Midnight or Lightning—he's named all the strays. It helped him keep track of them. . . .

His wife feels his resistance and withdrawal. "If we lose the house, what will we do?" she asks, reading his mind, knowing he doesn't have the answer. Hasn't she always been the one to supply that, with him simply the provider, bringing home the check, having learned it from his father, who had failed at being the Man?

"I'll think up something," he replies tightly, knowing he won't. Hasn't his role in life been to let her do the planning and budgeting, she having learned it from her mother, who had failed at being the Woman?

"Don't you think it's cold?" she says, putting ideas in his head. "Maybe you ought to come to bed. You know that whatever happens tomorrow you'll need your sleep."

He feels her manipulation, aware suddenly of how much of his life has been subject to that. At the sound of her voice he also feels a great weakness. He tries to remember how long he has been lying to her about small things rather than face her, and how long she has known about it and relished the power it gave her over him, treating him like a disobedient son. He tries to remember just when it was he lost control. Had it been the day he was hired by the company, learned to take orders, to depend blindly on the judgment of others, learned to hide his true feelings, stopped being a wild dog and accepted a collar, stopped being an outsider and became an insider?

And for what?

Did it matter to them that he was on their side—willing to close his eyes and harden his heart?

How quickly after the plant closed were their meager savings gone.

How quickly the union had proved itself impotent.

How quickly the unemployment insurance had run out while he was left standing in lines, filling out applications.

How quickly the utility companies had acted to stop service when the timely checks ended, forgetting years of prompt payments and talk of good credit.

How quickly the house had gone into foreclosure after a baffling exchange of letters with the insurance company that held the second mortgage.

How quickly he and his wife had been reduced in circumstance, chastened, humiliated, degraded, while time tightened about them.

"You never *talk!*" she cries. "How can I know what you're thinking?"

Didn't she know she could beat him at talking—that his power over her was his silence? Didn't she know that talking always led to his downfall—that he was only safe when he was silent, that the less people knew about him the better? The less *she* knew about him the better.

She waits vainly.

At last she says, "You'll get something."

"Sure," he says, not believing it anymore. "Go back to bed. I'll be there in a minute," and he knows that he'll never again in his life hold a job that pays seventeen bucks an hour.

He hears her go. He thinks he hears a sob. He hears the door close at the end of the hall.

He sits quietly, trying not to think of anything.

The groaning yowl of cats echoes and re-echoes, closer. The night is alive with menacing cries.

They'll come *that* way, he thinks, from the corner of the yard where the walls are tallest and the growth is deepest, a perfect staging ground for an assault upon the house. "Yes," he says softly. "That's the way they'll come."

He pictures them mounting the wall in single file to gather in the pool of ink under the branches of the neighbor's overhanging mulberry tree, their eyes glittering wickedly, exchanging cold smirky grins before descending to slink out over the dark ground, creeping invisibly in the tangled black shadows.

He stares into the blackness, shielding his eyes against stray city light, looking for movement.

His wife's careworn face appears before his mind's eye. He

searches her face for signs of reproach. He wants her to say, "You didn't do anything wrong." He wants her to say, "It isn't your fault."

After all, she isn't the one who has to face the smug bastards. She isn't the one who has to offer herself abjectly to their persistent refusal, knowing that the sands of the world have shifted, with the computer running the factories and the worker no longer needed. He stares into the pit where his job has vanished.

The back yard is silent, unmoving.

Has he heard footfalls on the roof?

The rake of claws against screen?

Scratching at the door?

He'd better go in to join her. She *is* right. In spite of everything he has to sleep.

He puts the slingshot down on the desk alongside the flashlight and feels his way to the bedroom door.

"Momma?" he says. "Are you asleep?"

"Come to bed," she says sleepily. "Nothing can be done until morning."

She is right.

He remembers the open window and the flashlight.

"I'll be with you in a minute," he says.

He feels the gods leaning in on him, attending his every move, plumbing the depths of his intentions; feels their presence as they pause to remember the perfidy of cats and the failures of men.

Touching the walls protectively, he makes his way to the den window and closes it carefully. The astonishing cam-action of the lever snugs it home, locks it tight.

Picking up the bulky flashlight, he flips the switch briefly to test the batteries. Revealed by the beam is his slingshot. He stares at what he sees, uncomprehending.

The rubber tubes have been clawed by sharp teeth, severed in several places, ruined.

He stiffens with shock.

He hears the scamper of claws on the wood floor close by.

While his back was turned one of the cats must have gotten inside.

He pictures the cat trapped in the locked house, desperate, alarmed, deadly.

He pictures it searching for escape down the hall into the front room where all the doors and windows are secured.

Fine. Now we'll find out who has the control. He feels a sense of power and outrage.

Guided by the flashlight, he goes searching for a cat who is too smart for its own good.

He hears soft footfalls on the living room rug. He hears the cat's quiet breath in the amazing silence.

He finds it crouched back in the corner under the couch, big and charcoal gray, marked with battle scars. *Bruiser.* When he flashes the light it spits and snarls, showing its needle teeth.

If he goes for a broom handle he may lose it.

He is momentarily baffled.

The cat shrinks back into the corner, eyes wide and blazing with reflected light, muscles flexed and ready, claws gripping the carpet, teeth threatening, throat hissing.

So it's going to be like that?

Adrenaline pops in his veins.

It is galling, impossible, the final insult. Inside his own house! Red rage flares through him.

Holding the light steady and without considering the consequences, he sticks his bare left fist under the couch, reaching, reaching farther. A dare.

The cat bites savagely, sinking its fangs into his hand. He unclenches his fist, jamming the cat's mouth wide open, the jaws powerless against his superior strength.

Surprisingly, there is no pain. Only a sense of triumph.

Locked in his hand, the cat's teeth can't release their hold. The teeth have gone into the bony knuckles and though the cat squirms and thrashes, it is helpless to escape. He feels the tug of jaws against ligaments, but everything holds.

Now we'll see!

He begins to draw the resisting cat toward him, pulling it out from under the couch. It twists and jerks in terror.

He raises the heavy flashlight and brings it down like a club on the now truly dangerous animal.

Feels the satisfying sting in his palm.

Feels the cat's spine break.

Feels the metal rim of the flashlight give, but the light holds steady. He raises the torch high and strikes again. The light is a dim yellow beam. The cat is still.

There!

His breath whistles through his teeth as he pries loose the dead jaws. He is bleeding like hell from the torn knuckles and his hand is beginning to ache.

He'll need a shot of penicillin and a couple of stitches.

He flashes the light on the cat's rigid body. Now they'll all know he means business.

He pictures the news of Bruiser's death flashing out from house to house, carried from cat to cat like a silent telegraph.

He pictures their consternation, realizing that the war they have triggered is to the death. That man accepts no compromises.

He pictures them rising to eliminate the threat, to restore the status quo.

He pictures them coming from distant neighborhoods, leaping, running along fences and tree limbs, across porch roofs and sheds, pausing invisible beneath parked cars, stalking him now as they grow in number.

He hears the faint cry of cats on the night air, sounding and resounding. Or are they tires on the freeway?

Pain from his damaged hand pulls him back into the dark living room.

He puts the knuckles of his now-throbbing fist to his mouth and begins to suck on it.

Now, with the taste of the hot blood in his throat, he suddenly *knows.* Abruptly he knows what those black Africans on TV were thinking and feeling, rising and falling behind wire fences, arms locked together like an army, heads thrown back, defiant, menacing—a powderkeg of hatred.

Oh, Masters, Lords and Rulers in all lands
How will the future reckon with this man?
How answer his brute question in that hour
When whirlwinds of rebellion shake all shores?

A crack of light appears in his brain. He sees the glimmering of a way out.

He doesn't owe anything to the others. He is on his own. They've made that clear enough.

Already he can hear cats scratching at the doors, the windows. He can hear their murderous keening.

With the kids gone there is just he and his wife.

Yes, he owes them nothing.

He sees everything through fresh eyes.

The bastards have revealed themselves!

How will it be with Kingdoms and with Kings—
With those who shaped him to the thing he is—
When this dumb terror shall rise to judge the world,
After the silence of the centuries?

He thinks of his rifle rusting away at Cousin Chuck's.

Cautiously he pushes open the back screendoor. Stepping into the garden he hears a hiss behind him and whirls. Poised on the edge of the low roof, shaped against the moon, ready to spring, is a black cat, back arched, all its fur aloft. He hears stirrings in the garden darkness surrounding him, a threat. He feels the hackles go up on the back of his neck.

Let them dare!

He raises the flashlight threateningly and with the gesture and the killing weight in his palm he finds himself thinking of his sleeping wife, thinking, "You could bust a man's skull with a club like this," thinking, let them come. He is ready.

And, later, walking over to Cousin Chuck's house he can feel the cats' wary eyes on him in the dark as he nurses his hurt hand against his chest and cuts at the air with his not yet useless flashlight, thinking, the flashlight will come in handy if Chuck tries to stop him. With that loaded rifle in his hands they'll play hell evicting him from his own home.

Are the gods hungry? Do they lust for more blood?

Yes, you gathered together against the wolf believing that there was strength in numbers. To your astonishment you discovered that there was weakness in numbers and when you learned that the group would not protect you, you were free to survive as best you could, but oh, my children, what of Honor?

But what of Grace?

Yes, there is no new truth, only that which is old. The dead past is alive in the present, and you never find the people that you go to meet in dreams.

GEORGE CLAYTON JOHNSON wrote a number of the original "Twilight Zone" episodes and shares screenplay credit on *Twilight Zone—The Movie.* He co-authored the novels *Ocean's 11* and *Logan's Run.* He wrote the premiere episode of "Star Trek" as well as segments of "Route 66," "Honey West," "The Law And Mr. Jones," "Mr. Novak" and "Kung Fu." His short stories have appeared in *100 Great Fantasy Short Shorts, Author's Choice #4, Masters of Darkness* and elsewhere.

LES DANIELS

They're Coming
for You

Mr. Bliss came home from work early one Monday afternoon. It was a big mistake.

He'd had a headache, and his secretary, after offering him various patent medicines, complete with their manufacturers' slogans, had said, "Why don't you take the rest of the day off, Mr. Bliss."

Everyone called him Mr. Bliss. The others in the office were Dave or Dan or Charlie, but he was Mr. Bliss. He liked it that way. Sometimes he thought that even his wife should call him Mr. Bliss.

Instead, she was calling on God.

Her voice came from on high. From upstairs. In the bedroom. She didn't seem to be in pain, but Mr. Bliss could remedy that.

She wasn't alone; someone was grunting in harmony with her cries to the creator. Mr. Bliss was bitter about this.

Without even waiting to hang up his overcoat, he tiptoed into the kitchen, and plucked from its magnetic rack one of the Japanese knives his wife had ordered after watching a television commercial. They were designed for cutting things into small pieces, and they were guaranteed for life, however long that happened to be. Mr. Bliss would see to it that his wife had no cause for complaint. He turned away from the rack, paused for a sigh, then went back and selected another knife. The first was for the one who wanted to meet God, and the second for the one who was making those animal noises.

After a moment's reflection, he decided to use the back stairs. They were more secretive, somehow, and Mr. Bliss intended to have a big secret just as soon as he could get organized.

He had an erection for the first time in weeks, and his headache was gone.

He moved as quickly and carefully as he could, sliding across the checkerboard linoleum and taking the back stairs two at a time in slow, painful, thigh-straining stretches. He knew there was a step which creaked, couldn't recall which one it was, and knew he would step on it anyway.

That hardly mattered. The groans and wails were reaching a crescendo, and Mr. Bliss suspected that not even a brass band behind him could have distracted the people above him from their business. They were about to achieve something, and he wanted very much to be there before they did.

The bedroom took up the entire top floor of the house. It had been a whim of his to flatter his young bride with as spacious a spawning ground as his salary would allow; the tastefully carpeted stairs led up to it in front as inexorably as the shabby wooden stairs crept up the back.

Mr. Bliss creaked at the appointed spot, cursed quietly, and opened the door.

His wife's eyes, rolled back in her head, were like wet marble. Her lips fluttered as she blew damp hair from her face. The beautiful breasts that had persuaded him to marry her were covered with sweat, and not all of it was hers.

Mr. Bliss didn't even recognize the man; he was nobody. The milkman? A census taker? He was plump, and he needed a haircut. It was all very discouraging. Cuckolding by an Adonis would at least have been understandable, but this was a personal affront.

Mr. Bliss dropped one knife to the floor, grasped the other in both hands, and slammed its point into the pudgy interloper at the spot where spine meets skull.

It worked at once. The man gave one more grunt and toppled over backwards, blade grinding against bone as head and handle hit the floor.

Mrs. Bliss was there, baffled and bedraggled, spread-eagled naked against sopping sheets.

Mr. Bliss picked up the other knife.

He pulled her up by the hair and stabbed her in the face. She blubbered blood. Madly but methodically, he shoved the sharp steel into every place where he thought she'd like it least.

Most of his experiments were successful.

She died unhappily.

The last expression she was able to muster was a mixture of pain, reproach, and resignation that thrilled him more than anything she'd shown him since their wedding night.

He wasn't done with her yet. She had never been so submissive.

It was late that night before he put down the knife and put on his clothes.

Mr. Bliss had made a terrible mess. Cleaning up was always a chore, as she had so frequently reminded him, but he was equal to the task. The worst part was that he had stabbed the water bed, but at least the flood had diluted some of the blood.

He buried them in separate sections of the flower garden and showed up late for work. This was an unprecedented event. The quizzical eyebrows of his colleagues got on his nerves.

For some reason he didn't feel like going home that night. He went to a motel instead. He watched television. He saw a movie about someone killing several other people, but it didn't amuse him as much as he'd hoped. He felt that it was in bad taste.

He left the "Do Not Disturb" sign on the doorknob of his room each day; he did not wish to be disturbed. Still, the unmade bed to which he returned each night began to bother him. It reminded him of home.

After a few days, Mr. Bliss was ashamed to go to the office. He was still wearing the same clothes he'd left home in, and he was convinced that his colleagues could smell him. No one had ever longed for the weekend as passionately as he did.

Then he had two days of peace in his motel room, huddling under the covers in the dark and watching people kill each other in a phosphorescent glow, but on Sunday night he looked at his socks and knew he would have to go back to the house.

He wasn't happy about this.

When he opened the front door, it reminded him of his last entrance. He felt that the stage was set. Still, all he had to do was go upstairs and get some clothes. He could be gone in a matter of minutes. He knew where everything was.

He used the front stairs. The carpeting made them quieter, and somehow he felt the need for stealth. Anyway, he didn't like the ones in the back anymore.

Halfway up the stairs, he noticed two paintings of roses that his wife had put there. He took them down. This was his house now, and the pictures had always vaguely annoyed him. Unfortunately, the blank spaces he left on the wall bothered him too.

He didn't know what to do with the paintings, so he carried them up into the bedroom. There seemed to be no way to get rid of them. He was afraid this might be an omen, and for a second considered the idea of burying them in the garden. This made him laugh, but he didn't like the sound. He decided not to do it again.

Mr. Bliss stood in the middle of the bedroom and looked around critically. He'd made quite a neat job of it. He was just opening a dresser drawer when he heard a thump from below. He stared at his underwear.

A scrape followed the thump, and then the sound of something bumping up the back stairs.

He didn't wonder what it was, not even for an instant. He closed his underwear drawer and turned around. His left eyelid twitched; he could feel it. He was walking without thinking toward the front stairs when he heard the door below them open. Just a little sound, a bolt slipping a latch. Suddenly, the inside of his head felt as big as the bedroom.

He knew they were coming for him, one from each side. What could he do? He ran around the room, slamming into each wall and finding it solid. Then he took up a post beside the bed and put a hand over his mouth. A giggle spilled between his fingers, and it made him angry, for this was a proud moment.

They were coming for him.

Whatever became of him (no more job, no more television), he had inspired a miracle. The dead had come back to life to punish him. How many men could say as much? Come clump, come thump, come slithering sounds! This was a triumph.

He stepped back against the wall to get a better view. As both doors opened his eyes flicked back and forth. His tongue followed, licking his lips. He experienced an ecstasy of terror.

The stranger, of course, had used the back stairs.

He had tried to forget what a mess he had made of them, especially his wife. And now they were even worse.

And yet, as she dragged herself across the floor, there was something in her pale flesh, spotted with purple where the blood had settled, and striped with rust where the blood had spilled, that called to him as it rarely had before. Her skin was clumped with rich brown earth. She needs a bath, he thought, and he began to snort with laughter that would soon be uncontrollable.

Her lover, approaching from the other side, was hardly marked. There had been no wish to punish him, only to make him stop. Still, the single blow of the TV knife had severed his spine, and his head lurched unpleasantly. The odd disappointment Mr. Bliss had felt in the man's flabbiness intensified. After six days in the ground, what crawled toward him was positively puffy.

Mr. Bliss tried to choke back his chuckles till his eyes watered and snot shot from his nose. Even as his end approached, he saw their impossible lust for vengeance as his ultimate vindication.

Yet his feet were not as willing to die as he was; they backed over the carpet toward the closet door.

His wife looked up at him, as well as she could. The eyes in her sockets seemed shriveled, like inquisitive prunes. A part of her where he had cut too deeply and too often dropped quietly to the floor.

Her lover shuffled forward on hands and knees, leaving some sort of a trail behind him.

Mr. Bliss pulled the gleaming brass bed around to make a barricade. He stepped back into the closet. The smell of her perfume and of her sex enveloped him. He was buried in her gowns.

His wife reached the bed first, and grasped the fresh linen with the few fingers she had left. She hauled herself up. Stains smeared the sheets. This was certainly the time to slam the closet door, but he wanted to watch. He was positively fascinated.

She squirmed on the pillows, arms flailing, then collapsed on her back. There were gurgles. Could she be really dead at last? No.

It didn't matter. Her lover crawled over the counterpane. Mr. Bliss wanted to go to the bathroom, but the way was blocked.

He cringed when his wife's lover (who was this creeping corpse, anyway?) stretched out fat fingers, but instead of clawing for revenge they fell on what had been the breasts of the body beneath him. They began to move gently.

Mr. Bliss blushed as the ritual began. He heard sounds that had embarrassed him even when the meat was live: liquid lurchings, ghastly groans, and supernatural screams.

He shut himself in the closet. What was at work on the bed did not even deign to notice him. He was buried in silk and polyester.

It was worse than he had feared. It was unbearable.

They hadn't come for him at all.

They had come for each other.

LES DANIELS's books include *Comix: A History of Comic Books in America, Living in Fear: A History of Horror in the Mass Media, Dying of Fright: Masterpieces of the Macabre, Thirteen Tales of Terror,* and three novels about the immortal vampire Don Sebastian de Villanueva: *The Black Castle, The Silver Skull* and *Citizen Vampire.* He is presently at work on a new Sebastian chronicle, tentatively entitled *Yellow Fog.* "They're Coming for You" is his first short story.

PART III

Walking the Headlights

RICHARD CHRISTIAN MATHESON

Vampire

Man.
Late. Rain.
Road.
Man.
Searching. Starved. Sick.
Driving.
Radio. News. Scanners. Police. Broadcast.
Accident. Town.
Near.
Speeding. Puddles.
Aching.
Minutes.
Arrive. Park. Watch.
Bodies. Blood. Crowd. Sirens.
Wait.
Hour. Sit. Pain. Cigarette. Thermos. Coffee.
Sweat. Nausea.
Streetlights. Eyes. Stretchers. Sheets.
Flesh.
Death.
Shaking. Chills.
Clock. Wait.
More. Wait.
Car. Stink. Cigarette.
Ambulance. Crying. Tow truck. Bodies. Taken.
Crowd. Police. Photographers. Drunks. Leave.
Gone.
Street. Quiet.

Rain. Dark. Humid.
Alone.
Door. Out. Stand. Walk. Pain. Stare. Closer.
Buildings. Silent. Street. Dead.
Blood. Chalk. Outlines. Closer.
Step. Inside. Outlines. Middle.
Inhale. Eyes. Closed.
Think. Inhale. Concentrate. Feel. Breathe.
Flow.
Death. Collision. Woman. Screaming. Windshield. Expression.
Moment. Death.
Energy. Concentrate. Images. Exploding.
Moment.
Woman. Car. Truck. Explosion.
Impact. Moment.
Rush.
Feeling. Feeding.
Metal. Burning. Screams. Blood. Death.
Moment. Collision. Images. Faster.
Strength. Medicine.
Stronger.
Concentrate. Better.
Images. Collision. Stronger. Seeing. Death.
Moment. Healing. Moment.
Addiction.
Drug. Rush. Body. Warmer.
Death. Concentrating. Healing. Addiction. Drug.
Warm. Calm.
Death. Medicine.
Death.
Life.
Medicine.
Addiction. Strong.
Leave.
Car. Engine. Drive. Rain. Streets. Freeway. Map.
Drive. Relax. Safe. Warm. Rush. Good.
Radio. Cigarette. Breeze.
Night.
Searching. Accidents. Death.
Life.

Dash. Clock. Waiting.
Soon.

RICHARD CHRISTIAN MATHESON has published scores of short stories in only a few years, while laboring over hundreds of scripts for shows such as "Simon & Simon," "Amazing Stories," "Three's Company," "MacGyver," "Magnum," and countless others. He has also worked as head writer for fifteen television series, including "Quincy," "The A-Team," "Hardcastle and McCormick," and "Hunter," and served as writer-producer on "Stingray" and "Stir Crazy." His latest work includes a movie for Steven Spielberg, several others for United Artists, a collection of twenty-five short stories titled *Scars and Other Distinguishing Marks*, and a forthcoming novel described as "a thriller set against a show business background."

CHELSEA QUINN YARBRO

Lapses

Just beyond the Marysville off-ramp, the big Chevy pickup suddenly braked and something came hurtling out of the back of the truck to crash and splatter into Ruth Donahue's windshield.

As she fought for control of her Volvo station wagon, she watched her hands in horror as red seeped through the splintered glass; the steering wheel was sticky with it. Ruth pulled onto the shoulder as much by feel as anything, since her vision was completely blocked by the . . . *thing* on the hood of the car. She was going little more than fifteen miles per hour then, but it felt to her as if she were racing along at seventy.

There was a whine of tires and her car rocked as it was struck a glancing blow. Ruth screamed as much from irritation as from fright. It was with difficulty that she forced herself to stay in the car once she had pulled on the brake. "I want out of here," she said in a soft, tense voice as she stared at the blood on her hands and arms and skirt.

The thing on the hood, she realized with revulsion, was a dog. She remembered seeing it in the back of the pickup. It was— had been—good-sized, faintly spotted, with floppy ears, and Ruth had wondered why the driver had neglected to put the tailgate up with an animal loose in the back. When the Chevy had slowed so suddenly, the dog had been thrown out of the truck bed and—

She lowered her head and vomited.

A sharp rap on the window caught her attention, and she looked up, embarrassed to be seen. A Highway Patrol officer (where had he come from?) indicated that she should roll down the window, and reluctantly she did.

"You all right, ma'am?" the officer asked her, concern on his face.

"I don't know. I . . ." Her words faltered and she began to cry, not soft, gentle tears, but deep sobs that left her trembling and aching.

"Hey, Gary, the lady's in shock," the officer called to another, unseen person.

"She hurt?" called the other.

"Scratches and bruises, and she's a mess, but I don't think she's hurt bad. They might want to check her over at the hospital, just in case."

Ruth tried to get the man to stop talking. She waved a hand at him and saw him wince at the sight. She forgot her gruesome hands until that moment, and now she hid them self-consciously.

"Shit, the sucker really landed hard, didn't he?" The officer opened the door and peered inside.

"I'm all . . . all right, Officer, or I will be, in a moment." She was finding the air and sunlight heady as wine. "Really."

"If you're certain," he said, with doubt. "But you better let me drive you to the hospital."

What is he seeing? she asked herself, dreading to inquire for herself. "You don't have to," she began, but he interrupted her.

"Look, lady, it's gonna take a while to get the animal off your car, and your windshield is broken. You can't drive anywhere in any case. And frankly, you look pretty rocky." He braced his hands on his hips, determined.

Ruth cleared her throat. "Okay."

"Is there anyone who can pick you up?" the officer went on.

"I . . . I'm from San Luis Obispo. I'm up here for the day." Who did she know back at home who would drop everything and drive for over five hours to get her?

"Well, look, we'll take you to the emergency room in Yuba City. You can call from there." He started to move away from her, as if her shock were contagious.

She could already imagine Randy Jeffers yelling at his secretary when he learned what had happened. Randy's main response to anything he could not control was to yell about it. He would be outraged at Ruth for her accident, the more so because she was in the Sacramento Valley on business for his company.

"You want to get out of the car, lady?" the officer asked.

"Oh. Yes." She opened the door, the movement making her dizzy. "And my name is Ms. Donahue. Ruth Donahue."

"Yeah," said the officer. Then, grudgingly: "I'm Officer Fairchild. Hal Fairchild."

Ruth could think of nothing to say. None of the admonitions she had received as a child covered meetings with law officers after accidents. I'm thirty-six years old, she thought, and I don't know what to say to a cop.

"You want to get in the car, Ms. Donahue?" Officer Fairchild offered. "Hey, Gary, how's the guy in the pickup?"

"I don't think the ambulance is gonna get here in time." The answer was flat, so without inflection that he sounded more like a machine than a man.

"Hey, Gary, get away from there." It was a friendly suggestion. Fairchild made it while holding the front door of his black-and-white open for Ruth.

"Somebody's gotta stay with him. Damn-fool bastard!"

"Don't let Gary bother you," Fairchild said quietly to Ruth. "It's his fifth bad accident in four days and it's getting to him." He closed the door and walked away.

"And I guess the SPCA'll have something to say about the way the dog was loose in the back of the truck."

"I beg your pardon," Ruth said, startled at finding Officer Fairchild beside her again and the car in motion. When had that happened? "My mind was . . . wandering."

"That's okay," said Fairchild. "Shock'll do that to you."

"How much longer until we reach the hospital?" She noticed that the farmlands had given way to smaller holdings and the first hint of urban sprawl.

"Ten minutes at the most. You be able to hold out until then?" He glanced at her swiftly. "Your color's a little off."

"I'm . . . doing fine." She was alarmed by her wandering thoughts, but she could not tell him so.

"Well, you hold on, Ms. Donahue. We'll make sure the doctors give you a good going-over before they let you out."

"Great." Her eyes felt solid and stiff in her head, like marbles, and she did not want to move them unless she had to. "The man in the pickup?"

"I don't know. Dispatcher says he was alive when the ambulance got there, but I don't know if he'll make it. He was pretty much of a mess."

"What happened?" Ruth asked. "Why did he stop that way?"

"Hard to tell. There was nothing on the road. We haven't had time to check the truck out. Maybe a bird came at his window. That happens around here. Ever have that problem down in San Luis Obispo?"

"I guess." She watched a school bus lumber out of a wide driveway, loaded down with young children. She followed it, thankful that there had only been a pickup in front of her and not one of those buses filled with kids.

"Just a couple more minutes," said Officer Fairchild.

"Good."

The doctor was middle-aged and harried; he ran his hand through his rumpled hair and made some hasty notes. "Well, Ms. Donahue, I don't know what to tell you. You're suffering from mild shock and that's not surprising. You could do with some sleep since there's no sign of a concussion. I'd recommend you get a checkup from your regular doctor."

"I don't have one," Ruth murmured. She had been in the hospital now for more than three hours and was disoriented.

"Then call a clinic or something," he said with asperity. "You've had a rough time of it, and it isn't good to neglect any symptoms."

"All right," she said, staring at the clock. She still had not called Randy; as far as the office knew, she was off checking on the County Planning Commission and the Zoning Commission regarding the possibilities for developing the old Standish Ranch. When he learned that she had lost more than half a day, things would not be pleasant.

"There's a motel near here. They're not too unreasonable. They can help you rent a car. But I don't think you should plan on driving for at least twenty-four hours." He cleared his throat.

"I'll have to be on the road tomorrow morning," she said.

"I'd advise against it," the doctor said, with a weary sigh. "Look, isn't there someone we can call for you? You're not married, I noticed, but there must be—"

"No one," she said, cutting him off. "I'll call my boss from the motel."

"If that's the way you want it," the doctor said. "I'm going to give you a prescription for something to help you rest and relax. Don't mix it with alcohol or dairy products. And wait at least an hour after a meal to take one."

"I'm not hungry," Ruth said softly.

"You will be," the doctor told her. "I'll call the pharmacy for your prescription. You can pick it up in about forty minutes."

"Thank you." Her mind was drifting and she found herself not wanting to resist.

"If you get any sudden headaches or other unusual symptoms, call me." He handed her a card. "My beeper number is the second one, and the answering service is the third. If it's late at night, insist that they wake me. I'll leave your name with them, just in case."

Ruth could not imagine calling this man, now or ever, but she took the card and put it into her purse. "I'll call if anything happens." What a ludicrous thing to say, she thought. Something had already happened—that's what all of this was about.

"The pharmacy is opposite the emergency admissions office." He gave her a last quick look, and then he was on his anxious way toward another examining room.

Very slowly Ruth got back into her clothes and gathered up her things. Her hands felt as if she were wearing mittens and nothing she donned seemed to belong to her. Her eyes ached, her jaw was sore from clenching her teeth, and there was a stiffness in her movements, the legacy of strain.

At the pharmacy window they asked her to wait. She found a badly shaped plastic chair, picked up a battered magazine, and thumbed through it.

The child at her elbow was screaming, his jacket sleeve soaked in blood. The two paramedics were trying to cut the material away, but the boy avoided them, kicking and yelling.

"He's in shock," one of the paramedics panted.

"Some shock," the other scoffed. "The little bastard just bit me."

How long had they been there? Ruth wondered.

The boy gave a yowl of pain and outrage as the paramedics

finally lifted him from the floor. His foot glanced off Ruth's cheek and his flailing left hand caught strands of her hair.

"Sorry, lady," said one of the paramedics as he forced the boy to open his fist.

"It's nothing," said Ruth. Her thoughts were still disordered. She could not remember the boy coming in. Certainly he must have been crying and making a fuss, and yet she could not bring this into any focus in her mind.

A thin, agitated woman with a tear-streaked face rushed out of the emergency admissions office, her eyes filled with dismay as she reached for the child. "Jerry . . ."

The boy shrieked, renewed his struggles, and succeeded in hitting one of the paramedics on the nose.

"Hey, fella," said the paramedic, doing his best to ignore the blood that had started to leak down his face.

"Let us handle this, ma'am," said the other paramedic to the woman. "We've got to get his jacket off him. We can't do much with his arm until we do."

"He wasn't this way in the car," the woman protested. "Jerry, let them help you."

Ruth moved two chairs away from the commotion, wishing she had not seen it. She was still distraught by what had happened on the highway, and to see the boy with a bloody sleeve was too much like the dog on her windshield.

"Ma'am, please tell this kid of yours we only want to help him," said the older paramedic.

"Jerry, let them—" his mother began, but her boy lashed out again with his good arm.

I must get away from here, Ruth said to herself. I must. She moved over two more chairs, but it was still not enough. Her breath came raggedly and she rose, prepared to leave through the first open door.

"Ms. Donahue," called the clerk at the pharmacist's window, repeating herself twice before Ruth was able to respond.

"Thank you," Ruth whispered as she scrabbled in her purse for her wallet and her MasterCard.

"Don't let the commotion bother you," the clerk advised. "Kids get that way when they're hurt sometimes. It's not as bad as it looks."

"How much do I owe you?"

Behind her, the paramedics succeeded in bringing Jerry under control; his screams turned to miserable sobs. Ruth could not force herself to look around.

"It comes to twenty-nine eighty-six." The clerk took the plastic card and ran it through the imprinter. "Did Doctor Forbes warn you about alcohol and dairy products?"

"Yes," Ruth said. She watched her hands tremble.

"Good. Sometimes they forget. Remember that you're likely to sleep for a long time—twelve hours isn't unusual. If you can arrange not to be disturbed, so much the better." She handed back the card and offered the receipt for Ruth's signature.

As she scrawled lines that looked nothing like her name, Ruth asked for a good motel nearby, repeating the name twice when the clerk offered her suggestion. "Can I call them from here?"

"Pay phone in the lobby," said the clerk with a hitch of her shoulders. "I'd let you use the phone here, but those are the rules."

It took almost an hour to get a taxi, for there were few of them operating in the city. After the brief drive, Ruth searched out the gifts-and-sundries shop to purchase a toothbrush and deodorant before she went to her room. The last thing she did was call San Luis Obispo to tell Randy Jeffers what had happened.

"Tough," her boss said after an initial show of concern. "Better rent a car tomorrow and head back. I'll tell Stan to take over for you. Hey, and drive carefully, won't you?"

At another time Ruth might have felt touched by this, but now it struck her badly, and she bristled. "If you didn't think I could handle this, why did you . . . ?"

"Hey, kid, easy," Randy interrupted. "I didn't mean anything like that. Jeez, you better get some rest. You sound worn out."

"I am worn out," she admitted, feeling tears start at the back of her eyes. "It wasn't very nice."

"Shit, no," Randy said with more feeling.

"I'll call you tomorrow before I leave. Tell Stan I've already got the material from Sacramento"—she realized her papers were still in her car; she would have to phone the police and find out where it had been taken—"and the man to see at County Planning is a Mister Garrick."

"Good work." Randy was clearly trying to help her feel better. "I'll tell him. He might be able to catch a shuttle out of Fresno. It could save us a little time."

Ruth wanted to ask him why he had made her drive when he was willing to pay for a shuttle airline for Stan, but the words caught in her throat and all she could do was sigh, hoping that she could hold off her tears until she was off the phone.

"Well, we'll see you soon, okay? If you can rent a compact, do it. I want to keep the costs down if I can. And, Ruth, take your time getting back. You've had quite a time of it, I can tell. So I won't expect you tomorrow or Friday. Take your time and get steady. We'll arrange for this to go on your sick pay."

His tone was indulgent, but Ruth did her best to accept the offer gracefully. "Thanks a lot," she said, knowing what was expected of her. By the time she put the receiver down, she could feel wetness on her face.

She called the Highway Patrol and requested that her brief-case be brought to the motel. It was in the trunk of her car, and she said she would need it in the morning. The woman who spoke with her assured her it would be done.

Last, Ruth called the front desk and asked that she not be disturbed. Then she took one of the capsules Doctor Forbes had prescribed, and in her pea-green motel room gave herself over to oblivion.

The Ford Escort was the cheapest car available from the local rent-a-car, and as she started to drive it, she realized that it did not have the performance she was used to from her Volvo. Driving made her nervous, and she kept to the slow lane as she made her way south toward Sacramento. Her hands were sweating although the day was cool, and from time to time she had to wipe them on her skirt.

Interstate 5 was mesmerizing, stretching out across the San Joaquin Valley. Ruth had driven it before, but this time there seemed to be many extra miles added to the road. She kept her speed at fifty-five and ignored the huge trucks barreling along at higher speeds. She promised herself that she would not stop for lunch until she reached Coalinga. Then she would take the time to have a good solid meal and collect herself for the last leg of the journey across the hills to 101.

Two Highway Patrol cars shot by and Ruth flinched at the

sight, hating to look at the road ahead in case there was another accident. She tried singing to herself—the Escort had no radio —but her voice sounded thin and cracked, so she fell silent again.

She could not recall the last thirty miles before Coalinga. The off-ramp came as a surprise and she nearly overshot it, blinking at the overpass as if it were a mirage. She decided that she had been driving too long, and gratefully pulled into the parking lot of Harris Ranch, resolving to dawdle over her food, giving herself enough time to calm down. She had heard of highway hypnosis, but until now had not experienced it, and it frightened her.

It was less than ten minutes after she left the restaurant that Ruth saw the animal lying beside the highway, drawn up into a protective half-ball in a last futile attempt to keep its guts in its shattered body.

Ruth was assailed by nausea, the excellent meal she had so recently eaten threatening to spill out of her. She stared ahead blindly, her face ashen, her breath fast and shallow. What was the animal? A cat? A raccoon? She had not seen it long enough to glimpse more than the destruction and dark striped fur. The headache, which had retreated to a painful itch behind her eyes, now gripped her skull in its vise.

It was all she could do to hold her car on the road. Dust was blowing from the west, reducing visibility with the tenacity of fog. The highway surface was made slippery by the sand, and she could not be certain how far she had come.

When had the wind come up? Ruth could not recall. It had to be her headache or the memory of the dead animal that had distracted her, but for how long? What had happened in the last —how many?—miles? She was not at all sure where she was. Had she taken the off-ramp to San Luis Obispo? Was she still on Interstate 5? *Where was she?* The question echoed in her mind in a shriek. She looked at the clock on the dashboard and saw that it was after three. She should be almost home by now, but instead she was caught here in the blowing dust.

She saw dimly another sign, an off-ramp beyond that, and after a moment of hesitation she took it, hoping that it would bring her quickly to a town where she could make a few phone calls and find out how far she had strayed.

Immediately adjacent to the off-ramp there was a service station, but as she drove up Ruth saw that it was closed. She pulled into the dust-covered parking area, her tires slithering for purchase on the asphalt. She opened the door of the Escort and felt the bite of the storm. There was a telephone booth not more than thirty feet away. She walked toward it, her purse held to shelter her face.

The telephone was not connected, and where there had been phone books the securing chains hung empty.

With a cry of vexation, Ruth flung herself out of the phone booth and struggled back to her car. She was moving against the wind now, and there was little protection. Dust made her blink, and when she sneezed her whole face hurt.

Back in the car, she lowered her head against the arch of the steering wheel and sobbed. Within a few minutes she was on the verge of hysteria. Everything she had endured for the last two days caught up with her at last. She was ashamed at her lack of control but powerless to remedy it. Sometime in the last forty-eight hours something crucial had deserted her and left her rudderless. The minutes and hours she could not remember, the panic that welled in her at this admission. Her body was shaking as with palsy. She looked, appalled, at her hands, which no longer seemed to be part of her.

Where am I now? Where?

As her high sobs dwindled, she tried to make a sensible decision, but was capable of little more than restarting the car. *I have to get back to the freeway,* she told herself, her thoughts moving as delicately as an invalid with a walker. *I have to find the exit for San Luis Obispo.*

Once in motion, she managed to feel her way through the blowing dust to the overpass and the on-ramp leading north. She was certain that, wherever she was, she had come too far south. But now she was determined to find her way back.

Driving was even more difficult than when she had been southbound, but she kept her hands locked on the steering wheel and her attention on the road ahead. She blinked often, as if that might clear the obscured windshield.

The street was almost empty and most of the storefronts were boarded up. Litter blew in the gutters and trash stood uncollected in overflowing bags at curbside. The stop sign canted at two o'clock, token of a mishap long past.

Ruth braked, staring around her.

It was night, late night by the look of it, and the few operating streetlights revealed that most of the block was deserted. Her dashboard clock said one twenty-seven; she stared at it for some little time, listening to her engine idle, refusing to believe what she saw. On the passenger seat there was a gasoline receipt from a Union station in Buttonwillow. She refused to touch it, fearing that it might be real. A quick look at the gas gauge showed that the tank was almost empty. Presumably she had driven more than two hundred miles since she left Buttonwillow, if the tank had been full then.

As she peered down the side street, she saw three motorcycles drawn up near a small metal-roofed building. The machines were large. Ruth did not recognize the symbols emblazoned on them, but their very strangeness added to her apprehension.

"I'd welcome a Hell's Angel," she said aloud, giggling in a way that made the fine hairs on her neck rise. "God. Oh, God."

A page of newspaper, open as a scudding sail, flew down the street, twisting and moving until it wrapped itself around a lamppost. Something metal clanged, perhaps a garbage can, perhaps a door. Its echo rattled off the buildings.

On a billboard angled precariously over the intersection ahead, Ruth saw enormous letters advertising Spring cigarettes. The whole thing was faded and there were slogans and symbols spray-painted over the face of it, but it was still possible to make out two faint figures walking in a meadow, long since turned from green to gray-brown. Ruth stared at the billboard for some time as if she hoped to learn something from it.

"I've got to find a phone. Ruthie, you've got to call someone." She said it sternly but in a girlish voice, the way she used to talk herself into doing her homework, a quarter of a century ago.

She put her car into gear once more and drove down the wider street. She looked for a lighted storefront or a business open at this time of night—a 7-Eleven or a gas station or a motel—and was dismayed when after several blocks she found nothing like that. True, the decaying brick buildings were behind her and now there were houses, vintage 1925, with faded paint and weed-grown front yards. Occasionally there were cars parked on the street, but nothing was moving. The houses were dark. She saw no one.

She did her best to ignore the wail of panic that was forming between her mind and her throat.

When, fifteen minutes later, she reached the outlying small farms beyond the empty city, she noticed a church with a light on over a discreet and old-fashioned billboard.

Lodi Methodist Church
"Learning to See through Others' Eyes"
11–12 Sunday Morning
Wednesday 8 p.m.
Discussion and Prayer

Lodi? The name came off the sign and hung in the air before her. Lodi was east of Interstate 5, and certainly north of Buttonwillow. Had she been driving in the wrong direction for most of the night? And why had it taken her so long to reach this place? Where had she been before that?

Reluctantly she pulled into the gravel-paved parking lot and stopped. She sat for some time, not thinking, not permitting herself to speculate. She decided that she needed to rest, to calm down. Obviously she was still in shock of some sort and the stress was causing her to do irrational things.

What things? demanded a treacherous voice within her. *What have you done that you can't remember?*

"I won't think about that now," Ruth said aloud in her most sensible tone, the one she usually reserved for business meetings. "The most important thing is to get back to San Luis Obispo and find a doctor. Just in case." She could not bring herself to wonder in case *what.*

Then, as she sought to avoid such probing, she drifted into unrestful sleep.

"Are you all right?" The knocking on her window was louder and the voice was raised almost to a shout.

Dazed, Ruth opened her eyes and tried to recall where she was. Scraps came back to her, each serving to make her more distressed. Carefully she rolled down the window. "I'm sorry," she began, not sure what she was sorry for.

The man standing by her rented Escort was over fifty and appeared to be both benign and ineffective. "Is there something wrong?"

Ruth cleared her throat. "I was driving late last night. I . . . got lost."

The man nodded. "That's the usual reason strangers show up on this road. Most travelers stick to the freeway and bypass us entirely." He stepped back and made a kindly gesture with his knobby hands. "Would you like a cup of coffee? We don't have much in the way of breakfast, but I can probably scare up a stale doughnut, if you want one." He smiled. "I'm George Howell. I'm the minister to this flock." This was said with a self-depre-cating smile that was clearly designed to put her at ease.

"I'm Ruth Donahue," she told him automatically. "I'm from San Luis Obispo and I was trying to find the way home . . . yesterday." She opened the door and stepped out.

"These side roads do get confusing," he agreed as he led the way to the side door of the church. "I was here for more than two years before I really learned my way around." He slipped a key into the lock, saying as the door swung inward, "There was a time we never closed the church, but these days, what with vandals and all, well . . ."

"Is it very bad?" asked Ruth, trying to make conversation with this mild-faced man while she worked up some explanation that he might accept.

"There have been problems. The cops try to hold the worst of them down, but they can't do everything. And you know how difficult it can be to establish some kind of order in a district like this. We're on the edge of things."

To her horror, Ruth laughed.

If the minister took offense, he made no sign of it. "I've heard that there have been problems in other places, too. I guess you've had your share in San Luis Obispo." He had led her to a pantry adjoining the kitchen, a large, featureless room designed to handle the occasional church dinner or wedding reception. A huge black stove squatted on the other side of the half-open door, six burners and a grill showing on its top.

"Sometimes," Ruth said. She found that the sight of the

kitchen was making her hungry. God, how many meals have I missed? she wondered, her thoughts slipping away from the question.

"The doughnuts are in here somewhere," George Howell said to her as he opened the old-fashioned cooler. "My secretary is always bringing me things to eat, and I can't convince her that it isn't necessary." He found the bag and pulled it out. "Not much left, but you take all of them if you like. She'll bring me something else at ten-thirty." He gestured toward the low table under the window. "Sit down and I'll make some coffee."

"Thank you," said Ruth, beginning to hope that her life was at last returning to normal.

The minister bustled happily about, clearly delighted to be of help to someone. He chatted about the weather—how strange for this time of year—and cuts in the county budget ("They expect us to provide charity, but how can we? Who has the money to spare?") and the progress his two children were making with their music lessons. It was all so wonderfully ordinary, so very predictable and sane, that Ruth felt herself smiling at her own boredom. What could be more normal? She was reassured.

"Do you take milk in your coffee?"

"No, thank you. Just black." As she accepted the mug, Ruth asked herself if she might find the caffeine too much on so little sleep and food, but she was so eager to make herself alert that she overruled her own caution.

"I always like a little milk in mine. I guess it reminds me of being a kid, having a cup of chocolate after school." He sat down opposite her.

Ruth smiled, recalling her mother and the many stern warnings about indulging in such treats. Her mother had had a dread of fat children, especially her own, and had instilled in Ruth a level of austerity that resulted in the lean angularity she now possessed. "This tastes very good," she said, though the scalding liquid nearly burned her mouth.

"I'm glad you like it. My secretary brings the coffee, too." He sipped at his cup.

"You're lucky, I guess," said Ruth, relaxing even more into the commonplace.

"Yes, I thank God for her often." He beamed, to show that

he had not intended for her to take his reference to God as introductory to any spur-of-the-moment sermon.

Ruth gazed at the blood on her skirt and blinked twice, as if she expected it to go away. The coppery smell was very strong in the room along with other, less pleasant odors. Blood festooned the pantry walls and swagged along the floor toward the sanctuary.

The coffee in her mug was cold.

"What?" Ruth whispered, shaking her head slowly at the carnage she sensed lay beyond the sanctuary doors. Her wrists ached, and she saw with amazement the distinct, raw impression of ropes pressed into her skin.

Obscenities were scrawled in spray paint on the walls of the kitchen and pantry, and from the grill of the stove, George Howell's head, gory and canted on one side, stared out at the wreckage of his church.

In her fright she fled westward, first to Stockton, and then along the narrow levee roads of Highway 4. She would pick up 580 or 680, whichever it was that would lead her back to Highway 101. All she would have to do then was to drive south.

At Oakley, she stopped and endured the sniggers of the high school boys pumping gas when she claimed that her period had started without warning and she had to wash her skirt. She had already got (another?) tank of gas in Stockton and hoped it would be enough to get her home. She considered calling her office again, but could not bring herself to attempt to explain what had happened. She was afraid that no matter what she said, it would mean her job.

Not that she would blame Randy if he did fire her after what had happened. She asked herself if it might be best for everyone if she simply resigned, but that in itself seemed too trivial a response. She was missing bits and pieces of her life and had no means of finding out what those losses were. Not that she wished to, for the aftermath was so dreadful that she was certain the events themselves must be hideous beyond her imaginings.

At Pittsburg, she pulled off the road, feeling light-headed from tension and hunger. She found a burger place with a drive-through window, and was horrified to discover that she had barely enough cash to pay for a frugal meal. She could not remember what had happened to her money, or even how much she had had. She noticed that she had a Visa card in her wallet, but thought that there should be a MasterCard as well. When had she lost it, if she had had one to begin with?

The food was tasteless to her, and she thought for a while that she would not be able to keep it down, but slowly she felt herself grow more calm, more *present*, less caught in the nightmare.

"It was only a nightmare, wasn't it?" she asked the air. "I got carried away after that trouble near Marysville and I fell asleep in the car, and that disoriented me. The rest was a nightmare. That's all."

Somewhere in the treacherous alleys of her mind, the image of the blood on her skirt remained, but she refused to look at it, confident that if there was any explanation needed, it was that the blood had come from the unfortunate dog that had fallen onto her windshield and died there, impaled on shattered glass. There was no minister in Lodi, she had never been in Lodi, and the rest was only the distortion of her memories of that terrible incident. She kept repeating this to herself as she drove toward Concord and the turnoff leading south, away from those dreadful visions.

She was southbound in little more than half an hour, and that refreshed her. The simple satisfaction of going in the right direction, of being in control, once again gave her a burst of confidence. It was a pleasure that truly delighted her. It would not be long before the entire ghastly episode was safely behind her. She would never have to endure such a thing again. She felt that her ordeal was finally over.

By three-thirty, she had reached Paso Robles, and was so near home that she was willing to get off 101 long enough to have a proper meal on her Visa card. She wanted to be refreshed when she walked back into her apartment. There were so many things to attend to once she was home—the return of her rental car, the arrangement to get her own once again, the whole business of filing necessary reports with the insurance company, they all piled up oppressively in her mind—that she decided a brief respite over an early supper or late lunch would give her the steadying influence she so truly sought.

She found a nice restaurant set back from the road, a building in a subdued Spanish style with tall willows growing around it. There were not many cars in the lot, but a discreet sign on the door assured her that the place was open.

Service was prompt and pleasant, the waitress taking her order with a smile. When she returned with the salad Ruth had ordered, she also brought a glass of wine.

"I didn't ask for this," Ruth said guardedly, afraid that she might have forgotten the request, or missed the order.

"No; it's on the house," said the waitress and set it down with the salad.

"I very much appreciate it, but since I still have a way to drive, I'd really rather have a cup of coffee, if you don't mind." Ruth said this politely, hoping her good manners would mask the fear that nearly choked her.

The waitress shrugged and took up the glass once more. "Suit yourself. Your broiled chicken will be ready in about ten minutes." She turned away and went back toward the bar.

Ruth ate the salad and, when the waitress brought the coffee, made a point of thanking her for it.

The man in bed beside her rolled over and touched her arm. Ruth almost screamed.

"Hey, did I wake you, Enid?"

"Enid?" Ruth repeated in disbelief.

"I ought be leave for work pretty soon. Want me to skip breakfast with you?" He smiled at her in easy familiarity, this stranger whom Ruth had never seen before.

"I—"

"You feeling okay, honey? You look a little strange." His concern was genuine, which made it worse than if he were as alien to her as she felt to him.

Ruth shook her head slowly, not daring to move too quickly, as if that might upset the precarious balance of this place. Did she dare ask the man who he was? Or how she came to be here with him? She gathered the blankets around her, making them tight and heavy, enclosing herself.

The man braced himself on his elbow and put his free hand on her shoulder. "Enid?"

Ruth turned away, knowing that she was about to cry. She was shaking, as weak as with a sudden fever. Did she have courage enough to look in the mirror? And what would she find there if she did? What place was this? Why did he call her Enid? Why had she lost herself—or was she lost at all?

"Honey?"

She flinched as he touched her.

"What's the matter?" He sounded genuinely concerned, but then the blood had been genuine, and the dog crashing into the windshield and the empty, disorienting freeway.

"I don't know—"

He tried to turn her toward him, but she pulled resolutely away, deep in her misery and her doubts. "You're like a stranger again."

Why did he say *again?*

"Enid?"

At last she met his eyes, finding them completely unfamiliar, their warmth and worry all the more terrible to her because he was so completely unknown to her.

The car was hurtling toward the embankment and she screamed.

CHELSEA QUINN YARBRO is the author of a series of books about the Count de Saint-Germain *(Hotel Transylvania, The Palace, Blood Games, Path of the Eclipse, Tempting Fate* and *The Saint-Germain Chronicles)* as well as dozens of other books and many short stories. Recent publications include *More Messages from Michael, To the High Redoubt, A Baroque Fable* and the collection *Signs & Portents.* She is currently at work on the first in a trilogy of novels about Olivia, a character from the Count de Saint-Germain series.

WILLIAM F. NOLAN

The Final Stone

They were from Indianapolis. Newly married. Dave and *stirring, flexing muscle, feeling power now . . . anger . . . a sudden driving thirst for* Alice Williamson, both in their late twenties, both excited about their trip to the West Coast. This would be their last night in Arizona. Tomorrow they planned to be in Palm Springs. To visit Dave's sister. But only one of them would make it to California. Dave, not Alice. *with the scalpel glittering*

Alice would die before midnight, her throat slashed cleanly across. *glittering, raised against the moon*

"Wait till you see what's here," Dave told her. "Gonna just be fantastic."

They were pulling their used Camaro into the parking lot at a tourist site in Lake Havasu City, Arizona. He wouldn't tell her where they were. It was late. The lot was wide and dark, with only two other cars parked there, one a service vehicle.

"What *is* this place?" Alice was tired and hungry. *hungry*

"You'll find out. Once you see it, you'll never forget it. That's what they say."

"I just want to eat," she said. *the blade eating flesh, drinking*

"First we'll have a look at it, then we'll eat," said Dave, *them getting out of the car, walking toward the gate* smiling at her, giving her a hug.

The tall iron gate, black pebbled iron, led into a picture-perfect Tudor Village. A bit of Olde England rising up from raw Arizona desert. A winged dragon looked down at them from the top of the gate.

"That's ugly," said Alice.

"It's historic," Dave told her. "That's the official Heraldic Dragon from the City of London."

"Is *that* what all this is—some sort of replica of London?"

"Much more than that. Heck, Ally, this was all built *around* it, to give it the proper atmosphere."

"I'm in no mood for atmosphere," she said. "We've been driving all day and I don't feel like playing games. I want to know what you—"

Dave cut into the flow of her words: "There it is!"

They both stared at it. Ten thousand tons of fitted stone. Over nine hundred feet of arched granite spanning the dark waters of the Colorado River. Tall and massive and magnificent.

"Christ!" murmured Dave. "Doesn't it just knock you out? Imagine—all the way from England, from the Thames River . . . the by-God-for-real London Bridge!"

"It *is* amazing," Alice admitted. She smiled, kissed him on the cheek. "And I'm glad you didn't tell me . . . that you kept it for a surprise."

glittering cold steel

They moved along the concrete walkway beneath the Bridge, staring upward at the giant gray-black structure. Dave said: "When the British tore it down they numbered all the stones so our people would know where each one went. Thousands of stones. Like a jigsaw puzzle. Took three years to build it all over again here in Arizona." He gestured around them. "All this was just open desert when they started. After the Bridge was finished they diverted a section of the Colorado River to run under it. And built the Village."

"Why did the British give us their bridge?"

"They were putting up a better one," said Dave. "But, hey, they didn't *give* this one to us. The guy that had it built here paid nearly two and a half million for it. Plus the cost of shipping all the stones over. Some rich guy named McCulloch. Died since then, I think."

dead death dead dead death

"Well, we've seen it," said Alice. "Let's eat now. C'mon, I'm really starving."

"You don't want to *walk* on it?"

"Maybe after we eat," said Alice. *going inside the restaurant*

*now . . . will wait . . . she's perfect . . . white throat, blue
vein pulsing under the chin . . . long graceful neck . . .*

They ate at the City of London Arms in the Village. Late.
Last couple in for dinner that evening. Last meal served.

"You folks should have come earlier," the waitress told them.
"Lots of excitement here today, putting in the final stone. I
mean, with the Bridge dedication and all."

"I thought it was dedicated in 1971," said Dave.

"Oh, it was. But there was this *one* stone missing. Everyone
figured it had been lost on the trip over. But they found it last
month in London. Had fallen into the water when they were
taking the Bridge apart. Today, it got fitted back where it belonged." She smiled brightly. "So London Bridge is *really* complete now!"

Alice set her empty wineglass on the tablecloth. "All this
Bridge talk is beginning to *bore* me," she said. "I need another
drink."

"You've had enough," said Dave.

"Hell I have!" To the waitress: "Bring us another bottle of
wine."

"Sorry, but we're closing. I'm not allowed to—"

"I *said* bring another!"

"And she said they're closing," snapped Dave. "Let's go."

They paid the check, left. The doors were locked behind
them.

The City of London Arms sign blinked off as they moved
down the restaurant steps. *to me to me*

"You'll feel better when we get back to the motel," Dave said.

"I feel fine. Let's go walk on London Bridge. That's what you
wanted, isn't it?"

"Now now, Alley," he said. "We can do that tomorrow, before we leave. Drive over from the motel."

"*You* go to the damn motel," she said tightly. "*I'm* walking on
the damn Bridge!"

He stared at her. "You're *drunk!*"

She giggled. "So what? Can't drunk people walk on the damn
Bridge?"

"Come on," said Dave, taking her arm. "We're going to the
car."

"You go to the car," she snapped, pulling away. "I'm gonna walk on the damn Bridge."

"Fine," said Dave. "Then you can get a *taxi* to the motel."

And, dark-faced with anger, he walked away from her, back to their car. Got in. Drove off.

alone now for me . . . just for me

Alice Williamson walked toward London Bridge through the massed tree shadows along the dark river pathway. She reached the foot of the wide gray-granite Bridge steps, looked up.

At a tall figure in black. Slouch hat, dark cloak, boots.

She was looking at death.

She stumbled back, turned, poised to run—but the figure moved, glided, flowed *mine now mine* down the granite steps with horrific speed.

And the scalpel glitter-danced against the moon.

Two days later.

Evening, with the tour boat empty, heading for its home dock, Angie Shepherd at the wheel. Angie was the boat's owner. She lived beside the river, had all her life. Knew its currents, its moods, under moon and sun, knew it intimately. Thompson Bay . . . Copper Canyon . . . Cattail Cove . . . Red Rock . . . Black Meadow . . . Topock Gorge. Knew its eagles and hawks and mallards, its mud turtles and great horned owls. Knew the sound of its waters in calm and in storm.

Her home was a tall, weathered-wood building that once served as a general store. She lived alone here. Made a living with her boat, running scenic tours along the Colorado. Age twenty-eight. Never married, and no plans in that area.

Angie docked the boat, secured it, entered the tall wooden building she called Riverhouse. She fussed in the small kitchen, taking some wine, bread, and cheese out to the dock. It was late; the night was ripe with river sounds and the heart-pulse of crickets.

She sat at the dock's edge, legs dangling in the cool water. Nibbled cheese. Listened to a night bird crying over the river.

Something bumped her foot in the dark water. Something heavy, sodden. Drifting in the slow night current.

Something called Alice Williamson.

* * *

Dan Gregory had no clues to the murder. The husband was a logical suspect (most murders are family-connected), but Gregory knew that Dave Williamson was not guilty. You develop an instinct about people, and he knew Williamson was no wife-killer. For one thing, the man's grief was deep and genuine; he seemed totally shattered by the murder—blamed himself, bitterly, for deserting Alice in the Village.

Gregory was tipped back in his desk chair, an unlit Marlboro in his mouth. (He was trying to give up smoking.) Williamson slouched in the office chair in front of him, looking broken and defeated. "Your wife was drunk, you had an argument. You got pissed and drove off. Happens to people all the time. Don't blame yourself for this."

"But if I'd stayed there, been there when—"

"Then you'd probably *both* be dead," said Gregory. "You go back to the motel, take those pills the doc gave you and get some sleep. Then head for Palm Springs. We'll contact you at your sister's if we come up with anything."

Williamson left the office. Gregory talked to Angie Shepherd next, about finding the body. She was shaken, but cooperative.

"I've never seen anyone dead before," she told him.

"No family funerals?"

"Sure. A couple. But I'd never walk past the open caskets. I didn't want to have to see people I'd loved . . . *that* way." She shrugged. "In your business I guess you see a lot of death."

"Not actually," said Gregory. "Your average Highway Patrol officer sees more of it in a month than I have in ten years. You don't get many murders in a town this size."

"That how long you've been Chief of Police here, ten years?"

"Nope. Just over a year. Used to be a police lieutenant in Phoenix. Moved up to this job." He raised an eyebrow at her. "How come, you being a local, you don't know how long I've been Chief?"

"I never follow politics—*especially* small-town politics. Sorry about that." And she smiled.

Gregory was a square-faced man in his thirties with hard, iced-blue eyes, offset by a quick, warm way of grinning. Had never married; most women bored him. But he liked Angie. And the attraction was mutual.

Alice Williamson's death had launched a relationship.

In August, four months after the first murder, there were two more. Both women. Both with their throats cut. Both found along the banks of the Colorado. One at Pilot Rock, the other near Whipple Bay.

Dan Gregory had no reason to believe the two August "River Killings" (as the local paper had dubbed them) had been committed near London Bridge. He told a reporter that the killer might be a transient, passing through the area, killing at random. The murders lacked motive; the three victims had nothing in common beyond being female. Maybe the murderer, suggested Gregory, was just someone who hates women.

The press had a field day. "Madman on Loose" . . . "Woman-Hating Killer Haunts Area" . . . "Chief of Police Admits No Clues to River Killings."

Reading the stories, Gregory muttered softly: "Assholes!"

Early September. A classroom at Lake Havasu City High School. Senior English. Lyn Esterly was finishing a lecture on William Faulkner's *Light in August.*

". . . therefore, Joe Christmas became the victim of his own twisted personality. He truly believed he was cursed by an outlaw strain of blood, a white man branded black by a racially bigoted society. Your assignment is to write a five-hundred-word essay on his inner conflicts."

After she'd dismissed the class, Lyn phoned her best friend, Angie Shepherd, for lunch. They had met when Lyn had almost drowned swimming near Castle Rock. Angie had saved her life.

"You're not running the boat today, and I need to talk to you, okay?"

"Sure . . . okay," agreed Angie. "Meet you in town. Tom's all right?"

"Tom's it is."

Trader Tom's was a seafood restaurant, specializing in fresh shrimp, an improbable business establishment in the middle of the Arizona desert. Angie, "the primitive," adored fresh shrimp, which had been introduced to her by Lyn, the "city animal," their joke names for one another.

Over broiled shrimp and sole amandine they relaxed into a familiar discussion: "I'll never be able to understand how you can live out there all alone on the river," said Lyn. "It's positively *spooky*—especially with a woman-killer running loose. Aren't you afraid?"

"No. I keep a gun with me in the house, and I know how to use it."

"*I'd* be terrified."

"That's because you're a victim of your own imagination," said Angie, dipping a huge shrimp into Tom's special Cajun sauce. "You and your fascination with murder."

"Lots of people are true-crime buffs," said Lyn. "In fact, that's why I wanted to talk to you today. It's about the River Killings."

"You've got a theory about 'em, right?"

"This one's pretty wild."

"Aren't they all?" Angie smiled, unpeeling another shrimp. "I'm listening."

"The first murder, the Williamson woman, that one took place on the third of April."

"So?"

"The second murder was on the seventh of August, the third on the thirty-first. All three dates are a perfect match."

"For what?"

"For a series of killings, seven in all, committed in 1888 by Jack the Ripper. His first three were on exact matching dates."

Angie paused, a shrimp halfway to her mouth. "Wow! Okay . . . you *did* say wild."

"And there's more. Alice Williamson, we know, was attacked near London Bridge—which is where the Ripper finally disappeared in 1888. They had him trapped there, but the fog was really thick that night and when they closed in on him from both ends of the Bridge he just . . . vanished. And he was never seen or heard of again."

"Are you telling me that some nut is out there in the dark near London Bridge trying to duplicate the original Ripper murders? Is that your theory?"

"That's it."

"But why *now?* What triggered the pattern?"

"I'm working on that angle." Lyn's eyes were intense. "I'm telling you this today for a vitally important reason."

"I'm still listening."

"You've become very friendly with Chief Gregory. He'll listen to you. He must be told that the fourth murder will take place *tonight,* the eighth of September, before midnight."

"But I . . ."

"You've got to warn him to post extra men near the Bridge tonight. And he should be there himself."

"Because of your theory?"

"Of course! Because of my theory."

Angie slowly shook her head. "Dan would think I was around the bend. He's a realist. He'd laugh at me."

"Isn't it *worth* being laughed at to save a life?" Lyn's eyes burned at her. "Honest, Angie, if you don't convince Gregory that I'm making sense, that I'm onto a real pattern here, then another woman is going to get her throat slashed open near London Bridge tonight."

Angie pushed her plate away. "You sure do know how to spoil a terrific lunch."

That afternoon, back at Riverhouse, Angie tried to make sense of Lyn's theory. The fact that these murders had fallen on the same dates as three murders a century earlier was interesting and curious, but not enough to set a hard-minded man like Gregory in motion.

It was crazy, but still Lyn *might* be onto something.

At least she could phone Dan and suggest dinner in the Village. She could tell him what Lyn said—and then he *would* be there in the area, just in case something happened.

Dan said yes, they'd meet at the City of London Arms.

When Angie left for the Village that night she carried a pearl-handled .32-caliber automatic in her purse.

If. Just if.

Dan was late. On the phone he'd mentioned a meeting with the City Council, so maybe that was it. The Village was quiet, nearly empty of tourists.

Angie waited, seated on a park bench near the restaurant,

nervous in spite of herself, thinking that *alone, her back to the trees, thick shadow trees, vulnerable* maybe she should wait inside, at the bar.

A tall figure, moving toward her. Behind her.

A thick-fingered hand reaching out for her. She flinched back, eyes wide, fingers closing on the automatic inside her open purse.

"Didn't mean to scare you."

It was Dan. His grin made her relax. "I've . . . been a little nervous today."

"Over what?"

"Something Lyn Esterly told me." She took his arm. "I'll tell you all about it at dinner."

lost her . . . can't with him

And they went inside.

". . . so what do you think?" Angie asked. They were having an after-dinner drink. The booths around them were silent, unoccupied.

"I think your friend's imagination is working overtime."

Angie frowned. "I knew you'd say something like that."

Dan leaned forward, taking her hand. "You don't really believe there's going to be another murder in this area tonight just because *she* says so, do you?"

"No, I guess I don't really believe that."

And she guessed she didn't.

But . . .

There! Walking idly on the Bridge, looking down at the water, alone, young woman alone . . . her throat naked, skin naked and long-necked . . . open to me . . . blade sharp sharp . . . soft throat

A dark pulsing glide onto the Bridge, a swift reaching out, a small choked cry of shocked horror, a sudden drawn-across half-moon of bright crimson—and the body falling . . . falling into deep Colorado waters.

Although Dan Gregory was a skeptic, he was not a fool. He ordered the entire Village area closed to tourists and began a thorough search.

Which proved rewarding.

An object was found on the Bridge, wedged into an aperture between two stones below one of the main arches: a surgeon's scalpel with fresh blood on it. And with blackened stains on the handle and blade.

It was confirmed that the fresh blood matched that of the latest victim. The dark stains proved to be dried blood. But they did not match the blood types of the other three murder victims. It was old blood. Very old.

Lab tests revealed that the bloodstains had remained on the scalpel for approximately one hundred years.

Dating back to the 1880s.

"Are you Angela Shepherd?"

A quiet Sunday morning along the river. Angie was repairing a water-damaged section of dock, briskly hammering in fresh nails, and had not heard the woman walk up behind her. She put down the claw hammer, stood, pushing back her hair. "Yes, I'm Angie Shepherd. Who are you?"

"Lenore Harper. I'm a journalist."

"What paper?"

"Free lance. Could we talk?"

Angie gestured toward the house. Lenore was tall, trim-bodied, with penetrating green eyes.

"Want a Coke?" asked Angie. "Afraid it's all I've got. I wasn't expecting company."

"No, I'm fine," said Lenore, seating herself on the living-room couch and removing a small notepad from her purse.

"You're doing a story on the River Killings, right?"

Lenore nodded. "But I'm going after something different. That's why I came to you."

"Why me?"

"Well . . . you discovered the first body."

Angie sat down in a chair opposite the couch, ran a hand through her hair. "I didn't *discover* anything. When the body drifted downriver against the dock I happened to be there. That's all there is to it."

"Where you shocked . . . frightened?"

"Sickened is a better word. I don't enjoy seeing people with their throats cut."

"Of course. I understand, but . . ."

Angie stood up. "Look, there's really nothing more I can tell you. If you want facts on the case, talk to Chief Gregory at the police department."

"I'm more interested in ideas, emotions—in personal reactions to these killings. I'd like to know *your* ideas. *Your* theories."

"If you want to talk theory, go see Lyn Esterly. She's got some original ideas on the case. Lyn's a true-crime buff. She'll probably be anxious to help you."

"Sounds like a good lead. Where can I find her?"

"Lake Havasu High. She teaches English there."

"Great." Lenore put away her notepad, then shook Angie's hand. "You've been very kind. Appreciate your talking to me."

"No problem."

Angie looked deeply into Lenore Harper's green eyes. Something about her I like, she thought. Maybe I've made a new friend. Well . . . "Good luck with your story," she said.

Lenore's talk with Lyn Esterly bore colorful results. The following day's paper carried "an exclusive feature interview" by Lenore Harper:

"Is River Killer Another Jack the Ripper?" the headline asked. Then, below it, a subheading: "Havasu High Teacher Traces Century-Old Murder Pattern."

According to the story, if the killer continued to follow the original Ripper's pattern, he would strike again on the thirtieth of September. And not once, but twice. On the night of September 30, 1888, Jack the Ripper butchered *two* women in London's Whitechapel district—victims #5 and #6. Would these gruesome double murders be repeated here in Lake Havasu?

The story ended with a large question mark.

Angie, on the phone to Lyn: "Maybe I did the wrong thing, sending her to see you."

"Why? I like her. She really *listened* to me."

"I just get the feeling that her story makes you . . . well, a kind of target."

"I doubt that."

"The killer knows all about you now. Even your picture was

there in the paper. He knows that you're doing all this special research, that you worked out the whole copycat-Ripper idea . . ."

"So what? I can't catch him. That's up to the police. He's not going to bother with me. Getting my theory into print was important. Now that his sick little game has been exposed, maybe he'll quit. Might not be fun for him anymore. These weirdos are like that. Angie, it could all be over."

"So you're not sore at me for sending her to you?"

"Are you kidding? For once, someone has taken a theory of mine seriously enough to print it. Makes all this work mean something. Hell, I'm a celebrity now."

"That's what worries me."

And their conversation ended.

Angie had been correct in her hunch regarding Lenore Harper: the two women *did* become friends. As a free-lance journalist, Lenore had roved the world, while Angie had spent her entire life in Arizona. Europe seemed, to her, exotic and impossibly far away. She was fascinated with Lenore's tales of global travel and of her childhood and early schooling in London.

On the night of September 30, Lyn Esterly turned down Angie's invitation to spend the evening at Riverhouse.

"I'm into something *new*, something really exciting on this Ripper thing," Lyn told her. "But I need to do more research. If what I think is true, then a lot of people are going to be surprised."

"God," sighed Angie, "how you love being mysterious!"

"Guilty as charged," admitted Lyn. "Anyhow, I'll feel a lot safer working at the library in the middle of town than being out there on that desolate river with you."

"Dan's taking your ideas seriously," Angie told her. "He's still got the Village closed to tourists—and he's bringing in extra men tonight in case you're right about the possibility of a double murder."

"I *want* to be wrong, Angie, honest to God I do. Maybe this creep has been scared off by all the publicity. Maybe tonight will prove that—but to be on the safe side, if I were you, I'd spend the night in town . . . not alone out there in that damn haunted castle of yours!"

"Okay, you've made your point. I'll take in a movie, then meet Dan later. Ought to be safe enough with the Chief of Police, eh?"

"Absolutely. And by tomorrow I may have a big surprise for you. This is like a puzzle that's finally coming together. It's exciting!"

"Call me in the morning?"

"That's a promise."

And they rang off.

Ten P.M. Lyn working alone in the reference room on the second floor of the city library. The building had been closed to the public for two hours. Even the staff had gone. But, as a teacher, Lyn had special privileges. And her own key.

A heavy night silence. Just the shuffling sound of her books, the faint scratch of her ballpoint pen, her own soft breathing.

When the outside door to the parking lot clicked open on the floor below her, Lyn didn't hear it.

The Ripper glided upward, a dark spider-shape on the stairs, *and she's there waiting to meet me, heart pumping blood for the blade* reached the second floor, moved down the silent hallway to the reference room, *pumping crimson* pushed open the door. *pumping*

To her. Behind her. Soundless.

Lyn's head was jerked violently back.

Death in her eyes—and the blade at her throat.

A single, swift movement.

pumping

And after this one, another before midnight.

Sherry, twenty-three, a graduate student from Chicago on vacation. Staying with a girlfriend. Out for a six-pack of Heineken, a quart of nonfat, and a Hershey's Big Bar.

She left the 7-Eleven with her bag of groceries, walked to her car parked behind the building. Somebody was in the back seat, but Sherry didn't know that.

She got in, fished for the ignition key in her purse, and heard a sliding, rustling sound behind her. Twisted in sudden breathless panic.

Ripper.

Angie did not attend Lyn Esterly's funeral. She refused to see Dan or Lenore, canceled her tours, stocked her boat with food, and took it far upriver, living like a wounded animal. She allowed the river itself to soothe and comfort her, not speaking to anyone, drifting into tiny coves and inlets . . .

Until the wounds began to heal. Until she had regained sufficient emotional strength to return to Lake Havasu City.

She phoned Dan: "I'm back."

"I've been trying to trace you. Even ran a copter upriver, but I guess you didn't want to be found."

"I was all right."

"I *know* that, Angie. I wasn't worried about you. Especially after we caught him. That was what I wanted to find you for, to tell you the news. We *got* the bastard!"

"The River Killer?"

"Yeah. Calls himself 'Bloody Jack.' Says that he's the ghost of the Ripper."

"But how did you . . . ?"

"We spotted this guy prowling near the Bridge. 'Bout a week ago. He'd been living in a shack by the river, up near Mesquite Campground. One of my men followed him there. Walked right in and made the arrest."

"And he admitted he was the killer?"

"Bragged about it! Couldn't wait to get his picture in the papers."

"Dan . . . are you *sure* he's the right man?"

"Hell, we've got a ton of evidence. We found several weapons in the shack, including surgical knives. *Three* scalpels. And he had the newspaper stories on each of his murders tacked to the wall. He'd slashed the faces of all the women, their pictures, I mean. Deep knife cuts in each news photo."

"That's . . . *sick*," said Angie.

"And we have a witness who saw him go into that 7-Eleven on the night of the double murder—where the college girl was killed. He's the one, all right. A real psycho."

"Can I see you tonight? I *need* to be with you, Dan."

"I need you just as much. Meet you soon as I've finished here at the office. And, hey . . ."

"Yes?"

"I've *missed* you."

That night they made love in the moonlight, with the silken whisper of the river as erotic accompaniment. Lying naked in bed, side by side, they listened to the night crickets and touched each other gently, as if to make certain all of this was real for both of them.

"Murder is an awful way to meet somebody," said Angie, leaning close to him, her eyes shining in the darkness. "But I'm glad I met you. I never thought I could."

"Could what?"

"Find someone to love. To *really* love."

"Well, you've found me," he said quietly. "And *I've* found you."

She giggled. "You're . . ."

"I know." He grinned. "You do that to me."

And they made love again.

And the Colorado rippled its languorous night waters.

And from the dark woods a tall figure watched them.

It wasn't over.

Another month passed.

With the self-confessed killer in jail, the English Village and Bridge site were once again open to tourists.

Angie had not seen Lenore for several weeks and was anxious to tell her about the marriage plans she and Dan had made. She wanted Lenore to be her maid of honor at the wedding.

They met for a celebration dinner at the City of London Arms in the Village. But the mood was all wrong.

Angie noticed that Lenore's responses were brief, muted. She ate slowly, picking at her food.

"You don't seem all that thrilled to see me getting married," said Angie.

"Oh, but I *am*. Truly. And I know I've been a wet blanket. I'm sorry."

"What's wrong?"

"I just . . . don't think it's over."

"What are you talking about?"

"The Ripper thing. The killings."

Angie stared at her. "But they've *got* him. He's in jail right now. Dan is convinced that he . . ."

"He's not the one." Lenore said it flatly, softly. "I just *know* he's not the one."

"You're nuts! All the evidence . . ."

". . . is circumstantial. Oh, I'm sure this kook *thinks* he's the Ripper—but where is the *real* proof: blood samples . . . finger- prints . . . the actual murder weapons?"

"You're paranoid, Lenore! I had some doubts too, in the be- ginning, but Dan's a good cop. He's done his job. The killer's locked up."

Lenore's green eyes flashed. "Look, I asked you to meet me down here in the Village tonight for a reason—and it had noth- ing to do with your wedding." She drew in her breath. "I just didn't want to face this alone."

"Face what?"

"The fear. It's November the ninth. *Tonight* is the ninth!"

"So?"

"The date of the Ripper's seventh murder—back in 1888." Her tone was strained. "If that man in jail really *is* the Ripper, then nothing will happen here tonight. But . . . if he *isn't* . . ."

"My God, you're really scared!" And she gripped Lenore's hand, pressing it tightly.

"Damn right I'm scared. One of *us* could become his seventh victim."

"Look," said Angie. "It's like they say to pilots after a crash. You've got to go right back up or you'll never fly again. Well, it's time for you to do some flying tonight."

"I don't understand."

"You can't let yourself get spooked by what isn't real. And this fear of yours just isn't *real*, Lenore. There's no killer in the Village tonight. And, to prove it, I'm going to walk you to that damn Bridge."

Lenore grew visibly pale. "No . . . no, that's . . . No, I won't go."

"Yes, you will." Angie nodded. She motioned for the check. Lenore stared at her numbly.

* * *

Outside, in the late night darkness, the Village was once more empty of tourists. The last of them had gone—and the wide parking lot was quiet and deserted beyond the gate.

"We're insane to be doing this," Lenore said. Her mouth was tightly set. "Why should *I* do this?"

"To prove that irrational fear must be faced and overcome. You're my friend now—my best friend—and I won't let you give in to irrationality."

"Okay, okay . . . if I agree to walk to the Bridge, then can we get the hell out of here?"

"Agreed."

And they began to walk.

moving toward the Bridge . . . mine now, mine

"I've been poking through Lyn's research papers," Lenore said, "and I think I know what her big surprise would have been."

"Tell me."

"Most scholars now agree on the true identity of the Ripper."

"Yes. A London doctor, a surgeon. Jonathan Bascum."

"Well, Lyn Esterly didn't believe he was the Ripper. And after what I've seen of her research, neither do I."

"Then who *was* he?" asked Angie.

"Jonathan had a twin sister, Jessica. She helped the poor in that area. They practically sainted her—called her 'the Angel of Whitechapel.' "

"I've heard of her."

"Did you know she was as medically skilled as her brother? . . . That Jonathan allowed her to use his medical books? Taught her. Jessica turned out to be a better surgeon than he was. And she *used* her medical knowledge in Whitechapel."

The stimulation of what she was revealing to Angie seemed to quell much of the fear in Lenore. Her voice was animated.

keep moving . . . closer

"No *licensed* doctors would practice among the poor in that area. No money to be made. So she doctored these people. All illegal, of course. And, at first, it seemed she *was* a kind of saint, working among the destitute. Until her compulsion asserted itself."

"Compulsion?"

"To kill. Between April third and November ninth, 1888, she butchered seven women—and yet, to this day, historians claim her *brother* was responsible for the murders."

Angie was amazed. "Are you telling me that the Angel of Whitechapel was really Jack the Ripper?"

"That was Lyn's conclusion," said Lenore. "And, when you think of it, why not? It explains how the Ripper always seemed to *vanish* after a kill. Why was it that no one ever *saw* him leave Whitechapel? Because 'he' was Jessica Bascum. She could move freely through the area without arousing suspicion. No one ever saw the Ripper's face . . . no one who *lived*, that is. To throw off the police, she sent notes to them signed 'Jack.' It was a *woman* they chased onto the Bridge that night in 1888."

Lenore seemed unaware that they were approaching the Bridge now. It loomed ahead of them, a dark, stretched mass of waiting stone.

closer

"Lyn had been tracing the Bascum family history," explained Lenore. "Jessica gave birth to a daughter in 1888, the same year she vanished on the Bridge. The line continued through her granddaughter, born in 1915, and her great-granddaughter, born in 1940. The last Bascum daughter was born in 1960."

"Which means she'd be in her mid-twenties today," said Angie.

"That's right." Lenore nodded. "Like you. *You're* in your mid-twenties, Angie."

Angie's eyes flashed. She stopped walking. The line of her jaw tightened.

Bitch!

"Suppose she was drawn here," said Lenore, "to London Bridge. Where her great-great-grandmother vanished a century ago. And suppose that, with the completion of the Bridge, with the placement of that final missing stone in April, Jessica's spirit entered her great-great-granddaughter. Suppose the six killings in the Lake Havasu area were done by *her*—that it was her cosmic destiny to commit them."

"Are you saying that you think *I* am a Bascum?" Angie asked softly. They continued to walk toward the Bridge.

"I don't *think* anything. I have the facts."

"And just what might those be?" Angie's voice was tense.

"Lyn was very close to solving the Ripper case. When she researched the Bascum family history in England she traced some of the descendants here to America. She *knew.*"

"Knew what, Lenore?" Her eyes glittered. "You *do* believe that I'm a Bascum." Harshly: *"Don't* you?"

"No." Lenore shook her head. "I know you're not." She looked intently at Angie. "Because *I* am."

They had reached the steps leading up to the main part of the Bridge. In numb horror, Angie watched Lenore slide back a panel in one of the large granite blocks and remove the Ripper's hat, greatcoat, and cape. And the medical bag.

"This came down to me from the family. It was *her* surgical bag—the same one she used in Whitechapel. I'd put it away—until April, when they placed the final stone." Her eyes sparked. "When I touched the stone I felt *her* . . . Jessica's soul flowed into *me,* became part of me. And I knew what I had to do."

She removed a glittering scalpel, held it up. The blade flashed in the reflected light of the lamps on the Bridge. Lenore's smile was satanic. "This is for you!"

Angie's heart trip-hammered; she was staring, trancelike, into the eyes of the killer. Suddenly she pivoted, began running.

Down the lonely, shadow-haunted, brick-and-cobblestone streets, under the tall antique lamps, past the clustered Tudor buildings of Old London.

And the Ripper followed. Relentlessly. Confident of a seventh kill.

she'll taste the blade

Angie circled the main square, ran between buildings to find a narrow, dimly lit alleyway that led her to the rear section of the City of London Arms. Phone inside. Call Dan!

Picking up a rock from the alley, she smashed a rear window, climbed inside, began running through the dark interior, searching for a phone. One here somewhere . . . somewhere . . .

The Ripper followed her inside.

Phone! Angie fumbled in her purse, finding change for the call. She also found . . .

The pearl-handled .32 automatic—the weapon she'd been carrying for months, totally forgotten in her panic.

Now she could fight back. She knew how to use a gun.

She inserted the coins, got Dan's number at headquarters.

Ringing . . . ringing . . . "Lake Havasu City Police Department."

"Dan . . . Chief Gregory . . . Emergency!"

"I'll get him on the line."

"Hurry!"

A pause. Angie's heart, hammering.

"This is Gregory. Who's . . . ?"

"Dan!" she broke in. "It's Angie. The Ripper's *here*, trying to kill me!"

"Where are you?"

A dry buzzing. The line was dead.

A clean, down-slicing move with the scalpel had severed the phone cord.

die now . . . time to die

Angie turned to face the killer.

And triggered the automatic.

At close range, a .32-caliber bullet smashed into Lenore Bascum's flesh. She staggered back, falling to one knee on the polished wood floor of the restaurant, blood flowing from the wound.

Angie ran back to the smashed window, crawled through it, moved quickly down the alley. A rise of ground led up to the parking lot. Her car was there.

She reached it, sobbing to herself, inserted the key.

A shadow flowed across the shining car body. Two blood-spattered hands closed around Angie's throat.

The Ripper's eyes were coals of green fire, burning into Angie. She tore at the clawed fingers, pounded her right fist into the demented face. But the hands tightened. Darkness swept through Angie's brain; she was blacking out.

die, bitch!

She was dying.

Did she hear a siren? Was it real, or in her mind?

A second siren joined the first. Filling the night darkness.

bleeding . . . my blood . . . wrong, all wrong . . .

A dozen police cars roared into the lot, tires sliding on the night-damp tarmac.

Dan!

The Ripper's hands dropped away from Angie's throat. The tall figure turned, ran for the Bridge.

And was trapped there.

Police were closing in from both sides of the vast structure.

Angie and Dan were at the Bridge. "How did you know where to find me?"

"Silent alarm. Feeds right into headquarters. When you broke the window, the alarm was set off. I figured that's where you were."

"She's hit," Angie told him. "I shot her. She's dying."

In the middle of the span the Ripper fell to one knee. Then, a mortally wounded animal, she slipped over the side and plunged into the dark river beneath the Bridge.

Lights blazed on the water, picking out her body. She was sinking, unable to stay afloat. Blood gouted from her open mouth. "Damn you!" she screamed. "Damn all of you!"

She was gone.

The waters rippled over her grave.

Angie was convulsively gripping the automatic, the pearl handle cold against her fingers.

Cold.

WILLIAM F. NOLAN has forty-five books and over six hundred stories and articles to his credit, many in the fields of science fiction, fantasy, mystery and horror. Recent books by the co-author of the novel *Logan's Run* include an anthology *The Black Mask Boys*, a horror collection *Things Beyond Midnight*, *Logan: A Trilogy*, and *Dark Encounters*, a compilation of his best verse. "The Final Stone" is a variant of the story he scripted for a 1985 NBC-TV movie, *Bridge Across Time;* readers who saw that production will note dramatic departures in this prose version, not the least of which is a new identity for the Ripper.

NICHOLAS ROYLE

Irrelativity

"So what we going to do for two hours?"

"Don't know. What can we do? I wonder."

"Well, you're the one who lives here. You should know. What's the best pub?"

"You don't want to sit in a pub for two hours."

"Why not? What's wrong with that?"

"Nothing wrong with it. It's just that we ought to be able to do better than sit in a pub. What do other people do?"

"Go to the pub."

"Well, why do we have to be like everyone else? I thought you were different. That's one of the things I liked about you. We didn't go to pubs last weekend when I came up to see you."

"I go with my friends."

"Oh, I see."

They walked on in silence for a while, stepping from black shadow into dead orange light and back into darkness again. Trees and lampposts trailed past them on one side, park railings on the other. The lights of the city center receded behind them. He wished she would say something, but knew she was probably waiting for him to speak up.

They'd exhausted the shops in the afternoon. Conlon's train had arrived at two-thirty and they'd spent the afternoon looking round the shops. Now at six they had time to kill before the film. Always a difficult gap to fill: not enough time to go home and too long for just a quick look at the park or cathedral. The situation was helped none by its awkwardness: the sense of the time spent together being an appointment. Arranged on the telephone, turning up at a particular time, hundreds of miles away from home for Conlon. But it wouldn't always be like this. When he and Carolyn got to know each other better, they shouldn't mind having awkward time on their hands.

"That abbey I told you about, it's just up here on the left. You want to see it?"

"Well, we've got to do something."

"Oh, that's annoying," Carolyn said, rattling the gate. "It's locked. Never used to be. You could walk round later than this. Anyway, it's a bit eerie and probably not very safe at this time of day."

"I'd like it then, wouldn't I? You know my tastes."

It was true, she did, after the afternoon's shopping. She hadn't known there were quite so many secondhand bookshops in her hometown. Crime novels, that's what Conlon had been looking for, and he'd found some as well: things he'd been after for a while. He'd been very pleased with the afternoon's purchases. It had occurred to him that maybe Carolyn would want to go somewhere for herself. He'd asked her, but she reminded him that as she lived there she could go anytime. It was his afternoon, he'd made the effort of coming down, they should go where he liked; she had seemed quite happy to follow. It pleased him also that she hadn't subjected his choice of reading matter to the usual pious criticism. Only when he'd picked up a case study of one of the recent heaven-sent murderers had she voiced an objection.

"It doesn't seem very healthy," she'd said. "It's morbid. The fiction should be enough." Conlon had found this curious but had let it pass, dropping the book and following her out of the shop.

Ahead colored lights blinked through the trees.

"What's that?" asked Conlon, pointing.

"It's a pub. The Dog and Swan. More studenty than most of the others."

"Shall we pop in and have a drink? Might be nicer than the ones in the town center."

"Could do. But I thought you only went with the lads."

"I'm with you now."

"You don't have to be, you know."

"Carolyn . . ."

"Well, you don't. I'm sorry you had to come all this way. You can go home if you'd rather."

"Look, Carolyn, I didn't mean it that way. I wouldn't be here if I didn't want to be. I want to see you. Anyway, I like long train journeys—you get a whole different perspective on the landscape and things."

The lights were getting closer; the transition from dark to light under the streetlamps less marked. Carolyn looked at Conlon but didn't say anything.

2

"What shall I get you then?"

"A Black Velvet. I'll go and find us somewhere to sit."

"A Black Velvet!" muttered Conlon to himself as he pushed through to the bar past young people wearing sweaters and spectacles, talking energetically. Carolyn had been right—students. Black Velvet, though; it was a long time since he'd bought a Black Velvet for anyone. If ever. . . . He'd just caught the barman's eye when suddenly the latter flicked his gaze away across the other drinkers at the bar. Seeing if anyone else should be first, thought Conlon, as he looked down the bar. He saw a television, bracketed to the wall and tuned to a soap opera. Then a figure caught his attention, light in color, its back to the crowd, moving slowly through the drinkers to the door. Déjà vu. But where? When? He flipped through memories of similar situations but came up blank. A dream maybe. But when had he dreamt such a figure? The barman was becoming impatient.

"Sorry?"

"What do you want?"

"A pint of lager and a Black Velvet."

"What?"

"Black Velvet, you know, Guinness and champagne, or sparkling wine in this case."

The barman's look said it all.

Conlon set the drinks down on the table.

"Thanks, Geoff."

"Cheers."

They drank.

"So, have you had a nice week?" she asked.

"Same as usual. No one buys clothes in that type of shop anymore. It's all Top Shop and Burtons now, but they won't listen. They're just old-fashioned, I suppose."

"It can't be very interesting for you."

"Interesting!" He laughed. "I'd rather get paid to watch paint dry."

"What about the evenings?"

"Go out with my friends. Like I said before, we go to the pub."

"Oh. Yes. What, every night?"

"Most nights."

"Don't you get a little fed up with it?"

"Nothing else to do, is there? Except do a bit of reading. But you can only read so much at a time."

"When I'm reading a book I like, I don't put it down until I've finished it. I can read a three-hundred-page novel in two days." What did she want? A medal? No, Conlon restrained himself, that was uncalled for. She was trying her hardest. If the conversation was flagging he was probably to blame.

"I tend to pick out stories under ten pages myself. They've got more impact. That's if I'm not reading a novel, of course, but even if I am I tend to lose concentration after twenty pages or so."

There was a pause. Conlon found himself reflecting on the differences between them. Carolyn changed the subject.

"I wonder why they'd shut the abbey."

Two tables away a girl with her back to them was slowly getting to her feet. Her dark hair disappeared in the dimly lit corner. A red-haired man rose above her, draping a beige cloth jacket around her shoulders. The jacket loomed. There it was again. It must have been in his dream of the night before. Now the man took the arms of the jacket and wrapped them around the body like bandages. The empty sleeves were of an improbable length: the image was absurd. Carolyn's voice came out of nowhere: "Why was it locked? I don't understand it. It's never been locked before." The girl had stood up; her off-white cloth-clad shoulders dominated the dark corner. He, Conlon, was outside, she within. Night was around them, or dusk. His eyelids began to close and the shape to move. Dread filled him: the déjà vu feeling turned on its head, accentuated. "They probably locked it because of the killer on the loose," he muttered.

"What? Geoff! What are you talking about?"

She touched his face; he jumped.

"What are you talking about?"

"I'm sorry. I must be tired." He looked at her. "It was my dream. The dream I had last night."

The girl in the jacket brushed past him on her way out. He turned round on his seat and craned his neck, but couldn't see her red-haired companion. He must have imagined him. Often he wouldn't remember anything at all of his dreams until later in the day when, unannounced, an image sparked off a memory. Or had the dreamed image conjured up the real one? he questioned. There was perhaps a further step he could take this logic? He thought for a moment there might be, but it dissolved before he could isolate it for definition.

"You work too hard," Carolyn said. "Don't you have a day off in the week?"

His mind refocused.

"Yes, but I had to swap it for Saturday so I could come and see you."

They both fell silent; Carolyn looked down; Conlon followed suit; then:

"I'm sorry."

Conlon glanced idly at the television set. The remonstrations of the actors wound themselves audibly into the melee of voices in the room. The harder Conlon tried to unravel the real from the unreal, the more inextricably the strands intertwined. Still Carolyn didn't say anything. The drama limped to the edge of a cliff and left the screen, to be replaced by a local news flash. "The parents of the missing girls . . ." the newscaster began to say, but was interrupted by Carolyn, who touched Conlon's arm.

"Don't let's ignore each other."

"No, I know, it's silly." Conlon smiled. "Shall we go?"

3

"This is the prison," she told him. They had left the pub and walked further up the road. "And over there on the other side is my old school."

Conlon stood reading the notice outside the prison while Carolyn ran over the road.

"Hey, the gate's open," she called. "Come on, let's have a look round the grounds. Then it'll be time for the film."

Conlon crossed the road and they went in. The grounds appeared to be extensive and grassy, rather than restricted to an asphalt yard.

"We're all right," she said. "There's no one here. They don't start back for another week or two. It is all right for us to have a walk round, isn't it?"

"Yes, of course it is. We're not doing any harm. Anyway, as you say, there's no one here."

They had reached the first of the buildings: low, squat blocks connected by covered passageways. Carolyn went up to a window and peered in.

"It's the main entrance hall," she said. "You go through those doors there and you get to the canteen. And if you go that way you get into those corridors over there that lead into the main building."

"How long is it since you were here?"

"Five years. God! Five years. It's a long time. And this is the first time I've been back."

"Really?"

"Yes. I was glad to get out. You know, it's funny it being opposite the prison. They used to say to us if we did anything wrong: 'You'll be sent over the road if you're not careful.' "

"And did you?"

"What?"

"Do anything wrong?"

"No, I don't suppose I did. Let's go this way." She took his hand and led him round the side of the building. They walked on a paved path bordered by grass: it seemed to lead to a series of long low huts fifty or sixty yards away. As they neared the first of the huts Conlon looked up and stopped dead in his tracks.

"What's wrong, Geoff?"

In the hut he saw a figure; the shape was human but it lacked a head, or so it seemed. He couldn't trust his eyes, not after the incident in the pub; there was something strange happening. The almost palpable sense of déjà vu was on him again, clinging to his scalp, drawing it tight. Colors blurred in and out of focus; shades really—twilight killed color. He blinked and narrowed his eyes to slits. Coarse linen, fine weave, the details were there. The shape appeared to move; a trick of the failing light. This was so familiar. Dimly Conlon became aware of Carolyn's urgent pleas for his attention: what was wrong?

"My dream," he muttered. "What is it?"

"It's a dressmaker's dummy, a mannequin. It's all right. You big baby, you're shaking. Come on, come here. Did you think it was someone in there?"

He looked at it over her shoulder as she hugged him; its ambiguity destroyed, it was harmless. Just a tailor's dummy, the torso and abdomen wrapped in off-white linen. He broke free of Carolyn, muttering thickly about the bad light, about how he was tired. He stepped up to the window and studied the mannequin. Below the linen-bound body a wooden shaft gently tapered down to its division into three curved spindles, like miniature table legs. The head was replaced by a wooden stump of a neck. Conlon blinked and looked down, catching apparent movement inside as he did so; a familiar trick of the angles of vision, but he did look in again. He hadn't noticed before that one of the three legs rested in a patch of light. He had thought them to be all in shadow. Then he caught sight of the moon, which he remembered cast light and shadow as it moved across the sky.

"I've always found them weird-looking, those things," Conlon said; he knew that he'd been too gruff with Carolyn.

"It's all right, Geoff," she said, taking his arm as they walked. Their path skirted a series of huts. Conlon saw mannequins standing guard among the desks and chairs, like teachers whose pupils were long dead and become dust.

"What are these huts, anyway?" Conlon asked. "They look like those permanent caravan things."

"They're called mobiles. See, they're just supported by these struts. They can fix wheels on and move them around. I don't know if they ever do. They haven't moved since I was here.

They're just classrooms. Geoff"—the subject changed with her tone—"did you get my letters last week?"

"Yes. I did. Thanks."

"I don't want to seem like a nagging old woman, but I didn't get any. You've only sent me one letter, and that took thirty seconds to read."

"Look, Carolyn, we've only known each other for three weeks. Don't start getting possessive. I'm busy during the week."

Again they were silent for a few minutes.

"There's a gate over there." Carolyn pointed. "Let's get out. It's getting a bit dark."

When they reached the gate it was locked and too high to climb.

"Damn!" Carolyn examined the heavy padlock. "There's another one further along. Let's try that."

This took them right to the back of the school grounds by the perimeter fence. On the other side of the fence was a public footpath, but the fence was too high. The gate, when they reached it, was locked as well. Conlon took Carolyn's hand and led her along the fence past a stand of trees.

"What are you doing?" she asked.

"Come on," he said. "It's all right."

He held her by the shoulders and kissed her. When she didn't respond he said: "Come on, Carolyn. We're alone. It's quite secluded. We've hardly had any privacy at all. Just a kiss. That's probably why we've been getting at each other a bit, you know. It's not good for you. Three weeks and we've scarcely touched each other."

He kissed her again and this time she relaxed. He cupped her breast through her jumper and squeezed. She lifted her hand to bring his away, but he whispered in her ear: "We won't have a chance to be alone at your house, you said so yourself. Not with your mother there." Her hand fell away and she let him. Her fingers now stroked the back of his neck as his hand crept inside her jumper. She shivered as his cold hand touched flesh, but she let him slip inside her bra and release her breast. He felt her swell under his hand; her excitement encouraged him. She didn't feel his other hand move out of the embrace to unbuckle his trousers. With both hands now he fumbled for the catch on her jeans. She broke the kiss and, realizing, pushed his hands away violently. His prick swung jerkily up at her, shocking him as much as her.

"You didn't ask me," she said, the words knife-edged with accusation.

"Oh come on, please, it's all right," was all he said as he took ahold of her again. He'd forced the catch and shoved his hand down inside her briefs before she hit him about the face and brought her knee swiftly up into his groin. He doubled up, squealing with pain; she'd already gone, careering across the grass, readjusting her clothing as she ran toward the main building of the school.

4

Anger was the first response. He observed her flight as he waited for the pain to ease enough to allow him to give chase. She disappeared in the shadow of the building. Wincing at every stride, he ran after her. The moon lit his way and also was caught in brief dancing reflections in the windows of the building, like sudden appearances, he fancied, of a sickly white-faced sentinel watching his progress. Straining his eyes, he saw Carolyn's white shoes disappear around a corner. He raced to the corner and almost fell negotiating it. She had vanished. There was not just one building here, he saw now: there were several low blocks as well as the main building, which was four or five stories high; all were joined by connecting corridors. He saw a pair of glass doors and ran to them. To his surprise the doors swung open; maybe there were decorators or cleaners at work in the daytime and they were lax about security. This was surely the way Carolyn had gone. But all the same he looked back the way he'd come. He'd been quick enough to have seen her had she made for the gap between this and the next building. He was about to turn and go through into the corridor when he caught sight of a door in the wall of the smaller block opposite. As it was down a short flight of steps, he hadn't noticed it when he'd run past that building. The door was open.

He barged back through the glass doors and ran across the narrow yard, almost taking a fall on the loose gravel.

He let his eyes become accustomed to the dim light diffused by the windows. He thought about flicking the light switch on the wall to his left, but decided it was better not to call attention to their trespass. He was in a large classroom; the only other door was between him and the blackboard. It had no lock; he entered a low-ceilinged corridor. There were doors to the right and to the left. He glanced through the glass in each one and saw only tables and chairs silhouetted in the moonlight. As he proceeded, turning corners where required, there was little change.

When, some time later, he turned a corner and saw a group of people standing fifty yards away, his heart leapt into his mouth. He stopped the scream in his throat when he saw what they were: mannequins. Moonlight, dappled by clouds, played over their bandaged bodies, giving them the illusion of movement. Sweat broke out on his face and neck and his stomach turned to acid. What was he going to do? They were only mannequins, he knew, but irrationality would have none of that. His fingers crept to his mouth and, his back to the wall, he slumped down until he was crouching. Unease had grown into fear. His predicament came home to him in terms of realization and guilt. He hadn't intended to be violent with Carolyn. He'd wanted her—God! How he'd wanted her, all of a sudden—the risk involved, of being outside, probably trespassing already although the front gate had been open, this had added to his excitement. And she had fed his fire as well, she'd allowed him to go so far. Maybe he'd appeared experienced to her, and she'd either feared the dominating aggression of his manhood or thought him mature enough to know when to stop. But he was a virgin, damn it! He didn't have the first idea what to do with it, other than what he'd seen, read, heard about and guessed at. She'd let him do what others had only ever denied him, and he'd got carried away. He was, in that sense, still very much a boy.

He would see if there was another way he could go. Through the glass in the next door he saw a room with a second door. Through the windows of the room he saw the beginning of a separate wing, to which the door in the far wall should give him access. He tried to visualize the layout in his mind: the mannequins had probably been stuck out of the way down a dead end. There would be a fire exit down there maybe, but his reason suggested the corridor ended behind them.

He was halfway across the room, surrounded by too silent sewing machines, when a gnawing fear gripped his stomach, turning it inside out: there was someone behind him in the corner, standing silently watching him. Please let it be Carolyn! he muttered to himself. He wanted to turn and see but couldn't. It took every ounce of courage he never thought he possessed to finish crossing the room and close the door behind him before turning to look. A flap of linen had been torn from the mannequin's breast at some time; it hung limply, catching a little light, like the end of a bandage.

Conlon struck off down the new corridor with panic threatening to snatch away his self-control. He was searching for Carolyn but didn't want her to feel hunted. She was frightened of him already. He wanted to find her and protect her. From what? From the indefinable menace impregnating the darkened corridors and empty classrooms? From himself? He was the only definite threat to her. In his confusion he had stopped and leant against a door, staring vacantly through the glass. It was a good minute before he saw the girl, although she had been in his field of view for that time. He doubted the reality of what he saw, wanting it to be a mannequin. Fear froze him. The girl was about fourteen years old, to judge from her body: she was quite naked. She stood between two desks like an innocent gazing at the moon, which fell full on her face. As Conlon watched, unable to tear his eyes away and run, she turned slowly toward him, so that her body was properly and sufficiently lit for him to see everything. A long scar, crisscrossed with crude stitching, described a backwards C on her abdomen, starting beneath the rib cage and finishing just above the pubis. More sickening— and this is what made Conlon retch and overturn his empty stomach—was the general condition of the girl's skin: it appeared to be completely dehydrated: tight narrow wrinkles were etched onto her body but did not change its form. The eyes alone still vital stared at Conlon. He wished he could move. A dampness in his trousers distracted him and gave him that power. He sprinted down the corridor—his failed bladder almost a blessing—rounded a corner and crashed into a hard object which fell beneath him as he sprawled across the width of the corridor. It was a mannequin; he squirmed away from it and dragged his body into a crouching position. The corridor, he saw now, was a thoroughfare; there must have been fifty of the things, sickeningly like people standing around in groups. He hallucinated human legs moving in amongst the throng, and beyond them all he thought he caught the flash of white shoes turning a corner. He prayed they hadn't got Carolyn. He had seen legs. Five girls, replicas almost of the one he'd just fled from, were threading their way through the mannequins toward him. Was he back in his dream of the night before, playing in its predicted performance? The dream wanted him to believe in a connection between the girls and the mannequins: they were bound by some unreal metamorphosis in conspiracy against him. But he would not yield to the dream's seduction, for he knew— as surely as a dreamer knows—that there was no connection. It was part of the machinery of the dream, which if he did not believe would not exist. Damn the philosophy, he thought, escape was imperative.

Conlon's fingers tugged frantically at a door handle, and he found himself in a high-ceilinged classroom empty of tables and chairs. Thank God there was another door, however! Over his shoulder he saw a girl enter the room as he left it at the other side. He ran, nearly falling, down concrete steps and reached a lower level. It was a tiled corridor; a faint luminous glimmer shed by a skylight showed the ceiling to be the same as the walls and floor. You could turn it upside down and no one would know, Conlon thought absurdly. Hearing the advance of his pursuers, he searched in the murk for a door. He found one. He slumped down inside his new room, his forehead against the door, praying that his entrance had not been observed. Please let them walk straight past the door! he begged of some imprecise divinity.

His scalp crawled. His exhausted brain had not recognized that this room was not in darkness. Slowly he turned round. The light came from six fluorescent strips suspended from the ceiling. They shone down with nightmare clarity on benches with gas taps and sinks. It was a chemistry laboratory. In the far left corner was an opening into what seemed to be a similiar room. Between the opening and Conlon a man stood naked. He was heavily built, in his late forties maybe. Red hair covered much of his body; sweat slick on his chest and brow. His massive erection suggested Conlon had interrupted something. Unless it was for his benefit, he thought, feeling his mind going. He fumbled behind his back for the door handle. It turned before he reached it. He spun round; the first desiccated girl stepped into the room, her face a seersucker mask. He backed away and turned again. The man took a step toward him. Conlon retreated to the wall. His only hope—his sanity demanding that he see it as such —was through the opening: there might be another door. He inched along the wall. The man swiveled to face him. As Conlon neared the corner the man took a step toward him. And another. Conlon played his last card and darted through the opening into the next room.

There was no other door. In the seconds that Conlon knew were all he had left, he took in the scene. The fittings were the same as in the first room; but it was different. On a shelf at the back were several jars marked NATRON. Stacked on a bench below this shelf were dozens of rolls of bandage. There was a girl in the room. Unlike the girls he had run from, this girl's skin was white and smooth. She was lying on a workbench, feet toward him, so that he couldn't see her face. But the body seemed younger and slighter than the one he feared to see. The man had obviously been at work: the incision in her stomach was stuffed with white crystals: one of the jars stood opened next to her. She appeared to be otherwise unmarked; however, her legs had been forced wide apart in an effigy of compliance.

Conlon heard movement behind him but did not swing round. He knew the scenario from his dream. The girls were standing in the opening, fingering their stitches; the man had picked up a scalpel from a bench and was coming at him. Suppressing his instinct for self-preservation, Conlon only sought to make sure of one thing before the dream played on. It was more important than comprehension the knowledge he coveted. He ran to see the girl's face, but knew, with the certainty of the dreamer, that the truth would elude him as surely as his next breath.

NICHOLAS ROYLE is an actor as well as a writer. Born in 1963, he has appeared in plays produced in London and Paris—including one, *Colossus*, that was written by another contributor to this volume, Clive Barker. His first short story saw print in *The 26th Pan Book of Horror Stories* (1985). He is presently at work on two series of interrelated stories, and a novel.

RAMSEY CAMPBELL

The Hands

Before long Trent wished he had stayed in the waiting room, though being stranded for two hours on the teetotal platform had seemed the last straw. He'd expected to be in London just as the pubs were opening, but a derailment somewhere had landed him in a town he'd never heard of and couldn't locate on the map, with only his briefcase full of book jackets for company. Were those the Kentish hills in the distance, smudged by the threat of a storm? He might have asked the ticket collector, except that he'd had to lose his temper before the man would let him out for a walk.

The town wasn't worth the argument. It was nothing but concrete: off-white tunnels like subways crammed with shops, spiraling walkways where ramps would have saved a great deal of trouble, high blank domineering walls where even the graffiti looked like improvements. He'd thought of seeking out the bookshops, in the hope of grabbing a subscription or two for the books he represented, but it was early-closing day; nothing moved in the concrete maze but midget clones in the television rental shops. By the time he found a pub, embedded in a concrete wall with only an extinguished plastic sign to show what it was, it was closing time. Soon he was lost, for here were the clones again, a pink face and an orange and even a black-and-white, or was this another shop? Did they all leave their televisions running? He was wondering whether to go back to the pub to ask for directions, and had just realized irritably that no doubt it would have closed by now, when he saw the church.

At least, the notice board said that was what it was. It stood in a circle of flagstones within a ring of lawn. Perhaps the concrete flying buttresses were meant to symbolize wings, but the building was all too reminiscent of a long, thin iced bun flanked by two wedges of cake, served up on a cracked plate. Still, the church had the first open door he'd seen in the town, and it was starting to rain. He would rather shelter in the church than among the deserted shops.

He was crossing the flagstones, which had broken out in dark splotches, when he realized he hadn't entered a church since he was a child. And he wouldn't have dared go in with jackets like the ones in his briefcase: the long stockinged legs leading up into darkness, the man's head exploding like a melon, the policeman nailing a black girl to a cross. He wouldn't have dared think of a church just as a place to shelter from the rain. What *would* he have dared, for heaven's sake? Thank God he had grown out of being scared. He shoved the door open with his briefcase.

As he stepped into the porch, a nun came out of the church. The porch was dark, and fluttery with notices and pamphlets, so that he hardly glanced at her. Perhaps that was why he had the impression that she was chewing. The Munching Nun, he thought, and couldn't help giggling out loud. He hushed at once, for he'd seen the great luminous figure at the far end of the church.

It was a stained-glass window. As a burst of sunlight reached it, it seemed that the figure was catching the light in its flaming outstretched hands. Was it the angle of the light that made its fingertips glitter? As he stepped into the aisle for a better view, memories came crowding out of the dimness: genuflecting boys in long white robes, distant priests chanting incomprehensibly. Once, when he'd asked where God was, his father had told him God lived "up there," pointing at the altar. Trent had imagined pulling aside the curtains behind the altar to see God, and he'd been terrified in case God heard him thinking.

He was smiling at himself, swinging his briefcase and striding up the aisle between the dim pews, when the figure with the flaming hands went out. All at once the church was very dark, though surely there ought to have been a light on the altar. He'd thought churches meant nothing to him anymore, but no church should feel as cold and empty as this. Certainly he had never been in a church before which smelled of dust.

The fluttering in the porch grew louder, loud as a cave full of bats—come to think of it, hadn't some of the notices looked torn?—and then the outer door slammed. He was near to panic, though he couldn't have said why, when he saw the faint vertical line beyond the darkness to his left. There was a side door.

When he groped into the side aisle, his briefcase hit a pew. The noise was so loud that it made him afraid the door would be locked. But it opened easily, opposite a narrow passage which led back into the shopping precinct. Beyond the passage he saw a signpost for the railway station.

He was into the passage so quickly that he didn't even feel the rain. Nevertheless, it was growing worse; at the far end the pavement looked as if it was turning into tar, the signpost dripped like a nose. The signpost pointed down a wide straight road, which suggested that he had plenty of time after all, so that he didn't sidle past when the lady with the clipboard stepped in front of him.

He felt sorry for her at once. Her dark suit was too big, and there was something wrong with her mouth; when she spoke her lips barely parted. "Can you spare . . ." she began, and he deduced that she was asking him for a few minutes. "It's a test of your perceptions. It oughtn't to take long."

She must open her mouth when nobody was looking. Her clipboard pencil was gnawed to the core, and weren't the insides of her lips gray with lead? No doubt he was the first passerby for hours; if he refused she would get nobody. Presumably she was connected with the religious bookshop whose window loomed beside her doorway. Well, this would teach him not to laugh at nuns. "All right," he said.

She led him into the building so swiftly that he would have had no chance to change his mind. He could only follow her down the dull green corridor, into a second and then a third. Once he encountered a glass-fronted bookcase which contained only a few brownish pages, once he had to squeeze past a filing cabinet crumbly with rust; otherwise there was nothing but closed doors, painted the same prison green as the walls. Except for the slam of a door somewhere behind him, there was no sign of life. He was beginning to wish that he hadn't been so agreeable; if he tired of the examination he wouldn't be able simply to leave, he would have to ask the way.

She turned a corner, and there was an open door. Sunlight lay outside it like a welcome mat, though he could hear rain scuttling on a window. He followed her into the stark green room and halted, surprised, for he wasn't alone after all; several clipboard ladies were watching people at schoolroom desks too small for them. Perhaps there was a pub nearby.

His guide had stopped beside the single empty desk, on which a pamphlet lay. Her fingers were interwoven as if she was praying, yet they seemed restless. Eventually he said, "Shall we start?"

Perhaps her blank expression was the fault of her impediment, for her face hadn't changed since he'd met her. "You already have," she said.

He'd taken pity on her, and now she had tricked him. He was tempted to demand to be shown the way out, except that he would feel foolish. As he squeezed into the vacant seat, he was hot with resentment. He wished he was dressed as loosely as everyone else in the room seemed to be.

It must be the closeness that was making him nervous: the closeness, and not having had a drink all day, and the morning wasted with a bookseller who'd kept him waiting for an hour beyond their appointment, only to order single copies of two of the books Trent was offering. And of course his nervousness was why he felt that everyone was waiting for him to open the pamphlet on his desk, for why should it be different from those the others at the desks were reading? Irritably he flicked the pamphlet open, at the most appalling image of violence he had ever seen.

The room flooded with darkness so quickly he thought he had passed out from shock. But it was a storm cloud putting out the sun—there was no other light in the room. Perhaps he hadn't really seen the picture. He would rather believe it had been one of the things he saw sometimes when he drank too much, and sometimes when he drank too little.

Why were they taking so long to switch on the lights? When he glanced up, the clipboard lady said, "Take it to the window."

He'd heard of needy religious groups, but surely they were overdoing it—though he couldn't say why he still felt they had something to do with religion. Despite his doubts he made for the window, for then he could tell them he couldn't see, and use that excuse to make his escape.

Outside the window he could just distinguish a gloomy yard, its streaming walls so close he couldn't see the sky. Drainpipes black as slugs trailed down the walls, between grubby windows and what seemed to be the back door of the religious bookshop. He could see himself dimly in the window, himself and the others, who'd put their hands together as though it was a prayer meeting. The figures at the desks were rising to their feet, the clipboard ladies were converging on him. As he dropped his briefcase and glanced back nervously, he couldn't tell if they had moved at all.

But the picture in the pamphlet was quite as vile as it had seemed. He turned the page, only to find that the next was worse. They made the covers in his briefcase seem contrived and superficial, just pictures—and why did he feel he should recognize them? Suddenly he knew: yes, the dead baby being forced into the womb was in the Bible; the skewered man came from a painting of hell, and so did the man with an arrow up his rectum. That must be what he was meant to see, what was expected of him. No doubt he was supposed to think that these things were somehow necessary to religion. Perhaps if he said that, he could leave—and in any case he was blocking the meager light from the window. Why weren't the other subjects impatient to stand where he was standing? Was he the only person in the room who needed light in order to see?

Though the rain on the window was harsh as gravel, the silence behind him seemed louder. He turned clumsily, knocking his briefcase over, and saw why. He was alone in the room.

He controlled his panic at once. So this was the kind of test they'd set up for him, was it? The hell with them and their test —he wouldn't have followed the mumbling woman if he hadn't felt guilty, but why should he have felt guilty at all? As he made for the door, the pamphlet crumpled in one hand as a souvenir of his foolishness, he glanced at the pamphlets on the other desks. They were blank.

He had to stop on the threshold and close his eyes. The corridor was darker than the room; there had been nothing but sunlight there either. The building must be even more disused than it had seemed. Perhaps the shopping precinct had been built around it. None of this mattered, for now that he opened his eyes he could see dimly, and he'd remembered which way he had to go.

He turned right, then left at once. A corridor led into darkness, in which there would be a left turn. The greenish tinge of the oppressive dimness made him feel as if he was in an aquarium, except for the muffled scurrying of rain and the rumbling of his footsteps on the bare floorboards. He turned the corner at last, into another stretch of dimness, more doors sketched on the lightless walls, doors that changed the sound of his footsteps as he passed, too many doors to count. Here was a turn, and almost at once there should be another—he couldn't recall which way. If he wasn't mistaken, the stretch beyond that was close to the exit. He was walking confidently now, so that when his briefcase collided with the dark he cried out. He had walked into a door.

It wouldn't budge. He might as well have put his shoulder to the wall. His groping fingers found neither a handle nor a hole where one ought to be. He must have taken a wrong turning— somewhere he'd been unable to see that he had a choice. Perhaps he should retrace his steps to the room with the desks.

He groped his way back to the corridor which had seemed full of doors. He wished he could remember how many doors it contained; it seemed longer now. No doubt his annoyance was making it seem so. Eight doors, nine, but why should the hollowness they gave to his footsteps make him feel hollow too? He must be nearly at the corner, and once he turned left the room with the desks would be just beyond the end of the corridor. Yes, here was the turn; he could hear his footsteps flattening as they approached the wall. But there was no way to the left, after all.

He'd stumbled to the right, for that was where the dimness led, before his memory brought him up short. He'd turned right here on his way out, he was sure he had. The corridor couldn't just disappear. No, but it could be closed off—and when he reached out to where he'd thought it was he felt the panels of the door at once, and bruised his shoulder against it before he gave up.

So the test hadn't finished. That must be what was going on, that was why someone was closing doors against him in the dark. He was too angry to panic. He stormed along the right-hand corridor, past more doors and their muffled hollow echoes. His mouth felt coated with dust, and that made him even angrier. By God, he'd make someone show him the way out, however he had to do so.

Then his fists clenched—the handle of his briefcase dug into his palm, the pamphlet crumpled loudly—for there was someone ahead, unlocking a door. A faint grayish light seeped out of the doorway and showed Trent the glimmering collar, stiff as a fetter. No wonder the priest was having trouble opening the door, for he was trying to don a pair of gloves. "Excuse me, Father," Trent called, "can you tell me how I get out of here?"

The priest seemed not to hear him. Just before the door closed, Trent saw that he wasn't wearing gloves at all. It must be the dimness which made his hands look flattened and limp. A moment later he had vanished into the room, and Trent heard a key turn in the lock.

Trent knocked on the door rather timidly until he remembered how, as a child, he would have been scared to disturb a priest at all. He knocked as loudly as he could, even when his knuckles were aching. If there was a corridor beyond the door, perhaps the priest was out of earshot. The presence of the priest somewhere made Trent feel both safer and a good deal angrier. Eventually he stormed away, thumping on all the doors.

His anger seemed to have cracked a barrier in his mind, for he could remember a great deal he hadn't thought of for years. He'd been most frightened in his adolescence, when he had begun to suspect it wasn't all true and had fought to suppress his thoughts in case God heard them. God had been watching him everywhere—even in the toilet, like a voyeur. Everywhere he had felt caged. He'd grown resentful eventually, he'd dared God to spy on him while he was in the toilet, and that was where he'd pondered his suspicions, such as—yes, he remembered now —the idea that just as marriage was supposed to sanctify sex, so religion sanctified all manner of torture and inhumanity. Of course, that was the thought the pamphlet had almost recalled. He faltered, for his memories had muffled his senses more than the dimness had. Somewhere ahead of him, voices were singing.

Perhaps it was a hymn. He couldn't tell, for they sounded as if they had their mouths full. It must be the wall that was blurring them. As he advanced through the greenish dimness, he tried to make no noise. Now he thought he could see the glint of the door, glossier than the walls, but he had to reach out and touch the panels before he could be sure. Why on earth was he hesitating? He pounded on the door, more loudly than he had intended, and the voices fell silent at once.

He waited for someone to come to the door, but there was no sound at all. Were they standing quite still and gazing toward him, or was one of them creeping to the door? Perhaps they were all doing so. Suddenly the dark seemed much larger, and he realized fully that he had no idea where he was. They must know he was alone in the dark. He felt like a child, except that in a situation like this as a child he would have been able to wake up.

By God, they couldn't frighten him, not any longer. Certainly his hands were shaking—he could hear the covers rustling in his briefcase—but with rage, not fear. The people in the room must be waiting for him to go away so that they could continue their hymn, waiting for him to trudge into the outer darkness, the unbeliever, gnashing his teeth. They couldn't get rid of him so easily. Maybe by their standards he was wasting his life, drinking it away—but by God, he was doing less harm than many religious people he'd heard of. He was satisfied with his life, that was the important thing. He'd wanted to write books, but even if he'd found he couldn't, he'd proved to himself that not everything in books was true. At least selling books had given him a disrespect for them, and perhaps that was just what he'd needed.

He laughed uneasily at himself, a thin sound in the dark. Where were all these thoughts coming from? It was like the old story that you saw your whole life at the moment of your death, as if anyone could know. He needed a drink, that was why his thoughts were uncontrollable. He'd had enough of waiting. He grabbed the handle and wrenched at the door, but it was no use; the door wouldn't budge.

He should be searching for the way out, not wasting his time here. That was why he hurried away, not because he was afraid someone would snatch the door open. He yanked at handles as he came abreast of them, though he could barely see the doors. Perhaps the storm was worsening, although he couldn't hear the rain, for he was less able to see now than he had been a few minutes ago. The dark was so soft and hot and dreamlike that he could almost imagine that he was a child again, lying in bed at that moment when the dark of the room merged with the dark of sleep—but it was dangerous to imagine that, though he couldn't think why. In any case, this was clearly not a dream, for the next door he tried slammed deafeningly open against the wall of the room.

It took him a long time to step forward, for he was afraid he'd awakened the figures that were huddled in the farthest corner of the room. When his eyes adjusted to the meager light that filtered down from a grubby skylight, he saw that the shapes were too tangled and flat to be people. Of course, the huddle was just a heap of old clothes—but then why was it stirring? As he stepped forward involuntarily, a rat darted out, dragging a long brownish object that seemed to be trailing strings. Before the rat vanished under the floorboards Trent was back outside the door and shutting it as quickly as he could.

He stood panting in the dark. Whatever he'd seen, it was nothing to do with him. Perhaps the limbs of the clothes had been bound together, but what did it mean if they were? Once he escaped he could begin to think—he was afraid to do so now. If he began to panic he wouldn't dare to try the doors.

He had to keep trying. One of them might let him escape. He ought to be able to hear which was the outer corridor, if it was still raining. He forced himself to tiptoe onward. He could distinguish the doors only by touch, and he turned the handles timidly, even though it slowed him down. He was by no means ready when one of the doors gave an inch. The way his hand flinched, he wondered if he would be able to open the door at all.

Of course he had to, and at last he did, as stealthily as possible. He wasn't stealthy enough, for as he peered around the door the figures at the table turned toward him. Perhaps they were standing up to eat because the room was so dim, and it must be the dimness that made the large piece of meat on the table appear to struggle, but why were they eating in such meager light at all? Before his vision had a chance to adjust they left the table all at once and came at him.

He slammed the door and ran blindly down the corridor, grabbing at handles. What exactly had he seen? They had been eating with their bare hands, but somehow the only thought he could hold on to was a kind of sickened gratitude that he had been unable to see their faces. The dimness was virtually darkness now, his running footsteps deafened him to any sound but theirs, the doors seemed farther and farther apart, locked doors separated by minutes of stumbling through the dark. Three locked doors, four, and the fifth opened so easily that he barely saved himself from falling into the cellar.

If it had been darker, he might have been able to turn away before he saw what was squealing. As he peered down, desperate to close the door but compelled to try to distinguish the source of the thin irregular sound, he made out the dim shapes of four figures, standing wide apart on the cellar floor. They were moving farther apart now, without letting go of what they were holding—the elongated figure of a man, which they were pulling in four directions by its limbs. It must be inflatable, it must be a leak that was squealing. But the figure wasn't only squealing, it was sobbing.

Trent fled, for the place was not a cellar at all. It was a vast darkness in whose distance he'd begun to glimpse worse things. He wished he could believe he was dreaming, the way they comforted themselves in books—but not only did he know he wasn't dreaming, he was afraid to think that he was. He'd had nightmares like this when he was young, when he was scared that he'd lost his one chance. He'd rejected the truth, and so now there was only hell to look forward to. Even if he didn't believe, hell would get him, perhaps for not believing. It had taken him a while to convince himself that because he didn't believe in it, hell couldn't touch him. Perhaps he had never really convinced himself at all.

He managed to suppress his thoughts, but they had disoriented him; even when he forced himself to stop and listen he wasn't convinced where he was. He had to touch the cold slick wall before the sounds became present to him: footsteps, the footsteps of several people creeping after him.

He hadn't time to determine what was wrong with the footsteps, for there was another sound, ahead of him—the sound of rain on glass. He began to run, fumbling with door handles as he reached them. The first door was locked, and so was the second. The rain was still in front of him, somewhere in the dark. Or was it behind him now, with his pursuers? He scrabbled at the next handle, and almost fell headlong into the room.

He must keep going, for there was a door on the far side of the room, a door beyond which he could hear the rain. It didn't matter that the room smelled like a butcher's. He didn't have to look at the torn objects that were strewn over the floor, he could dodge among them, even though he was in danger of slipping on the wet boards. He held his breath until he reached the far door, and could already feel how the air would burst out of his mouth when he escaped. But the door was locked, and the doorway to the corridor was full of his pursuers, who came padding leisurely into the room.

He was on the point of withering into himself—in a moment he would have to see the things that lay about the floor—when he noticed that beside the door there was a window, so grubby that he'd taken it for a pale patch on the wall. Though he couldn't see what lay beyond, he smashed the glass with his briefcase and hurled splinters back into the room as he scrambled through.

He landed in a cramped courtyard. High walls scaled by drainpipes closed in on all four sides. Opposite him was a door with a glass panel, beyond which he could see heaps of religious books. It was the back door of the bookshop he had noticed in the passage.

He heard glass gnashing in the window frame, and didn't dare look behind him. Though the courtyard was only a few feet wide, it seemed he would never reach the door. Rain was already dripping from his brows into his eyes. He was praying incoherently: yes, he believed, he believed in anything that could save him, anything that could hear. The pamphlet was still crumpled in the hand he raised to try the door. Yes, he thought desperately, he believed in those things too, if they had to exist before he could be saved.

He was pounding on the door with his briefcase as he twisted the handle—but the handle turned easily and let him in. He slammed the door behind him and wished that were enough. Why couldn't there have been a key? Perhaps there was something almost as good—the cartons of books piled high in the corridor that led to the shop.

As soon as he'd struggled past he began to overbalance them.

He had toppled three cartons, creating a barrier which looked surprisingly insurmountable, when he stopped, feeling both guilty and limp with relief. Someone was moving about in the shop.

He was out of the corridor, and sneezing away the dust he had raised from the cartons, before he realized that he hadn't the least idea what to say. Could he simply ask for refuge? Perhaps, for the woman in the shop was a nun. She was checking the street door, which was locked, thank God. The dimness made the windows and the contents of the shop look thick with dust. Perhaps he should begin by asking her to switch on the lights.

He was venturing toward her when he touched a shelf of books, and he realized that the gray deposit was dust, after all. He faltered as she turned toward him. It was the nun he had seen in the church, but now her mouth was smeared with crimson lipstick—except that as she advanced on him, he saw that it wasn't lipstick at all. He heard the barricade in the corridor give way just as she pulled off her flesh-colored gloves by their nails. "You failed," she said.

RAMSEY CAMPBELL's books include the novels *The Doll Who Ate His Mother, The Face That Must Die, The Nameless, The Parasite* (U.K.: *To Wake the Dead*) and *Incarnate,* as well as the collections *Dark Companions, Demons by Daylight, The Height of the Scream* and *Cold Print.* He is also the editor of the anthologies *Superhorror, New Terrors, The Gruesome Book* and *New Tales of the Cthulhu Mythos.* His most recent books are *Scared Stiff,* a collection, and the novels *Obsession* and *The Hungry Moon.*

RAY RUSSELL

The Bell

Ding-dang-dong . . . ding-dang-dong . . . ding-dang-dong . . .
The damned, he thought, the forgotten souls in Hell: do they
suffer more than this? Can they possibly scream louder? Sweat
more? Do they feel more excruciating pain? Then he told himself: Don't be a fool. You don't believe in all that.

She showed up once wearing a small cross around her neck.
Got it through the mail, she said, from one of the charities she
contributed to. It was a bit gaudy—mock gold, the basic shape
swollen here and there by rococo digressions, studded with imitation diamonds and pearls, suspended on a slender chain—but
its appeal, apart from the religious significance it had for her,
was the stone located at the intersection of the crossing bar and
vertical beam. This was not really a stone at all, not even a false
one, but a drop of clear glass, a tiny convex lens in fact, and
when you closed one eye and looked through it, holding the
talisman up to a strong light, you saw a simple line drawing of a
kneeling figure and, under this, the Lord's Prayer: the one with
"trespasses" instead of "debts" and without the symphonic "For
Thine is the Kingdom" finale. In magnification, it seemed the
size of a billboard.

Squinting through the lens at the prayer, he asked, "Are you a
Christian?"

She shrugged. "I'm thinking about it." Her voice was a soft
contralto mist. "But it's hard to be a Christian. A good Christian."

He uttered a favorite phrase of his father's: "It's hard to be a
good anything."

The first time she came to his place, he asked her what she'd like to drink, and she said, "It's not what *I* like, it's what my ulcer likes, and *she* likes Scotch Cows."

"Coming right up." He got out the milk and whisky, saying, "I like them, too, and I don't even have an ulcer. They taste sweet, somehow, I wonder why. Scotch isn't sweet, milk isn't sweet, but put them together . . ." He handed her a glass. They drank. The mixture was thick and silky. "You really have an ulcer? You don't seem the type. You stay cool, unhassled."

"Maybe that's the problem. Maybe I hold in too much."

"We'll have to fix that."

"Will we?"

"Two or three of these Cows ought to help. Doctor's orders."

"Yes, Doctor." (He had just made Ph.D.)

He taught an extension course in music appreciation one night a week, and she was one of his pupils. She had maybe half a dozen years on him; he clocked her at thirty-five or thereabout.

During Lent, she denied herself Scotch Cows, sweets, and all forms of bread except for kosher Passover matzos, although she wasn't Jewish, explaining that the Last Supper of Our Lord— she always called him that—was, after all, a Passover feast, at which unleavened bread had been served, the first eucharist.

"The Singing Bread," he contributed from his private fund of lore.

In bed with him one day, smooth and subtly fragrant, wearing nothing but the cross, she reached behind her neck and unfastened the clasp, her breasts lifting so beautifully. She slipped the holy bauble off her neck and fastened it around his. He expected the metal to feel cold, but it was warm from her flesh. "Now we're married," she said.

He almost replied, You're already married. But it wasn't necessary. Her face furrowed at the unspoken thought. He was often tempted to ask her how she reconciled her infidelity with her obviously genuine religious convictions; what kind of deal or bargain had she made with God? This time, he did ask her.

"Don't be silly," she snapped. "You can't make deals with God."

"People do it all the time, don't they? 'Dear God, please help me pass my exams and I'll never take your name in vain again.' That sort of thing. You scratch my back and I'll scratch yours."

She frowned. "You sound like my husband."

"Heaven forbid." To distract her, he said, "Let's have some music. I bought a new record yesterday for the class. Old Blue-Eyes."

"Sinatra?"

"Bach."

He climbed naked out of bed, into the late-afternoon chill, and put the record on the machine. Quickly, he returned to her warmth. She wasn't really musical, but she liked the record and asked, a little later, if it was "religious."

"No," he said. "Bach wrote a lot of stuff to liturgical texts, of course, but this is pure music. It's called *The Art of Fugue*. The last thing he wrote. Summed up his whole life's work. So, in a way, maybe you *could* call it religious. Hear those four notes? . . . That's his name, B, A, C, H."

"I didn't know there was a note H."

"There is in German. It's B natural. Their B is our B flat. Listen now . . . hear that?" The music had come to an abrupt unresolved end, and the machine turned itself off with a click. "That's where Bach died," he said. A moment later, he added, "In 1750. But *The Art of Fugue* wasn't performed publicly until 1927! Can you believe that? That's when Lindbergh crossed the Atlantic, wasn't it? A good year. But for *The Art of Fugue* to be premiered so late!"

"Speaking of late," she said, glancing at the bedside clock, "I'd better get home and start dinner." She was always alert to the priorities of duty. She was the mother of two children, a boy and a girl.

Her husband, he had learned a bit at a time, was unsympathetic to her religious feelings, making them the butt of his wit, sometimes in the presence of others. It was this, she said, that had turned her against him. "You're different," she told him. "You understand. You're interested." His interest was unfeigned, but he also liked the way her eyes looked when she talked about it. She said he was a religious man. He denied it.

"I'm moved by the B Minor Mass," he said, "and the *Missa Solemnis* and the Verdi Requiem and all that. But I'm moved by the *sound* and maybe a little bit by the language. It's an esthetic response, not a religious one."

"Are you sure there's a difference?"

"Of course there is."

She said, "You're devoted to music. Dedicated. Almost like a priest. I read somewhere that the word 'religion' really means 'bound,' being bound to something."

He smiled and kissed her. "Come on, I don't go in for that bondage stuff."

With the small bright snap of the clasp behind his neck, lust became love. Deliver us from evil. When she said they were married, he knew it was true.

The night of that day, he had a dream about the little cross. In the dream, he wondered what the prayer would look like if he peered at it from the other side: would it be reversed, as in a mirror? He turned the cross around and put his eye to it.

Foam-topped waves under a robin's-egg sky and clouds like drifting cottonballs. A color slide, he thought at first, but the waves were moving, rolling in and shattering on the rocky shore. He marveled at the wizard-work of miniaturization that had packed microscopic motion-picture equipment into so small an object. Sound equipment, too: breakers crashing, music soaring . . .

When he awoke in the morning, the cross was still around his neck. He removed it and looked eagerly into the wrong side.

Nothing. A gray blur. He got out of bed, smiling at the sudden recollection of an old friend who had owned a novelty fountain pen with a similar peephole at one end. When you looked into it, you saw a pair of pink young people coupling. (But why should the devil have all the best tunes?)

After showering, he slipped the cross around his neck again. As he was stepping into his slacks, the bedside phone rang.

It was his father. "Oh, good, you're home." The voice was weak. "Called a few minutes ago . . ."

"I was in the shower. Anything wrong, Dad?"

"Well, I started to get these pains."

"Did you call the doctor? Where are the pains?"

"In the gut. Yeah, he said he'd meet me at the hospital."

"I'll pick you up right away."

"I could get a cab . . ."

"No, no, I'll be right over."

His father was folded in two by agony. At the hospital, an injection dulled the pain and made him drowsy. His face was gray and, without dentures, collapsed in upon itself. Hours after sunset, standing in the drab alcove called a solarium, the doctor explained the situation to the son. Both men were dim with fatigue. The intestinal disorder, something with a Greek or Latin name, often could be controlled by special diet, but with an attack as severe as this one, immediate surgery was usually the only answer.

"An operation?"

"Two operations, actually. Weeks or months apart."

"At his age?"

"I know. And I won't kid you. It will be hell on earth for him. The convalescence will be awful. Both convalescences. He'll wish he were dead." The doctor went on to explain the operations in detail.

"If my mother were alive, she'd know what to do."

"The decision is yours, that's what it comes down to. He's in no condition to make it."

"What if he doesn't have the surgery?"

The doctor shrugged. "He *might* recover without it. But he'll probably die. Not peacefully."

"Do I have to make up my mind right now?"

"Go home and sleep on it."

A fly landed on a dusty plastic plant, wrung its hands, and flew away.

He couldn't eat dinner. He chewed absentmindedly on a shard of stale matzo from an old box she had left in his kitchen some weeks before. "How can you eat this stuff?" he once had asked her. "It tastes like the Dead Sea Scrolls." He drank a glass of milk. He turned on the TV and looked at it for an hour without seeing it.

Curled fetally in his bed, sweating, he muttered into the pillow. "He'd never survive all that cutting," he said. "He couldn't take it. All that pain. On his back for weeks. Then the whole thing all over again. The old guy never hurt anyone in his life. I can't do it to him." His muttering had merged into unvoiced thought. Tightly, he clutched the cross that still hung from his neck. Listen, he said silently. Can we make a trade? I'll give you something if you give me something. You scratch my back, I'll scratch yours. I want you to spare my father. Tell me what you want. What have I got that you could possibly want?

The sharp points of the metal and the facets of the glass gems bit into his palm. "All right," he said aloud. "You've got a deal."

Seconds later, he was sound asleep, peering through the dream lens of the dream cross at the pink young couple in motion, going at it hell-for-leather, under a flaming sky.

That was all three years in the past. She hadn't understood his reasons for the breakup, and he couldn't explain. He'd said sanctimonious things like "It's the only right way" and "It's better for your family" that rang false as lead coins. She'd dropped out of the class, as well. He'd given her *The Art of Fugue* as a parting gift.

The morning after making the deal, he had gone to the hospital, where he'd found his father sitting up and complaining about the food. The color had returned to his face and he was wearing his dentures. He had greeted his son by growling, "When can I get the hell out of this joint?"

He'd got out the following week, waving and winking at the nurses.

The doctor hadn't tried to explain it. "I *said* he might recover. Well, he did."

Now the son, three years older and beginning to bald prematurely, sat in the same bleak solarium and listened to the same doctor. "No, there's no point in surgery this time," the medical man was saying. "It's gone too far. And he's too weak now, too old."

"You've got to do *some*thing."

"We are. We're trying to keep him comfortable."

"Until what?"

"There's only one way it can end."

Two weeks later, his father was still hanging on, but the drugs had begun to lose their efficacy. "Hurts like the devil," the old man said, trying to smile.

Another two weeks, and the doctor said, "I don't understand what's keeping him alive. He's so old and frail. I've never seen anything like it."

"Can't you do anything about the pain?"

"He's doped to the eyeballs. The stuff just doesn't work anymore."

His father looked like a brown, shriveled mummy, small in the broad whiteness of the bed. His lips were dry and caked.

After some minutes, his eyes opened and focused on his son. They were fogged by suffering. When his son leaned over to kiss his forehead, the sick man asked him something, but it was inaudible.

"What's that, Dad?"

The old man licked his lips and repeated the question. The voice, once so strong and virile, was like a puppy's whimper: "Why can't I die?"

The question followed him home, repeating itself in endless playback like a loop of tape.

The thought of death, his father's longing for it, made him slowly gravitate to a dresser drawer where he kept a black necktie. He had last worn it years before, at his mother's burial. There was a dot of grease still on it from the post-interment meal. The funeral baked meats. Next to it was a small leather case containing old cuff links, tie pins—gifts, he never wore them—and the cross. He held it up to the light and looked into the center stone. But the lens had become cracked and the only word of the Lord's Prayer that still could be seen was "evil."

He gripped the cross, remembering the bargain muttered into his sweaty pillow three years before. Turning decisively, he walked over to the bedside phone and punched out the old number. He hadn't forgotten it. He hoped it hadn't been changed; hoped she hadn't moved; divorced and married again; died.

The phone was answered by an adolescent boy whose voice had deepened in the three-year interval.

"Is your mother there?" he asked the boy.

"Hold on. Hey, Mom? . . ."

In a moment, she was speaking. She sounded the same. He identified himself and added, "Can you talk?"

"It depends."

"Right. The thing is, I'd like to see you. Is it possible?" She didn't answer. "Are you still there?"

"I was just thinking about it. I mean, why?"

"I really do want to see you. I . . . I need you."

"All right. When?"

"Whenever you can. As soon as possible."

"Yes, Reverend . . ."

"What?"

". . . I'll be glad to take over the Bible class tonight. I'll be there at eight."

"Wonderful. I'm still at the same place."

Twice before she arrived, he phoned the hospital, only to hear the expected immutable report: "No change."

She looked no older. She wore the same delicate perfume. His dormant feeling for her returned in a flash of warmth. He embraced her and they kissed. She tasted the same, too.

"What's in the package?" he asked. "Got to be either a pizza or a record."

"Old Blue-Eyes," she said, slipping *The Art of Fugue* out of the wrapping.

"You still have that?"

"I've grown fond of it. And you still have *that.*" (The cross dangling from his neck.)

He said, "So you made the plunge."

"Plunge?"

"Became a Christian."

"Why do you say that?"

"All that 'Reverend' business on the phone."

"Oh. No, I'm still on the brink. But I do attend a Bible history class in the neighborhood. And sometimes I stand in for Reverend Huebing if he's called away. He says I'm his star pupil! We have all kinds in the class. A Jewish lady, a Catholic, a couple of Methodists, even an atheist."

"Your husband?"

"No."

"How about a Scotch Cow?"

"Fine."

"I'll whip 'em up. Put on the record why don't you?"

Only token sips were taken of the drinks, for they were both impatient to make up for three years' lost time, and as the glowing spiral of music spun near its unconcluded end, he probed her, deeply, surely, trustful that his flesh was a blade of mercy, severing the bargain, delivering the good old man from pain, from life.

While she was still in his arms, the phone rang. He reached out from the bed and answered it. The doctor announced the sad, welcome news. "Thank you," he said quietly, and hung up. When he turned back to her, he saw that her face was suddenly contorted. She gasped and desperately clutched her naked belly.

Later, in the same hospital, the same doctor was saying, "The injection we gave her will start working right away." She was screaming piteously in the bed, sweat streaming from every pore of her flesh, eyes rolling in terror and disbelief.

"I didn't bargain for this," he whispered. The doctor looked at him blankly.

She once had said: You can't make deals with God.

(The damned, he thought, the forgotten souls in Hell: do they suffer more than this? Can they possibly scream louder? Sweat more? Do they feel more excruciating pain? Then he told himself: Don't be a fool. You don't believe in all that.)

A hospital functionary was asking him the name of her next of kin. He gave the husband's name, address, phone number. Meanwhile, the doctor was muttering, "No, I think it's a little bit more complicated than an ulcer. Looks like it may be the same sort of thing your father had, but we can't be sure without tests. Has she been sick very long, do you know? Any medical treatment at *all,* other than those damn Scotch Cows? I wish I knew her doctor's name, because the condition appears to be pretty far progressed. I guess the husband will be able to give us that information when he gets here . . ."

She sank finally into drugged torpor and soft moans, so he let himself stagger out into the corridor and into the solarium. Somebody had left a newspaper on one of the chairs, folded to a garish advertisement for a sale: BARGAINS BARGAINS BARGAINS were promised in a bold headline across the top of the page. Bargains, he thought, there are all kinds of bargains. Another fly hovered over the same plastic plant—or was it the same fly, another plastic plant? he wondered dully. It touched down briefly. As it buzzed off, he said silently, indignantly: Damn it, I thought we had a deal.

The fly buzzed past his head. He brushed it away as he felt a cold response from deep inside himself.

You did have a deal, the dark unspoken voice assured him. *But with whom?*

The three syllables clanged in his mind over and over, like a triplet of notes struck on an underground bell, ding-dang-dong, sour and hollow, a fearsome fugue, eternally entwining, endlessly repeated. Ding-dang-dong. Ding-dang-dong. But-with-whom. Ding-dang-dong.

He left the hospital quickly, to escape the husband and Anyone Else. He knew there would be no escaping the bell. That he would hear forever.

RAY RUSSELL's books include the novels *The Case Against Satan, The Colony, Incubus, Princess Pamela,* and *The Bishop's Daughter,* and the collections *Sardonicus and Other Stories, The Book of Hell* and *The Devil's Mirror.* His latest book is *Haunted Castles.* At present, the former executive editor of *Playboy* is occupied with the writing of another novel, a long poem "and, of course, short stories. Always short stories."

CLIVE BARKER

Lost Souls

Everything the blind woman had told Harry she'd seen was undeniably real. Whatever inner eye Norma Paine possessed—that extraordinary skill that allowed her to scan the island of Manhattan from the Broadway Bridge to Battery Park and yet not move an inch from her tiny room on Seventy-fifth—that eye was as sharp as any knife juggler's. Here was the derelict house on Ridge Street, with the smoke stains besmirching the brick. Here was the dead dog that she'd described, lying on the sidewalk as though asleep, but that it lacked half its head. Here too, if Norma was to be believed, was the demon that Harry had come in search of: the shy and sublimely malignant Cha'Chat.

The house was not, Harry thought, a likely place for a desperado of Cha'Chat's elevation to be in residence. Though the infernal brethren could be a loutish lot, to be certain, it was Christian propaganda which sold them as dwellers in excrement and ice. The escaped demon was more likely to be downing fly eggs and vodka at the Waldorf-Astoria than concealing itself amongst such wretchedness.

But Harry had gone to the blind clairvoyant in desperation, having failed to locate Cha'Chat by any means conventionally available to a private eye such as himself. He was, he had admitted to her, responsible for the fact that the demon was loose at all. It seemed he'd never learned, in his all too frequent encounters with the Gulf and its progeny, that Hell possessed a genius for deceit. Why else had he believed in the child that had tottered into view just as he'd leveled his gun at Cha'Chat? —a child, of course, which had evaporated into a cloud of tainted air as soon as the diversion was redundant and the demon had made its escape.

Now, after almost three weeks of vain pursuit, it was almost Christmas in New York; season of goodwill and suicide. Streets thronged; the air like salt in wounds; Mammon in glory. A more perfect playground for Cha'Chat's despite could scarcely be imagined. Harry had to find the demon quickly, before it did serious damage; find it and return it to the pit from which it had come. In extremis he would even use the binding syllables which the late Father Hesse had vouchsafed to him once, accompanying them with such dire warnings that Harry had never even written them down. Whatever it took. Just as long as Cha'Chat didn't see Christmas Day this side of the Schism.

It seemed to be colder inside the house on Ridge Street than out. Harry could feel the chill creep through both pairs of socks and start to numb his feet. He was making his way along the second landing when he heard the sigh. He turned, fully expecting to see Cha'Chat standing there, its eye cluster looking a dozen ways at once, its cropped fur rippling. But no. Instead a young woman stood at the end of the corridor. Her undernourished features suggested Puerto Rican extraction, but that—and the fact that she was heavily pregnant—was all Harry had time to grasp before she hurried away down the stairs.

Listening to the girl descend, Harry knew that Norma had been wrong. If Cha'Chat had been here, such a perfect victim would not have been allowed to escape with her eyes in her head. The demon wasn't here.

Which left the rest of Manhattan to search.

The night before, something very peculiar had happened to Eddie Axel. It had begun with his staggering out of his favorite bar, which was six blocks from the grocery store he owned on Third Avenue. He was drunk, and happy; and with reason. Today he had reached the age of fifty-five. He had married three times in those years; he had sired four legitimate children and a handful of bastards; and—perhaps most significantly—he'd made Axel's Superette a highly lucrative business. All was well with the world.

But Jesus, it was chilly! No chance, on a night threatening a second Ice Age, of finding a cab. He would have to walk home.

He'd got maybe half a block, however, when—miracle of miracles—a cab did indeed cruise by. He'd flagged it down, eased himself in, and the weird times had begun.

For one, the driver knew his name.

"Home, Mr. Axel?" he'd said. Eddie hadn't questioned the godsend. Merely mumbled, "Yes," and assumed this was a birthday treat, courtesy of someone back at the bar.

Perhaps his eyes had flickered closed; perhaps he'd even slept. Whatever, the next thing he knew the cab was driving at some speed through streets he didn't recognize. He stirred himself from his doze. This was the Village, surely; an area Eddie kept clear of. His neighborhood was the high Nineties, close to the store. Not for him the decadence of the Village, where a shop sign offered "Ear piercing. With or without pain" and young men with suspicious hips lingered in doorways.

"This isn't the right direction," he said, rapping on the Perspex between him and the driver. There was no word of apology or explanation forthcoming, however, until the cab made a turn toward the river, drawing up in a street of warehouses, and the ride was over.

"This is your stop," said the chauffeur. Eddie didn't need a more explicit invitation to disembark.

As he hauled himself out the cabbie pointed to the murk of an empty lot between two benighted warehouses. "She's been waiting for you," he said, and drove away. Eddie was left alone on the sidewalk.

Common sense counseled a swift retreat, but what now caught his eye glued him to the spot. There she stood—the woman of whom the cabbie had spoken—and she was the most obese creature Eddie had ever set his sight upon. She had more chins than fingers, and her fat, which threatened at every place to spill from the light summer dress she wore, gleamed with either oil or sweat.

"*Eddie,*" she said. Everybody seemed to know his name tonight. As she moved toward him, tides moved in the fat of her torso and along her limbs.

"Who are you?" Eddie was about to inquire, but the words died when he realized the obesity's feet weren't touching the ground. *She was floating.*

Had Eddie been sober he might well have taken his cue then

and fled, but the drink in his system mellowed his trepidation. He stayed put.

"Eddie," she said. "Dear Eddie. I have some good news and some bad news. Which would you like first?"

Eddie pondered this one for a moment. "The good," he concluded.

"You're going to die tomorrow," came the reply, accompanied by the tiniest of smiles.

"That's good?" he said.

"Paradise awaits your immortal soul . . ." she murmured. "Isn't that a joy?"

"So what's the bad news?"

She plunged her stubby-fingered hand into the crevasse between her gleaming tits. There came a little squeal of complaint, and she drew something out of hiding. It was a cross between a runty gecko and a sick rat, possessing the least fetching qualities of both. Its pitiful limbs pedaled at the air as she held it up for Eddie's perusal. "This," she said, "is your immortal soul."

She was right, thought Eddie: the news was not good.

"Yes," she said. "It's a pathetic sight, isn't it?" The soul drooled and squirmed as she went on. "It's undernourished. It's weak to the point of expiring altogether. And *why?*" She didn't give Eddie a chance to reply. "A paucity of good works . . ."

Eddie's teeth had begun to chatter. "What am I supposed to do about it?" he asked.

"You've got a little breath left. You must compensate for a lifetime of rampant profiteering—"

"I don't follow."

"Tomorrow, turn Axel's Superette into a Temple of Charity, and you may yet put some meat on your soul's bones."

She had begun to ascend, Eddie noticed. In the darkness above her, there was sad, sad music, which now wrapped her up in minor chords until she was entirely eclipsed.

The girl had gone by the time Harry reached the street. So had the dead dog. At a loss for options, he trudged back to Norma Paine's apartment, more for the company than the satisfaction of telling her she had been wrong.

"I'm never wrong," she told him over the din of the five televisions and as many radios that she played perpetually. The cacophony was, she claimed, the only sure way to keep those of the spirit world from incessantly intruding upon her privacy: the babble distressed them. "I saw power in that house on Ridge Street," she told Harry, "sure as shit."

Harry was about to argue when an image on one of the screens caught his eye. An outside news broadcast pictured a reporter standing on a sidewalk across the street from a store ("Axel's Superette," the sign read) from which bodies were being removed.

"What is it?" Norma demanded.

"Looks like a bomb went off," Harry replied, trying to trace the reporter's voice through the din of the various stations.

"Turn up the sound," said Norma. "I like a disaster."

It was not a bomb that had wrought such destruction, it emerged, but a riot. In the middle of the morning a fight had begun in the packed grocery store; nobody quite knew why. It had rapidly escalated into a bloodbath. A conservative estimate put the death toll at thirty, with twice as many injured. The report, with its talk of a spontaneous eruption of violence, gave fuel to a terrible suspicion in Harry.

"Cha'Chat . . ." he murmured.

Despite the noise in the little room, Norma heard him speak. "What makes you so sure?" she said.

Harry didn't reply. He was listening to the reporter's recapitulation of the events, hoping to catch the location of Axel's Superette. And there it was. Third Avenue, between Ninety-fourth and Ninety-fifth.

"Keep smiling," he said to Norma, and left her to her brandy and the dead gossiping in the bathroom.

Linda had gone back to the house on Ridge Street as a last resort, hoping against hope that she'd find Bolo there. He was, she vaguely calculated, the likeliest candidate for father of the child she carried, but there'd been some strange men in her life at that time; men with eyes that seemed golden in certain lights; men with sudden, joyless smiles. Anyway, Bolo hadn't been at the house, and here she was—as she'd known she'd be all along —alone. All she could hope to do was lie down and die.

But there was death and death. There was that extinction she prayed for nightly, to fall asleep and have the cold claim her by degrees; and there was that other death, the one she saw whenever fatigue drew her lids down. A death that had neither dignity in the going nor hope of a Hereafter; a death brought by a man in a gray suit whose face sometimes resembled a half-familiar saint, and sometimes a wall of rotting plaster.

Begging as she went, she made her way uptown toward Times Square. Here, amongst the traffic of consumers, she felt safe for a while. Finding a little deli, she ordered eggs and coffee, calculating the meal so that it just fell within the begged sum. The food stirred the baby. She felt it turn in its slumber, close now to waking. Maybe she should fight on a while longer, she thought. If not for her sake, for that of the child.

She lingered at the table, turning the problem over, until the mutterings of the proprietor shamed her out onto the street again.

It was late afternoon, and the weather was worsening. A woman was singing nearby, in Italian; some tragic aria. Tears close, Linda turned from the pain the song carried, and set off again in no particular direction.

As the crowd consumed her, a man in a gray suit slipped away from the audience that had gathered around the street-corner diva, sending the youth he was with ahead through the throng to be certain they didn't lose their quarry.

Marchetti regretted having to forsake the show. The singing much amused him. Her voice, long ago drowned in alcohol, was repeatedly that vital semitone shy of its intended target—a perfect testament to imperfectibility—rendering Verdi's high art laughable even as it came within sight of transcendence. He would have to come back here when the beast had been dispatched. Listening to that spoiled ecstasy brought him closer to tears than he'd been for months; and he liked to weep.

Harry stood across Third Avenue from Axel's Superette and watched the watchers. They had gathered in their hundreds in the chill of the deepening night, to see what could be seen; nor were they disappointed. The bodies kept coming out: in bags, in bundles; there was even something in a bucket.

"Does anybody know exactly what happened?" Harry asked his fellow spectators.

A man turned, his face ruddy with the cold.

"The guy who ran the place decided to *give* the stuff away," he said, grinning at this absurdity. "And the store was fuckin' swamped. Someone got killed in the crush—"

"I heard the trouble started over a can of meat," another offered. "Somebody got beaten to death with a can of meat."

This rumor was contested by a number of others; all had versions of events.

Harry was about to try and sort fact from fiction when an exchange to his right diverted him.

A boy of nine or ten had buttonholed a companion. "Did you smell her?" he wanted to know. The other nodded vigorously. "Gross, huh?" the first ventured. "Smelled better shit," came the reply, and the two dissolved into conspiratorial laughter.

Harry looked across at the object of their mirth. A hugely overweight woman, underdressed for the season, stood on the periphery of the crowd and watched the disaster scene with tiny, glittering eyes.

Harry had forgotten the questions he was going to ask the watchers. What he remembered, clear as yesterday, was the way his dreams conjured the infernal brethren. It wasn't their curses he recalled, nor even the deformities they paraded: it was the smell off them. Of burning hair and halitosis; of veal left to rot in the sun. Ignoring the debate around him, he started in the direction of the woman.

She saw him coming, the rolls of fat at her neck furrowing as she glanced across at him.

It was Cha'Chat, of that Harry had no doubt. And to prove the point, the demon took off at a run, the limbs and prodigious buttocks stirred to a fandango with every step. By the time Harry had cleared his way through the crowd the demon was already turning the corner into Ninety-fifth Street, but its stolen body was not designed for speed, and Harry rapidly made up the distance between them. The lamps were out in several places along the street, and when he finally snatched at the demon, and heard the sound of tearing, the gloom disguised the vile truth for fully five seconds until he realized that Cha'Chat had somehow sloughed off its usurped flesh, leaving Harry holding a great coat of ectoplasm, which was already melting like overripe cheese. The demon, its burden shed, was away; slim as hope and twice as slippery. Harry dropped the coat of filth and gave chase, shouting Hesse's syllables as he did so.

Surprisingly, Cha'Chat stopped in its tracks, and turned to Harry. The eyes looked all ways but Heavenward; the mouth was wide and attempting laughter. It sounded like someone vomiting down an elevator shaft.

"*Words*, D'Amour?" it said, mocking Hesse's syllables. "You think I can be stopped with words?"

"No," said Harry, and blew a hole in Cha'Chat's abdomen before the demon's many eyes had even found the gun.

"*Bastard!*" it wailed, "*Cocksucker!*" and fell to the ground, blood the color of piss throbbing from the hole. Harry sauntered down the street to where it lay. It was almost impossible to slay a demon of Cha'Chat's elevation with bullets; but a scar was shame enough amongst their clan. Two, almost unbearable.

"Don't," it begged when he pointed the gun at its head. "Not the face."

"Give me one good reason why not."

"You'll need the bullets," came the reply.

Harry had expected bargains and threats. This answer silenced him.

"There's something going to get loose tonight, D'Amour," Cha'Chat said. The blood that was pooling around it had begun to thicken and grow milky, like melted wax. "Something wilder than me."

"Name it," said Harry.

The demon grinned. "Who knows?" it said. "It's a strange season, isn't it? Long nights. Clear skies. Things get born on nights like this, don't you find?"

"*Where?*" said Harry, pressing the gun to Cha'Chat's nose.

"You're a bully, D'Amour," it said reprovingly. "You know that?"

"*Tell me . . .*"

The thing's eyes grew darker; its face seemed to blur.

"South of here, I'd say . . ." it replied. "A hotel . . ." The tone of its voice was changing subtly; the features losing their solidity. Harry's trigger finger itched to give the damned thing a wound that would keep it from a mirror for life, but it was still talking, and he couldn't afford to interrupt its flow. ". . . on Forty-fourth," it said. "Between Sixth . . . Sixth and Broadway." The voice was indisputably feminine now. "Blue blinds," it murmured. "I can see blue blinds . . ."

As it spoke the last vestiges of its true features fled, and suddenly it was Norma who was bleeding on the sidewalk at Harry's feet.

"You wouldn't shoot an old lady, would you?" she piped up.

The trick lasted seconds only, but Harry's hesitation was all that Cha'Chat needed to fold itself between one plane and the next, and flit. He'd lost the creature, for the second time in a month.

And to add discomfort to distress, it had begun to snow.

The small hotel that Cha'Chat had described had seen better years; even the light that burned in the lobby seemed to tremble on the brink of expiring. There was nobody at the desk. Harry was about to start up the stairs when a young man whose pate was shaved as bald as an egg, but for a single kiss curl that was oiled to his scalp, stepped out of the gloom and took hold of his arm.

"There's nobody here," he informed Harry.

In better days Harry might have cracked the egg open with his bare fists, and enjoyed doing so. Tonight he guessed he would come off the worse. So he simply said, "Well, I'll find another hotel then, eh?"

Kiss Curl seemed placated; the grip relaxed. In the next instant Harry's hand found his gun, and the gun found Kiss Curl's chin. An expression of bewilderment crossed the boy's face as he fell back against the wall, spitting blood.

As Harry started up the stairs, he heard the youth yell, "Darrieux!" from below.

Neither the shout nor the sound of the struggle had roused any response from the rooms. The place was empty. It had been elected, Harry began to comprehend, for some purpose other than hostelry.

As he started along the landing a woman's cry, begun but never finished, came to meet him. He stopped dead. Kiss Curl was coming up the stairs behind him two or three at a time; ahead, someone was dying. This couldn't end well, Harry suspected.

Then the door at the end of the corridor opened, and suspicion became plain fact. A man in a gray suit was standing on the threshold, skinning off a pair of bloodied surgical gloves. Harry knew him vaguely; indeed had begun to sense a terrible pattern in all of this from the moment he'd heard Kiss Curl call his employer's name. This was Darrieux Marchetti; also called the Cankerist; one of that whispered order of theological assassins whose directives came from Rome, or Hell, or both.

"D'Amour," he said.

Harry had to fight the urge to be flattered that he had been remembered.

"What happened here?" he demanded to know, taking a step toward the open door.

"Private business," the Cankerist insisted. "Please, no closer."

Candles burned in the little room, and by their generous light, Harry could see the bodies laid out on the bare bed. The woman from the house on Ridge Street, and her child. Both had been dispatched with Roman efficiency.

"She protested," said Marchetti, not overly concerned that Harry was viewing the results of his handiwork. "All I needed was the child."

"What was it?" Harry demanded. "A demon?"

Marchetti shrugged. "We'll never know," he said. "But at this time of year there's usually something that tries to get in under the wire. We like to be safe rather than sorry. Besides, there are those—I number myself amongst them—that believe there is such a thing as a surfeit of Messiahs—"

"Messiahs?" said Harry. He looked again at the tiny body.

"There was power there, I suspect," said Marchetti. "But it could have gone either way. Be thankful, D'Amour. Your world isn't ready for revelation." He looked past Harry to the youth, who was at the top of the stairs. "Patrice. Be an angel, will you, bring the car over? I'm late for Mass."

He threw the gloves back onto the bed.

"You're not above the law," said Harry.

"Oh *please*," the Cankerist protested, "let's have no nonsense. It's too late at night."

Harry felt a sharp pain at the base of his skull, and a trace of heat where blood was running.

"Patrice thinks you should go home, D'Amour. And so do I."

The knife point was pressed a little deeper.

"Yes?" said Marchetti.

"Yes," said Harry.

"He was here," said Norma, when Harry called back at the house.

"Who?"

"Eddie Axel; of Axel's Superette. He came through, clear as daylight."

"Dead?"

"Of course dead. He killed himself in his cell. Asked me if I'd seen his soul."

"And what did you say?"

"I'm a telephonist, Harry; I just make the connections. I don't pretend to understand the metaphysics." She picked up the bottle of brandy Harry had set on the table beside her chair. "How sweet of you," she said. "Sit down. Drink."

"Another time, Norma. When I'm not so tired." He went to the door. "By the way," he said. "You were right. There *was* something on Ridge Street . . ."

"Where is it now?"

"Gone . . . home."

"And Cha'Chat?"

"Still out there somewhere. In a foul temper . . ."

"Manhattan's seen worse, Harry."

It was little consolation, but Harry muttered his agreement as he closed the door.

The snow was coming on more heavily all the time.

He stood on the step and watched the way the flakes spiraled in the lamplight. No two, he had read somewhere, were ever alike. When such variety was available to the humble snowflake, could he be surprised that events had such unpredictable faces?

Each moment was its own master, he mused, as he put his head between the blizzard's teeth, and he would have to take whatever comfort he could find in the knowledge that between this chilly hour and dawn there were innumerable such moments—blind maybe, and wild and hungry—but all at least eager to be born.

CLIVE BARKER was already known as a playwright *(Franken-stein in Love, The History of the Devil,* etc.) when his *Books of Blood I–III* were published in 1984. Only a year later three more volumes of *The Books of Blood* appeared, as did a novel, *The Damnation Game.* That same year he saw a feature film, *Underworld,* made from his original screenplay, and he won both the British Fantasy Award and the World Fantasy Award. Upcoming: more films, a children's book, a fantasy novel, and further short stories.

PART IV

Dying All the Time

ROBERT BLOCH

Reaper

After the kids have grown up and moved away, a new child comes into your house.

His name is Death.

He comes quietly, without the wail of an infant, and he won't keep you up at night or make daily demands on your attention. But somehow you'll know he's there to stay. As he keeps growing, getting bigger and stronger with each passing day, you become smaller and weaker. Sooner or later there'll be the inevitable confrontation—and when it comes, you're the one who'll have to go.

Ross wrote these lines on the morning of his sixty-fifth birthday, then put them aside.

He was tired of writing about Death with a capital *D*. As an author of dark fantasy he'd done more than his share of dramatizing man's mortality, and it was difficult to find a fresh approach. Too many writers had exhausted the idea—Death as an angel, Death setting an appointment in Samarra, Death taking a holiday, Death trapped up a tree, Death forestalled, Death deceived. And it was all wishful thinking. There's nothing angelic about the Grim Reaper; he takes no holidays, he won't be fooled or forestalled. Death is an impersonal force, not an articulate and articulated skeleton swinging a scythe.

Ross shrugged and left his desk. After all, a man is entitled to take time off and celebrate his birthday, even if nobody else cares whether he lives or dies.

His parents and relatives were long gone and he'd never married. During the years he spent here in an old house on the peninsula of upper Michigan, Ross formed no friendships. He corresponded with his agent and editors, but his only personal contact with other people came when he drove into town for groceries.

Ross was a loner, but he never felt lonely. Newspapers, magazines and books came from his mailbox, and his children kept him company.

His children stood on the bookshelves of his workroom, row on row—the novels with their stiff spines and sturdy skins, the short stories secure within the pages of magazines and anthologies. Some of them, transformed by translation, spoke in foreign tongues. Others appeared only in original editions, their voices weakened to a whisper by the passing years. But here and abroad, in or out of print, they still lived, still possessed the power to speak to new readers in time to come.

Ross regarded them with parental pride, for even the least of the lot contained something of himself. He loved his children—and envied them, because they would outlive him. Eventually, of course, they too must die—their spines would sag, their bindings fall apart, their pages crumble. But long before that happened his own spine would cease its support, the skin binding his body would wrinkle and wither until what was within disintegrated.

It was already beginning to happen now. Now, as the years took their relentless toll; as eyes blurred, teeth decayed, aches and pains proliferated, memory dimmed and thought strayed from his control to focus on fear.

Ross sought the sunlight outside his house and went for a walk in the woods. But there were shadows lurking among the trees, and fear walked with him. Try as he would, he couldn't shake off the thought of Death—Death with a capital *D*. Sooner or later it would come, bringing eternal sleep.

To sleep, perchance to dream—

This was what he really feared. The mind continues to function when you sleep. Suppose it continues to function when you die. Suppose consciousness lives on, even in the grave, in the deep, damp darkness where the brain lies buried within a rotting corpse, imprisoned yet aware, unable to escape from the ultimate eternity of hopeless horror.

Does pain still register? If you avoid the terrors of entombment, will cremation bring a torment like the fires of hell?

His mind dwelt on the ways the end might come—the sudden violence of accident or even murder, or the slow agonies of terminal illness. As Ross walked on the sunlight faded and the shadows deepened. There was no solace to be found here in the woods.

Back at the house he prepared a solitary meal, then had a few drinks, but it was hardly a birthday celebration. The thought obsessed him—how would he meet Death?

And that night, after sinking into troubled slumber, he met Death in a dream.

There he was, the King of Terrors himself, a gleaming skeleton standing at the foot of Ross's bed. The bony fingers dangling from his left wrist were curled around an old-fashioned hourglass; the fleshless talons below the right wrist grasped the handle of a scythe.

Ross stared at the cruel curve of the scythe blade—the blade of the Grim Reaper. Death, he realized, was not a child. The apparition before him embodied all the attributes of legend, the skeletal symbol of tradition and the Tarot.

Ross also realized he was dreaming.

"Wrong."

There was no sound, but Ross heard the word, even as he saw the movement of the jutting jaw.

"No!" Ross was talking in his sleep. "You *can't* be real—you're just a figment of my imagination."

Death laughed soundlessly, but Ross heard him, heard the unspoken words that followed.

"What about those books and stories you've written? All of them are figments of your imagination too, but they're real enough. They exist because you created them."

"I didn't create you," Ross murmured.

"That's because there was no need," said Death. "Imagination possesses a power of its own. And the imagination of millions of men before you gave me semblance and substance. Believe me, I'm as real as you are. Even more so, since you will die and I'll go on forever." Once more the soundless chuckle came.

"Why are you here?" Ross whispered.

Death motioned with his scythe and the sound of the swishing blade was audible enough. "Your hour has come."

Ross's head stirred on the pillow. "But I don't want to die!"

"Few men do, unless prompted by unbearable agony. Consider yourself lucky to be spared such suffering."

Ross shuddered. "Please, I beg of you—"

"Beggars die. And so do kings. That's true democracy."

Suddenly Ross became conscious of the creeping chill. His body was invaded by a numbing cold that turned blood into ice.

"No!" he gasped. "There's got to be some way—"

Slowly the skull nodded atop its bony perch. "You want to make a bargain, I take it."

"Can that be possible?" Ross murmured.

"Of course." Skeleton fingers stroked the scythe blade with a rattling sound. "Once I walked the world with this weapon and wielded it upon each man, woman or child at the appointed time."

Death shifted the hourglass cradled against his rib cage. "But the world changed. Instead of a few thousands, there are millions of mortals, far too many to fall beneath a single scythe.

"At first I had help. Famines and pestilence, epidemics of cholera, bubonic plague, a score of other fatal diseases. But medicine advanced and the numbers of survivors grew again.

"For a while wars solved my problem. Genghis Khan, Attila, Tamerlane and a hundred others in the past—men like Napoleon, Hitler, Stalin—gave me battles where fifty thousand fell in a single day.

"I still have wars, even new drugs and bugs, but it's never enough, not in this era of population explosion. That's why I'm prepared to make an offer."

Ross scowled in sleep. "I'm not a ruler or a general—just an ordinary man."

"I don't expect anything extraordinary," said the voice that was not a voice. "But every little bit helps. What do you say to dealing with me on a one-to-one basis? One extra year of life for each death?"

"Immortality?"

"I don't promise that. You may grow weary and decide to end our bargain. Meanwhile let's call it a stay of execution." The jawbone of the skull quivered in silent mirth.

Again Ross frowned. "But you're asking me to become a murderer—"

"You've already committed murder many times in your mind and described the deeds on paper."

"That's different. I couldn't actually kill another human being."

"Why not? Life is meaningless. Everyone dies, sooner or later." The skull's grin gleamed. "And you can choose whoever you wish. Think of the power I'm giving you."

"I don't want such power!"

"Not even if it's power to do good?" Once more the bony fingers caressed the scythe. "Look around you. The world is filled with those who deserve to die. Make the proper choices and you won't be dealing death—you'll be dealing justice."

"It's still murder," Ross whispered.

"Consider yourself an Avenging Angel," Death murmured. "Isn't there someone you know of who has forfeited the right to live?"

Ross hesitated, then nodded in slumber. "You're right, there *is* someone. A man named Wade, the one who butchered all those women and got off with a life sentence, which means he'll be out again in a few years. I wouldn't mind killing a mass murderer."

"Sorry," Death told him. "Wade happens to be one of my emissaries. We made a deal long ago and he still has years to live, in or out of prison."

Ross sighed. "Then I'll settle for the people who permitted such a miscarriage of justice. His scumbag lawyer, the nit-picking judge, the stupid jury—"

The skull's grin seemed to broaden. "Don't forget the parole officer who was supposed to keep an eye on him after a previous conviction, or the juvenile authorities who turned him loose before that. If you expect to do away with everyone connected with the case you'll be quite a mass murderer yourself."

"But there must be somebody who's ultimately responsible!"

"You decide. The power to slay or spare will be yours alone. I'll never force you to act if you don't want to. That's part of our contract."

"I still don't like the idea—"

Death swung his scythe. "Do you like this better?" He leaned forward over the foot of the bed. "Think of what I'm offering.

One whole year in return for one little life. Choose your own time, your own candidate, your own method."

"Suppose I get caught."

"You won't. Your whole career has been devoted to devising fictional fatalities, putting perfect crimes on paper. Use the same ingenuity in your own behalf and there's no danger." The bony arm raised the scythe and a blast of freezing air fanned Ross's face. "So what will it be? Do or die?"

Ross stirred restlessly. "And if I accept your offer—what then?"

Skeleton shoulders shrugged. "Nothing. No contracts signed in blood, no hocus-pocus. Just a verbal agreement. One life, one year. Call it a birthday present." The skull's eye sockets fixed on Ross's face. "Well?"

"Done," Ross whispered.

Death raised the hourglass and reversed it. Slowly the sand began sifting down into the lower half, grain by grain.

"One year," Death murmured.

And vanished.

If, indeed, he had ever been there.

In the light of the morning sun Ross wasn't sure. The mind plays tricks.

So does the body.

By midafternoon he was back in bed, shivering in the sudden onslaught of chills and fever. Dreams can herald illness, he told himself. But as darkness deepened, the fever flamed, bringing visions—Death, with his fleshless face and soundless voice, his scythe and hourglass. How soon would the sand run out? When it did, the scythe would swing, and he feared that scythe. *Isn't there someone you know of who has forfeited the right to live?*

Ross tried to think. The mind is a computer, and in delirium the computer was down. Those rich writers with their fancy word processors—did their expensive equipment ever go down too? His mind was blank, blank as a computer screen, but now something flickered into view.

A face was forming. He'd seen it many times before, in close-up on television talk shows, peering out at him from newspaper pages, smiling smugly on the backs of book jackets.

Kevin Colfax. He knew the name. Thanks to the media,

everyone knew Kevin Colfax. Famous author. Owner of a villa on the Riviera, a fleet of classic cars, a sixth wife and a dozen mistresses.

Romans à clef, that's what they called his books. He cannibalized from the pages of *The National Enquirer* and *People* magazine, took the lives of celebrities and turned them into pornography—grossly explicit sex and vulgar violence to feed the fantasies of mindless millions bent on mental masturbation. His steamy sleaze boosted him to best-seller lists and the A lists of parties where lines of coke were snorted by upwardly mobile arrivistes who no longer had any place to go except where tripping might take them. But now he was where he really belonged —on Ross's hit list.

The face faded in the flush of fever and Ross murmured through dry, cracked lips. "Kill Kevin Colfax." Perspiration bathed his body as he sank into slumber.

When he awoke the following morning the fever was gone but resolution remained. Kevin Colfax deserved to die.

The only question was how— there must be a way that left no cluc.

Poison?

Over the years Ross had researched toxicology and amassed an imposing number of reference works. Amazing how many lethal compounds existed that were easy to procure, or concoct from simple substances found in almost every household. Fast-acting, fatal and almost undetectable if proper precautions were taken.

Once he knew what to look for, Ross lost no time in finding it. The insecticide had been outlawed years ago but he'd never bothered to throw it away and still had half the contents in a spray can. A bit of boiling on the stove and the stuff condensed, leaving a deady distillate that would kill on contact.

But how to make that contact?

He didn't know Kevin Colfax or anyone in the privileged circles which he orbited. There was no way of introducing a pinch of the poisonous substance into his food or drink or the powder he inhaled through his nasal passages. Colfax was surrounded by personal security designed to protect him from friends, foes and fans alike.

Fans.

Ross sat down at the typewriter and wrote a letter. A fan letter to Kevin Colfax, asking for an autographed photo.

He typed it quickly; the rubber gloves he'd donned didn't interfere with his speed. Nor did they interfere as he added a drop of water to a smidge of the poisonous powder, turning it to a paste, which he carefully smeared on the gummed flap of the stamped self-addressed return envelope enclosed in his letter.

The name and address on the envelope were faked, of course, but the poison was real. Real and reliable. One lick and the tongue would absorb the fatal dosage, bringing death in a matter of minutes.

Ross found Colfax's address in Who's Who, copied it on the outer envelope, affixed a stamp. Then he drove to a town thirty miles away from his own zip-code area and his gloved hand dropped death into the mailbox.

After that, all he had to do was wait.

Four days later he read the item in his morning paper.

POLICE PROBE
MYSTERY DEATH

NEW YORK (UPI) — Authorities here are investigating possibilities of foul play in the sudden death of Florence Rimpau, 23, personal secretary of best-selling novelist Kevin Colfax. According to her employer, Miss Rimpau appeared to be in perfect health at the time of her collapse while working on correspondence. Paramedics were unable to revive her and an autopsy has been ordered after medical reports indicated poison as a possible cause.

Ross let the paper slip from trembling fingers, and several anxious days followed before a follow-up story appeared. Florence Rimpau was more than a secretary; she had ambitions of pursuing a writing career herself, and according to grieving family members, she was eagerly awaiting the publication of her first novel when death came.

There was more. Results of the autopsy confirmed the poison theory but investigation uncovered no clues. Kevin Colfax himself was quickly exonerated of any connection with the case. Apparently the source of the poison and the method used to employ it were not discovered by police or pathologists. Ross could congratulate himself; he'd never be caught. It was indeed a perfect crime.

The perfect crime—but the wrong victim.

Ross read and shuddered. He was responsible for the death of an innocent girl, blighting a bright future and bringing sorrow to her family and friends. Why hadn't he anticipated such a possibility?

He knew the answer, of course. His eager act had been prompted by envy; it was jealousy, not justice, that motivated him to murder.

And to what end? His self-appointed enemy, Kevin Colfax, was still alive. If anything, the publicity surrounding the mysterious tragedy actually boosted the sales of his books.

The following months passed quickly, but to Ross each day seemed an eternity, and the nights were endless agonies of guilt-haunted dreams.

But time has a way of healing trauma and mending memories; as his next birthday neared, Ross realized that he had indeed survived another year.

Of course it really had nothing to do with his bargain, he told himself. That was only a dream. He would have lived on even without the nightmare about dealing with Death. And once the pangs of guilt lessened he found life sweet again. Just as he'd wished, there was time to read, relax and enjoy comforts and diversions.

And then time ran out.

Time ran out one night as Ross lay in bed, tossing and turning and cursing himself for a fool.

Diversion had been his downfall. Diversion, in the shapely form of one Janice Coy. Coy, he reflected bitterly, was hardly an appropriate surname for the young lady he'd casually picked up a month ago during an impromptu visit to a bar in a town nearby. At his age sex was hardly an imperative—at least he'd thought so until his encounter with Janice. He'd gone to the bar just for a drink, and it came as something of a surprise to find himself engaged in byplay with an attractive female. Byplay turned to foreplay, then fulfillment. When he discovered that his pleasure was Janice's business, Ross merely shrugged and paid. Goodbye, Janice.

Two weeks later it was Hello, Doctor.

Herpes. That's what the slut had given him. Dirty little tramp. Now he was suffering, but the sores would heal, there would be periods of remission. It could have been worse, he told himself; at least his condition wasn't fatal.

Only the scythe was fatal. The scythe, swinging in a silver arc through the darkness of his dreams.

Death stood beside his bed.

The scythe swung idly, but he knew its purpose. Death held up the hourglass and Ross saw that the last grains of sand were dwindling down into the lower half. And now, as the sand descended, the scythe rose. Suddenly the darkened room was very cold.

Death grinned.

"No!" Ross shook his head. "Not now—give me another chance!"

Death's grin was fixed, but the scythe wavered.

"You wish to renew our bargain?"

The voice that was not a voice echoed in Ross's ears and he nodded quickly. "Please—"

The grinning jaws moved. "As I recall, you meant to kill someone who deserved to die. But it didn't turn out that way, did it?"

"That was an accident," Ross quavered. "I made a mistake."

"A mistake which you still regret." Death paused, and then the question came. "Are you willing to take such a risk again?"

"Trust me," Ross whispered.

"It's your conscience I don't trust," said Death. "Are you really sure you can go through with this?"

Ross stared at the emptying hourglass as the final grains fell. Then he stared at the scythe as it rose, stared at the bright broad blade. If that blade descended its brightness would blur, bathed with his blood.

"I'm certain!" Ross cried. "I promise you!"

"Agreed."

The scythe withdrew, the hourglass reversed and once again the filled half of the double globe was uppermost. It would take a year for the sands to run out—the sands of Time.

"Happy birthday." Death turned, still grinning.

And disappeared.

* * *

It proved to be a happy birthday for Ross after all, because this time he knew what he must do.

This time he already had decided who deserved to die—Janice, the whore who'd infected him, who was still spreading disease among the innocent victims of her corrupt charms.

Once again it was merely a matter of method.

Ross knew nothing of Janice aside from his brief encounter, but in order to be successful the hunter must first learn the nature of the beast. Only when familiar with its habits and habitat can he stalk his prey.

So Ross hunted Janice out, hunted her down.

Finding her at the bar again was no problem. To pretend to be pleased at his second meeting was more difficult, and carrying the encounter through to its lustful conclusion was almost impossible in view of what he knew. But Ross managed.

To Janice, in the weeks that followed, Ross was just one of her regular tricks—an elderly john who made few demands on her professional skills and could always be counted on for a fast buck. Wham-bam-thank-you-ma'am.

She never realized he was a hunter studying his intended quarry, seeking a method to bring it down.

Ross already knew he possessed the means to ensure a foolproof fatality; his poison would leave no clue.

But how to use it? Janice's fans—if they could be called such—didn't write letters. It wasn't her autograph they were after. The poor fools never realized she was leaving them with a signature of another sort, the kind she'd left him. The filthy disease-spreader descrved to die, and die she must.

The good hunter is patient, and Ross's patience paid off. By the time of their third assignation he'd become familiar enough with Janice's habits to find his solution.

It was in the bathroom that he discovered it—the liquid solution of the bath oil she used. And the little plastic container which held it was almost empty.

During the course of their fourth encounter he excused himself and checked again. There was, he noted, just about enough oil left for one more loll in the tub. She'd probably bathe after he left, and neither she nor anyone else would detect the tiny amount of odorless, colorless liquid he added to it from the vial he carried. With any luck, the poison wouldn't take effect for a few minutes; by then she would have left the tub and prepared for bed. Of course there was the problem of the bath-oil container, which she'd probably empty and toss into the trash, but chances were that no one would notice. In any case he must be prepared to take that risk—and he did.

Once again he suffered the torments of waiting, but Janice didn't suffer at all. The following week, when he went back to the bar, the bartender gave him the sad news.

Only yesterday Janice's body had been discovered, sprawled across the bed in her crummy little apartment up the street. There wasn't a mark on her, outside of a few telltale herpes blisters; apparently she'd had a heart attack and there was no talk of an autopsy.

That was the bad news, and Ross took it calmly enough. It was the sad news that really shook him.

Janice hadn't died alone. What nobody knew—and what Janice never mentioned—was that the second bedroom of the shabby apartment was occupied by her child. The six-month-old baby boy had lain untended during the days following her death, and succumbed to starvation.

Ross left the bar in a daze. He went home but found no peace there. Even though the bartender had been right and there was no investigation, even though the police never knocked on his door, Ross took no comfort in his safety.

His mission was successful, but it hadn't stopped there. He was no Avenging Angel—he was the killer of an innocent child.

Inner torment turned to outer agony. It wasn't a herpes flare-up, but *psyche* tormented *soma*. Ross couldn't work, couldn't read or relax. Worse still, he couldn't eat or sleep. When at last he summoned a doctor he was too weak to walk. He ended up in the hospital with an IV in his arm and twenty-four-hour nursing care. They force-fed him, pumped him full of medication, until eventually he came around.

But the doctor was profoundly and professionally puzzled. "Frankly, I don't know what to tell you," he admitted. "EKG, CAT scan, all those lab tests, and I still can't come up with a damned thing. Except the herpes, of course, and that's in remission. If I had to make a guess, I'd say the problem is geriatric."

"Meaning what?" Ross said.

"You're sixty-six, going on sixty-seven. According to actuarial tables you should be good for quite a while yet. Trouble is, the human body doesn't always go by statistics. I've seen cases a damn sight younger than you get a clean bill of health, and two days after the examination—bingo." The doctor tried to soften his statement with a smile. "I guess it all comes down to the old saying. When you gotta go, you gotta go."

"But I don't feel old," Ross murmured. "Just weak—"

The doctor shrugged. "That will pass. Once you get your strength back, chances are you'll be okay. Your vital signs check out. But from now on you'd better settle down and take things easy. I'm sending you home on a strict diet, no more alcohol, no smoking. Aside from that, the only thing I can tell you is to watch yourself."

Ross watched himself when he got home but he didn't like what he saw. Whether the result of his crime or the ravages of illness, the face staring back at him in the mirror was that of an old man.

When you gotta go, you gotta go.

If his appearance startled him, he was even more shocked by other physical changes. Although he gradually gained weight he still hadn't the strength to cope with daily routine. Cooking and housekeeping chores drained him to a point where leisure pursuits became pointless. Running errands became a burden, going up the stairs was like climbing Mount Everest.

Ever rest? Not here, not any longer. *When you gotta go—*

Finally, he went.

Though his mind balked and his body rebelled, Ross forced himself to make the rounds of local facilities. Rest homes, retirement homes, convalescent homes—none were really homelike, and most were mere warehouses for weary wretches on their last legs, wheelchairs or deathbeds.

But Ross wasn't afraid of dying; even though he'd taken a life by mistake his debt to Death was paid up for months to come. And though his search was depressing, he continued until he found a place which seemed comparatively comfortable. It was by far the most expensive of the lot but he could afford the extra outlay, once his house was sold.

Putting it on the market and making the sale took longer than he'd expected, and so did the escrow period which followed.

Even with the extra time, Ross had his hands full. Emptying them was the real problem; emptying them of all he'd accumulated over the years. The hardest part was saying farewell to his children, disposing of them to a book dealer who carried them off in cartons that looked like miniature coffins. Ross wondered what kind of a coffin Janice's child had been buried in, then thrust the thought away. Forget the past, let the dead bury the dead. His job was to run the ads, confer with buyers of second-hand furniture and appliances, strip the house until only a bare box remained for him to rattle around in while waiting for the end.

Not the end, Ross reminded himself. *This is a new beginning.*

The Sunset Crest Rest Home proved to be a better choice than he'd hoped. Located in the suburbs of a nearby city, the building was modern and well equipped. There was laundry and cleaning service, a bus line nearby for shopping excursions into town. Meals were decently prepared, with special diets for those in need of them. His room was large, with plenty of closet space, a private bath, a comfortable bed and a view overlooking the grounds. Best of all, there was Sheila.

Sheila was one of the three RNs living in their own quarters on the premises. Tall, slender, brown-haired and blue-eyed, she might be close to fifty but didn't look her age. Since she was assigned to his floor Ross came to see quite a bit of her, and what he saw he liked.

To his surprise she had identified him as a writer, even claimed to have read some of his work. True or false, he was flattered by her recognition and pleased with her presence. Gradually Sheila's professional reticence relaxed and he found out more about her. As a young woman she'd worked in a major hospital, then left it for an apparently happy marriage. Three years ago, after her husband died, she returned to nursing. She bore widowhood well, but as acquaintance ripened Sheila confided that she sometimes missed the daily domesticity and privacy of her own home. This Ross could easily understand, for he missed his home too.

The thing that bothered him the most was his daily contact with fellow residents at mealtime, in the recreation room, the corridors or the outer grounds.

Ross couldn't make friends with his fellow residents. He

didn't like the way their minds dwelt on the past or how their bodies dealt with the present. He was irritated by the click of false teeth, the tremor and twitching of aging limbs, the continual counterpoint of coughing and throat-clearing. It disturbed him to see walkers and wheelchairs, depressed him when some familiar faces disappeared into darkened rooms equipped with oxygen tanks and hospital beds.

He did his best not to think about such things—cancer, strokes, heart attacks, Alzheimer's disease. No matter what the mirror told him, Ross didn't feel old. In fact, since getting to know Sheila, it seemed he was both looking and feeling younger. Hadn't the doctor said that if he took care of himself he could live for many years?

There was a future ahead for him and he needn't spend it here. Perhaps he couldn't manage living in another house, but there were apartments in the area. And Sheila had said she missed having a place of her own. She could make a home for herself, a home for him.

He thought about it one night as he lay in bed and stared up at the ceiling in the dark. His life wasn't over. After all, he was still in his sixties—come to think of it, he'd turn sixty-eight tomorrow—

"Will there be a tomorrow?"

The question came with chilling clarity. Only it wasn't *his* question, and the chill fastening him in freezing fingers was really present in the room. His eyes darted to the foot of the bed and the phosphorescent figure standing there.

Death grinned a greeting, raising the hourglass as the sand in the upper half emptied out.

But it was the scythe Ross watched—the scythe, swinging up in an inexorable arc, then swooping down swiftly, surely, bare blade moving to menace his bare throat.

"Stop!" he cried.

The scythe wavered.

"Another year?" Death whispered.

"Yes." Ross nodded eagerly. "Another year."

But the scythe did not withdraw; it remained poised, sharp and shimmering, ready to complete its relentless swing.

"You know the price," Death murmured.

"I'll pay it—you can be sure of that."

"Can I?" The scythe hung there, so close that even in shadow Ross could see the dark stains along its edges, the dried droplets encrusting the surface of the blade.

Death fixed him in an eyeless stare. "How do you know? Have you already selected your next victim?"

"Don't use that word! This time there'll be no mistake. No innocent will suffer."

Death shrugged. "But who is innocent? All must die, sooner or later." The scythe began to move forward again. "I can't trust you to be judge and jury any longer. There is only one law—a life for a life."

The blade swung down.

"Please!" Ross gasped. "You'll have your life. I swear it!"

The blade drew back. But Ross didn't stop trembling until Death's bony claw grasped the hourglass and turned it over again.

"Quickly," Death muttered. "It must be done quickly."

His voice was audible only to Ross's inner ear; outwardly it was as soundless as the shifting sands. And now voice and vision blurred, fading into the depths of sudden slumber.

That night Ross slept like the dead, but in the morning sunlight he was alive, basking in the bright promise of days to come. Death had vanished for another year, leaving only a faint, phantasmal echo of a parting word.

"Quickly."

But how could he obey? Ross pondered the problem as he shaved and dressed. Memories of his previous errors returned and stayed with him as he fled to the outer grounds. Sitting in the garden, he stared out at the street beyond, filled with a yearning to be a part of the life there once again.

A car sped by, its driver oblivious to his presence. Somehow cars always seemed to pick up speed when passing hospitals, sanatoriums or places like this. No one wanted to be reminded of what lay within. Life is for the living. *Have a good day.*

Ross's day didn't improve until he returned to his room that afternoon. To his surprise he found mail awaiting him—a single envelope, but an unusual one. Generally he received nothing but his monthly pension check and a few junk prize-contest items destined for the wastebasket. Ross was puzzled; outside of the mail-order advertisers, who cared about him?

Sheila.

Somehow she'd made it her business to learn his birthday, and sent him a card. Sheila cared.

Sunlight faded, but to Ross the world was bright again. Sheila cared, and he cared too.

That night when she looked in on him, he told her how he felt, what he hoped for the future.

"Our future," he said. "Together."

Ross awaited her reply, hoping for acceptance and steeling himself against rejection. But Sheila remained silent and there was no answer in her eyes.

"Don't you understand?" he murmured. "I'm asking you to marry me."

She sighed. "Of course. The Last-Nurse Syndrome."

Ross stared at her and Sheila nodded. "That's what the lawyers call it. An older man, bachelor or widower, falls ill, and a nurse attends him. When he recovers he proposes to her out of gratitude—"

"It's not just gratitude." Ross reached for her hand, capturing warmth and softness.

Warmth kindled into heat, softness firmed in response. Then she was in his arms and it was easy to speak, to pour out his plans.

Sheila listened, her smile broadening, eyes brightening. "Not so fast," she said. "It sounds wonderful, really it does, but you've got to give me a chance to think. We can't walk out of here tomorrow, you know. We must be practical—make sure there's enough for us to live on—find an apartment, furnish it. There's a million and one things to take care of. And I'd have to give notice."

"Then do it!" Ross said. "Now. Quickly."

When at last she left him his glow remained, dimmed only by a single shadow—or was it an echo again?

Quickly. Death's word. *It must be done quickly.*

That night he forced himself to consider the meaning behind the phrase, to think about the unthinkable.

And for the first time since his arrival here he sought his suitcase in the closet. To all appearances it was unpacked and empty; only he knew about the little pouch concealed in a zippered pocket at its base. Inside the pouch was the tiny glass vial and in the vial was the final potion of poison. At least he'd thought of it as the final potion when he packed it—a potion reserved for himself in case life here became unbearable.

But life was unbearable no longer and he needn't be spending it here. Which meant that now the potion would be final for somebody else.

Ross stared at the colorless contents swirling silently. Then he put the vial away and the swirling ceased. Now it was only his thoughts that swirled; poisonous thoughts which could not be put away any longer.

Tossing and turning through the night, he pondered. It must be done quickly—but to whom?

He had no enemies here. And bitter experience had taught him revenge was a meaningless motive. Ross remembered his resolve—no innocent would suffer.

"But who is innocent?" Death's words again. "All must die, sooner or later. A life for a life."

Questions in the dark, awaiting an answer. Then, just before dawn, Ross heard his own voice whispering a name.

"Mrs. Endicott."

There was his answer. Mrs. Endicott, the oldest resident here at the home. Ninety-three years old, blind and bedridden; she never ventured from her room down the hall but everyone knew about her. Sheer longevity made her an institution in the institution. "Imagine that—been here over twenty years and she still hangs on. Got to hand it to the old girl, having such a will to live."

Ross grimaced at the thought. Didn't the fools realize the truth? Couldn't they at least imagine what it must be like to lie sightless and helpless year after year without hope? Nobody had a will to live under such conditions; it was just that the poor blind body refused to obey the will to die. "Got to hand it to the old girl," they said. Well, he would hand it to her—hand her the release she longed for. It wouldn't be murder. This was euthanasia, an act of mercy.

Ross rose on Saturday morning strangely refreshed despite his lack of sleep. Now he knew what to do; better still, he knew he *wanted* to do it. The rest was just a matter of ways and means.

This was Sheila's day off, which made things even easier. She stopped by his room before leaving and told him she was going into town to consult with some rental agencies. "Don't worry, I'm going to stick to it until I find the right place for us. In case I get back late, I'll see you first thing in the morning. Oh, darling, I'm so excited—"

Her smile and embrace told him even more than her words, and Ross rejoiced as she went on her way.

As for him, he went to work.

He asked questions; careful, casual, unobtrusive questions. Mrs. Endicott's room was 409, halfway down the corridor to the left on this floor. Meals were brought to her at regular serving times; staff members looked in at intervals during the day. At nine the lights went off—not that it made any difference to the poor old lady. Bed checks came at three-hour intervals during the night, routine inspections by whoever was on floor duty at the opposite end of the hall. Tonight the orderly in charge was Bill Hawthorne, a nice enough young man but a bit on the lazy side. He tended to spend much of his time at the desk reading comic books between his appointed rounds. So much the better for all concerned, Ross thought. *Be patient, Mrs. Endicott. Help is on the way.*

It was he who had to be patient as the day dragged on. By evening he was really uptight. Sheila hadn't returned and the final hours seemed endless.

The first bed check came at midnight. When Hawthorne looked in on him Ross was under the covers, apparently fast asleep. But moments later, after Hawthorne closed the door, Ross rose and groped his way through darkness to the closet. Once he procured the vial he carried it back to bed and waited. In half an hour Bill Hawthorne would be back at his desk in the alcove at the far end of the hall. From there the orderly had no view of the corridor itself and only sounds would summon him forth to investigate their source.

But there would be no sounds.

Ross's door swung open silently at twelve-thirty. Ross's footsteps were noiseless as he started off slowly to the left. Hawthorne couldn't hear the pounding of his heart.

Quietly he made his way to room 409. Quietly he opened the

door. Quietly he entered, closed the door behind him, then tiptoed to the bed.

At first he saw only a blurred outline of the form nestled beneath the blankets. Gradually his eyes grew accustomed to the deep darkness. The room was cold, smelling faintly of disinfectant mingled with a sour scent, the odor of age. It emanated from the half-open mouth of the old woman as Ross gazed down at the wrinkled ruin of her face, the white wisps of hair which framed it. She wasn't sleeping, for the blind eyes were open in a sightless stare.

In a way the milky whiteness of the cataracts covering her pupils confirmed his conclusions; surely here was someone who would welcome the promise of relief, even though she'd never know how it came. Ross knew what to do now.

He would identify himself as Dr. Morgan, the new resident physician, come to bring her a sedative. All he need do was to pour the contents of the vial into the half-filled water glass on the nightstand and help guide it to her shriveled lips.

Softly, he spoke. "Mrs. Endicott?"

No response. Hearing isn't keen at ninety-three, Ross reminded himself, and he bent closer. "Mrs. Endicott—"

Still no answer. Gently he reached down and placed his hand on the bony brow. The cold brow—the icy brow that turned at his touch as the face pivoted on the pillow and the mouth yawned wide. No breath issued from it, only a telltale stench, and then he knew.

Mrs. Endicott was dead.

Somehow he managed to turn, leave, retrace his way along the corridor to the safety of his room. But there control ceased and he sank down upon the bed, still holding the useless vial he'd carried on a useless mission. Ross lay shuddering in silence as the vial slipped from trembling fingers and he closed his eyes in despair.

When he opened them again he had a visitor.

Despair gave way to horror, for this time Ross knew he wasn't dreaming. The fleshless figure beyond the end of his bed was quite real—either that or he'd gone mad. He shut his eyes once more, willing mind and vision to clear.

But when he blinked the figure was still there; it had moved closer, standing now at the side of his bed.

"You!" he whispered.

The skull bobbed slightly.

"What are you doing here?" Ross said.

"I had a call to pay down the hall."

Ross read mockery in the reply, read it in the ghastly grin. "You knew what I was going to do," he muttered. "You could have waited—"

"Her hour had come."

"You cheated me!"

"I do not cheat," Death said. "Remember, I warned you to act quickly. But what's done is done."

"Then why are you here?"

Death shrugged. "I think you already know the answer."

The skull was coming closer. Now Ross could see the greenish splotches of mold rotting in the yellowed cranial ridges. He could see the bloodstained edge of the scythe blade directly above him, see the hourglass clutched closely to the hollow rib cage, its upper half still packed with sand.

He shook his head. "It isn't time!"

"That's for me to decide," Death told him. "Your time is up."

"But we made a bargain—"

"A bargain you couldn't keep. I'll take no risk of further failure."

"I won't fail!" Ross's words came in a rush. "Give me a chance and I'll prove it. You make the choice—I don't care who's the victim as long as I stay alive."

"You really mean that?"

"I promise. Tell me who to kill, just give me the name."

"Very well." Death nodded. "The name is Sheila."

"Oh no!" Ross gasped. "Not Sheila—I can't—"

The grinning skull bent closer. "You see? Your promise is worthless." Death raised his scythe. "And so are you!"

Suddenly the blade came down, slashing at Ross's throat.

Frantic with fear, Ross jerked his head aside as the scythe descended, ripping into the pillow only an inch away from his neck. Blind instinct sent his hands forward, grasping the bony wrist as Death tugged to free the blade. In desperation Ross tightened his hold, twisting with all his might until the wristbones crunched under the squeezing pressure.

Then Death's grip loosened and the scythe fell free. As it dropped, Ross released his hold and his fingers closed around the handle of the weapon.

Clutching it, he felt the sudden surge of strength coursing up his arm. The power was in the scythe, and he possessed it now.

Death's soundless voice rose in a wail. "Give it back!"

Ross shook his head. "No. It's mine now."

"But you have no right—"

"This is my right." Ross waved the scythe.

The skeletal figure retreated and a wordless whisper came. "You fool—do you really think you can trick me so easily?"

"But I *have* tricked you!" Ross cried. Rising from the bed, he swirled the weapon and Death fell back.

Death's jaws opened and closed convulsively. "Give me my scythe!"

The power Ross held infused his arm and his voice. He lunged forward, shouting, "No—get out—"

The skeleton shape shrank to one side, hourglass clutched tightly to its bony breast. Once more Ross struck out, but the blade missed its mark.

For a moment there was silence; then the skull bobbed and its rotted teeth parted in a rustling reply. "I warn you. No one cheats Death."

Ross shook his head. "*I* am Death now!"

Ross raised the scythe, slashing at empty air, then blinked. The figure was gone.

He blinked again, eyes widening. Or was he merely opening them for the first time? Had he been talking and walking in his sleep again, was it another dream?

Then he glanced down at what he held in his hand. Death had disappeared but the scythe remained, and it was real. Death's weapon was here, its power pulsing from the blood-stained blade. *His* power, now.

As he stared at it, elation gave way to apprehension. Ross didn't want such power. All he'd meant to do was save himself, but he could never play the role of the Reaper, never wield the scythe. His power was useless.

Or was it?

As long as he possessed the weapon Death couldn't strike down his victims; he was vanquished. For an instant Ross warmed to the thought, but then warmth gave way to a wave of cold fear.

He stared at the blade again as the questions came. Suppose Death returned to claim the scythe while Ross slept. He couldn't stay awake forever, couldn't guard it night and day from now on. And what would happen if others saw the weapon; how could he explain its presence?

There was only one answer. He had to hide it. Hide it from others, hide it from Death.

Ross glanced at the bedside clock. Ten after two. In less than an hour the orderly would be making his rounds again. Whatever must be done had to be done quickly.

Gripping the handle of the scythe, he moved to the door, opened it, peered down the deserted hall. The orderly would be at his desk in the alcove at the far right and there was no way of passing him unnoticed. But to the left the hall ended in a back stairway.

It was to that stairway Ross tiptoed now, then descended silently to the first floor and the rear door leading to the grounds outside.

At the far end of the grounds was the garden, and in the garden roses bloomed, petals closed in protection against the night.

Ross inhaled their scent in darkness as he neared, knelt, then scraped away moist earth with the blade of the scythe. He dug deeply until the opening yawned clear. Taking a deep breath, he smashed the handle of the weapon down across his bended knee. The worn wood splintered and broke under the impact. His groping fingers found a rock. Raising it, he hammered at the scythe blade, hammered again and again until the metal twisted and bent, then sheared into shards. Gathering up the fragments, he thrust them into the depths of the hole. Covering it with loose dirt, he patted the soil flat so that no disturbance was detectable.

Panting, Ross rose to his feet. It was finished now. Not even Death would know where his weapon had been buried. And even if he found the hiding place it didn't matter, for the scythe was destroyed.

As he walked back across the garden, relief returned. Mounting the stairs, gliding silently down the hall to his room, Ross felt the possession of a power even greater than that of the scythe he'd stolen. No one could stop him now. Tomorrow, when he saw Sheila, they'd carry out their plans, find their future.

Tired but triumphant, Ross sank back across his bed. He stared into the darkness but he no longer feared it. No need to fear, for the Grim Reaper was no longer grim. The King of Terrors had been toppled from his throne.

Ross realized he'd erred in imagining Death as a child—perhaps the real truth was that Death was old. Wrenching away his scythe had been unexpectedly easy, for the old lack strength to resist. Hiding the weapon had been easy too, for wits are dimmed with age.

"No one cheats Death." Ross smiled at the memory of the threat, for it was feeble too. The passage of countless centuries had taken its toll; Death's only remaining power lay in his scythe, and now that power was broken and buried.

There was still another possibility which Ross, thinking clearly now, did not totally discount. Perhaps his vision of Death *had* been a dream after all; a recurrent dream born of vivid imagination. Maybe everything was part of nocturnal illusion; even his trip to the garden could be the product of a somnambulistic fugue in which he broke and buried something which didn't exist. But whatever the truth, he was free of it forever. Whether in nightmare or reality, the scythe would never strike him down, and he was safe at last.

Still smiling, Ross drifted into sleep.

It was sometime later that the orderly made his rounds and entered the room. He was smiling too, but not for long. What he saw there sent him stumbling out into the hall, summoning others with his screams. Others came to stare and search, but discovered no evidence of forced entry or any intruder.

What they did find, and could never explain, were the broken fragments of an empty hourglass on the floor at the bedside. And Ross, lying dead in the bed above, with his mouth wide open—and the sand stuffed down his throat.

ROBERT BLOCH's many novels include *The Scarf*, *The Kidnapper*, *Spiderweb*, *The Dead Beat*, *Firebug*, *The Couch*, *American Gothic*, and the classic *Psycho* and *Psycho II*. Collections include *The Opener of the Way*, *Pleasant Dreams*, *Yours Truly, Jack the Ripper*, *Bogey Men*, *The Skull of the Marquis de Sade*, *Tales in a Jugular Vein*, *Chamber of Horrors*, *Dragons and Nightmares* and *Such Stuff As Screams Are Made Of*. His latest novel is *The Night of the Ripper*. He is currently assembling three new collections and writing a new novel; meanwhile his stories continue to be dramatized on such television programs as *Alfred Hitchcock Presents* and *Tales from the Dark Side*.

EDWARD BRYANT

The Transfer

Something is not right.

My name is Doris Ruth MacKenzie, and I am forty-three years old. When I was a little girl, everyone around me called me Dorrie. I hated that. Nowadays, only a few friends remember—and they still call me that—but it's all right.

And then there's Jim. It's fine for Jim to call me Dorrie. I haven't loved many people, but those I *have* loved—they can do anything.

Jim? *Jim.* Where are you?

James Gordon MacKenzie has been my husband for twenty-two years. We've known each other only slightly longer than that. He's a tall man, slightly stooped, and kind. Always very kind. *And he's wearing a red mask.* Something's not right at all.

Jim? My wrists are numb. There is so much I can't touch. Behind my eyes, the pain zigzags madly. It feels like there are shards of broken glass grinding in there. I can't see anything, except what I can think of.

Jim . . . Where are you?

Talk to me, love.

Won't anyone speak to me? I'm talking to myself.

But I'm not going crazy. I'm *not!*

He wears a scarlet mask. It shines, glistens like— What is it I'm not seeing?

I can still feel. People always said I had empathy. Even at the beginning, when I first could frame ideas in words, I knew I could feel for others, actually *feel* others. "Equalizing potentials," my high school physics teacher said, even though he never knew what those two words actually meant to me. He was

266

speaking of something else entirely. It was a metaphor I couldn't phrase, but I knew it fit.

"A high-pressure area's generated to the west of the Quad Cities . . ."

That's the practical application of my teacher's words.

Reading from the wire copy: "The low-pressure system in central Illinois is holding steady."

I'd smile again and use my breathy, little-girl voice.

"The storm's coming in fast, folks. Bring in your doggies and kitty cats. The Weather Bureau says—"

We still called it the Weather Bureau back then. It was 1963, I was twenty-three, and I was working at WWHO-TV in Aurora. I hadn't made it into Chicago yet—at least professionally—but finally I was past Peoria.

I had thought the forecast was still variable.

Oh, God. The weather report. The patterns with their smooth whorls. The transfer of energy, sometimes violently. The shapes from the contour maps swirling around me, humming monotonously, distorting all the clear, sharp angles . . .

At WWHO they hired me because I was cute. The station manager let me know that right away. I didn't want to go out to dinner with him, but he was very insistent, and I was hungry.

Over his medium-rare liver and onions, he said, "We'll get you the numbers. You'll be the sexiest, most watched weathergirl in the Midwest. You'll be able to write your own ticket in New York or L.A., wherever you want." But first, of course, he'd have to punch my ticket in Aurora.

The smell of liver and onions and sex made me want to throw up. I said no. But it was close, dangerously so. The compulsion to touch his soul, satisfy his need, to draw near and meld with him, actually *be* him, perhaps to become even worse than he . . . that frightened me so much that I drew back.

I wouldn't have phrased it this way, back then, but I wanted to remain my own person.

The next night, there were messages scrawled on my weather board; they were terrible, obscene things. The Chroma-Key didn't pick them up, so only the crew and I could see them. I finished the evening news block, and then I quit. I didn't have many choices, but at least that one I could make.

So that's why I ended up in Chicago sooner than I'd expected, on the streets looking for another job; maybe I could be a weathergirl again. I don't think there are many weathergirls now. Every station has its own staff meteorologist and they usually are men. But back then, looks counted.

At least for more than they do now. I think. I haven't tried to trade on looks for a long, long time, and that's all to the good.

When I finally got a job, it was at an advertising agency on North Michigan. The company was called Martin, Metzger, and Mulcahy, and appearances certainly counted there. The men who ran the agency had a crystalline vision of how we should all look and act, whether we were at the office or not. You always represent the agency, they said. All of us had to measure up to their expectations.

It's not easy defining yourself that way, but I tried. I worked hard and did what they wanted for six months, until nearly my twenty-fourth birthday. I was a pretty good secretary. It seemed to work—I was in line for a promotion. Then I met Cody.

That's blood, isn't it? Blood, all liquid and running down— Stop it, Dorrie! Think. Remember . . .

My parents, my father especially, used to tell me, don't be so impressionable, Dorrie. Use your own head. But how could I do that when I used the heads of others? When I saw through their eyes and felt what they felt. And, and—

What, Dorrie? I looked back, confronted the child I was then, the person I am now.

I—I became like— No, I *became*—

Please . . . Damn it. Please, no, I'm me. Me, Doris Mac-Kenzie. I am forty-three years old, though I overheard one of my neighbors at the market talking to a woman from across the street and guessing that I was in my fifties. That's as old as Jim, my husband. They didn't know I'd overheard, because there was a pyramid of paper-towel rolls between us.

It's not that I mind being that old. No, it's being reminded of him. We were so much alike. My dearest, dearest. His face is so red. And it drips. Oh, Jim.

I met Cody Anderssen on my lunch break while I was walking slowly along the lakefront. At first I thought he was just another hippy. There weren't many hippies downstate in Macomb, at least none I'd ever been aware of, and certainly I'd never met one, much less talked to any. If my mother had been along, I'm sure she would have turned and walked twice as fast the other way, maybe shrieking for police at the same time. I was braver. When the freakish-looking man said, "Hi," I just kept on walking in the same measured pace.

He followed in step beside me. "You look awful nice," he said. "Will you just stop a minute and talk?"

My step faltered and I really looked at him. He was young, perhaps even younger than I. Blue eyes—I remember those well. They were the same deep blue I sometimes saw in the winter sky above the lake. He wore a broad-brimmed leather hat and a fringed leather jacket that looked like it had been sewn at home. His goatee and long hair were blond. The hair made me feel uneasy, but the clean shine of it somehow triggered me to speak.

"You look like Buffalo Bob—"

"—Bill," he said, correcting me, apparently unamused.

I laughed. After a moment, so did he.

He told me his name and then spelled "Anderssen." "It's not so remarkable where I come from—northern Minnesota—but at least down here the s's and the e make me something different. It's groovy."

I blinked. I wanted to ask if Cody really was his first name, but felt too shy.

At first Cody made all the conversation. He told me about leaving Minnesota and coming here, of living on the streets for months before finding a job in a pet store and an apartment he could afford. He talked about drugs, a topic that scared me. It was the question of control. "And you?" he finally said.

I talked about growing up in Macomb and hardly ever going to the city, and how, when I graduated from high school, I went against my parents and didn't enroll at Western Illinois. The first brave thing I ever did in my life was to take the bus to Peoria, then on toward Chicago.

My parents had talked so often of my striking out on my own, I thought that was what they really and truly wanted of me. The conflict made me sick for days. As ever, I stored up the tension like a battery.

But I ended up in Aurora as a weathergirl at a tiny TV station, and then immersed myself in the city.

"That's great," Cody said, and then laughed. "You oughta be a hippy too. You've got the spirit of freedom in you."

No, I didn't, but I didn't say my doubts aloud.

"It's late," I said, looking at my watch. "My lunch hour's gone. I've got to go back to the office."

"Meet me after work," said Cody. "Please?"

I stared at him. I'd never met anyone at all like this.

After work, in the mob of rush hour, I found him. The next morning, which was Saturday, I met him again and we went out to the Museum of Science and Industry and toured the coal mine. That night I accompanied him back to his apartment and lost my virginity.

And two decades later, I wish I were back in Chicago. In a different bed than where I lie now.

Two weeks later I moved into Cody's apartment. My original apartment had been larger, but I was too shy to let him move there. I kept going back to my old apartment for a month to pick up my mail. Finally Cody convinced me to tell my parents I'd moved to a nicer place. I got a post office box and hoped my folks wouldn't come visit Chicago. I told them I would come home for Christmas.

I quit my job. I wore the same kind of clothing Cody did. I let my hair grow long and straight. I started learning guitar. I used the same drugs he did. I sold the same things he did. We finished each other's sentences. We got along all right.

Cody took real delight in being special, different. It was his name, his clothes, everything. But we were both alike in so many ways now. He noticed it too.

"It's so freakin' weird," he said one night. "You and I. It's almost like looking in a mirror, except that a mirror image's reversed. You're *me*, darlin'." He shook his head.

I couldn't contradict him. Only a portion of it was wanting to be what he wished me to be. Part of it too was *being* him. I didn't know what it meant—just that it had always been so. And it worked both inside and out. Cody had an ulcer. I had an ulcer.

"I don't want you to be me," he said.

"Don't you?"

He shook his head again. "We're all free," Cody said. "It's the time of liberation."

I just stared at him. He looked back at me and finally kissed me long and hard. The gaze from his blue eyes fixed me.

"I like what I see," said Cody.

But a week later he died. I never was sure what all he took. The hardest thing I've ever done was to avoid following Cody into the abyss. It wasn't easy, but I tried to absorb the compulsion within myself.

I still had the clothing I'd brought to Chicago. I resumed my colorless, invisible presence. No more beads. No more fringe. The ulcer went away.

My name is Dorrie MacKenzie and I'm older than that now. There are songs I can almost remember, images I can nearly recall. The portrait of Jim on my dresser at home swims into focus. But it isn't Jim. It's something I look at in my mind and then discard. Whatever it is, it can't be him. He is a pleasant, attractive man. And this thing on the dresser is, is—I don't know. It could be anything. It reminds me of the skinned head of a rabbit. I throw the image away. I will not think of it.

The dresser and the picture on it evaporate. Our house in Kansas City dissolves into fragments and then to blackness.

I see nothing. But I can listen. What I hear sounds like a man stripping away a stubborn Velcro panel.

Probably I think of that because of Jim. There is an inflatable leg-setting sleeve with Velcro seams in his bag. He's a doctor, a GP, and he even still makes occasional house calls. Takes his bag wherever he goes, even on vacation.

Vacation . . . See the wild beasts. Don't think about it. Red beasts. Scarlet. Dripping scarlet, shining—

Wet.

I can feel the high-pressure area all through me. My skull wants to explode. Energy flows, deepens, prepares to flood. I have so little control anymore.

Storm warning.

It was wet, raining heavily, when I met Jim. He never realized the melodramatic circumstances of how it happened. All he knew was that he happened upon a bedraggled woman trudging toward the midway point of a highway bridge over the Chicago River in the middle of a driving rainstorm. He thought I must have had automobile trouble, so he stopped to see if he could help. What he did was save my life, since I'd been planning to jump from the center of the span into the muddy current. I never let him know that. I would have turned down his offer of a ride except for his eyes. They were kind eyes, a deep liquid brown, and intelligent.

I got in his car. That was the beginning. I forgot about the attraction of the abyss, of the fatal temptation that had continued to haunt me after Cody's death.

It was love, or something similar. At least it was the need, the necessity that always tugged me toward others.

It's not that I'm a chameleon. I'm not. Transference and transformation—those are the key words. What they mean is less important than what I feel. In truth, I adapt to my environment. It's the way I survive.

Jim and I lived in Chicago for another two years, then went to Cleveland when he was offered a good clinic position. It didn't work out as well as he'd have liked, so then it was back to Chicago. Finally we came to Kansas City, where some of Jim's medical school friends had set up a partnership and invited him in.

It was peaceful. For years, the only real conflict was my having to convince Jim that I really couldn't have children. I didn't want to tell him the truth—that I didn't want to. That was our only difference, and I think I only had the will to carry it out because he secretly, in his heart of hearts, didn't want to share his life with anyone else. At any rate, my forty-fourth birthday would be in just one more week, on the seventh; procreation was getting to be ever less of a real possibility.

For all those years, Jim urged me to be myself. It was only partially successful. I've stored up so much.

The forecast . . . Storms? Earthquake? Tidal wave? Apocalypse? I don't really know. All I do know is that my head hurts, as though the skull wants to come apart at the cranial fissures.

Jim? Touch me, stroke me, tell me things are all right. If I could just see you again.

But I would have to open my eyes.

Something I learned to notice with both Cody and Jim: it wasn't just that I came to resemble them in so many important aspects; to whatever degree, to *be* them as I was defined by each. There was always something a little extra, a lagniappe.

As they perceived me, they had what they wanted, and a little bit more.

Simple physical proximity was enough to trigger the process, closeness of bodies and souls carried it through. I discovered that sex speeded it. Sharing served as an accelerator. And trauma—

Because Jim knew many people through his work, we socialized quite a lot, and our friends sometimes remarked that we looked *so* much like each other.

Jim would allow his easy Midwestern chuckle and make a joke about the psychological studies of how so many human beings and their pets come to resemble each other. Transference.

And who was who? he'd say. Everyone would laugh.

The storm is breaking.

And here we are at the Sleepaway Motel in Bishop, California.

I will open my eyes; I *will*.

Here we are in a forsaken desert town I've never seen before and hope I never will again. Jim. Dorrie. And the new man in my life. I sound so flip only because it keeps the hysteria at bay. I had enough of trying to scream through the gag.

The heat lightning had flashed over the mountains as we checked in. One more long day to San Diego. Our first vacation in years. The Wild Animal Park on my birthday—that was Jim's promise.

We checked into the motel, that damned motel, that motel of the damned, and then— Shut up, Dorrie! There is nothing left to do. Only one thing left undone.

The knock.

Must be the manager, Jim had said. Probably didn't get a clear impression on the credit card or something.

When he unlatched the door—

Don't scream, Dorrie, don't.

—it burst open, Jim flung aside, the nameless man with the gun, the pistol, the metal dark and shining, the threat and the darkness.

It is our vacation. My birthday is in only a few days. These things don't happen to people, not to normal people, good people.

Oh, but they do, Dorrie, the man said. I know your name. Your husband—Jim?—said it before I took care of his tongue. Did you appreciate my giving him the Demerol before I worked on his face?

Not to normal people, they don't. I'm not normal.

Oh, said the man, you look normal enough to me, as normal as any other woman tied to the bed with her husband's two neckties, an Ace bandage, and a roll of gauze. Taste in ties a little conservative, eh? I figure you'll act normal enough when I get around to you. That's it. Keep your eyes open.

I am bound tightly, my shoulders hard against the headboard, my limbs stretched apart, my body open and vulnerable. I have no choice but to face Jim. He is roped upright into the wooden chair at the foot of the bed.

The weather, Dorrie. My voice now is solely in my head. The storm is breaking. The smooth contour swirls. The rain and the wind will come. If only they would rush in and cleanse—

Oh yes, Dorrie, says the man. I'm glad your husband was a doctor. Handy he brought his bag along. Saved me no end of trouble. He holds up the disposable scalpel in one hand, the mask that Jim wore in the other. No. No, Dorrie. It's not a mask at all.

The hemostats, the glittering clamps are set out on the bedspread. The fabric's pattern is designed to hide anything. But I can see the instruments. I look away from Jim to the waldo— the long, curved forceps. Beside it are the incision clips, stylized clothespins with teeth.

All told, there are three of us in the room, but in every real way, I am now alone. I begin to know with final sureness what will happen.

And yet . . . and yet I know I am not the person I was for all my early years. I know that somewhere inside, I do have a core that will not be bent, cannot be warped, and maybe, just perhaps, I can draw upon it.

But the forecast is bleak.

What I feel is like the pulling back of a nail from the quick of a finger. No, Dorrie, I tell myself, that is too soft, too gentle. It is more like the wrench of my heart being taken away, torn from me.

Jim's kiss was always gentle. This man's will be rough.

Jim's embrace . . . His touch was kind. The man's will be brutal.

When Jim entered me, it was joyfully. This man— I cannot

imagine his touch. Not yet. It will tear. Burn. Like the lightning, only not clean.

The crimson, the sheen, the mask, the blood. I will say goodbye to Jim in my soul and look ahead. The man with the gun and the scalpel. I have read of killers like him and his fellows, though I didn't think people like us ever encountered them. It was always another depressing story on the news, just before the weather.

Some people win lotteries.

Jim and I— Forget that, Dorrie.

I look forward again. Storm fronts. Equalizing potentials . . . The man stares down at me, and is that a gentle smile? It is a smile. He holds Jim's mask in his free hand.

I think I am ready to give it up. He will possess me here on this soaked bed in the Sleepaway Motel in Bishop, California, before he pulls the trigger or pushes the blade.

His lips, shiny, part. I'll want you to wear the mask, he says, for you and me. Just for us, Dorrie. He leans down toward me.

That is when I decide.

What a surprise for him. He will comprehend the trauma of my transformation. Frankly even I do not know the extent of the power, the energy released by storm fronts colliding.

I wonder what he will encounter beyond the mask: something with horns, fangs, scales, fur? Something as bestial as only he can imagine? Or just himself enhanced? Whatever the sum, it will only be the result of his terrifying addition.

Goodbye, Jim. Farewell, love. This nameless man in the motel, regardless of how I am transformed, will get no less than he deserves.

And probably more.

EDWARD BRYANT's short stories have been appearing since 1970 in a wide variety of magazines and anthologies. Two of these stories, "Stone" (1978) and "giANTS" (1979), won the Nebula Award, the science fiction field's highest honor. His collections include *Cinnabar, Among the Dead, Wyoming Sun,* and *Particle Theory,* the most recent. He is presently at work on a novel.

WHITLEY STRIEBER

Pain

When I encountered Janet O'Reilly I was doing research by "networking" into the community of prostitutes. This is more difficult than it might seem. To connect with a prostitute for business purposes isn't hard; to question her about the nature of her trade and her experience is practically impossible.

My research was for a novel. In the early eighties I was just beginning to see the novel as a form of political art. Previously I had viewed it as entertainment, and what political content my work had was no more than fortuitous.

I have always felt the need to do a great deal of research for my books. *The Dark* required me to track wolves in Canada and Minnesota. For *Red Moon* I studied five or six historical eras with care.

For my new book, to be called *Pain*, I wanted to know not only about prostitution but also about the various perversions that attach themselves to it. There are sexual desires so exploitative that people will not gratify them without being paid even in our exploitative society. These have to do for the most part with pain and death. For death is connected to sexuality—witness the spider. Who hasn't wondered what the male spider feels, submitting at the same time to the ecstasy of coitus and the agony of death?

For almost all of human history it has been believed that there is something to be gained by human sacrifice. There are lurid tales of it in ancient times, when it was practiced formally. In the *Golden Bough* Frazer comments that "worship of the feminine principle was everywhere and in all times associated with human sacrifice." This is, naturally, an outrageous misstatement of fact. All early religion was associated with sexuality and so with death; human sacrifice was an integral part of much ritual. There has forever been the notion that something higher than men had to be fed on human souls. Janet has taught me both the truth and the error in this concept. She has taught me with my own life's blood.

Because of the belief that the importance of the victim matters, the sacrifice of kings is an ancient Western tradition. It persisted in organized form into the Roman Empire. The emperors were not assassinated for political reasons, as is normally supposed, but in a secret religious ritual that formed the center of the Roman state cult. Only a few emperors escaped this fate —Hadrian by letting the Vestals drown his beloved catamite in the Nile, Trajan by suffering such a terrible illness that they decided his torment was more satisfactory to the gods than would be his death. All of this is chronicled in the recently discovered books of Grammius Metarch, whose deposit lay undisturbed in the Vatican library until February of 1985.

The slow torment and abnegation involved in the great rituals of sacrifice—where a haughty lord was humiliated and tortured before his former subjects—derived from the conclusion that death was not the only thing wanted. Suffering was also wanted. We make an error by trying to interpret the motives of higher beings. To learn from them we must first accept their presence, and then their primacy over us. Western culture, with its dependence on empiricism and its exaltation of the individual, equips us for neither of these things.

It takes the fire of great agony to burn away these confused notions. That is the reason for the suffering associated with sacrifice.

Suffering leads people to understand themselves. This is perhaps why there is a tremendous and subtle mechanism of destruction in human life. We are not here for the wine, but for the stones. What might spread the boundaries of Camelot is destroyed by those who love us the most.

It has been whispered that President Kennedy was killed in an alchemical ritual entitled "The Death of the White King," the purpose of which was to open the door to new suffering in the world, perhaps to bring about the long and complicated series of events that would end in nuclear war. Even a small nuclear war might touch off atmospheric changes that would lead to cooling short of "nuclear winter," but intense enough to cause the one fatal summer of snow that could lead to a new ice age. After Kennedy's death a famous Scottish prophet saw the snows spreading down from Ben Bulben to cover the whole world. Other prophets have also seen snows.

Even if we save ourselves from war, the environment is turning against us. There is increasing volcanic activity throughout the world, almost as if the planet itself were beginning to do battle on behalf of suffering.

The eruption of El Chicón in 1983 spread ash into Texas six hundred miles to the north. The Mexican government closed off the area of the volcano. It remains closed. It is known that El Chicón ejected more debris into the atmosphere than six thousand hydrogen bombs. We are still feeling the effects. The El Niño that took place in the Pacific in 1984–85 and led to the vast Borneo Conflagration which burned an area of the rain forest the size of New England was a direct result of El Chicón. And the world is getting colder because of El Chicón and numerous other volcanoes.

Right now Buffalo is struggling under a deeper snow cover than ever before in recorded history. If there comes a year when the snows do not melt across Canada and the northern United States, the glacier will come back. This will be an abrupt thing: the snow will reflect so much heat and light that the next winter will be more intense, the next summer colder. Then the glacier will begin to move.

Human sacrifice has also been thought of as a form of appeasement of the gods. The Nazi destruction of the Jews was a particularly vicious exception to this rule: Hitler killed the Jews to consolidate his power. They owned too much of the German economy, and nothing he did would ever make them trust him. They formed a certain reservoir of opposition and so had to be destroyed. Weren't they sacrificed for the sake of Nazism?

At the beginning of my studies with Janet O'Reilly I would have contended that there was something which accepted their sacrifice and in return destroyed Nazism. The Jews thus gave their lives to destroy Hitler.

They did indeed, but not for the reason I thought. We do not give our sacrifices, we receive them. The greatest sacrifice produces the greatest learning. The most blessed are those who suffer the most. That is the prime esthetic of death, at once the horror of it and the miracle. Thus Hitler's victims are among the greatest of all heroes. But we only mourn them, we do not celebrate their valor, because we do not understand what they really did.

The one thing that became clear to me from my association with Janet is that there is something that feeds on human suffering. It is not a principle or some nebulous spiritual presence, but a real civilization, albeit with higher goals, motives and understanding than our own.

Except on rare occasions it does not act directly in our world, but rather affects it indirectly. The farmer does not live in the pigsty; he conceived it, created it and manages it from afar. Day to day, it remains the possession of the pigs.

This is an example of its indirect action. Back in 1926 and 1927 my uncle lived in Munich. Hitler was there, and so was one Karl Haushofer, the leader of a group called the Vril Society. In 1961 I found in an old desk a picture of this uncle lying in a coffin in what seemed to be a North African background. He took it from me and furiously tore it up. After his death twelve years later my father told me that this had been a photograph of his initiation into Haushofer's Vril Society. There has long been a rumor that this group raised up a demon in the body of one of its less exalted members, Adolf Hitler. Of course they did not "raise a demon." There are no demons. But Hitler believed they had, and if—as he had—you discard empiricism, belief is also a reality.

The final goal of the Vril Society was the ritual known as "The Death of the White King." In the weeks before the Kennedy assassination my uncle became morose and irritable. A few days before, he narrowly escaped death when his car exploded due to a faulty gas line. The day before, he had a terrible heart attack on a plane he had chartered in an effort to leave the United States. Afterward he died a lingering death due to congestive heart failure. Over those twelve years, I do not think he spoke a thousand words. He grew thinner and thinner, became a haunted shadow and died.

At first I assumed that I met Janet O'Reilly by accident, but this is obviously not true. To explore the reason that the meeting was contrived, I must digress broadly once more, into the largely buncombe world of "ufology."

There is evidence all around us of the presence of the hidden world. We reject it, though, as silliness and foolery.

Because it knows that this hidden civilization feeds on us, the government does everything possible to hide reality. It does not want us to know that our lives, our culture, our very history has been designed for the purpose of causing us suffering, and that there is nothing whatsoever that any of us can do to relieve ourselves of this burden.

Ten years ago, in the course of another research effort, I met a man—since dead—who claimed that the National Security Agency had a document a hundred and thirty pages long which told the truth about UFOs, making an almost irrefutable case for the fantastic notion that they are the artifacts of an intelligent civilization so far in advance of our own that we literally cannot see its manifestations except on rare occasions when they probe into our temporal space, much as the farmer enters the pigsty to check the health of his animals.

The underlying thesis of the paper is that this higher species is native to earth, and that—by their own lights—they use us just as we use the pigs. I know that this is true because Janet has shown me that it is true. For reasons that will become clear, I was earmarked for special suffering. As my understanding has increased, I have come to love my tormentors, and share with them their own sorrow.

I was astonished to see in 1983 that NSA had been approached by CAUS (Citizens Against UFO Secrecy) under the Freedom of Information Act to divulge what it knows about UFOs. Officially, the government has made a massive effort to debunk the whole notion of "flying saucers," claiming that they are all either hoaxes or misperceptions. However, when it was time for it to give up certain information about UFOs, it took a very different stance. The Justice Department fought furiously on behalf of NSA to retain exactly one document, which is the "core truth" of the matter. Its length is a hundred and thirty pages.

If what I was told was truly the content of this paper, then the obvious conclusion is that they use us for their own reasons, gaining something we do not understand from our suffering and

our slaughter, gaining strength perhaps, or pleasure, or maybe
even the fundamental energy of their civilization. As the burning of oil fuels human civilization, moving planes and cars, providing electricity and heat, so also the carnage of human beings
might provide this invisible higher civilization with its prime
energy source. Perhaps there is a burst of very fine energy as the
soul explodes from the body—an energy which can be used for
the most subtle and powerful purposes. Or perhaps the soul is,
simply, food for finer bellies.

Our suffering does not benefit them directly, but rather the
growth our suffering brings us. To wreak mayhem in the world is
not the responsibility of demons, but of angels. It is their greatest and most painful duty, the one they hate for the agony they
must cause, but love for the riches of understanding it brings.

This is a slaughterhouse, but we the victims are not offered
the blessing of a quick club to the head or the slitting of the
throat. The greater our learning, the happier the angels.

Why must we suffer to learn? Because pain breaks down the
barriers of ego, of personality, of false self. It separates us from
ourselves and allows us to see deep. Witness the Book of Job,
which in the secret texts Janet uses is called the Book of Man.

The best death would be an ecstatic mixture of loving acceptance and deepest despair.

I met Janet O'Reilly at the Terminal Diner at the corner of
Twelfth and West streets in Greenwich Village. I was there
because of my research. The Hellfire Club is nearby, a haunt of
New York's sadomasochistic community. I particularly wanted
to connect with some of the people who went there to make
money. I wasn't interested in the compulsive participants, but
rather in the men and women who preyed on them.

It was three o'clock in the morning, and the diner was nearly
empty. In the week I had been going there, I had drawn three
interesting specimens into my net, and learned a great deal from
them. When she sat down in my booth, I assumed that Janet
had heard about me from one of them. My standing offer was
twenty-five dollars for fifteen minutes of talk. "I've been doing
pain for about two years," she said without so much as an introduction.

SM is to some degree a matter of costume and makeup. The
people involved in it are fantasists at heart, and they enjoy elabo-

rate regalia and ritual. A good part of torture is contained in the drama and the waiting that accompanies lengthy preliminaries and preparations—the strapping of cuffs, arrangement of tools, application of leather appliances and so forth. Janet revealed no hint of the exotic in her dress.

She wore a fresh-looking blue frock. Her hair was golden brown and conventionally waved. Her face was soft, the face of a girl, with inviting, delicate lips, a straight nose and eyes softly rimmed by big lashes, framed by arching brows. It was a completely winning face, as pure a face as I have ever seen. Her eyes were light green and were the only thing in her face that suggested anything more than sock hops and torrid back seats. It was not that they were dazed or shadowed or cruel—not at all. They were the eyes of a surpassingly intelligent person—bright and quick and full of life. More than that, they were kind eyes. Looking into them, one sensed a true place of rest.

I smiled at her. "You heard about my deal?"

"What deal?" Her voice was fluid and soft. She was not at all like the other people I had met in her profession. I ought to say that I found them hard or exotic or slitheringly dangerous but I didn't. Their chief distinguishing characteristic was that they were just ordinary people. To one degree or another all of them dressed up, but scratch the studded surface and you revealed Flatbush.

"I have a deal. People tell me about their trade, and I give them twenty-five bucks. It isn't much money, but I'm a safe ear, and people like to talk."

"I don't know anything about it."

"Why did you sit down here, then?"

She looked at me dubiously, as if she couldn't believe that I would ask such an obvious question. She folded her arms. I wasn't going to get an answer.

"I would like to hear about what it is you do."

She reached across the table and touched my cheek. Her fingers were cool and firm; her hand did not shake like it would have if she'd been on drugs. Many of the women who get into pain do it because the money is good and the johns usually don't demand youth or beauty. Many even want a degree of ugliness and dirt. Pain is the last refuge of the demolished whore.

"Like I said, I do pain." Again her eyes found mine. "I do it the way it was meant to be done, and I do it for the right reason."

It was an invitation. "You've drawn the wrong conclusion about me. I'm not a john."

"Every man is a john."

"If you mean an exploiter of women—in that sense—"

"Every man is a john. And every man wants what I have to give. When I want a john I just hit the next guy I see. I never miss."

At that moment my life was ruined. I did not discover a masochist within myself, and become addicted to the whip. What happened to me is more terrible than that. Indeed, I have seen so much of the unusual in life that I tend to think that all perversions are mild, no more than slightly startling variations on the theme of relationship that dominates human experience. In fact, the adoration of the submissive for the dominant in a moment of high sexual drama is a beautiful thing to witness. Like all real love, it is innocent, and is only intensified by the studied indifference of the skilled sadist.

"I don't want to break your record," I said.

She smiled, color coming into her cheeks. "They never do. What's your fantasy?"

I thought at once of my wife. I have been married for eighteen years. I have three children. My eldest daughter could not be much younger than this woman, whom I still knew as "Lauren Stone." Not until I became a part of her inner circle did she tell me her real name. Even now when I think of that first meeting, I think not of Janet but of Lauren Stone. She is, of course, an excellent actress. Lauren Stone was not an assumed name. It was a character. Janet is also a character. No doubt she has many others, as many as she wants, potentially one for each person she meets.

"I don't have a fantasy. I told you, I'm not into this. It isn't my—"

"Don't say 'bag.' You can explain yourself more cogently than that."

"It isn't my way. I'm afraid that I have normal sex with my normal wife, and that's all."

"I told you, I do pain. Pain and sex are not the same thing. They aren't even similar."

"In many minds they're bound up together. A lot of people can't have pleasure without intermingling pain."

"They don't interest me. You can't *want* to suffer if you're really going to. If you seek it out, it becomes a variant of pleasure. I don't give pleasure, I give pain. And in return you get a gift."

"I'm listening."

"The gift is, I lift the burden of self from your shoulders. You can see clearly then. You can see the truth of the world, when you are no longer encumbered by will. That's why nobody ever turns me down, once they understand what that truly means."

She was glowing. There is no other word to describe how ineffably beautiful she was at that moment. That the human form could express such loveliness still amazes me. I want so badly to see her again. One day I know that I will see her. The thought makes me colder than the wind that is howling around my cabin.

At the present moment I am in a tiny log cabin in the woods west of Ellenville, New York. The north wind roars down from the mountains, a cataract in the night. Across the room my wife snores softly. Downstairs my children sleep in silence, each one under a down comforter, snuggled with a cat or, in the case of my son, his dog.

When I go to her and submit myself, a part of my suffering will be the certain knowledge that all of their lives will be damaged by my act. My pain will be infinitely greater for understanding that it will lead to theirs. To know that you will cause grief to those you love is a very hard thing.

That first night I made my fatal mistake: I allowed her to take me to her apartment, a miserable, filthy cellar on Thirteenth Street. In the diner a sort of coldness overcame me, a shuddering of the heart that left me breathless, but also in some peculiar way in her power.

As I walked along beside her, I visualized an elegant den, perhaps the top half of a brownstone or an enormous loft space. I was not prepared for the two dark rooms, and the roaches scuttling away as she turned on the light. In the first room there was an old iron bed and a tiny Victorian servant's tub, the sort that you crouch in. A two-burner gas ring stood on a small

counter near a clear plastic dish full of withered salad greens and
a plate of deteriorating tofu.

Beside the bed was a low shelf containing a few books. I saw
Swann's Way, Castle to Castle and *The Best of P. G. Wodehouse.* Marking a place in the Wodehouse was a small black
pincers.

"I stay here when I'm working with somebody," she said. She
smiled up at me, a bright, heartbreakingly lovely smile. "I hope
you like it."

There was no sensible reply. I just shook my head. The rooms
were quite cold, clammy. There was an unpleasant smell, the
odor of rancid sweat. Her turning on the light in the first room
darkened the doorway into the second. From this darkness came
a soft, pleading moan. She ignored it, tossing her car coat on the
bed and sitting down. "Sorry I don't have any chairs." She
touched a cushion on the floor with her toe. "It beats standing,
but only just." She seemed to be trying to win me in a feckless,
almost adolescent manner. When I sat down on the cushion I
found myself at her feet. Something in me recoiled. I did not
wish to be in such a position before this girl. In fact, I would
have been uncomfortable crouching at the feet of the Tsar.

And yet I did not get up. She touched my knee with her toe.
"The cushion's only for show. You don't have to use it if you
don't want to."

"What choice do I have?"

"A lot of them prefer the floor. It establishes a correct relationship from the beginning."

"Prefer the floor? I hope I don't seem stupid. What are you
getting at?"

She tossed a ringlet of hair out of her eyes. "Prefer to kneel
on the floor. But the cushion's fine. I don't mind."

There came again that clear, direct look, the hint of amuse-
ment around the mouth, the coldness deep in the eyes.

"Don't be scared," she said quickly. "Nothing's going to happen that you don't want to happen. Everything at your speed."

Protests filed through my mind. I controlled them, speaking
smoothly. "I told you before, I'm not into an S and M trip."

"Fine. Neither am I. I thought we'd agreed on that."

"I don't understand."

She kicked me in the chest, not hard, but in such a way that I felt a thrill of pain right up to my heart. It is hard even now to understand how that gesture began the process of my death. But it did.

As I caught my breath she spoke, and her voice had a harsh edge to it. "You certainly do understand. Personality won't admit to itself what essence knows very well. You didn't run when I sat down at your table, did you? I started off by telling you exactly what I do and what I am. Unlike you, I didn't lie about myself. Now you're here and you're still having difficulty submitting." She tossed her head. "Look, my name is Janet O'Reilly. Janet Claire O'Reilly. I'm in the phone book, and if I move you can always call information. You need some time alone with this. When you're ready to see me again, call me."

She stood up. I was shocked and confused. I demurred, but she was resolute. A few moments later I found myself standing on her dark cellar stair, listening to her lock click behind me. I was about to turn and go when I heard what at first I thought was another woman in the apartment, speaking in a low voice.

"How dare you make a noise like that when I bring in an outsider. You could have frightened him away. Then he would have lost his chance. You need to learn the importance of responsibility, I think. We're going to do a little heat."

Light flickered under the door. In a moment there came a wail. It was so real and so raw with agony and despair that I recoiled. Yet the sound fascinated me as well. I did not leave, not at once.

New York is a big, strange city and in its corners one can certainly find the odd and the dark. Who knew what I had encountered here. No matter how attractive this person was, how inoffensive and even innocent she appeared, she must be terribly dangerous. The cries went on and on, rising it seemed forever in intensity. Sometimes the light flickered and sometimes it glowed deep red, and at length there came an acrid odor from the apartment, like the smell of hot wax.

When the cries stopped I left, striding off down the street, and found that I was shaking so badly I could barely control myself when I stopped at a crossing. My stomach turned. Unexpectedly, I vomited into the street.

When at last I arrived home the sky was gray with impending dawn. I moved through our warm, quiet living room, was greeted in the hall by Seymour, our most active cat. He rubbed up against me with a friendly meow. I knelt down and picked him up.

Never have I been so grateful for the touch of the familiar. He oozed and stretched in my hands. Cats seem to have been created for touching. I went into my bedroom, kicked off my shoes and stripped. I was going to get straight into that lovely warm bed with Sally when I noticed perfume around me. Some of Janet O'Reilly's scent was clinging to my hair.

When I showered the steam seemed to intensify the scent. I washed my hair and used body shampoo as well. Free at last of the slightest residue of the night, I slipped between the sheets. My wife moaned and drew close. She was warm and I was grateful.

I was too sleepy to react to the fact that I could still smell that perfume. It must have gotten into my clothes.

I was swept at once into a dreamscape. Many of my dreams take place in a shadowy land that is partly the neighborhood where I grew up and partly a dark country of my own imagining. Journeys there are accompanied by a strange and delicious poignance. It is always night in those dreams, and always autumn.

On this night I found myself in a terrible situation. I was to be executed. My tormentors were not unkind—in fact they were sweet and friendly.

She was there. She came to me and supported me while one of the others loaded a high-powered rifle. I was slack with terror. The bullets clattered into the magazine, and one of them clicked into the breech. She held me under my arms, keeping me erect so that the bullet would pierce my chest in the right place. As the ritual moved slowly along, she spoke kind words to me. "Is there anything we can do to help you?"

"Somebody could hug me."

"Oh, okay, I can do that."

As we remained there together something quite unexpected happened to me. My will, the core of my identification as a separate self, ebbed slowly away. The ebbing of will was like black water parting to reveal a drowned cathedral.

To be free of oneself is to escape a great blindness. A palace universe spread around me, and I found that my tormentor was an angel who in her abiding kindness was willing to suffer with me the very real torture of tearing down the stones of my personality in order to allow my true, essential self to join the hidden dance for which it was made and intended. My whole will was in her hands: I was so free of myself that I even lost the wish to beg her for my life. She spoke softly and insistently. I realized quite clearly that she was giving the executioners their orders.

Then the door of the bedroom flew open and I was assaulted by a cheerful parade of kids. It was Sunday morning and here came Alex Jr. and Patty and Ginger along with assorted cats and dogs and stuffed toys. Sally moaned and laughed as our bed filled with children and animals.

My happiness surrounded me. The love, the joy, the warmth banished all my brooding dreams. The dreary landscape receded. I remembered only that wonderful face, and the delicious moment when I realized just how much a relief it is to surrender oneself to a higher will.

Although the perfume lingered for days, a poignant harbinger of my own death, I found that my ordinary life quickly reasserted itself. I did not forget about Janet exactly, but I discovered that my mind was turning away from the book I have called *Pain* and toward stronger, richer subjects.

Three months later I was well into the book that became *The Night Man* and no longer troubling my mind with the odd and repellent world of sadomasochism.

We were here in this house when I had the dream that made me remember her. It wasn't really a dream, but a sort of possession, an agony of the soul that came upon me in late afternoon. The family was out riding. I had taken a swim and spent ten minutes in the hot tub listening to the birds sing out by Sally's suet feeder. I'd gone into the house in my long cowled robe and opened a beer. The next thing I knew I was in a tiny, droning airplane with Janet. At first I didn't recognize her. Then I saw that she was flying the plane, watching me out of the corner of one eye. She spoke in a language I could not quite understand.

I saw the whole world as a single, coherent entity, an enormous living organism. It is hard to express the impact of this sense of wholeness. There was tremendous detail: a man gently breathing his last, his hand in his child's hand; babies wriggling; the inner stones of the earth radiant with teaching heat; a young woman singing in a sunny backyard. The vision went on and on, until I saw the world as a tiny dot of light, a bright ark forever voyaging.

Then I saw the missile silos and the atomic warheads, and the images of the powerful, the President leaning against a doorway with a glass of orange juice in his hand, three Russians speaking intently in a room, and in one of their faces the same expression that *she* had, the same fatal kindness.

Over it all there was a soft and gentle song. They love us. They do. We are their grass, their trees, their rooting piglets. They have grown immense on us, sapping us, whipping us with war and famine and pestilence, designing brain and body for more and more breeding, until the world is choked with billions upon billions of shining, brilliant human souls ready for the slaughter. Ready also, for growth.

The point of a sacrifice is that it satisfies the need of a higher being. This need is not for suffering, though, or death: it is for the enrichment of the soul. Janet was striving mightily that I would learn my own truth. Only then would I be of real value to her. The concept of sacrifice as appeasement is merely wishful thinking. The angels will never be appeased, not by anything except the expansion of true wisdom in our world.

While I swooned on my couch with beer foaming down my robe to the floor, she remained close to me, nursing me with the hands of death, speaking in her light voice, encouraging and explaining.

I awoke to the long evening sun, the whinny of horses and the voices of my returning family.

I was so exhausted that I could not raise myself from the couch. Later that week my doctor told me that it was not my first heart attack, and that I needed to revise my life. Exercise. A healthy diet. Less stress. Early heart attacks are dangerous because they are so often silent—a period of fatigue, a slight tightening of the chest.

Summer waned and autumn came. We returned to another city winter. The kids went back to school. Sally and I settled back into the satisfactory routine of our marriage.

Hardly a day passed, though, that I did not think of Janet O'Reilly. Her face, so grave and gentle—so very beautiful—had been fired on the center of my consciousness. Again and again my mind returned to the moments I had spent in her apartment, the cushion, the gentle, hurtful push, the subtle confirmation of my place.

I wished that I had done things differently. She had wanted me to submit to her in some way. I was still unsure about the details. If only I had humbled myself on the bare wood, had given myself to her will, might I not have somehow escaped?

What was she—an angel, a demon, some being from the world beyond the barnyard fence . . . or my anima, the feminine principle that Carl Jung believed resides at the center of every male?

Whatever she was, I was uneasy with the growing urgency of my hunger to submit myself to her.

My third heart attack was a stunning cataclysm of pain. I was in my room writing when the color seemed to drain from the leaves outside my window. I sat helplessly watching the world become dark and gray, then the pain came clubbing up from the center of my chest: Moloch's flaming jaws gaped where my heart had been.

Sally found me lying on my side on the floor and I was taken to the hospital in an ambulance. I could hardly breathe and even the oxygen didn't seem to help. Sally's silence, her tears, hurt me to my quick. Her hand never left mine.

A week passed in the hospital bed. Then the machines told the doctor something I was glad to hear: it was time for me to go home.

Janet came to me one afternoon when Sally was out shopping and the kids were at school. She appeared in my bedroom. My eyes were closed. At first when I smelled her perfume I assumed that I was dreaming, she had come on such silent feet.

"Hello, Alex. Would you like to take a walk with me?"

"You! Where did you come from?"

She looked at me with kindly condescension. "Alex, I like your invincible adherence to the expected. I'm going to take you for a walk now. We're going to my apartment."

"My God, I can't possibly! Look at me, Janet, I can't get out of bed."

But I did get out of bed. When she got me up I simply could not resist. She took me into the bathroom, she shaved me and washed me up. "Now how do you feel?"

"Better."

"I thought so. It's a sunny day. You need some sun."

I dressed, and by the time I was wearing fresh clothes again I really did want a walk. Seeing her dreary brownstone in the light of afternoon, though, almost made me turn back. "No," she said, and drew me on.

I forced myself to continue. When we got to the house I forced myself to descend the stairs. Then I heard her voice behind me, melodious with laughter. "What are you doing?" She was standing on the stoop of the main entrance. The light fell on her. Despite my familiarity with her I was not prepared for the purity of this vision of beauty. Looking up, gaping, I almost tottered backward. She laughed aloud. "You look like a surprised ostrich. Come on up, we're just in time for coffee." With shaking steps I ascended the stairs.

Inside, the upper floors of the brownstone were beautiful, a perfect Federal restoration. I've not much of an eye for furniture, but I do know good antiques when I see them. Contrasted to my memory of the basement, these palatial surroundings were all the more remarkable.

She walked ahead of me, casually swaying her hips in her jeans. We went into a sun room full of orchids, a truly magnificent and intimate space. It smelled of sweet tropical flowers and rich coffee. "Mom and Dad, I'd like you to meet a student of mine."

Her words flashed through my mind like a whip of lightning. I realized that it was true. I was indeed the student of this remarkable being. I was grateful for it, but I was also embarrassed. Before two of my peers in age, I felt mawkish.

They seemed indifferent to my discomfiture. As if prepared for a formal portrait, they sat together on a love seat. They were more than handsome, they were regal. The man was tall with a mane of blond hair and ash-gray eyes. His wife was a serene version of her daughter. It occurred to me that Janet was also a student. By working with innocents, she was learning patience.

Did they know what their daughter did in the basement? What a question—of course they did. This was their home.

I realized that there was hidden in their faces an expression of suppressed glee. They were triumphant: their Janet was a hunter home with a shattered stag. They had sifted the leaves of men and chosen me; I had been caught in a net of careful intention.

Janet glanced at me. "I take two sugars. A little half-and-half."

In a kind of red daze of panic and disbelief, I poured her coffee. Such was the extremity of my emotion that the world around me had receded into dreamy unreality. I began to wonder if I was not in some sort of dream state even yet. But I was here, there was no doubt about that. I sipped my own coffee. Janet was watching me carefully, but also with that merry gleam in her eyes.

She seemed to follow my thoughts. "I'm so proud of you," she said. "It took courage to come back." My heart hammered. I could feel their eyes searching into me. I had never felt so naked, so revealed. Her small compliment flushed me to my toes with embarrassed pride, I couldn't help it. I felt my face grow hot. I could not look up from the black steaming cup. I was a praised dog.

"Thank you," I managed to mumble. My words seemed to have been spoken by another person, or rather a machine that I only controlled from a distance. Why I would react so strongly to this family was clear to me. Seeing them in their serene presence told me something I would have preferred to deny. I had to face how glorious they were, and so to see my own inadequacy.

Janet took my cup and put it on the saucer. Her hand entered mine, guided me to my feet and toward a door at the far side of the room. "It's going to be difficult for him," she said over her shoulder.

"I never listen," her mother said quickly.

"I don't think he'll be noisy." She laughed softly, in which sound I detected a small but deeply unsettling measure of contempt. "He's too proud." She drew me along. "I think he might try to leave." Her hand tightened. "Do you think that, Alex?"

"No. I won't do that. I've made my decision."

Her hand was extremely powerful, and she was hurting me. "No matter what you think, you haven't made a decision. I made the decision."

We went together down a dark stairway into that other world. We were in the back room, the one I had not seen. It was a dreary a little chamber as I have ever entered. Against one wall was a small steel closet. There was a bare metal bed frame under the low, barred window that looked out into the back garden.

The view from this window was the only nice thing about the room, and it was very nice indeed. Observed from these surroundings, the sight of the garden with its careful borders, its climbing vines and floral shrubs was heartbreaking.

It hit me with the shocking force of unexpected insight that this room was not devoted to the decadent amusements of the people I had been studying for *Pain* but for another purpose. This was the place of death.

Her arm slipped around my waist. She did not come up to my shoulder, but still I leaned my weight against her. In a soft voice, speaking quickly, she explained the purpose of the steel closet. "It's called the Standing Room. You can't stand up, not quite, and you can't sit down. It is what I have chosen for you. There are many other ways, but they tend to be more intimate and less prolonged. You need conditions that will force you to face yourself. You have a lot still to see, and I know the effect that small places have on you."

When I was a child I'd been stuck in a telephone booth. The thing was awful and black and stifling and I hadn't been able to get out for what seemed like hours. All of my life I've had a nightmare about being buried alive, where I wake up and I am in a coffin and I feel horribly alone and I start to suffocate.

"Would you like to try it?"

I stepped back, my eyes searching for the stairs. I felt sick, about to retch, dizzy with terror. My heart was weighted with the deepest sorrow. I thought of my family, of our precious happiness. Again she took my hand. Firmly, she drew me toward the box. "It might be fatal," I babbled. "My condition—"

"It won't be fatal, not this time."

"I can't. I know you want me to and that makes me want to, but I just can't. You should have left me alone."

"You have it in you, I know you do."

"It's true, then?"

"You understand the purpose of the sacrifice. You have always understood it. You were born for it, raised and educated for it. You have eaten your fruit in the sun. Now it is time for you to pay."

I wanted to protest, but truth in her words could not be denied.

"Undress, Alex. Go in the box."

Ashamed, I turned away from her. I forced my hands to stop shaking. "It won't be fatal," she had said. I did as I was bidden, removing the familiar blue sweater that Sally gave me for my birthday ten years ago, taking off my shirt and undershirt, my shoes and trousers, my socks, my shorts. Standing behind me, she took me by the arms and pushed me toward the miserable little closet.

What a stupid thing. Why was I doing this? Why was I here?

Before me danced visions of the demons of war, pestilence and upheaval. In their eyes there gleamed the same flicker of genius that so drew me to this young woman. "Your death will not stop the harvest," she murmured. "That's just your imagination. You aren't that important. None of you are."

Her words caught my attention. I blinked, started to speak. Instantly she pushed me in and shut the door. The clang resounded in my ears, sparked in my brain. She'd given no thought to my position. I was contorted, my head thrown back, my face pressing against the ceiling of the thing. One arm was behind my back, the other twisted between my left hip and the back wall. "Please, I'm all twisted!"

Silence.

"Please!"

She laughed. It was a merry noise. Then there was silence again. I tried to turn myself, could not. What had been a discomfort soon became the utmost torment. All the while I could hear her outside. She made more coffee for herself in the other room. She played the radio for a time. I could hear pages turning occasionally. She was reading.

Then she went out. She went out! I jerked, gasped, in a claustrophobic panic. My heart thuttered like a thing of paper. Finally exhausted, I wept.

She was gone for hours and hours and hours. There was no way to lessen the torment. My neck felt like a column of red-hot wire. My left arm was tingling, both of my legs were numb, my feet were throbbing with agonizing pins and needles and I was nauseated.

I would fall down a well of unconsciousness, only to be

dragged back by my agony. I would call out into the thick, suffocating silence. But she was never there.

I lost track of time. I was frantic to get back to Sally and the kids. They would miss me by now, they would be terrified. Nobody would find me back here in this basement, nobody, not ever.

Then I heard her. My heart leaped up, tears of relief stung my eyes. My mouth was so dry that I could barely make a sound. I moaned, it was all I could do. A short silence followed, then voices. She had somebody with her? Her parents? No. A man. A friend, she had brought some demented friend to enjoy my suffering with her.

But the voice was so gentle, so firm and decent. So full of awe and love. It could have been my own voice a year ago.

My blood went cold. This was a repeat of that situation, an exact repeat, only now I was the victim moaning in the dark. I remembered the flickering light, the red glow that had followed my last departure from this place.

Pray God she hadn't heard my own careless moan. I tried to be as quiet as humanly possible. I barely breathed. I prayed. Long and hard, I prayed.

The door opened and closed, the guest left. Immediately there were footsteps, rat-tat-tat right up to the wall of my prison. "How dare you moan like that when I'm working with somebody! That was a potential student, you stupid fool! What if you scared him away, think how much he will lose. Think of it!"

I saw the other man, saw inside his mind as Janet must see inside minds. There was a fuzzy, confused jumble of ideas and thoughts, a great gabble of voices. There was no wisdom at all, nothing more than the empty fear of an animal. To be truly human there must be clarity. We must know the body and understand its relationship to the soul. If he did not return here, he would lose his precious chance to understand. I might have denied it to him.

"I'm going to have to explain obedience to you. I will not do it in words, but in the body's language." There was a crackle, then a pop followed by a sustained hiss. "You'll have to take some heat, Alex." Her voice was not mean, not even hard. It was simply, absolutely final.

I have never known such suffering as I knew over the period

of time she applied the torch to the outside of the steel box. She did not burn me but rather baked me slowly. I sweated, tickled, itched. The box became a humid hell. I screamed helplessly, totally given over to my pain. I cannot fully describe in words what I felt in those hours. But I can say that my spirit separated from my body, yet remained very intimately a part of it. The lesson I learned was of incalculable value. I understood the limits of my body, and its tragedy. *It* has done my real suffering in life. *It* must do the real dying. As the cup is not the wine, Alex is not me. Understanding this, I began to know myself a little.

To learn this lesson was the reason she had brought me here and submitted me to such suffering. The whole torment of a lifetime had been concentrated into a few hours. I was now at the threshold: she had taught me what is essentially needed to be well prepared for death.

The heat stopped.

"Can you speak?" I tried, but nothing came out. I wanted to speak, though, and she knew it. "Try harder, Alex."

Finally my voice cracked to life. "Thank you."

"Well said. You've understood. Say it again."

"Thank you, *thank you.*"

When that door opened it was as if I had been delivered to the threshold of heaven. A rush of holy air caressed me and strong hands pried me loose from my confinement. With powerful ease she carried me to the bed frame. There she affixed cuffs to my wrists and ankles and stretched me mercilessly, unknotting muscles without regard for the sensation she caused. I thought she was tearing me to pieces.

At last, though, I lay spread-eagled on the bed, every muscle in place, neither tingling nor numb. I ached, of course, but I was otherwise undamaged. "Let me bring some strength back into your limbs." She touched me, and I went from a state of aching exhaustion to one of increasing strength. I have never been massaged by such delicate or knowledgeable fingers. I have never felt such light, clear energy flowing through me. Inside of half an hour I was a new man.

She smiled when I sprang up before her. "You'll see me soon." I was still arrogant enough to assume that it was a question.

"Of course," I replied as I dressed. Inwardly I jeered: what a lie. I'd never come near this poor, mad creature again. In my weakened condition I was lucky to have survived.

"The next time we'll go the whole way."

"Certainly. I'm looking forward to it."

"Yes, you are. At last, you really are."

I have never been so glad to get home in my life. I wept in Sally's lap. I told her as much of the story as I dared, saying that I'd been abducted by some of the lunatics I'd met when I was researching for *Pain*. She was furious, she wanted to call the police.

The thought made my blood stop in my veins. I could do nothing that might bring harm to my precious Janet. Too much depended on her. The same man who had left her house an hour before with the firm intention never to return already saw her again as a shining angel to be loved and protected. Frantically I explained to Sally that a call to the police might embarrass me.

A few days later I was alone in my office working. Janet's hands had rejuvenated me to an amazing degree. I had entered the final stages of recovery from my heart attack with a speed that delighted my doctor.

Sally was off watching a school play. I was not really surprised when Janet walked through my office door, having gotten past the doorman and into the locked apartment with no difficulty at all.

The shock gave way almost at once to a strange, awful feeling, more a sensation. My body seemed to want to drop to its knees. It was silly. I was embarrassed at myself. "Why resist?" she said lightly.

I did it, and was rewarded with the understanding that what stood before my crouching form was no young woman. My feeling of worshipfulness changed to awe. I could not move, let alone look up. I thought I might not be able to bear what I would see. Then a hand came down and raised my head.

"Surprise."

She was the same as ever. She took my chair, began bustling through my personal papers. I saw her take my tax returns, my accountant's reports, my net worth statement, copies of leases and contracts, everything of any financial significance.

"You've earned the knowledge that your end is coming," she said. "Don't ignore your obligation to prepare."

A week later she returned and reviewed my will with me. Her knowledge was expert, and we made revisions together. When we were finished she laid her hand on mine. I could feel her watching me. "Do I have to come with you now?"

"Do you want to?"

My impulse was to say no, to scream it, to howl it out. But I had grown cunning at this game. "I might as well get it over with."

"You'll wait a little longer. The next time we meet I will call, and you will come."

It was a small triumph, or so it seemed at the time. I had no idea that years would pass. Day after day I have waited for Janet. I have lived in a grim ecstasy of suspense. I hear her footstep behind me, see her pushing through a crowd. Once she was standing silently in the door of my office. But she turned and left without a word.

My family has grown closer, more full of love, happier. My work has prospered as never before. My reviews are excellent, there's talk of awards. Most painful of all, Sally and I have reached a new level of closeness both sexually and spiritually. Sensing what awaits it, my whole being is clinging to life. I am a tower of sexual urgency. An old marriage has become new again, full of delight and play and fun. Night after night I go to her side of the bed, and she meets me with open arms. She sings all the time. We have gone together into undreamed universes of love.

The wind shakes the cabin. Somewhere out there I know that Janet waits in the cold. One day, she will come for me.

When she does, she will tear my heart from my chest like the priests once did to their anointed victims on the altars of the Aztecs. This time there will be no reprieve: she has graduated me from her school. I will watch her squeeze out the pumping life, and my soul will be caught in her hungry jaws.

Once this frightened me, but no more. I thought that I was alone, among a select few victims of the sacrifice. But this is not true. Every human being is sacrificed; all death has value.

Janet is nothing more to me now than the progress of the clock. The horror of the sacrifice is an illusion, for the end

beyond—the soul absorbed into the breast of these mighty beings—is rapture as well as oblivion.

I do not hate Janet. Because she has given me a glimpse of
what beyond the walls of life is true, I can only love her. I wait
as she comes scything down the rows of autumn. Although her
call will mark the last stroke of my life, it will also say that my
suffering is not particular, and in that there is a kindness. She
comes not only for me, but also for those yet unborn, for the old
upon their final beds, and the millions from the harvest of war.
She comes for me, but also for you, as in the end for us all.

WHITLEY STRIEBER is the author of *The Wolfen, The Hunger, Black Magic, The Night Church, War Day* (written with
James Kunetka), the award-winning *Wolf of Shadows* and *Communion.* "Pain" is the last thing he wrote while he was still
unconscious of the events recounted in *Communion.*

RIDLEY PEARSON

"A HOT NEW THRILLER WRITER!"
—Los Angeles Times

NEVER LOOK BACK

The supercharged novel of an obsessed American manhunter, a brilliant Russian assassin and a very small—very deadly—secret. "Breakneck action!"   —Kirkus Reviews

_____90528-9 $3.95 U.S.   _____90529-7 $4.95 Can.

BLOOD OF THE ALBATROSS

Innocent Jay Becker is chosen to be a crucial link in a chain of spies carrying the latest U.S. defense weapon to the Soviets. Now he has to save his country—and his life!
"The writing is ebullient, the author has a good time with the conventions, and so should the reader."   —The New York Times

_____90607-2 $3.95 U.S.   _____90608-0 $4.95 Can.

"ONE HOPES PEARSON WILL PUBLISH AGAIN AND AGAIN."   —UPI